SHEENA AND
OTHER GOTHIC TALES

Borgo Press Books by BRIAN STABLEFORD

Alien Abduction: The Wiltshire Revelations * *Asgard's Conquerors* (Asgard #2) * *Asgard's Heart* (Asgard #3) * *Asgard's Secret* (Asgard #1) * *Balance of Power* (Daedalus Mission #5) * *The Best of Both Worlds and Other Ambiguous Tales* * *Beyond the Colors of Darkness and Other Exotica* * *Changelings and Other Metaphoric Tales* * *The City of the Sun* (Daedalus Mission #4) * *Complications and Other Science Fiction Stories* * *The Cosmic Perspective and Other Black Comedies Critical Threshold* (Daedalus Mission #2) * *The Cthulhu Encryption: A Romance of Piracy* * *The Cure for Love and Other Tales of the Biotech Revolution* * *Designer Genes: Tales of the Biotech Revolution* * *The Dragon Man* * *The Eleventh Hour* * *The Face of Heaven* (Realms of Tartarus #1) * *The Fenris Device* (Hooded Swan #5) * *Firefly: A Novel of the Far Future* * *Les Fleurs du Mal: A Tale of the Biotech Revolution* * *The Florians* (Daedalus Mission #1) * *The Gardens of Tantalus and Other Delusions* * *The Gates of Eden* * *A Glimpse of Infinity* (Realms of Tartarus #3) * *The Golden Fleece and Other Tales of the Biotech Revolution* * *The Great Chain of Being and Other Tales of the Biotech Revolution* * *Halcyon Drift* (Hooded Swan #1) * *The Haunted Bookshop and Other Apparitions* * *In the Flesh and Other Tales of the Biotech Revolution* * *The Innsmouth Heritage and Other Sequels* * *Journey to the Core of Creation: A Romance of Evolution* * *Kiss the Goat: A Twenty-First-Century Ghost Story* * *The Legacy of Erich Zann and Other Tales of the Cthulhu Mythos* * *Luscinia: A Romance of Nightingales and Roses* * *The Mad Trist: A Romance of Bibliomania* * *The Mind-Riders* * *The Moment of Truth* * *Nature's Shift: A Tale of the Biotech Revolution* * *An Oasis of Horror: Decadent Tales and Contes Cruels* * *The Paradise Game* (Hooded Swan #4) * *The Paradox of the Sets* (Daedalus Mission #6) * *The Plurality of Worlds: A Sixteenth-Century Space Opera* * *Prelude to Eternity: A Romance of the First Time Machine* * *Promised Land* (Hooded Swan #3) * *The Quintessence of August: A Romance of Possession* * *The Return of the Djinn and Other Black Melodramas* * *Rhapsody in Black* (Hooded Swan #2) * *Salome and Other Decadent Fantasies* * *Sexual Chemistry* * *Sheena and Other Gothic Tales* * *Streaking: A Novel of Probability* * *Swan Song* (Hooded Swan #6) * *The Tree of Life and Other Tales of the Biotech Revolution* * *The Undead: A Tale of the Biotech Revolution* * *Valdemar's Daughter: A Romance of Mesmerism* * *A Vision of Hell* (Realms of Tartarus #2) * *War Games* * *The Walking Shadow* * *Wildeblood's Empire* (Daedalus Mission #3) * *The World Beyond: A Sequel to S. Fowler Wright's The World Below* * *Writing Fantasy and Science Fiction* * *Xeno's Paradox: A Tale of the Biotech Revolution* * *Year Zero* * *Yesterday Never Dies: A Romance of Metempsychosis* * *Zombies Don't Cry: A Tale of the Biotech Revolution*

SHEENA
AND OTHER
GOTHIC TALES

BRIAN STABLEFORD

THE BORGO PRESS
MMXIII

SHEENA AND OTHER GOTHIC TALES

FIRST BORGO PRESS EDITION

Published by Wildside Press LLC

www.wildsidebooks.com

SHEENA AND
OTHER GOTHIC TALES

CONTENTS

INTRODUCTION

Once upon a time, all stories were told rather than being written. They had tellers rather than authors, who posed as mere transmitters of tales whose authority was based on their antiquity. They were set in a past that was qualitatively different from the present rather than merely displaced in history—as they had to be, because oral cultures, by definition, have no history. The past of "once upon a time" is a mythical past, in which magic worked, supernatural beings interacted with humans on a routine basis, and which might be subject to other fanciful embellishments, such as animals that talk. The people who told such tales, and listened to them, sometimes believed in the possibility of some of or all these things, but were very conscious of the fact that they no longer happened *ordinarily*. The tacit assumption of tales of the mythical past is that that the world has been—and still is—subject to a process of "thinning" that has leached the supernatural out of the mundane and banished it to the edges of experience.

Whenever and wherever oral cultures were displaced by literate ones, the early phases of literary development began with written versions of oral tales: the mythical past was recorded, not merely as history but as pseudo-history. Once there were documents, however, the raw material of actual history began to be produced, and the possibility developed of transforming pseudohistory by degrees into actual history, and of replacing stories set in the mythical past by stories set in the historical past.

The history of literature is largely the history of that process of replacement, not merely in the settings of stories but in their narrative methods: the unsteady but inexorable growth of narrative realism, and the replacement of what Plato called the diegetic mode of narration by the mimetic, as enshrined in the central mantra of all modern handbooks on writing ("show, don't tell"). To many writers and almost all literary critics this has always seemed to be a progressive sequence, a matter of sophistication and maturation—but it was never completed, for the simple reason that fiction is not history, and has no need to be its handmaiden. The recent history of literature has been complicated by a massive, but not unproblematic, resurgence of mythical elements.

In the realm of history, the thinning of the mythical past came close to complete, at least in the sense that the supernatural was banished from the explanatory roles it had once monopolized, but even the most scrupulous history has never quite shaken off the pseudohistorical burden it inherited from oral culture. In the realm of literature, the supernatural inevitably proved to be far more stubborn, and also far more perverse. It not only refused erasure as an explanatory resource, but actually became rebellious, defiantly reasserting its claim on the imagination in a series of ingenious ideological campaigns. The labels employed as banners under which such reassertive crusades might be undertaken have been many and various, but one of the most significant—if only because of its unrepentant flamboyance— is "Gothic."

The term was initially borrowed from architecture, but its first literary use was to denote the dark underbelly of Romanticism: a spirited re-examination and sophistication of the aesthetics of horror. The term has acquired many other nuances of meaning since then, but the core significance remains the same: "Gothic" fiction is calculatedly, arrogantly and ingeniously perverse. It is far more interested in the aesthetics of the sublime than the aesthetics of beauty, because its principal function is to disturb and horrify rather than flatter and comfort. It often refuses to employ the same strategies of closure as more conventional forms of fiction, refusing normalizing and rewarding endings in favor of tragic and ironic subversions of such narrative conventions. It sometimes also refuses to grant the superiority of the mimetic narrative mode over the diegetic, and routinely prefers a more even balance than naturalistic fiction will nowadays allow.

The original Gothic novels—whose supernatural apparatus now seems sadly crude to connoisseurs who have had two hundred years to sophisticate the aesthetics of horror—could not offer a straightforward reversion to fiction that referred to a mythical past rather than a historical one. Even recycled fairy tales (which Nathan Drake characterized as "sportive Gothic" fiction) could not do that, no matter how hard they pretended. Once history exists, it cannot be ignored, let alone unlearned. What the first wave of Gothic fiction did, however, was to insist that the explanatory coherence of history was fragile, and perhaps false: that the supernatural elements rendered liminal by thinning had not been deprived by their marginalization of the power to alarm, but had in fact been perversely re-empowered by the denial of their actual possibility.

In the mythical past of oral tales and imitations thereof, human characters confronted by the supernatural may be terrified, but they are never required to doubt their sanity. In the historical past of written stories, human characters confronted with the supernatural have to battle not merely the implicit supernatural menace itself, but also the corrosive skepticism that insists on ruling their experience insane. This necessity recomplicates their anxiety and redoubles their potential distress; the double bind in question was to become the imaginative bedrock of modern horror fiction and the powerhouse of its aesthetics.

Other aspects of the interaction of the historical and mythical pasts have also been vitally important to the sophistication of modern Gothic fiction. The most important harks back to one of the earliest side-effects of the development of the historical past: the invention of scripture-based religion. In oral cultures the mythical past is not only largely taken as given—it does change, but it changes slowly, subtly and invisibly, bogged down by the inertia of its seemingly-passive transmission—but is also essentially nebulous; its contents and limits cannot be clearly specified and maintained. The invention of writing, which made the development of history possible, also permitted much more sweeping, arbitrary and decisive revisions of the mythical past; the particular form of pseudohistory that adopted the form of religious scripture took full advantage of this facility. Indeed, the advantage acquired by these calculated rewritings of the mythical past was so immense that they remain powerful adversaries to history even today, continuing to fight fierce ideological battles against the calculated thinning of their most cherished delusions.

Gothic fiction is, in consequence, not merely rebellious against the corrosions of history but also against the crystallizations of religion. The mythical past it champions is a fluid one that retains all its flexibility and imaginative potential, which resists faith even more determinedly than it resists emaciation. Like the tales of oral culture, Gothic fiction accepts as a fundamental assumption that "thinning" has taken place and is continuing; it does not deny the fundamental assumptions of history as a matter of empirical fact, but contradicts them on the far more sophisticated grounds that fiction, unlike history, need not and should not confine its ambition to the strict reproduction of starveling mundanity. For the same reason, it flatly denies—or, at least, ought to deny—the imperialistic and totalitarian claims of any dogmatic version of the mythical past based in sacred writings.

In consequence of this logic, another of the key assumptions of Gothic fiction is that nothing is, or ever could be, sacred. This essential sacrilegiousness is a subcategory of its perversity, but it is a specific corollary of sufficient importance to be worth emphasis. Contrary to superficial appearances, Gothic fiction is not anti-scientific, although it is often anti-scientistic. Quite the reverse; Gothic fiction not only admits but rejoices in the fact that it deals in the substance of myth, madness and mendacity. It claims, proudly and insistently, that such artful dealing is one of the things that fiction is *for*. Gothic fiction is not anti-religious either, in the broader sense of the word although it is implacably anti-faith; it is entirely sympathetic to the kind of tolerant paganism promoted by neo-Platonic philosophers like Iamblichus, who preached that all the religions of the decadent Roman Empire had something to recommend them except Christianity, which had disqualified itself from such sympathy by denying that very precept.

The ten stories collected here are all *contes cruels*, not so much because they have "unhappy endings"—although all but two of them do—but because they attempt to count the cost of "happiness" with the kind of scrupulous accuracy that people with no talent for moral arithmetic call "cynicism." They also make more use of variant of the diegetic narrative mode than is currently fashionable, even in the commercialized and commodified fringes of neo-Gothic fiction. Most readers do not like stories of that sort, and editors desirous of appealing to large audiences invariably take the view that there is no point in writing or publishing them, but I make no apology for them. I am glad that there are perverse readers in the world as well as perverse writers, and even a few perverse publishers—a fact for which there is no earthly reason to thank God—but I hope that I would be sufficiently stubborn in my perversity to keep writing stories like these even if there were no perverse readers and publishers to lend them heroic endorsement.

ROSE, CROWNED
WITH THORNS

Barbara was the first on my list, because she was the source of my distress. It wasn't all her fault, of course—how could it be?—but she had been the prime mover in every phase of the unfolding tragedy.

I didn't have to visit her at home in order to pick up stray hairs from her bathroom; I'd always been a collector and I'd had plenty of reason, over the years, to think that I might one day have need of a little dead Barbie: hair, skin cells, even a little dried blood. I had bits of almost everyone I knew stored in my secret cabinet, along with the tallow, the pins and the needles, and all the other paraphernalia. Going to see her was a different thing; a matter of pride and balance as well as tactics. We'd been rivals and opposites so long that it wouldn't have been right to do what I intended to do without an actual confrontation, even if it had been possible. I needed to stand face to face with her and look her in the eye, as if I were a sinister reflection lurking in the depths of a darkened mirror, staring out at my bright and gaudy doppelganger in the world of artifice.

She lived, as a Barbie would, in a red-brick house with freshly painted woodwork, on a tidy new 'model village' estate south of Marlow, nice and handy for the M4 and the M40. The garage door was aluminum, but it was painted the same shade of burgundy as the window frames. The front door had frosted glass panels and three locks; the burglar alarm was ostentatiously positioned above it and to the left. The door chime sounded like tubular bells.

I watched the expressions flit across her face when she opened the door and saw me there. Surprise, confusion, suspicion and anxiety all showed, briefly, before the professional smile took over and her face reverted to its plastic Barbie mask.

'R...Rose!' she said, swallowing her first impulse and calming the exclamation so that it implied pleasure rather than alarm. 'Why didn't you call?'

Nowadays, everyone says *Why didn't you call?* if you turn up unexpectedly. It's impolite, these days, to do anything without warning, although that doesn't stop people doing things in secret.

When I moved forward she stepped reflexively aside to let me in. Inside, the carpets were royal blue and the wallpaper was cream, patterned in silver. Because I hadn't answered her question she said, 'You were lucky to catch me in.' Luck had nothing to do with it; I knew that she was in, and alone—but she was right to be surprised; if I'd turned up at random the chance of finding her in that precious combination of circumstances would have been slim. Whenever her so-called job wasn't keeping her busy, adultery was.

I went into the sitting room and sat down on a leather-clad armchair. She didn't know what to do, but she stayed on her feet. 'Would you like a drink?' she said, still cruising on automatic. 'How's John?'

'No thanks,' I replied. 'You probably know better than I do.'

It took her a moment or two to figure out that the two remarks were unrelated to one another because I'd answered both her questions, in strict chronological order. That was when she sat down, in the armchair that was twin to mine. Rumor has it that people's faces are supposed to go pale when they find out that they've been rumbled by their lovers' spouses, but Barbie's didn't. Plastic never loses its hue, and mischief knows no shame.

'How long have you known?' she asked, matter-of-factly.

I nearly said *Since it began*, but it wouldn't have been true. Witch or not, I'd had to pick up the usual clues, and my first reaction had been exactly the same as anyone else's: denial. There was a sense in which I'd known long before it began that Barbara could never be satisfied with what she originally wanted, of course; Barbie had always wanted everything, because she was the kind of person who could. When she'd given John to me—or, as she presumably saw it, had given me to him—she'd always intended to take him back as and when the whim struck her, to fit him in when she found a gap in her life, a window in her schedule. Even so, I'd been taken by surprise when the inevitable finally became manifest.

'Long enough,' I said, for want of any better answer.

'Long enough for what?' she came back, her poise recovered and her delicate sneer back on line—but I'd rehearsed and she hadn't; for once I was quick enough to join in.

'Long enough to decide what to do,' I told her.

She'd known me long enough not to really see me, even when she looked at me long and hard, but the way her gaze travelled from my boots to my eyes, taking in the whole Stygian ensemble, suggested that she might be making a new appraisal. She probably contemplated making the suggestion that I was certainly dressed for a funeral, but she'd used it too many times before—and what was worse, had heard other people use it. When you always dress entirely in black, it's the kind of comment everyone stumbles over as they search for something apposite to say; for once, though, it would almost have been appropriate.

'And what have you decided to do?' she asked, in a carefully neutral tone. 'Name me as co-respondent in your divorce petition?'

'I won't need a divorce,' I told her. 'Nor will you.'

For a moment, she must have toyed with the notion that I was being civilized; I'm sure there was nothing in my tone to suggest otherwise—but she had known me too long. She knew that the last thing I could be accused of was any kind of orthodoxy.

'Howard wouldn't divorce me,' she said, uneasily aware of the probable irrelevance of the remark. 'We tolerate one anoth-

er's little adventures. I'm surprised, in a way, that you and he....'
She trailed off, too nervous to be thoroughly vicious.

'I think you managed to put him off, when we were all nineteen,' I said, blandly.

'Are you sure you don't want a drink?' she said, abruptly getting to her feet again. 'If this is going to be intense, I think I need one.'

'I'm not staying long,' I assured her. 'I just came round to tell you what I'm going to do, so that if it works, you'll know that it was me. I wouldn't like you to think that it was just some kind of virus.'

She really did want the drink, but she didn't want to go over to the cabinet with that kind of tease unresolved.

'Are you planning to kill us all?' she said, sharply. 'Or is it just me? What are you going to do—make a doll that looks like me and stick pins in it?'

'I don't have to make a doll that looks like you,' I told her. 'For your effigy, I can just buy one off the shelf. I'll have to mould a photograph to its face, of course, and bind the other identifiers to it with sealing wax, but you're easy. You've always been easy.'

She noticed the *double entendre*, but her mind was on other matters. 'Rose, darling,' she said, mustering all the vitriol she could, 'I know that this witchcraft stuff has always been more than a pose with you, but surely even you must know that you can't hurt someone by sticking hatpins in a doll—not even if you call to see them first, to let them know you're going to do it. It's all very well for witch doctors in Africa to point the bone at their credulous tribesmen and order them to lie down and die, but it certainly doesn't work in Marlow.'

'That,' I said, patiently, 'remains to be seen.'

'Have you tried it before?' she asked, arching a neatly painted eyebrow.

'I never had any reason to,' I told her, not entirely truthfully.

'I think, darling,' she said, 'that you ought to give serious consideration to the possibility that you're going mad. It's one thing to be weird, but quite another to....'

This time she broke off because I'd stood up again. She stood too, so that she could look down at me. She was only five foot seven, and she wasn't wearing heels, but she still had the advantage endways as well as sideways. She took a deep breath, as if to assert that no one with a conventional B-cup had any right to threaten or insult the proud wearer of a C-cup Wonderbra.

'We'll see, shall we?' I said.

'We'll see all right,' she assured me, as I went past her into the hallway. The silver patterns in the wallpaper glistened with obliquely reflected sunlight as I passed them by.

'Anyhow,' Barbie called after me, as I reached out both hands to open the security-conscious door, 'isn't that sort of thing supposed to rebound on the ill-wisher? You're supposed to be a white witch, aren't you?—although you certainly don't look it.'

'The question is,' I told her, before I closed the door on her, 'what kind of witch are you?'

I had closed the door behind me before she could formulate a reply. I had, after all, had the benefit of my rehearsals.

She was right, of course. The first thing Mrs. Cole told me, when Mum sent me to her to receive instruction in witchcraft, was that the Art should only be used to achieve good ends. 'Beware of curses, Rose,' she said. 'They work, but they always rebound. You never can tell how many people will get hurt, but you'll always be among them.'

The name on my birth certificate is Rosemary but everybody called me Rose until Barbara Schiff gave me a new nickname— and even Barbie, who was now Mrs. Fletcher, had thought better about using that when she found me on her doorstep while she was in the middle of a red hot affair with my husband.

I didn't take Mrs. Cole seriously, about curses or anything else. How could I? I was eleven years old and it was 1989. I'd got used to Mum being a witch, having grown up with it, and I'd got used to being included, the way Keith got included in all Dad's hobbies, but I spent seven hours a day in school and another three watching TV. I couldn't take any of it seriously. Not that it stopped me doing it, of course. Keith played football and went fishing; I did witchcraft. It was the way things were. Keith learned ball skills and line-casting; I learned recipes and rituals. We did it because it was expected of us. Mum and Dad had divided us up almost from birth, without ever really thinking about it; they'd just taken it for granted that their son would follow in his dad's footsteps and their daughter in her mum's. Maybe Mum wouldn't have been heartbroken if I hadn't shown willing, but she'd have been disappointed, and if Keith wasn't going to disappoint Dad then I certainly wasn't going to disappoint Mum. We weren't the kind of family that went around disappointing one another more than was strictly necessary.

I never told Mum that I didn't take it seriously, of course. It was easy to keep the secret. You soon become used to keeping secrets when your mother's a witch. Not that she was ashamed of it, of course. If anyone brought the subject up, she'd talk about it gladly, explaining with minute care that she was a worshipper of the Mother Goddess, not a Satanist, a healer, not a fortune-teller. It was different for me; most kids can't be made to see distinctions like those, and would refuse to understand them even if they could. When other kids asked me if it was true that my mother was a witch, I'd say yes but wouldn't elaborate; if they asked me if I was one too, I'd refuse to talk about it—and I wouldn't yield to pressure.

When I was sixteen Mum started taking me to the Annual Conference of the Pagan Federation. It was her idea of taking note of the fact that I'd reached the age of consent. We'd sit through all manner of lectures and workshops on rituals and alternative medicine, and I'd listen to it all with saintly patience, waiting for last thing Saturday night, when there'd be a big party with a rock band—usually Inkubus Sukkubus—playing live.

I liked the music; it was the one thing that seemed to me to be worth taking seriously—that and the style that went with it. All the rest, it seemed to the awkwardly shy teenager I then was, was just so much hot air, just like any other kind of religion—

including football and fishing.

I never thought of myself as a truly weird kid, but I suppose I must have been, or else I'd never have got into my twenties without ever trying to curse anyone or anything, and without ever finding out that Mrs. Cole was right.

Curses rebound, and you never can tell how many people will get hurt.

I was in my upstairs room, putting the finishing touches to the last figurine, when John arrived home. I had Funeral Nation on the mini-system, playing as loud as the little speakers would allow; he would have timed it better if 'Graveyard Eyes' had been playing, but in fact the title track had just given way to 'Sacred Cities'.

John was late, of course, but not that late. He'd stopped off for a double, or maybe a couple of doubles, at the Rat & Parrot or the Newt & Cucumber or one of the other ghastly newfangled pubs that had sprung up all over the town centre in the mid-90s. He'd probably gulped the booze down in ten seconds flat, with no time to spare for anything more than a nod to anyone he knew; parking and unparking the Peugeot was what had taken up the extra time.

Barbie had phoned him on his mobile, of course. 'Better get along home, Coldheart,' she would have told him. 'Rag Doll's found us out and flipped. Better calm her down before she goes over the edge.'

If the nickname Barbie had stuck on him had been apt, he wouldn't have needed the top-up at the Rat & Parrot, or wherever, but it wasn't warmth he was after in the whisky. I knew he hadn't had enough—he wouldn't have dared to have enough, even though the double or two he'd had must have pushed him over the legal limit—and I knew full well that the first thing he'd do when he came stumbling through the door was have another, and another after that.

I was right, of course. He gulped those too before he came up to my room. By the time he arrived in the doorway, aesthetic propriety had been restored; the speakers were booming out the 'resurrected' remix of 'Chaos Mind'.

John had never liked Midnight Configuration; he didn't mind the poppier goth rock, but he hated anything with guttural vocals and a real edge. 'Chaos Mind' wasn't his sort of thing at all, although at that particular moment in time I couldn't think of anything that would have suited me better. When he saw that I wasn't going to switch it off he did it himself, with what was intended to be an angry flourish.

The fact that I'd been to see Barbara had licensed his anger, but it was still a mask for shame and guilt and terror. When he turned towards me from the mini-system he didn't know whether to yell at me or beg forgiveness, but when he saw the figurines on the desktop the choice became more complicated.

In the end, he could only manage, 'What the hell are those?'

'Didn't Barbie tell you?' I said, picking up the Barbie doll—one of two that wasn't entirely my own work. I knew she wouldn't have; it would have sounded too silly, and she would have known that he'd find out as soon as he confronted me.

I watched his brow furrow, and I knew he was wondering why there were four figurines instead of only two—but all he said was: 'Well, I can understand why you might want to stick pins in both of us—but it doesn't mean anything, Rose. It really doesn't. It needn't affect you and me. We can get past this, if we can just talk it through. The thing with Barbara's over—I give you my word.'

By my count, that was four clichés; I had to keep count because I'd promised him a needle for every cliché, starting with the thinnest one and making my way through the packet towards the thickest.

'It means something to me,' I said. 'Even you must have an inkling as to just how much.' I picked up a big hatpin and held it up alongside the Barbie doll, but it was just for show; I was keeping my real first move in reserve, because I knew it had to be timed exactly right.

'That's not going to help,' he said. 'Even if it makes you feel better, it's not going to solve anything.'

'It's not supposed to solve anything,' I told him. 'It's supposed to dissolve something.' All that rehearsal-time was really paying off.

He turned the spare chair around and sat down lumpenly. His face was flushed by confusion and alcohol; he had never seemed less deserving of the nickname Barbie had foisted on him. 'Hell, Rose,' he said, 'we have to be adult about this. I'm sorry it's happened, but it's happened. It can't be undone. We have to get past it.'

That boosted the cliché-count to seven, with one repetition. I decided to forgive him the repetition; it was the only thing I did intend to forgive him.

'She had no right,' I told him. 'It was bad enough that she gave you up, but she could at least have stuck to it. She had no right to take you back. I swore that I wouldn't let her do that. I couldn't stop her twisting Howard round her little finger, or throwing me to you like some kind of consolation-prize, but I swore that I wouldn't let her take you back. I swore that I wouldn't let her turn the gift into a curse. Curses rebound, you know. Of course you know—even Barbie knows that curses rebound on the sender. Mischief should have stopped her mischief when she wasn't a Miss any longer—but Barbie doesn't know how to stop, does she?'

'It will stop,' my errant husband said, not following the argument at all. 'I swear that it will.'

Was that eight clichés in all, I wondered, having momentarily lost track, or seven and two forgivable repetitions? I hadn't expected him to be quite so prolific. Carefully, I laid the Barbie doll down, on its back. I picked up one of my humble efforts, molded from candle wax.

Its arms and legs weren't very good, but the photograph of John was neatly sealed to the front of its head. It was clipped from a wedding photograph, of course; that was one cliché I had to count against myself. Not a needle-through-the-belly sort of cliché, but a cliché nevertheless. On the other hand, I had promised myself a whole crown of scathing thorns, so I could still be reckoned to be in credit, cliché-wise.

'Go ahead,' he said, bitterly. 'Stick the pins in, if it'll make you feel better. I deserve it. If there's any justice at all, I'll feel the pain. In fact....'

I couldn't let him finish. There wasn't time. I ran the hatpin into the abdomen of the doll, aiming for the stomach, just as the cramps began to hit the real thing.

I had never seen anyone look so astonished in my entire life. I hope I managed to control the grim certainty of my own expression.

'By my count, John, dear,' I said, 'that's eight clichés and two repetitions. I'll forgive you the repetitions, but you get a needle for every one of the stupid, shabby, pathetic things you borrowed from the standard script. The hatpin's for the sin itself.'

He clutched his belly, still unable to believe that the hatpin's penetration was echoing inside him, unleashing sharp and horrid pain. I showed him the packet of needles, and I showed him which end of the array I intended to start from.

He was still fully occupied by amazement. For the moment, his astonishment was taking the edge off the pain and blocking the fear, but only for the moment.

I took out the thinnest of all the needles, and stuck it into the doll; this time it went in through the side, but the point was still aimed at the stomach.

'But I don't believe...,' he said, and then interrupted himself with a strangled obscenity. He pressed both hands into his booze-softened belly and fell off the chair. If it had been an armchair he'd have been able to stay in it, but I'd never kept armchairs in my room. The one I was sitting on was a swiveling-chair, the kind that some office typists use.

'It really doesn't matter what you believe,' I told him. 'A witch is a witch regardless. A sin is a sin, and a needle in the eye is a needle in the eye. How do you think I felt? Do you think it would have made one little bit of difference if I hadn't believed in marriage, or loyalty, or love, or jealousy, or common decency? Do you?'

Needle number two went in, and then needle number three, their points aimed at the small intestine. Coldheart John broke into a cold sweat, and the sweat was pure fear. If he hadn't believed before, he certainly believed now—if not in marriage, in magic; if not in love, in hate.

'I'm having a fucking heart attack,' he moaned, demonstrating his complete ignorance of the relevant warning signs and symptoms as well as a perverse inclination to heed his own fears. 'Call a fucking ambulance, will you!'

I used my right hand—the one that wasn't holding John's effigy—to pluck the receiver from the phone, which lay amid the litter of all my hard labor. I used the forefinger of the same hand to peck out the numbers. It must have been perfectly obvious to John, even in his distressed condition, that I wasn't dialing 999.

Barbie picked up almost immediately. She must have been waiting by the phone—waiting to hear the news.

I held out the receiver to John, knowing that he could just about reach it if he condescended to remove one of the hands that was clutching at his terrorized stomach.

'Tell her,' I commanded him. 'Tell her what a real witch can do.'

'You're crazy,' he said. His voice was raw and guttural, almost tortured; for the first time in his life he could have sung 'Graveyard Eyes' the way it was meant to be sung.

'I'm not crazy, I'm a witch,' I told him. 'And you'd better tell her that while you still can, because you and I have six needles still to go, and you might not be in any fit condition to tell her anything by the time I've finished.'

In spite of his agony, he reached out and he took the phone. For the first time in my life, I felt that I was in control, that I had authority. For the first time in my life, I knew that John Coulthart was truly mine. For the first time in my life I was Rosemary for remembrance, and it all seemed to be worth it, even though I knew that I'd end up as mere Rose, crowned with thorns.

'Tell her!' I said—and he actually screamed.

I don't know why we had to have nicknames, or how it came about that they got assigned when they did. I suppose it was a kind of bonding—the sort of thing young people do when they're hurled out of the family nest into a world where relationships have to be made instead of found.

Because I was a year older than Keith, I was the first to go away, although I'd never really thought about it as going until I was actually gone. Applying to university had just been the next expected step—expected even by Mum, although she knew full well that you couldn't study witchcraft at any British university. She'd never tried to encourage me to study one subject rather than another at school, obviously figuring that the instruction from Mrs. Cole and our dutiful association with the Pagan Federation would supplement any kind of orthodox education as well as any other. If Mum was relieved that I clung hard to English Literature and refused to interest myself in science she never showed it. If she was desolate when she and Dad unloaded my stuff outside the hall of residence where I'd been allocated a room she didn't show that either. Every week, though, she'd send me a brand new phonecard, to ease the ritual of keeping in touch.

I don't know how exactly how it came about that I became a part of a little group of four. It wasn't entirely a matter of chance, and it certainly wasn't entirely a matter of convenience. I suppose, looking back, that it was because I liked Howard Fletcher that I gravitated into his orbit, and because Howard knew John Coulthart from school that he turned out to be already occupying the next orbit in—and it was probably because John thought that Barbara Schiff looked gorgeous that he tried with all his might to bring her into our combined gravitational field. Once we were together, though, that initial chain of causation gave way to a much more complicated combination of attractions and movements.

Howard's nickname must have been left over from school.

John had obviously been calling him 'Flasher' for years, and wasn't about to be put off just because Howard wanted to make a clean start—quite the reverse, in fact. I don't think Howard ever retaliated in kind; it was certainly Barbara who first started calling him 'Coldheart', deliberately echoing the kind of transformation that he insisted on wreaking upon his friend's name. I didn't want to get involved—I never called Howard 'Flasher'—but they wouldn't leave me out of it. I even explained to them that Rose already was a nickname, because my name was actually Rosemary, but they wouldn't be content with that.

'We could call you Ophelia,' John said, after I'd told him what my full name was, 'because Rosemary's for remembrance.'

'She's not Rosemary now,' Howard pointed out. 'She's Rose.'

'But she has no thorns,' John said, still trying to be clever, 'and a Rose by any other name would smell as sweet. If only Ophelia hadn't gone mad....'

It was Barbara who took the next step. Like any new girl, not knowing what to expect, I'd come to university liberally equipped with notebooks and files, all neat and new and far more brightly-colored than anything I ever wore, and I'd punctiliously stenciled my name on every one of them, in formal capitals: R. EDGELL.

'Rag doll,' said Barbara. 'They called her Rag Doll.' She was quoting an old song by the Four Seasons, that must have been her mother's or her grandmother's vintage. She'd never even heard of Inkubus Sukkubus or Midnight Configuration or All Living Fear, or any of the bands I liked. Not many people had—which was one of the reasons I liked them so much.

Maybe she wasn't being vicious, at least not consciously. Maybe she was just looking to apply the same methodology to my name as she'd applied to 'Coldheart' John's. She certainly didn't have any good reason to attack my clothes, which were no worse than hers. I was used to people remarking on the fact that they were uniformly black, but no one had ever criticized their quality.

Perhaps, if I'd been quick enough, I could have derailed the entire train of thought. Perhaps, if I'd only known how, I could not only have kept myself in their minds as Rose but made her Barb or Barbie in our everyday usage—but the suggestion was rejected on the grounds that the contractions were too obvious, and too commonplace to qualify as a private joke. I suppose it must have been John who took up the baton and dubbed her 'Mischief'—on account, of course, of the fact that her surname was Schiff and she was, for the moment, single.

'Mischief's no good,' I pointed out. 'It won't make sense after she gets married.'

'Nor will Rag Doll,' Barbara was quick to point out. 'But that won't matter. When you marry John, you can be Mrs. Coldheart.'

She only said it to make mischief, of course. She only said it because she knew full well that it was Howard I liked. It was the first inkling I'd had that she liked him too—and that she had already considered, as coolly as you please, the possibility that if John's obvious desire for her might be deflected, I was the direction in which he ought to be encouraged to look.

Even if the nickname itself hadn't been a kind of curse, that supplementary remark certainly was—and like all the worst curses, it unwound over time, rebounding as it went, and it kept on and on rebounding.

'It wouldn't be as bad as Mrs. Flasher,' John contended, but even I could see that it all depended how flash she was to start with—and Barbie was very flash indeed. Not that beautiful, and not that rich, but certainly flash. She thought she could have everything she wanted, and she would probably have been right, if she hadn't tangled with a witch. We were tangled already, of course, but only by common-or-garden friendship. It wasn't until the business of the nicknames that the tangles became thorny, catching like curses. Until then, it hadn't mattered that I was a witch, but afterwards....

I didn't swear anything there and then, but that was when it all began in earnest. John had been right about my having no thorns. Until then, in spite of my being Rose instead of

Rosemary, I'd been entirely innocent of thorns. From that moment on, though, I was fated to be crowned with them.

Howard arrived at half past eleven. If he'd only had to drive from Marlow it wouldn't have taken him nearly as long, but he hadn't been at home. Lately, he'd been spending a lot of time away from home, exactly as John had, and probably for much the same reason: fucking someone else's Barbie while his own got fucked in her turn. No witchcraft involved, of course: no love potions, no real glamour. Just the everyday routines of ordinary folk, supposedly hurting no one. But a needle in the eye is a needle in the eye, and you feel what you feel, even when the needle isn't literal, especially if you're a witch.

Flasher Fletcher rang the doorbell in an uncommonly assertive manner, although I didn't take more time than was warranted letting him in.

'Hello Howard,' I said. 'Would you like a drink?'

'Where's John?' he demanded. He was already looking up the stairs, wondering if he ought to bound up them two at a time and hurl back the door of the room I had claimed as a counterpart to John's 'study': the room in which I kept my cabinet, and my recipes, and my pathetic apology for a sewing kit.

'Why?' I asked, innocently. 'Do you want to beat the living daylights out of him for fucking your wife?' My assiduous rehearsals were still paying dividends.

Howard cast one last look up the staircase, and then turned to look down at me. He looked down from a much greater elevation than Barbie, greater even than John. From way up there I must have looked very tiny indeed, and utterly harmless. I must have looked meek, too, because he relaxed perceptibly.

'You'll never believe this, Rose,' he said, perhaps hoping that it might even be true, 'but Barbara's got some stupid idea into her head that you might have killed him. She only insisted that I came round to make sure that he was all right.'

'Only insisted,' I echoed. 'That doesn't sound like Barbie at all. She was never one to take things one at a time.'

'She said that you were pretty pissed,' Howard said, blundering on regardless. 'I can understand that, of course. I mean, I was exceedingly pissed myself when she told me what had happened. It's not the first time she's got off with one of my mates, but I would have thought that John, of all people, was way out of bounds. You're supposed to be her best friend, for Christ's sake! And what on Earth could he be thinking of? It's one in the eye for us both—but we do have to be adult about these things, don't we?'

There was a tiny hint of self-congratulation in his voice, born of the tacit assertion that he wasn't the kind of guy who would go around fucking his best friend's wife. In all the years I'd known him, I'd never once heard Howard the Flasher say 'There, but for the grace of God, go I.' It was difficult to understand, at that particular moment, why I'd ever been besotted with him.

Then he smiled, and I remembered.

'I know you better than Barbara does,' he said, mistakenly. 'I know you're tougher than you look, and smarter than any of us. You wanted to throw a scare into her, didn't you? It was something you and John cooked up together, wasn't it?'

I smiled too. 'I wanted to throw a scare into her all right,' I said. 'And you're absolutely right—it was something I cooked up, with John in mind. Are you sure you don't want that drink?'

'I knew it,' he said. 'I knew you couldn't really be sitting upstairs sticking pins and needles into voodoo dolls. I knew it had to be a joke—like all that awful music you like so much.'

He laughed. That was Howard all over; whenever he was in doubt, he laughed. The first time he'd found out about his wife's little adventures he'd probably had to choke back a tear or two, but in the end, he would have decided to laugh about it. He would have pursed his lips, gritted his teeth, and matched her adventure for adventure, so that they could both laugh at life's little ironies, and congratulate one another on how civilized they were.

I had to put a stop to that train of thought, or I'd have merited far too many thorns to fit into any mere crown. I'd already opened the door to the sitting room and I was standing there like some midget butler, trying to usher him through. 'Drink?' I said, again. Men are like dogs; if you reduce communication to one-word sentences and repeat them often enough they usually get the message eventually.

'Well, OK,' he said. 'Just one—I'm driving. Bloody Mary, if that's OK.' His BMW was bigger than John's Peugeot, but he had two more points on his license. He'd never have sunk two doubles in the Rat & Parrot or the Newt & Cucumber and then got back behind the wheel.

When he sat down on the settee, though, the Flasher looked around yet again, furtively. 'Where is John?' he asked.

'Oh, he's already gone,' I said. 'Barbie knew that, of course. If I had to guess, I'd say that she probably only sent you round here in the hope that I'd beg you to fuck my brains out, so that I'd lose the moral high ground in this business between John and her. I think she'd prefer me to get even in the ordinary way, rather than stick her effigy into a candle flame and watch it burn. Well, she would, wouldn't she?'

I handed him the Bloody Mary; I knew that Howard never drank whisky, so I'd already poured the stuff in the doctored bottle down the sink. He looked at me in complete confusion, although I thought I'd detected a faint hopeful gleam in his eye when I mentioned the possibility of his fucking my brains out. Flashers are always teed up to respond to sweet nothings of that kind.

'I always loved that dry sense of humor,' he said. 'It drives Barb crazy, though. I really am sorry, you know—about her and John. I can take it, but I know how cut up you must be. If I'd known...I really am sorry. She is too, you know. She just didn't think....'

'If you were John,' I informed him, 'I'd owe you half a dozen needles by now—and I only have the thicker ones left. But you're not John, are you? You were never that cold-hearted.'

He laughed again, in a curiously dutiful fashion, even though he didn't have a clue what the remark about the needles signified.

'Come upstairs,' I said to him, opening the door again. 'There's something I want to show you.'

The gleam came back into his eye, flashing at me as he turned his head. He honestly thought I meant the bed. He honestly thought that if I really believed that Barbara had sent him around to give me a chance to even the score, I might have given her the satisfaction of taking the bait. He didn't know me at all, and never had.

I suppose I would have wondered again what I could ever have seen in him, if he hadn't already been flashing his smile

I'd hung around with girls prettier than myself long before I met Barbara Schiff, of course. At school, I'd gone with better-looking acquaintances to discos—even to gigs when the rare opportunity presented itself to see one of my favourite bands outside the hallowed environs of the Pagan Federation Conference. I knew well enough how such things worked: how predatory boys hunted in pairs, eyeing up their paired targets with assumed expertise, mouthing the usual clichés like the oldest rituals in the grimoire: *Don't fancy yours much. You take the little one; I'll handle the Wonderbra. You take the thin one—she won't need as much oiling.* In my teens, though, that sort of thing had all been safely confined to the odd evening out, after which—no matter what might develop or how far things might go—everybody went home.

With Howard and John and Barbara it was different; we already were home. We lived on the same corridor, shared the same kitchen. John and I even attended the same lectures—but Howard was a historian and Barbara, thinking herself more fashionable by far than the rest of us, was doing Media Studies.

Left to ourselves, Coldheart John and I would probably have kept our distance from one another, or collided once and moved apart, never pausing overlong thereafter as our paths criss-crossed—but we weren't left to ourselves. We were part of something larger and more complicated. We were entangled, by Flasher's flair and animal magnetism, by Mischief's leadership and Machiavellian scheming.

When Mischief decided that she must have Flasher she also decided that Rag Doll, whose initial attraction had been to him, must be fobbed off with Coldheart, whose initial attraction had been to her, thus neutralizing both potential inconveniences. It was probably unnecessary, and could easily have proved pointless, but that was the way she saw it. Once the precedent had been set, she returned time and time again to that same formularistic curse: 'When you marry Coldheart'.

Never once did Barbie say, 'When I marry Flasher', but she never needed to. All she needed to do was to repeat her own spell over and over, until the people around her began to take it for granted. I never did, of course, but I was a witch and had been trained to know witchcraft when I saw it, even when it was being used by someone who would have laughed her socks off at the thought of the Pagan Federation's Annual Conference. John and Howard had no idea, any more than Dad or Keith would have done. They accepted the assumption without ever realizing that they were being bound by a spell. By slow degrees, as our first year progressed, we stopped being a quartet and became two pairs.

Maybe, if I'd cast a counter spell soon enough, I could have turned the thing around—but I didn't have Barbie's advantages. I'd had a lifetime of knowing what to look for, but I'd never been able to take any of it seriously. She'd had a lifetime of blissful ignorance, and was able to take what she was doing very seriously indeed because she thought of it as common sense instead of magic, as everyday lust instead of demonic possession, as playing with words instead of laying curses.

If I'd been able to tell my mother, she would probably have helped me out. If Mrs. Cole hadn't 'passed over', I could have consulted her, but she had gone to sleep in the bosom of the Goddess three years after I'd started secondary school. All I had to console me was my music: Corpus Delicti and All Living Fear, Ataraxia and Midnight Configuration, Faith and the Muse and Faith and Disease.

I should have fought back, but I didn't. All I could do, then, was to swear that if Mischief ever took back what she had given, running needles into my eyes to start my bitter tears, then I would make her suffer in return—even though I knew that any curse I laid would hurt me too.

It didn't seem appropriate to change the record, so I put 'Funeral Nation' on again while I showed Howard the two dolls I'd adapted and the two dolls I'd made. He tried to laugh, but 'Subterrania' was already pounding in his ears, and he couldn't quite manage it.

'Barbie wasn't making it up,' I told him, 'and she wasn't being stupid, although I'm sure you must have told her that she was. When she heard John screaming, he really was screaming—and when he left, he didn't go to the hospital, because he was utterly and absolutely convinced, by that time, that he had to do exactly what I told him to do. He went to Barbie's. He's there now. By now, he must have been screaming and moaning at her for the best part of an hour, as well as vomiting all over her royal blue carpet and shitting his pants. He won't die, of course, but he doesn't know that—and neither does she.'

'Sinister Sinister' was booming from the speakers, and even Howard had the grace to be more than a little bit frightened.

'What have you done, Rose?' he asked me, in a tone that suggested that all thought of fucking my brains out had vanished from his fickle head.

'Exactly what you said—I cooked something up, from one of Mummy's old recipe books. Not exactly eye of newt and toe of frog but something not dissimilar. Natural selection has devised all manner of tasty trifles for the benefit of innocuous creatures that need a little something to discourage all the predators who might otherwise make a meal of them. Not fatal, of course—the whole point of such devices is that the predators need to learn from bitter experience. Rumor has it that mixing the brew with the alcohol increases the intensity of the spasms, but I've never actually experimented with it before.

Howard the Flasher looked down, horror-stricken, at the empty glass clutched in his hand. I let him stew for three or four seconds by saying: 'I put it in John's whisky—the vodka's just for guests, and it's as pure as the day it left Warrington.'

'I don't understand,' he said, truthfully.

'That's good,' I assured him. 'Because this is where we move into unknown territory. By now, you see, Barbara must be just as confused as you are. She still doesn't believe, of course, but it's not what you believe that counts: it's what you feel. Barbara's heart was always a few degrees colder than John's, but even she can't be ice-cool right now. Not with John groaning like a sinner in hell in front of her, and with all the anxiety and shame and guilt and everything else that goes with the territory. No matter how civilized you and she may think you are, the sickness must already be creeping upon her. All it needs is one last twist.' While I was talking I picked up the phone, hit REDIAL and handed the receiver to Howard.

He took it.

'Now, Howard darling,' I said, as sweet as sweet could be, 'I want you to do exactly as I tell you to. When Barbie answers, tell her who you are and where you are—and then describe, as neatly and as accurately as you can, exactly what I'm doing.'

I picked up the Barbie doll, and I drew out the next needle from the pack. Only the thicker ones were left, but there were plenty of them.

Howard looked at me as if I were mad—but only for a second. Then he saw the logic of it.

He could have refused, of course. Barbie was, after all, his wife, and they were both civilized people, who tolerated one another's little adventures. As I'd already told him, though, it doesn't really matter what you believe; what matters is how you feel. He had a bitter taste in his own mouth, which hadn't come from the Bloody Mary, and it was his royal blue carpet too.

'Barbara,' he said, 'it's me. I'm in Rose's upstairs room. She has a Barbie doll in her left hand, which has a photograph of you mounted on its face, and a needle in her right hand. Now she's resting the point of the needle on the doll's stomach, and....'

He had the tone of voice exactly right, but he wasn't entitled to any credit for that. For the moment, just like his effigy, he was all my own work.

When Howard had finished I took the receiver back and replaced it in its cradle. I didn't bother to listen to the strangled sounds that were coming from the other end. I knew that the power of suggestion had done its work, and done it well.

I picked up the figurine that had Howard's face and passed it over to him; he took it meekly.

'It's up to you to keep it safe, Howard,' I told him. 'For as long as it exists, it's the only image of you that has any power. If you look after it, no witch will ever be able to do you harm—but if you break it, or allow it to become distressed, you'll suffer. Whether you believe in it or not, you'll suffer. Do you understand that?'

He nodded, like a child confronted with the earnest admonition of a trusted parent. Later, no doubt, he'd tell himself that he'd been foolish, and that of course the makeshift doll had no power to harm him—but he'd keep it safe anyway. He wouldn't dare to test the proposition by running a needle through the effigy's waxen flesh, or breaking it in two, because he'd figure that it was best to be on the safe side.

Howard was the kind of man who always figured that it was best to be on the safe side. He'd married Barbara Schiff instead of somebody capable of loving him, but even that, in its way, was a matter of being on the safe side.

'You'd better go now,' I told him. 'They might need an ambulance, and they might not have the guts to call for one themselves.'

I wasn't absolutely sure, at that particular moment, whether the suggestion I'd planted might even be powerful enough to destroy them. I'd demonstrated to Barbie that Marlow wasn't quite as far from the dark heart of Africa as she had assumed, and even I couldn't be sure how much margin there really was.

Howard got up to go, carrying the figurine as if it were the most precious thing he owned.

If only I'd had such confidence in my art at nineteen, I thought, the whole farce might have been unnecessary. If only I'd had the courage and the imagination, I might have spoiled Barbie's spell and claimed Howard for myself. As I heard the front door close behind him, though, I wondered whether the situation might not have reproduced itself anyway, with Flasher Fletcher as the errant husband of poor Rag Doll and Coldheart Coulthart as the hapless Mister Mischief.

Reflexively, I reached out to hit the PLAY button on the mini-system, starting Funeral Nation yet again. It was playing far too loudly for that hour of the night, but I needed the oppressive rhythm and the dark sentiment of the words. I had no rhymes of my own to serve as incantations, so I had to borrow some.

I picked up the last of the four dolls: the rag doll to which I'd attached my own photograph, about whose neck I'd placed a noose woven from my own black-dyed hairs. Then I opened a little plastic box of dressmaker's pins: the kind that have little colored spheres in place of flat no-nonsense heads.

I began to take pins from the box, one by one; I pushed them into the head of the doll, so that the colored spheres marked out the arc of a halo. As I pushed them in I exerted every atom of my will to the magical task in hand. I commanded the points of those pins to delve into the depths of my own tortured mind, to kill the terrible thoughts and cauterize the horrid feelings, and give me the strength not to care.

I wouldn't have minded paying a price for what I wanted, in ordinary pain. Any pure and simple headache would have been preferable to the kind of hurt I actually felt: the hurt compounded out of raging jealousy, the sense of my betrayal and the awful awareness of my own implicit worthlessness. I was perfectly prepared to wear a crown of thorns, and to endure its pricking, provided that I could be free of ire and guilt and dreadful self-pity.

But it didn't work.

Witchcraft had worked on John, with a little help from one of Mum's grimoires, and it had worked on Barbara, with a little help from John's awful example, and it had worked on Howard, with a little help from my own dark intensity, but it still wouldn't work on me.

I just couldn't take it seriously.

In spite of my newfound power, my proven authority, I simply couldn't take it seriously.

That was the manner in which my curse rebounded on me—or, at least, the manner in which it began its rebounding. I don't believe that the crown of thorns actually intensified or prolonged my misery, but that's not the point. The point was that hurting John and Barbara—and showing them that I had the power to hurt them—didn't make me feel the least bit better. It simply didn't help

John was discharged from hospital two days later, having made a complete recovery. He didn't tell the doctors there the truth about what had happened to him; he just kept on assuring them that it must have been something he ate. Barbara was released the following day, having steadfastly made the same assurances. If the doctors knew or thought differently, they made no public declaration of the fact; all that mattered to them, it seemed, was that their patients had got better.

John came home to pack his things, and then left again. Barbara went home with Howard, and they resumed their lives, sensibly putting the incident behind them. I stayed where I was, alone.

And so the curse unwound, and kept on unwinding.

I threw the effigies of John and Barbara away, with all the needles sticking in them. They were only dolls, and only needles. The last needles I'd inserted—the ones I'd stuck into the dolls' eyes—had only deprived Coldheart and Mischief of the ability to see clearly enough to repent what they had done. I hung on to my own doll, as Howard presumably hung on to his, but I couldn't keep it safe.

I still look at it occasionally, and reflect on the foolishness that inspired its ridiculous crown of thorns. Sometimes, I'm a little rough with it. I just can't seem to help myself.

Unlike Barbies, rag dolls come apart at the seams.

RENT

At first, Jez thought that the vamp was just another freak, just another weirdo, just another shit with a screwed-up soul.

Jez knew lots of freaks. Some people—including the female whores who strutted their stuff on the King's Cross meat rack with the rent boys—would have said that all his johns were freaks, but that was just naked prejudice. Jez was a liberal, and he didn't give a damn where his johns wanted to squirt their semen, as long as they paid the going rate for the location in question; but even he had to concede that more than a few of the guys were seriously weird and definitely freaky.

At first, he thought the vamp was one of those.

The vamp drove a black BMW, polished so assiduously that it gleamed. Jez couldn't imagine the neatly manicured vamp laboring over the machine with an old rag and an ozone-friendly can of Mr. Sheen, so he assumed that the job was contracted out. The first time he ever saw the BMW kerb-crawling the rack, he noticed the girls edging out with a little more enthusiasm than usual, not just because they smelled the money but because they smelled the pride behind that polish. But the vamp wasn't interested in girls, and they soon learned to turn away in disgust when it came nosing up from the station.

That first night, Jez thought the vamp just had to be crazy. For one thing, he took Jez home to a brand-new glass-faced block in the Docklands, to the place where he actually lived. Not many johns did that, certainly not on a first date; even the ones who lived alone and only wanted hand relief were nervous of the neighbors and scared half to death of becoming blackmail targets. The vamp ought to have been twice as scared, given the nature of his nasty little habits, but he wasn't. The vamp didn't seem to be scared of anything. He had nerves of steel.

Even that seemed like one more symptom of serious weirdness, in the beginning.

The vamp didn't have fangs, of course—not Christopher Lee-type extended canines, anyhow. Nor did he go straight for the jugular, the way vampires were supposed to do. He looked for veins in the same places the regular mainliners did, in the soft white flesh of the arms and the legs. He'd break into them very carefully, nibbling away with his pearly-white front teeth, then suck for twenty or thirty minutes at a stretch. It took the vamp far longer to take his drink than it did to shoot his wad, which he always did afterwards, into Jez's mouth, but he paid well enough for the time he used. It hurt, of course, but so did lots of other things, and hurt was just one more thing that got added on to the rent.

The bites certainly didn't look like the little round holes that Christopher Lee left; they were more like ragged love bites. They healed very quickly, though, and they never got infected, and Jez soon decided that the horror stories that passed up and down the rack about the things you could catch from human bites must be exaggerated. Most of the horror stories that passed up and down the rack were exaggerated, though some weren't; it was difficult to figure out which were which, but Jez was fifteen years old and learning fast.

The first couple of times with the vamp, Jez found the business moderately sickening, but for that sort of rent he was always prepared to swallow his pride, along with everything else if necessary. After the first couple of times, it got much easier. He got used to it. He had plenty of opportunity, because the vamp was a man of regular habits, and the BMW always made straight for his spot; one of the other kids told him that if the car came cruising when Jez was otherwise occupied, it just went straight on through and out the other side.

Jez wasn't stupid enough to reckon that the vamp used him regularly out of affection; he figured that it was probably because his veins were easy to get at, because he was strictly a snorter and a dragon-chaser and never used a needle. Even so, he began to award the vamp a leading role in his fantasies of making a big enough score to skip the rack altogether and go independent. Like all the boys, he resented having to hand over so much of his take to the management—after all, he was the one renting out his tender young flesh to be poked and chewed; all they were renting to him was a square yard of pavement that they didn't even own. They supplied the junk too, of course, and an eight-by-twelve in a converted Victorian semi, but Jez knew how easily replaceable those services were, as long as you could come up with enough pictures of the queen.

It was only natural, in the circumstances, that Jez was able to think positively about the possibility of being taken on permanently by the vamp, in spite of the ragged love bites. It was, after all, far less blood than the usual kind of donor was required to give, and the vamp never asked any awkward questions about HIV. Jez had never been tested and didn't intend to be; he couldn't afford to care, or even to try to figure out the odds as to whether the junk he smoked and sniffed would kill him before his immune system's season ticket finally expired.

Apparently the vamp didn't care either, maybe because he already had it, maybe because he had nerves of steel. Either way, he qualified for a starring role in Jez's dreamland—for a while. In fact, the vamp didn't stop being a prominent figure in Jez's dreams even when Jez started wondering whether he might, after all, be something other than one more freak, something more ominous than one more shit with a screwed-up soul, in a world where shits with screwed-up souls were by no means scarce.

Their conversation mostly consisted of mocking jokes. The vamp had a great line in deadpan answers to teasing questions.

'Will I become a vampire after I die?' Jez asked, once. 'That's what's supposed to happen, right?—a vampire's victims generally become vampires themselves.'

'You don't have to wait until you die, Jez,' the vamp told him, serenely. 'You could start right away, if you saved your money the way I do instead of blowing it all on synthetic endorphins and ersatz ecstasy. You could buy your own place and pick up some kid fresh off the train, and bleed him to your heart's content—or even her, if your fancy goes that way. If you really want to be a vampire, that's the only way to do it. There's no way to extend a lease on a body.'

By degrees they built up quite a double act.

'Hey, Vamp,' said Jez, when he felt entitled to be a little more familiar, 'I bet I know what you do for a living—you're in the city, right? You're a bloodsuckin' capitalist who got filthy rich by exploitin' the toilin' masses, right?'

'Got it in one,' the vamp conceded. 'I'm the sole proprietor of one of the oldest and most respected firms in the Golden Square Mile. My family has been managing investments since the beginning of the Industrial Revolution.'

'Bullshit,' said Jez. 'You don't expect me to believe you got a family, do you? I bet you've been doin' it all yourself since day one—except you sometimes have to disappear for a while and then come back pretendin' to be your own son, so that nobody gets suspicious.'

'Alas,' the vamp replied, wistfully, 'even vampires aren't immortal. I only wish we were.'

Jez enjoyed the conversations, at first. It made a change—most johns were too paranoid to say much more than 'How much?' and 'This'll do.' Most johns wouldn't look Jez in the eye, but the vamp did, without the least trace of embarrassment or shame or shiftiness. Nor was his stare at all mesmeric, as might have been expected if he'd been a real vampire—'real' meaning, in this paradoxical instance, the kind you could watch at work for a couple of quid on a rented video. The vamp had a gaze much softer and infinitely less haunted than Klaus Kinski's, although he was sexy enough in a dignified kind of way. Jez figured that if the vamp had girls working at his offices in the city the air was probably heavy with unrequited lust.

'How come you got garlic in the kitchen, vamp?' Jez asked him once, after he'd done a bit of snooping. 'Not to mention mirrors all over the place. Ain't you got no sense of propriety? Why don't y'hang a crucifix on the wall, for Christ's sake?'

'Like every other species, vampires are subject to the rigors of natural selection,' the vamp assured him, calmly. 'All the ones who could only go out at night, or who couldn't be seen in mirrors, or got frightened half to death by the sight of a crucifix, ended up with sharpened stakes through their hearts. My kind is the only one left. But I don't go in for crucifixes—one ought to show a little respect for the lost undead, don't you think?'

'Great,' said Jez, laughing. 'All the true blue Draculas got impaled, and only the harmless ones survive. With us normals, it's always been t'other way around.'

'Oh, we're not harmless,' the vamp corrected him, in a voice as mild as milk. 'We're civilized, discreet, modest...but not harmless. Only the fittest survive, Jez—only the cleverest, and the strongest, and the best.'

It was good fun, for a while. It might have been a fraction sicker than talking about what the greenhouse effect was doing to the weather or why England's batting had collapsed in the test match, but it certainly wasn't as sick as exchanging merry quips about the first signs of Karposi's sarcoma, or what you get when you cross a green monkey with a traffic warden, or any of the other contributions that the great gay plague had made to the oral cultural intercourse of the London Underworld. Jez was tempted once or twice to ask whether vampires were doomed to extinction now that AIDS was here to stay, but he never did; he figured that if anything were to qualify as overstepping the mark, that would probably be it.

There was no particular point in time when Jez's attitude to the vamp began to change. There was no sinister clue to catch his attention and make him shiver with unease, let alone a ghastly revelation. In fact, it didn't seem to be anything to do with the vamp's behaviour at all; Jez thought that the change was purely in himself, and didn't make much sense. It took the form of a creeping paranoia, which stole up on him like a wasting disease. If there was a single starting point, it must have been some fugitive dream that he had forgotten completely by the time he woke up, or came down.

Logically, the relationship ought to have continued to become more comfortable; the two of them might even have learned to trust one another. As the weeks of their acquaintance turned into months, Jez found out more and more about the vamp. He knew not only his real name and his real address, but which bank and credit cards he used, where he got his groceries, where he had been to school, what kind of music he liked...all the little data that fleshed him out into the perfect image of a human being. But the more Jez found out—the more intimately he came to know the innocence of the image—the more the suspicion stole upon him that it really was all image, all sham, and all disguise, and that the only real and true thing about the vamp was the particular way he used his teeth and his prick, in that order, in the course of their expensive rituals.

At first, Jez was happy enough to construe his suspicions about the vamp's fundamental unhumanity as a natural extension of their joking relationship—was it not the case, after all, that such suspicions were a tacit assumption of all their humorous banter? But in time, although Jez and the vamp did not cease to joke with one another, the comedy wore thin. The idea that the vamp was just another freak seemed to shrivel up inside Jez's head, of its own accord, soon to be reborn as an anxiety that the vamp might in fact be thoroughly and utterly normal—by his own alien, unhuman, diabolical standards.

That anxiety was all the more pernicious, and all the more persistent, because Jez did not know exactly what it implied. He became gradually afraid, without quite knowing what it was that he was afraid of.

That was when his questions gradually became more

pointed—and, inevitably, when the answers became gradually more evasive.

'Who'd you put the bite on before you took up with me?' Jez asked. 'The old-timers on the rack say they never saw you before.'

'Does it matter?' the vamp countered. 'It was no one special—I paid him the way I pay you, and at much the same rate, allowing for inflation. Rents are cheaper up north, I hear, but that's because no one wants to live there.'

Jez was from the north himself; the rack was full of north-erners, put there by the state of the nation.

On another occasion, Jez asked whether everybody's blood tasted the same, and whether the fact that he was so often coked up to the eyeballs made his blood more addictive than the blood of a non-user.

'A connoisseur gets to notice subtle differences after a while,' the vamp informed him, punctiliously. 'But it's not as obvious as the difference between burgundy and claret. As to the hypothesis that my compulsion might have intensified by virtue of drinking the nectar of too many drug-addicts, I can only say that it sounds just a little far-fetched.'

Later still, Jez asked what would happen to the vamp's considerable personal fortune, given that he had no son and heir to leave it to, adding the sarcastic suggestion that he might care to leave it to the Blood Transfusion Service.

'Oh, I intend to have an heir,' the vamp assured him, blandly. 'There's plenty of time for that, dear boy...plenty of time.'

The vamp looked to be well on the downside of fifty; he kept Grecian-2000 in his bathroom as well as a mirror, and there was not one jot of evidence to suggest that he ever kept company with members of the opposite sex. Maybe that was the crucial incongruity that finally sowed the seed of something crazy in Jez's addled brain—although the crack through which it crept was, of course, already there.

Truth to tell, it wasn't just the vamp who had begun to seem a little less sick and freaky to Jez; the whole world was beginning to appear ordinary by its own implicit and thoroughly unhuman standards.

Jez wasn't particularly worried when he first began to feel the movement in his guts. It didn't seem to be painful, even when he hit dirt after a high; to begin with it was just there, disturbing simply by virtue of its presence. But it got steadily worse.

As time went by, he found it more and more difficult to sleep. Every time he lay down—whether he was drunk or sober, high or low—the quietness of his own limbs showed up by contrast the activity of whatever was inside him. Sometimes, he watched his own stomach, trying to see the skin bulge and stretch where the thing was shifting in its restless fashion. He began to run a tape measure around his waist every day, worried about the possibility that he was expanding from within; but he wasn't—in fact, he was getting thinner.

He thought that he was getting paler too, but it was difficult to tell. The rack was full of pallid faces, which grew gradually whiter as careers progressed along their customary trajectories. No one else on the rack saw anything in his face or his gait or his manner that seemed worthy of comment, and if ever he mentioned to one of the other boys or one of the more maternal whores that his guts felt as if they were practicing their boy-scout knots they would just laugh, and tell him he ought to have their problems.

Jez was no wimp, and he would have ignored the feeling if he could, waiting patiently for it to go away, but the nature of the feeling simply wouldn't permit that. It was too intrusive, too consistent, too close to the core of his being. He couldn't help but worry about it, and he couldn't help his anxiety transforming itself by inexorable degrees into an obsession.

Although he never actually saw the thing shifting under the skin of his belly he became absolutely certain that something was in there, that it was alive, and that it was feeding off him. He knew it wasn't a tapeworm or a tumor, but imagined it instead as something resembling a newborn rat or a blind mole, with massive jaws filled with tiny teeth, which it used to clamp on to his intestine in order to draw out the best of his blood—blood newly-enriched by the products of digestion.

It didn't take long to guess what the entity might be—to 'formulate a hypothesis' about the thing, as the vamp would undoubtedly have phrased it. At first, the idea that came into his mind seemed too way-out, and Jez knew that even the vamp, despite his love of understatement, would have found a dismissive description far more colorful and contemptuous than 'just a little far-fetched'. But he couldn't shake the idea loose, and the longer it stayed with him, the more its incredibility was eaten away by familiarity. Every night, while he took his place on the rack, waiting and waiting while the creepy-crawlies inched past in their Astras and Cortinas and Volvos and Datsuns, the thing would gnaw away at his entrails—gently and painlessly enough, but no less horrid for that—and the idea would gnaw at his mind, gently and painlessly but no less horrid in its turn.

As the creature in his belly grew, so did the idea in his brain. They grew together, like shadowy twins, until the one was a mature homunculus, as sleek as strong as any fond parent could wish for, and the other was a full-grown fantasy, as vivid and venturesome as anything that morphine or magic mushrooms could ever hope to compose.

The fantasy that possessed Jez's mind took off from the supposition that the vamp wasn't just a shit with a screwed-up soul, like every other city gent who liked a bit of rough from the rack, but that his taste for blood was merely a matter of the routine nourishment of his species. Perhaps, Jez somehow could not help but think, this was one john who wasn't even queer, because he belonged to a kind that didn't have two sexes at all, but only one. Perhaps, Jez somehow could not help but fear, this was one john who was only doing exactly what came naturally, for the proper purpose that nature intended. Perhaps, Jez somehow could not help but believe, the heir that the vamp fondly intended to have had already been conceived, after the fashion of his alien kind.

When Jez first wondered whether the strange stirring in his belly might have something to do with the vamp his immediate inclination was to share the joke, but he couldn't. He didn't see the vamp that week, and by the time the black BMW came cruising again he was well past the point where he could think the churning in his gut was anything trivial and temporary. He didn't want to mention it to the vamp, because he didn't want to see the vamp's reaction. It was like the blood test he'd never taken—one of those moments of possible confirmation that were best postponed forever. He was scared that if he told the vamp that something was eating away at his guts, the vamp would smile—not an amused smile, but a proud smile; the smile of an expectant father.

Jez thought—and believed, despite one or two brave attempts to doubt it—that the vamp had shot an alien spore into his fertile gut, where it had taken root and begun to grow after its alien fashion, and from which it would, in the fullness of time, emerge, the moment of its birth a baptism of blood

In time, it became a little more painful, but never unbearable. Without hurting him unduly, the thing simply wore him down. By the time the creature in his abdomen had been gnawing at him for two months, Jez was so listless and so starved of sleep that simply taking his place on the rack became an ordeal. The intervals between enquiries began to get longer, and the management began to quiz him about the decline of his takings. If it hadn't been for the vamp, the management might have decided that he wasn't worth his spot, given that more fresh meat arrived just around the corner with every intercity 125, but the vamp was still a regular, and one well-used to meeting sky-high city rents without a murmur.

The vamp never commented on the way Jez looked, or enquired after the state of his health. The blood, it seemed, was still good—and the vamp, in any case, had other reasons for keeping in touch. Those reasons didn't have to be spelled out;

their relationship had reached that magical pitch at which they no longer seemed to needed words to help them understand one another's motives and desires.

It still went on, day by day and week by week. Jez lost twenty kilos, and became as weak as a kitten. Eventually, after one more quiz administered more in sorrow than in anger, he lost his place on the rack, and he knew that he couldn't complain. The management had had no choice, in the end; they were men of business, after all. The vamp hadn't been around for a while, and no one except Jez could be certain that he wasn't gone for ever.

The management even overrode his strenuous objections and sent him to the hospital, but the hospital couldn't make a bed available and the doctors sent him back to the eight-by-twelve after leeching a generous helping of his blood in order to carry out tests. Jez didn't tell them about the creature inside him, because he could tell that they didn't want to know, and would refuse to see it on an X-ray. He could tell that the doctors didn't want to take him in—that they'd rather he simply vanished, or at least had the elementary courtesy to die somewhere else instead of wasting time that they would far rather devote to the deserving sick.

By this time, Jez was in bad trouble. The worst of it wasn't that he was playing host to the vamp's offspring but that he was cut off from his connection.

If the hospital had admitted him, they'd have been obliged to feed his habit after some sort of fashion, rather than see him shrivel up to nothing at all, but the management worked on a strictly cash basis. They had done their bit, and owed him nothing; he'd never taken the trouble to pay into any kind of pension fund. He didn't have any friends among the other rent boys, and although some of the older whores sometimes seemed to experience a ghostly maternal affection for the prettier boys, there was no way that sort of pantomime affection was going to be convertible into any kind of supply.

Even so, Jez was home for two whole days, in bed but not

sleeping, before he called the vamp and begged for help.

Any run-of-the-mill freak or weirdo would have put the phone down on him, but the vamp didn't. The vamp listened. Jez wasn't particularly glad about that, but he wouldn't have been glad if the vamp had cut him off either; he knew that there was no way out.

The vamp brought the black BMW to the semi, and came upstairs to Jez's room. He didn't waste any time; he just picked Jez up in his arms, all wrapped up in a blanket, and carried him down to the car. He laid Jez out on the back seat and he drove home to the brave new world of the half-reconstructed Docklands. He installed Jez in the spare room, and brought him a cup of hot, sweet tea.

'That's no good,' Jez pointed out, politely. 'I need some stuff—white and pure. I can't feed your lousy kid unless you can feed my head as well as my guts.'

The vamp only held the cup to Jez's lips, patiently but insistently, and in spite of what he'd said, Jez drank it. He knew, somehow, that the vamp wasn't going to get him any hard stuff, or give him any money so that he could get it himself. Now Jez was in the spare bedroom, it was Jez who owed rent, in cash or in kind—and Jez knew that if it were to be paid in kind, it wouldn't be paid in the usual kind.

'Why me?' asked Jez, when he'd finished the tea. 'Why'd you pick me?'

'Why anybody?' countered the vamp, with a shrug. 'We can't even pick and choose our own selves with any degree of rationality or any semblance of good aesthetic judgment, so why should we be any better at picking the others on whom we elect to inflict ourselves?'

He was a philosopher to the bitter end, was the vamp. Jez might have admired him for it, if he hadn't been so desperately in need of a hit.

When the vamp left him alone, Jez thought that it would soon be all over. In fact, he felt so close to the end that he was certain that the vamp had misjudged it, and would be too late returning to witness the birth of his son and heir—but he didn't know whether or not that would matter to the vamp, who was, after all, unhuman.

As things turned out, though, Jez had longer to wait than he thought, and the vamp had come back

It was nighttime when the moment finally came, but the light was on. The vamp was sitting by the bed, patiently waiting. When Jez began to retch and gasp, the vamp unhurriedly pulled the duvet back, and unbuttoned Jez's shirt to expose the pale white belly within. Then he stood back to watch while the thing inside chewed its way out, ripping and slashing and tearing with its tiny, clawed fingers and its tinier teeth.

The vamp could have brought a razor or a carving knife to help it on its way, but he didn't. His kind obviously didn't believe in cosseting their young; the ones who couldn't make it on their own must simply be deemed unfit to live. The vamp just stood and watched, his face devoid of any expression, while his son and heir fought his messy way out through the surprisingly resilient flesh of the host who had carried him to term.

Jez watched too, though he would rather have been shocked into insensibility. He watched the rip in his belly from the moment it first appeared until the much later moment when the thing that was so laboriously making it was ready to squeeze through, stained top to toe with blood and flushed with the triumph of its first success in the harsh and hazardous game of life.

The pain had always been muted before, but it was given free rein while the thing was extracting itself, and the agony increased steadily all the while. Jez would have given anything for a hit powerful enough to blast him into orbit, but he was down at ground level, flat in the gutter without a shooting star in sight. There was nothing he could do to fight the pain except stuff his knuckles into his mouth and bite down hard, as if the self-inflicted pain might somehow exorcise the other. Strangely enough, it did help.

Eventually, though, the creature was free. It didn't look much like an ordinary baby, but there wasn't any particular reason to expect it to.

The vamp picked it up.

Jez looked down at the bloody wreck of his abdomen, and slowly unclamped his teeth from his bloody hand. He realized, pathetically, that he wasn't going to die. In spite of everything, he wasn't going to die.

He didn't immediately understand why he wasn't going to die, but in the end he looked up from his rapidly healing wound to stare at the vamp. Then he saw that father and son were looking down at him with earnest concern, sincerely glad to see that he was getting better.

Jez's mouth was full of the taste of his own blood, and as the pain gradually ebbed away, he realized for the first time how supremely sweet and nourishing that blood must be, in the mouths of those who were that way inclined.

TENEBRIO

John Hazard had just started on the pile of first-year essays when there was a rap on the lab door. He didn't get the chance to say, 'Come in'. Steve Pearlman wasn't the type to wait for an invitation. Instead, Hazard said, 'No. Absolutely not. I told you last time—never again.'

'Hi, Doc,' Pearlman said, breezily. 'Got something here that might interest you.' The young man reached into the leather pouch attached to his belt and pulled out a map, which he threw on the desk while he rummaged around for something more deeply buried.

Pearlman was in his full ecowarrior regalia: faded blue jeans that hadn't been washed for a month, a fawn sweater so thick and lumpy it might have been knitted with chopsticks, and mud-spattered Doc Martens. His blond hair was no longer in dreadlocks, but it looked less tidy than ever. Pearlman had been Hazard's tutee during the three years he had spent at the University, notionally studying ecology. Hazard hadn't seen a lot of him in the lab or the lecture theatre but had been forced to spend time with him at the beginning and end of every term to discuss the various complaints that invariably accumulated. It had been a great relief to Hazard when Pearlman had actually contrived to get a third-class degree; he hadn't expected to see or hear from him again after the post-graduation piss-up— Pearlman wasn't the kind of student who required his teachers to produce references for dozens of different jobs—but he hadn't been so lucky.

Although Steve Pearlman had never shown overmuch interest in entomology while he'd been studying, the veterans of Crookham Heath had taught him that academics had their uses, and the battle of Egypt Mill had sent him scurrying back to his alma mater in search of an expert on the habits of hawk moths. Hazard was more a beetle man, but he'd been so flattered that he'd agreed to appear at the press conference set up to argue that the area between Egypt Mill and Cramborne Barrow ought to be designated a Site of Special Scientific Interest and that the railway line north of Sutton station ought not to be diverted across it in order to allow the road to be widened. Unfortunately, the tabloid press had decided to take the other side, and Hazard's name had been an open invitation to pun-hungry headline-mongers. By the time the bulldozers had actually moved in, Hazard felt as if he'd done a stint on the Somme in 1914, and the Dean of the Faculty had been seriously displeased by the damage he'd supposedly done to his department's reputation for objectivity and scientific seriousness.

A full thirty seconds had passed by the time Pearlman found what he was searching for in the bottom of his bag. He hauled out a plastic specimen-bottle a little longer and a little thicker than a tube of Smarties, which he passed to Hazard. It was full of small beetles—hundreds of them. They'd probably been alive when Pearlman had scooped them into the tube, but crowding and lack of air had done for most of them by now. Hazard released the cap in order to provide belated relief for the survivors, but he was careful not to spill any on to his desk. They weren't all the same species, but most of them were very similar. Hazard didn't require a magnifying glass to identify the dominant genus, although he suspected that he'd need a microscope to figure out exactly how many species were represented.

'*Tenebrio*, except for three or four undersized carabids and a couple of others,' he said. 'Common as muck. Thanks to agriculture, *Tenebrio* species are the most cosmopolitan of all beetles, although most of their immediate cousins prefer a warmer and drier climate. They're farmed in their own right because their larvae are used as fishing bait—mealworms, they're called.'

'I knew they weren't woodworm beetles,' Pearlman replied, cheerfully. 'I wish I could say that you taught me that, but I had plenty of opportunity to get acquainted with that kind of critter when I was at the squat in Curzon Street.'

'Some *Tenebrionidae* are wood-borers,' Hazard told him, holding the specimen tube up to the light and peering at the interior, trying to find something more interesting than he'd so far seen, 'but none of these guys have the jaws for it. Look, Steve, I can't see the point. They're perfectly ordinary species— pests, even—and even if they weren't, they'd be no help to the cause. The hawk moth fiasco must have taught you that no self-respecting tabloid will ever go out on a limb for an insect. Newts maybe—but even that colony of snails on Twyford Down was simply relocated. There's not a single instance on record of a road development being stopped, even at the pie-in-the-sky stage, for the sake of an insect—and this one has to be way past the pie-in-the-sky stage if the Friends have mobilized the Last-Ditch Brigade.'

'It's not actually a brigade at present,' Pearlman confessed. 'Hardly a platoon, so far. Even the Friends don't think this one is worth fighting, but that's because they don't have any domino players on the steering committee. *Tenebrio* is what they call a darkling beetle, no?'

Hazard's eyebrows went up in response to the revelation that Steve Pearlman actually knew what a darkling beetle was. 'You've already shown these to someone else, haven't you?' he said.

'I can use a library,' Pearlman retorted, as he took up the map again and unfolded it. It was just a road map, not an ordnance survey map—but that made a sort of sense, given that Steve Pearlman's vocation was trying to make sure that today's road maps didn't go out of date as fast as earlier editions. The army he'd joined had been so successful back in the nineties, in the wake of the Newbury bypass fiasco, that no brand new road had been built for a decade within a hundred miles—but that had only served to shift the war into a new phase. Road widening was all the rage now, and it was very difficult for the protesters to defend sites that already sat alongside significant traffic arteries. The tide of public opinion that had briefly got behind them was dead against them now. Everybody but the Friends' Last-Ditch Brigade figured that the inevitable cost of not building any new roads was making the most of the ones that already existed.

'There,' said Pearlman, passing him the map.

Hazard looked at the place where the younger man's finger was pointing and frowned. 'That's the A303,' he said. 'I didn't know they had any plans to widen the A303 this year.'

'They don't,' said Pearlman. 'They're widening this one here.'

Hazard had to squint to see it. The 'road' that Pearlman was indicating was so small that it didn't even have a B-number. 'But it doesn't go anywhere,' he said.

'Yes it does,' said Pearlman. 'It goes to Tenebrion Farm. Tenebrion Farm's in the Domesday Book—I checked online. So far as I can tell, it was a thriving enterprise from the eleventh century all the way through to the nineteenth—then it began to fade because its owners couldn't or wouldn't fall in with new fashions. It must have been losing money for two generations before the Common Agricultural Policy gave it a new lease of life. If the owner had switched entirely into cereals and rapeseed he'd probably be OK, but he didn't. He built up his dairy herds instead—then BSE and the supermarket price-lock came along and the whole operation crashed. He tried a few desperation measures—even planted potatoes at one stage—but nothing could stem the cash-hemorrhage and he had to sell out to a developer. All the developer could do to begin with was revamp the actual farm buildings—but there were three big barns as well as a row of workmen's cottages. He converted the lot into dwellings, with the encouragement of a local council that had been ordered by Central Government to make room for 600 extra homes in the next five years, and Tenebrion Farm was suddenly a village ripe for expansion. The only problem with that plan is this stupid cart-track connecting it to the A303. It's not even wide enough for two cars to pass one another. That didn't matter while the farmer was driving his tractors back and forth, but once you've got eight separate family dwellings with two cars apiece, you've got what your bog-standard planning application calls a pressing need for improvement.'

While Pearlman was talking Hazard had worked out how his ex-student had found out that *Tenebrio* was a darkling beetle. He must have taken the name of the farm to the dictionary and the Britannica. The name of a farm recorded in the Domesday Book couldn't possibly have anything to do with the name assigned to a beetle in the Linnaean classification, but *Tenebrio* was so cosmopolitan that you could probably find specimens on every farm in England if you could be bothered to look. Pearlman had obviously bothered to look—but Hazard still couldn't see what good it was going to do him.

'Well,' the entomologist said, carefully, as he put the cap back on the specimen tube, 'it seems to me that the developer has a good case. Presumably, you're worried about the possibility that once the road is there, he'll start angling to build more houses either side of it.'

'That's the least of it,' Pearlman said. 'The real point is that the A303 offers an easy connection to the M3. Look to the north, at that cluster of newish villages west of Hurstbourne Priors. At present, their access roads all connect to the A343, which means that the local yuppies have to make their way over to the M4, with Newbury sprawling right across their path. The bypass was supposed to make that access easier, of course, but that was fifteen years ago. It's Nightmare Junction now—but once the cart track connecting Tenebrion to the A303 is a real road, the temptation to extend it northwards to give the villagers a new way out will become enormous. The New Tenebrionites won't like it, of course—all they want is to be a nice cozy cul-de-sac—but you can bet your pension that the developer always had it in mind. He understands the domino principle, if no one else does. Once he's got the go-ahead to expand Tenebrion

Village he's going to send his bulldozers northwards to plant the spine of a whole bloody town. That's why the battle's worth fighting and why it's worth fighting here and now, between the farm and the A-road. The strip either side of the road's mostly hedgerow, but there's a little patch of woodland here that must have been there from the very beginning, untouched by the hand of cultivation since the Norman invasion. The Domesday Book identifies it as Tenebrion Wood—my bet is that the farm was named after it.'

'It's not entirely untouched,' Hazard said, raising the specimen tube. 'No matter how long Tenebrion Wood's been there, this *Tenebrio*'s an invader, carried into the British Isles with European grains. These may have adapted to local produce, but they're no more native to the wood than you are. I suppose you've considered the argument that setting up tree houses, digging tunnels and getting set to fight a pitched battle against the developer's security men will completely wreck the fragile ecology of your precious wood. Even if you did save it from the bulldozers—which you won't—you'd destroy it in the process. Anyway, I already told you I'm not getting involved. I can't afford the hassle.'

'That's what they'll put on the ecosphere's tombstone,' Pearlman said, predictably. 'We might have saved it, but we couldn't afford the hassle. I just want you to take a look, Doc. I just want you to stroll around the site, and tell me whether there's anything better than darkling beetles there—anything we can actually use in an all-out propaganda war. It's an exceptional site in more ways than one, and the leaf-litter seems to be beetle heaven. I scooped that lot up in two minutes flat, in daylight. You don't have to lead the charge—just give us the benefit of your expertise. One day, the frontline will reach your back yard, and you'll be screaming for my help.'

'My back yard is a cemetery,' Hazard pointed out.

'You think that makes a difference? You think that because you're living in a redundant vicarage next to a derelict church you're safe? Come on, Doc, even you aren't that naive. It won't be nearly so much fun living next to that folly once they've connected your little lane to the A33—and they'll do it. Inch by inch, wood by wood, they'll do it. Just take a look. That's all I'm asking.'

'It's pointless,' said Hazard.

'It's better than marking first-year essays,' Pearlman retorted. 'It's coming on summertime, and I'll bet you haven't been out in the field since September last, even if you do live in the darkest heart of the green belt.'

Hazard could feel himself weakening. Summer was coming on, and he hadn't been in the field since the start of the autumn term. Even if there was nothing to see but darkling beetles, it would be a day out.

'Tomorrow's Friday,' he said, finally. 'I'm teaching till three, but I can wrap up after that. Probably reach you by five, traffic permitting.'

'Tonight would be a lot better,' the ecowarrior retorted, unable to suppress a wide grin of self-satisfaction. 'The beetles mostly come out at night. That way, you could give me a lift.'

'Tomorrow,' Hazard said, flatly. He figured that he'd made enough compromises.

'I'll leave you the map,' said Pearlman, who was prepared to be generous now that he's got what he wanted. 'Leave your car in the lay-by west of the turn-off—it's a good three-quarters of a mile, but the walk will do you good. Bring your wellies.'

Because it was Friday the traffic was dire, so Hazard didn't get to the relevant stretch of the A303 until five-thirty. What Pearlman had described as a 'lay-by' was just a gap in the haw-thorn hedge that already had one car parked in it: a red Citroen Saxo. Having received no attention for at least two years, the hedge was so overgrown that it was difficult to manoeuvre his Daewoo in beside the Saxo, but Hazard managed. He pulled his wellington boots out of the front seat and put them on. He threw his loafers on the seat and put his mobile phone out of sight in the glove compartment before locking the vehicle and setting forth.

Although the gate guarding the 'cart track' had been tied open—presumably by the new residents of Tenebrion Farm—it still bore a notice saying PRIVATE ROAD: NO RIGHT OF WAY. It hadn't occurred to Hazard until he saw it that Pearlman's Last-Ditchers would be trespassing, thus requiring him to break the law even to look at the site, but he had come too far to turn around. Cursing himself for allowing himself to be sucked in, he began to walk up the narrow lane.

The unkempt hedges were seething with small birds and the fields beyond hadn't been ploughed or planted for as long as the hedges hadn't been trimmed. Spring had been warm and wet, as spring usually was nowadays, and grasses had run riot in the fallow fields. To the uneducated eye, it might have seemed that the land to either side was already halfway returned to wilderness, but Hazard's eye was not uneducated. He knew that the patchwork of hedges and square fields that even country folk tended to think of as 'natural' was entirely the product of technical artifice. If Tenebrion Farm really had been a thriving operation when the Domesday Book took account of its productivity, the artifice in question might go back a thousand years—but it was no more 'natural' for that.

For the first half-mile, during which the track curved gently to the left, there was little or no change in the surroundings. Then Hazard came to the border of what Pearlman had called Tenebrion Wood—although his earlier description of it as 'a little patch of woodland' seemed far more accurate. The hedges dissolved into a chaotic mess of thin-boled trees and thick-leaved undergrowth, which crowded more closely upon the track than the hedges. The foliage loomed over the pathway with dismal effect, although the arching branches hadn't quite contrived to form a tunnel roof.

Hazard observed, wryly, that this really could pass for 'natural' woodland. It was crammed with sickly and diseased specimens, having nothing of the airy spaciousness of a well-managed and carefully coppiced wood. It was certainly plausible that the site of Tenebrion Wood had never been brought under cultivation since the Norman invasion—although, as he'd pointed out to his former student, that was a far cry from being 'untouched'. If Steve Pearlman could scoop up *Tenebrio* beetles by the dozen, even by day, Hazard was prepared to bet his last sixpence that other invaders would be equally at home here: grey squirrels, brown rats, black-and-white magpies as well as hundreds of invertebrate species. Supermarket supply chains, cross-channel trains and global warming were combining forces to import alien species into southeast England on a massive scale. Whatever Pearlman's Last-Ditch Brigade was striving to defend, it wasn't the native ecosystems of Ancient Britain; those were currently in the process of being shot to hell for the fourth or fifth time since the Celts allegedly imported agriculture to this not-very-green and not-very-pleasant land during the last-little-ice-age-but-one.

It wasn't difficult for Hazard to find Steve and his half-dozen friends, although they were discreet enough not to reveal the extent and nature of their operation to passing cars until they had established a defendable coign of vantage. The wood was so dense that there weren't many places within spitting distance of the road where any sane person would try to pitch a camp. As he approached the Last-Ditchers' base, Hazard could see that the canopy squad were having some difficulty getting their tree houses and rope bridges into shape, and the diggers had only managed to sink a single shaft. By the time he came into the camp the sentry had whistled a warning, and a mud-caked head had bobbed up out of the shaft.

'Oh hi, John!' said the muddy head. 'Steve said you were expected.' He raised his voice to shout, 'OK, boys, he's on our side!' before lowering it again to say, 'You remember me, don't you?'

Hazard would never have recognized the face of the boy beneath the mask of mud, but the voice finally clicked. 'Um... Adrian,' he said. Hazard knew perfectly well that because he was a digger named Adrian his compatriots inevitably called the boy Moley, but that would have seemed an intimacy too far, in spite of the fact that Moley had used his first name. 'Where is Steve?' he asked.

Moley pulled himself out of the hole, revealing a body that was every bit as filthy as his head. 'He's showing the skirt round. He'll have heard the signal—won't be long.' Hazard knew that the digger's use of the word 'skirt' wasn't a symptom of thoughtless sexism. In road-protest parlance, 'skirt' referred specifically to a female outsider—female ecowarriors never wore skirts.

'I take it that the developer doesn't know you're here yet,' Hazard observed.

'I think the residents might have caught on,' Moley told him. 'We're not expecting the opening salvo of blustery threats any time soon, though. You're a scientist, right? You know about soil structure. We're having a hell of a job digging this tunnel—stuff's like black treacle, keeps seeping between the boards no matter how tightly we place 'em. Need more wood underground than up top at this rate. Appreciate it if you could take a look and give us an expert opinion.'

'I'm a beetle man,' Hazard said, unable to think of anything more foolhardy than taking a look at a tunnel whose walls had communicated so much filth to the young man's body. 'I sift leaf-litter when I have to, but everything below the surface is out of my jurisdiction. Sorry.'

'Well, there's plenty of dead leaves,' Moley replied, unresentfully. 'Never seen so many creepy-crawlies before either. I figured out that all woods aren't the same when we were at Egypt Mill, but this baby is seriously yucky.'

'That's how things go when they're left to themselves,' Hazard said, patronizingly. 'If the woodcutters don't keep coming in to clear out the old growth and thin out the saplings, none of the acorns ever grow into mighty oaks. Mother Nature's a real slut when it comes to housekeeping. As for the creepy-crawlies, every frostless winter we have sets off a new population explosion—just one damn plague after another. *Tenebrio* came to raid our granaries, but it's as versatile as any other vermin. Rats, people, even cockroaches—you name it and *Tenebrio* will give it a run for its money.'

Steve Pearlman had now become visible between the densely packed and crooked tree trunks now, so Moley must have figured that he had done his bit for the cause of courtesy. With a casual wave of a black hand he disappeared back into his shaft.

The woman with Steve was indeed wearing a skirt, but she'd had the sense to bring wellingtons. Her hair was cut short, but not as severely as the general run of Steve's female friends. She was older, too—more Hazard's age than Steve's.

'Hi, Doc,' said Steve. 'Glad you made it.' To his companion he added: 'This is the entomologist I mentioned—taught me at uni, or tried. John Hazard. John, this is Claire Croly.'

Claire Croly was clean enough for Hazard not to mind taking the hand she extended. His slight hesitation was caused by the thought that she might be a reporter. 'What pretext did he use to drag you out here?' was the politest way he could think of to ask.

'He says the place gets lively after dark,' the woman said.

'I'll bet it does,' Hazard countered. 'But it's not the kind of party you wear your best clothes to—and the gatecrashers sometimes get ugly.'

'We're not expecting the opposition yet,' Steve Pearlman said, sharply. 'And we won't be doing any partying. We're undermanned and way behind schedule. Claire's here for the same reason you are: to see how weird the site is.'

'You're a biologist?' Hazard said, looking quizzically into the woman's clear brown eyes.

'Not exactly,' she said, wryly. 'I'm on the staff of the *Fortean Times.*'

Hazard felt as if his face had been slapped. The worst suspicion he'd so far entertained was that she might be from the local rag; this was far worse. He rounded angrily on Steve Pearlman, who was wearing the same infuriating grin that had possessed his face when he'd initially closed the trap on his old tutor. 'You little shit!' he said. 'I can't believe you'd set me up for this! Jesus, it's bad enough being fucked over by the *Sun*. Plastering my name all over the *Fortean Times* will just about kill my career.'

'I told you yesterday would be better,' Pearlman replied, unrepentantly. 'You insisted on double-booking yourself.'

'I can assure you that I've no intention of plastering your name anywhere, Dr. Hazard,' Claire Croly was quick to add. 'Your presence here is of no relevance to me. Even if something were to happen—and I see no reason, as yet, to think that it will—I'm perfectly prepared to leave your name out of any report I might make, if that's your wish.'

Hazard gulped air as he fought to control his outburst of temper. He didn't want to make a worse fool of himself by blustering. His gaze flickered back and forth between Pearlman and the woman. 'So I'm an afterthought, am I?' he said, trying to speak lightly. 'I'm your last hope, if the Fortean Society can't give you any ammunition to fight with.'

'If you'd come when I asked,' Pearlman pointed out again, 'you'd have been in and out before Claire arrived. Short notice, I admit, but still—for you, I took the trouble to collect the beetles. All I offered Claire was a cupful of unease—and the name, of course.'

'What name?' Hazard asked, although he knew as soon as he said it that he'd been cleverly wrong-footed.

'Tenebrion Wood. You didn't think it was named after the beetles, did you?'

'Of course not,' Hazard said, knowing that it wouldn't sound convincing in spite of the fact that it was the truth.

'According to my admittedly-brief research,' Pearlman said, 'the beetle genus was probably named after the same thing as the farm.'

'*Tenebra* is Latin for darkness,' Hazard said, trying to regain the intellectual high ground. 'Hence darkling beetles.'

'Yes,' said Pearlman, 'but Tenebrion with an 'n' is Old French for goblin, and there's even an obsolete English word tenebrio, referring to a kind of night-spirit.'

'Are you telling me that you brought me out to hunt for ghosts and fairies?' Hazard said, coldly.

'No,' said Pearlman, patiently, 'I brought *you* out here to look at insects. I brought *Claire* to hunt for ghosts and fairies. It's called not putting all your eggs in one basket. We are the Last-Ditch Brigade, remember? Even the Friends aren't wholly behind us on this one. Do you know how the circulation of the *Fortean Times* compares with that of *The British Journal of Entomology*—or *New Scientist*, come to that?'

Hazard did know; he had always thought it a sad comment on the times in which he was living. 'I should never have come,' he said.

'Yeah,' said Steve Pearlman, 'well, you knew that yesterday, and you came anyway. Now you're here, you might as well take a look around, mightn't you? Then you can go back to your ivory tower and your graveyard, protect your reputation as a scrupulous bore, and pray that urban blight won't come marching over your own personal horizon for a few years yet.'

Hazard clenched his jaw, but decided against striking back. He knew that the young man had a point. He'd overreacted. On the other hand, he did have to hope that this reporter's promise was worth more than the average. He could really do without a mention in the *Fortean Times*—a mention that one of his students was, alas, guaranteed to spot. 'OK,' he said, eventually. 'Show me what you've got.

What Pearlman had, it transpired, was little more than Hazard had already guessed from his first sight of the little wood. The ecowarrior had elected to defend a little corner of Nature that had already been more than half-choked by Nature's own fecundity. The wood had been unhealthy for centuries. Far from bringing it back from the brink, the recent string of mild winters and benign springtimes had given a tremendous boost to its parasites. More than three in every five of the standing trees were dying, and the leaf-litter that had accumulated with undue rapidity had begun to rot down with almost tropical alacrity.

Pearlman had called the wood 'beetle heaven' but that had just been a come-on. Moley had been spot on when he'd described it as 'seriously yucky'. All kinds of insects were having a high old time here, including the mealworms that were the larvae of darkling beetles, but the only message implicit in their unusual activity was that this thousand-year-old stand of trees was doomed, regardless of whether or not bulldozers were allowed to pulverize it in the interests of transforming a farmer's access-track into two lanes of neatly-laid tarmac.

Hazard did, however, play his part. He let Steve Pearlman show him a couple of muddy hollows six or seven feet in diameter, which would allegedly become seething pools of insectile flesh when darkness fell. They were not exactly 'clearings', because the emaciated tree branches clustered just as densely above them as they did everywhere else, but they were the only patches of almost-bare ground to be seen except where Moley and his fellow excavators were at work.

'Odd, no?' said Pearlman, as Hazard tested the second concavity with his fingertips.

'Maybe,' said Hazard, cursing the sticky mud that clung to his fingertips. He borrowed a few leaves from a nearby tree to wipe it off. The leaves seemed dry and peculiarly autumnal, considering that the saps of spring ought to be rising lustily.

As Pearlman beckoned Hazard on, a host of slender branches drew their tips across his face, but they didn't get tangled in his hair and they didn't leave scratches. They too seemed oddly limp and effete. It was almost as if the wood knew that it was doomed, and had become listless in the face of adversity.

'Don't worry about the stroking,' Pearlman said. 'The spirit of the wood's just trying to get acquainted. No thorns. It'll like you, with you being a biologist and all. It doesn't seem to like me much, even though I've come to help it out. The tips are always catching in my hair.'

'You should get it cut occasionally,' Hazard suggested.

'Anyhow, if trees were capable of forming relationships at all, I expect these would want to keep a polite distance until they'd been properly introduced. They're English, after all. They can't take kindly to having shanties connected by ropy ratlines erected in their canopy.'

Pearlman laughed at that—but then he got called away by one of his fellow climbers. Hazard continued his investigations solo, shoving his way through the seemingly amorous under-growth with as much delicacy as he could, pausing now and again in order to inspect all kind of chewed and pockmarked leaves. If nothing else, pottering around in Tenebrion Wood gave his spotting skills a thorough and much needed workout. There were *Silvanidae* as well as *Tenebrionidae* left over from the days when cereals had been grown on the adjacent fields, numerous *Rhizophagidae* and, perhaps most interestingly, a couple of *Acanthoceridae* that were a very long way from their normal subtropical habitat. There was a possibility that these might be the first ever sighted north of Southampton, but who would care?

He took the trouble to collect a few of the more interesting specimens, but even after two hours of assiduous study he couldn't believe that he'd found anything that might be of the slightest relevance to Pearlman's frail hope of mustering public sympathy behind the wood. The simple truth was that it wasn't a Site of Special Scientific Interest. The old cemetery behind Hazard's house was much more interesting, in an objective sense, although it wasn't nearly as well populated with beetles.

When Hazard eventually found himself, rather unexpectedly, on the fringe of the wood, he figured that it was time to give up and go home. Then everything changed again.

Having caught sight of something tiny and black-and-yellow out of the corner of his eye, he took three paces towards it, and knelt down. He hadn't even stabilized his crouching position when a groan of despair escaped his lips.

For a moment, Hazard wondered again whether Pearlman might have set him up, and whether he'd been brought in merely to find something that the ex-ecology student had already found. But that didn't make sense. If Pearlman really had seen and identified what Hazard had just found, he'd have known full well that his petty crusade was futile, and that the technologically-assisted execution of the wood was a mere formality waiting to be recognized.

On the other hand, Hazard thought, even if Pearlman hadn't set him up, he had exposed him to the attention of a reporter from the *Fortean Times*, and made him a hostile witness to the front end of a ghost- and fairy-hunt. He had enough resentment left in him not to spell out what he'd found, or what its consequences would be, when he made his way back to the encampment.

All he said to Pearlman was, 'Give it up. It's hopeless. There's nothing here worth defending—quite the contrary, in fact.'

'Even if it were hopeless,' Pearlman told him, 'I couldn't give it up. Come on, Doc—this is your life's work, for heaven's sake. Insect Utopia. Give me something I can make a fuss about. I'll keep your name out of it—all I want is ammunition.'

'I can assure you that it is hopeless,' Hazard insisted. 'Even if you trapped a whole bloody family of Norman goblins and stuck them in a cage at Whipsnade, you couldn't save this wood. You have my solemn word on that.'

'That's not enough for me,' said Pearlman, unwisely. 'You can't be a conscientious objector in this war, Doc. If you're not part of the solution, you're part of the problem.'

'You don't know how true that is,' said Hazard, with a sigh. 'I'm sorry, Steve. If you'd paid more attention to my lectures, you'd be able to see how badly you'd misjudged this battleground—but all you brought to show me was darkling beetles and carabids. I hope you're a better judge of goblins.'

Pearlman protested that he would see far more when darkness fell, but Hazard had already seen enough. He walked back to the Daewoo as fast as he could and he took his mobile phone out of the glove compartment. Then he called the Department of Agriculture to notify them of the bad news, as he was bound by law to do.

The next day was Saturday, which was Hazard's shopping day. He still followed the same ritual that he and Jenny had adopted when they first moved into their little haven of peace, before Jenny had decided that she was a city girl after all and couldn't stand the isolation. Mercifully, they'd never actually tied the knot, so there was no divorce to fight—and no threat to Hazard's tenure in the Old Vicarage. He drove into town, stopping at the baker's for fresh bread before going on to Sava-centre and stocking up for the week. He filled up the Daewoo on the way out, collecting double reward points in the process.

After lunch, he went out into the cemetery, to reassure himself that it really was more deserving of the title of Site of Special Scientific Interest than Steve Pearlman's disgustingly fecund wood. It was man-made, of course, but that wasn't the point at issue; the simple fact was that it was a unique environment: a special habitat with precious few parallels. There had, of course, been a village here in the days when the church had been functional and the vicarage had been occupied by a resident clergyman, but when the great migration to the towns had begun in the early nineteenth century the forward-looking landowner had seized the opportunity to modernize his methods.

He'd concentrated his declining labor-force in the hamlets on the north side of the estate and he'd taken down the houses north and west of the church brick by brick, so that he could extend his oblong fields into greatly elongated rectangles. He'd been the first man in the county to use a steam traction engine to pull a plough, and one of the consequences of his revolutionary spirit had been that he'd been able to obliterate an entire village and put the land under cultivation. He'd obviously taken his freethinking ways very seriously, because he'd elected to destroy the village rather than the smaller hamlets, isolating the church.

The church commissioners had refused to sell their own parcel of land but they hadn't been able to maintain the living.

They'd closed the church and the cemetery and sold the vicarage with the proviso that its exterior aspect was preserved. When he'd bought it, Hazard had become the official key-holder of the church, although he had no more than a couple of enquiries a year from tourists wanting to look inside—mostly American Mormons hunting down scraps of evidence relating to the lives of their remoter ancestors.

The abandonment of the cemetery more than a hundred years before had allowed the graves to develop their own peculiar ecosystems, in which alien flowers still vied for space with grasses and the old headstones supported extraordinary tapestries of lichen and moss. The flowers attracted butterflies and wild bees, but Hazard's favorite neighbors were the *Lampyridae* that lit the cemetery by night and the death-watch beetles that were slowly clicking their way through the timbers of the dead church.

Hazard was still immersed in his desultory contemplation of the peculiar ecology of the derelict graveyard when a police car pulled up in the lane and a uniformed man got out. Hazard made his way back to the narrow gap in the wall on the opposite side of the cemetery to the more imposing lich-gate.

'Can I help you?' he said.

'Dr Hazard?' the policeman enquired, for form's sake. 'I'm Constable Potts, Sherfield. I'm making enquiries about an incident at Tenebrion Wood last evening. I believe you were there.'

'It's hardly a police matter,' Hazard said. 'I reported the infestation to the Department of Agriculture. They'll take care of it.'

The constable frowned, quizzically. 'I'm sorry, sir,' he said, uncertainly. He obviously didn't have the faintest idea what Hazard meant.

'My fault,' said Hazard. 'I reported an infestation of Colorado beetle in some potatoes growing on the edge of a field where they'd once been cultivated. You must be referring to some incident that occurred after I left. I take it that the residents had found out about the fledgling demonstration and notified the developer.'

'No, sir,' the policeman said. 'I'm afraid there was an accident. A young man named Adrian Stimpson was killed when a tunnel collapsed.'

There was a moment of shock, when Hazard's mind refused to recognize that Adrian Stimpson was Moley, but then the pressure of reality asserted itself. 'Oh,' he said, finally. 'I'm sorry.'

'Did you speak to the young man?' the policeman asked, his words falling with appalling weight on Hazard's stunned consciousness.

'Yes,' Hazard said, numbly remembering the seemingly trivial conversation whose ominous quality now stood fully revealed. 'He asked me if I knew anything about soil structure. He said that he was having difficulty shoring the tunnel up. He asked me to take a look but I said that I wasn't a soil scientist and couldn't help him. I really couldn't. I'm an entomologist. He knew more about soil than I ever did—he spent days underground at Crookham Heath and Egypt Mill. What could I have done?'

'It was an accident,' the constable said. 'No one was at fault, except for the boy. The coroner might call it misadventure, but it was just one of those things. There'll have to be an inquest, I'm afraid, but I doubt that you'll be called. A statement will probably be sufficient—but your testimony is relevant.'

'Yes,' said Hazard, still dazed. 'Wasn't there anything they could do? I mean, there were half a dozen people there.' *And they all had mobile phones*, he added, silently. *My going didn't make any real difference. I'd only have been one more pair of hands.*

'Nothing,' said the policeman. 'He didn't have a chance to call for help, but they were checking on him at regular intervals. As soon as they became aware of the collapse they started digging, in case there was an air pocket, but he must have asphyxiated very quickly. He was long dead when the fire brigade finally got the body out.' The policeman turned as he spoke, having heard the sound of another vehicle drawing up behind his own. It was a red Citroen Saxo. 'If you could drop into the station at

Sherfield some time soon, Dr Hazard,' Potts added, 'we'll take a formal statement. Shouldn't take long.'

'Of course,' Hazard said. The entomologist stood where he was while the policeman went back to his car, nodding politely to Claire Croly and Steve Pearlman as he passed them

Pearlman had obviously changed his clothes within the last couple of hours, and the *Fortean Times* reporter was no longer clad in the skirt she'd been wearing the previous evening. They had both showered recently, presumably separately. Hazard hoped that he knew Pearlman well enough to be reasonably sure that the only reason the woman from the *Fortean Times* was with him was that he'd been desperate for a lift. The ecowarrior didn't own a car, and Hazard's house wasn't on a bus route.

'You could have told me about the Colorado beetle,' Pearlman said, accusingly.

'Would it have made a difference?' Hazard countered, fearing the possibility that it might have. 'Would you have told Moley to fill in the tunnel and pack up if I had?'

'No,' said Pearlman. 'Even if you'd spelled out exactly what the ecopolice would do, we'd have stayed. We're still determined to defend as much of the wood as possible. We think we still have a chance to save something.'

Steve Pearlman was far too young to remember the days when they'd had posters in post offices identifying Colorado beetle as a significant public enemy. They'd still been on show when Hazard was a toddler in the mid-sixties: a stubborn hangover from the late forties, when potatoes had been just about the only significant foodstuff that wasn't on ration. If Hitler had only had an entomologist on his General Staff to advise him to equip the Luftwaffe with jars full of Colorado beetles—plundered by his Japanese allies from occupied China if his American spies couldn't oblige at source—he might never have had to suffer D-Day. Instead, he'd stuck to incendiary bombs and had generated the spirit of the Blitz.

'They aren't going to stint on the pesticides, Steve,' Hazard said. 'They have to make sure the infestation doesn't spread to fields where potatoes are still being grown for market. Colorado beetle may not be rabies, but it could do a hell of a lot of economic damage if it became endemic. The wood's already nine parts dead—the sprayers will kill it off completely.'

'It'll regenerate, if it's given the chance.' Pearlman said.

'True—but you can't defend a dead wood on the grounds that it will probably resurrect itself in twenty or thirty years' time. Anyway, that's not the issue any more, and you know it. You got someone killed, Steve. It's time to give it up.'

'We all knew the risks,' Pearlman retorted, obstinately.

'Oh, sure. You all knew the risk of falling out of a tree when the cherry pickers moved in. Poor Moley probably thought he knew the risk of being caught in a collapse if the JCBs came on site before it was completely clear—and probably thought of it as a heroic risk to run—but what killed him was his own inability to cope with the sloppy soil. He was just a boy, Steve! He didn't have a clue what he was doing!'

'Yes he did,' said Steve. The determination in his voice was tangible.

'Oh, shit!' said Hazard, finally catching on to the reason why Pearlman was here. 'You're going to try and use it, aren't you? You don't give a damn about the Department of Agriculture's clean-up squad. You're going to try to build Moley's death into some kind of martyrdom. Worse than that—you're going to claim that the goblins did it, aren't you? You're going to splash the whole sorry incident over the front page of the *Fortean Times* and make a fucking circus of it. What about the poor kid's parents, for Christ's sake? What are they going to make of it? Do you really imagine that you can stop the developer widening the access road by establishing the wood as a Site of Special Pseudoscientific Interest? You're off your fucking head—and you can leave me out of it, you hear. No more. Ever.'

'You're in it,' Steve Pearlman said, ominously. 'You were there. He asked you to take a look, and you refused.'

Hazard had already turned to look at Claire Croly. 'Aren't

Forteans supposed to be agnostics?' He said. 'Aren't you supposed to pretend to be objective, or at least not to be completely bonkers? You can't be willing to go along with this!'

'It's not as simple as that,' the woman replied. 'Steve's got it backwards, actually. The problem isn't that you were there, but that you left so soon.'

Hazard was beyond shock by now. His blood was no longer capable of running cold. The realization that the woman was in on Pearlman's new master plan was just one more faint rap on his tired skull. 'You actually think the goblins did it,' he said, slowly. 'You spent the night in the dark and deathly wood, and you saw exactly what you'd been primed to see. Every shadow a *Tenebrio*, every rustle a night-spirit. Then someone shouts out that the tunnel's collapsed and Moley's trapped, and bang— the goblins did it. Are you absolutely sure that it wasn't a giant Colorado beetle, resentful of the fact that I'd discovered their invasion force before they could run riot?'

She didn't flinch. 'You weren't there, Dr Hazard,' she reminded him. 'You left, as soon as you'd found something that satisfied your spirit of enquiry.'

'That's right,' Hazard said, softly. 'I was long gone. Be sure to mention that in your report, won't you? I spotted the infestation, and I left. I am not part of your crazy stunt. Now, I'd like you both to leave. It's very kind of you to warn me that the shit will be hitting the fan, but now you've done it I don't think I ever want to see either of you again.'

'It's not as simple as that,' Pearlman said, deliberately echoing Claire Croly's formula. 'We've got something to show you. It won't take a minute. It's in the boot of the car.'

'Fuck off,' said Hazard.

'You have to look,' said Pearlman, doggedly. 'Afterwards, you can tell us to fuck off—but first you have to look. We've come a long way.'

Hazard let loose an almighty sigh, but he followed Pearlman when the youth led the way back to the Citroen. He waited patiently while Claire Croly unlocked the boot and raised the hatch.

Inside, sitting between a toolbox and a petrol can, there was a huge glass jar with a capacity of at least three gallons. It had a narrow neck and a rubber stopper, so it was sealed as tightly as the specimen tube Pearlman had brought to Hazard's office, with much the same result. Most of the insects enclosed in the jar were dead—but that still left thousands, perhaps tens of thousands, that were not yet motionless.

Hazard had no idea how many *Tenebrio* beetles would be required to fill a three-gallon jar, but he knew that it was a lot—perhaps a million. He could see, too, that there were more than a few carabids mixed in with this lot, and maybe forty or fifty other species. He could even see a couple of brightly colored burying-beetles. For the most part, though, the beetles were *Tenebrionidae*, genus *Tenebrio*, in a profusion that had surely never been seen outside a mealworm farm.

Now, at last, Hazard admitted to himself what he hadn't quite admitted before. *Tenebrio* was basically a grain beetle, a granary pest. It had no business being in a dying wood in any considerable numbers, certainly not in such awful profusion as this. Not even a dying wood called Tenebrion Wood, which had Colorado beetle in the margin that had once marked the edge of a potato-field. The hot weather was causing all kinds of unexpected outbreaks—plague after plague after plague—but global warming wasn't scapegoat enough to explain why Tenebrion Wood was full of darkling beetles. That was odd—damnably odd, in fact.

'Twenty minutes,' said Steve Pearlman. 'I wasn't entirely sure that you weren't coming back, so I thought I'd better make provision to get you back. I certainly didn't know Moley was going to die. All I knew was that something was happening that shouldn't be, and maybe couldn't be. It was as if they just came up out of the ground, like oil from a well.'

'That's ridiculous,' Hazard said.

'Yes, it is,' said Pearlman. 'Where do you think Moley started to dig? Where else but in one of those funny hollows—

the biggest of the three. Maybe the worst place he could have chosen.'

'You have to make up your mind,' Hazard said, tight-lipped. 'Either the goblins did it, or the beetles did it. They're both impossible, so it really doesn't matter, but it really has to be one or the other.'

'No it doesn't,' said Claire Croly. 'The forms this thing takes are probably arbitrary. The point is that the wood's not as nearly dead as it seems, and that the life it has is a strange kind. You left before it came into its own, Dr. Hazard. You really ought to give us a second chance to convince you.'

'It'll be just the three of us,' Pearlman put in. 'When the Dep of Ag's hit squad turned up we made a tactical withdrawal— but it'll take them all weekend to figure out exactly how much ground they have to spray. There are a lot of stray potatoes on the farm. They won't start spraying until Monday. No one will disturb us if we go back tonight—no one except whatever's kept that wood free of cultivation for a millennium and more.'

'You're quite mad, you know,' said Hazard.

'The only way you'll be able to say that with authority,' Pearlman retorted, 'is to come and meet the goblins yourself. Until you've faced them, you can't say for sure that they don't exist.'

Hazard disagreed. He knew perfectly well that the goblins didn't exist, and that a million beetles and one dead boy couldn't possibly prove that they did. But Steve Pearlman had been able to push his buttons ever since he'd found out where Hazard lived. One day, the bulldozers really would put in an appearance on his own doorstep—and when that day came, Hazard would be screaming for help from the Friends and anyone else who would condescend to listen. Come that day, he'd be perfectly prepared to populate his private cemetery with imaginary ghosts, and pretend that the empty church had once played host to the Holy Grail. Anything to hold back the tide. Tenebrion Wood wasn't his back yard, and the people whose back yard it was wanted it gone, but that wasn't really the point.

'I'm not going out to bat on page one of the *Fortean Times*,' Hazard insisted. 'Whatever you talk me into seeing, I'm not putting my own head on the public chopping block. Not for the Angel of Death with a flaming sword, let alone a night-spirit that takes the form of a horde of beetles.'

'For your eyes only, Doc,' said Steve Pearlman. 'I just want you to know that I'm not as mad as you think I am.'

'I'll be there,' Hazard said. 'Eleven o'clock suit you? If your goblins haven't come out by midnight, though, I'm done with it, once and for all.'

'That's fine,' Pearlman replied. 'Eleven till midnight it is. I'll let the wood-spirit know. It might not like me as much as it likes you, but good news is always welcome.'

'Quite mad,' Hazard repeated, determined to have the last word, at least for the time being. Pearlman had won enough to give it to him. Claire Croly shut the boot, then the two of them got into the car and drove away.

Hazard went indoors; he had had enough of the cemetery for one day.

This time, thanks to the thin Saturday night traffic, Hazard was bang on time. He pulled into the lay-by on the stroke of eleven, sliding the Daewoo in alongside Claire Croly's Citroen.

He slipped on his wellington boots before getting out of the car. He had taken the precaution of changing the battery in his flashlight before setting forth, and he pocketed a spare just in case. Unlike Jenny, he wasn't in the least afraid of the dark, but he didn't have a cat's eyes and was just as likely as any common-or-garden coward to get himself filthy or hurt while blundering blindly around.

A few stars were visible amid the clouds, but the light pollution from Newbury collaborated with the usual oxides and micro-particles to impart a curious salmon-pink stain to the strip of sky visible above the lane. The hedgerows seemed taller and closer by night than they had by day, and the impression was enhanced by a background susurrus that owed more to the stirring of slender branches in the breeze than to the movement of rodents and birds. He heard an owl hoot once, but it didn't come from the direction of the wood, whose branches were far too dense to allow fliers to hunt therein.

It was just as easy to find the way to the Last-Ditchers' camp-site by night as it had been by day—easier, given the number of booted feet that had tramped back and forth since Adrian's accident and Hazard's report of the presence of Colorado beetle on the wood's further fringe. As Hazard moved away from the lane he played his light over the ground expectantly, but the only beetles he saw were glossy carabids out hunting. The beam reflected back more than once from tiny pairs of eyes, but they were only mice.

The track he was following was now a well-worn path and there was no need to fight his way through tangled branches. A few trailing tips brushed his arms, but he was wearing a protective tracksuit top over his shirt and there didn't seem to be anything intimate in the way the leaves slid across its synthetic surface.

Steve Pearlman and Claire Croly had torches of their own, but they'd turned them down low in order to conserve power. Hazard switched his own light off when he joined them, knowing that his eyes were already half-adjusted to the gloom. By the light of Pearlman's torch he could see where the hole that Adrian Stimpson had dug had been filled in again, leaving a convex mound like an oversized molehill. Hazard knew that one always took more dirt out of a hole than was required to fill it again; it was a matter of compaction.

'Well?' said Hazard.

'It feels strange,' Pearlman said.

'That's why I'm here,' Hazard said. 'It's supposed to feel strange. Goblins to the right of us, kobolds to the left....'

'It's not like that,' Claire Croly said. 'It wasn't like that last night—but it wasn't like this either. Something's changed.'

'Sure,' said Hazard. 'You're down half a dozen ecowar-riors—one of whom is lying in a mortuary—and you're up one skeptic, who can't feel a damn thing. Maybe it's the breeze. Last night was still, and that must have made a big difference to the background noise. Ears adjust their sensitivity in much the same way that eyes do, and they can play peculiar tricks on the town-bred. Your brain gets used to screening out familiar noises, but unfamiliar ones can seem very eerie when they become newly obtrusive. That was what spooked Jenny when we moved into the vicarage. I kept telling her that it was just a matter of adaptation, but she couldn't wait.'

'Jesus, Doc, you really are full of bullshit sometimes,' Pearlman told him. 'I've spent a hell of a lot of time sitting in trees at night, and Claire's no novice. Did it ever occur to you that the fact that your girlfriend had already been living with you for ten years without ever pushing you to marry her might be a symptom of a deep-lying unease that had nothing whatsoever to do with the silence of the countryside?'

That speech was followed by an uncomfortable silence. The crowns of the trees quivered in the breeze, as if in the grip of a sudden chill. 'Show me your beetle heaven, Steve,' Hazard said, quietly. 'Let's see what kind of plague it is that afflicts your goblin wood.'

Pearlman led him to the smaller of the two hollows that he'd shown Hazard by daylight. It was just as empty and dull now as it had been then.

'Douse your light, Claire,' Pearlman said. 'If we all stand still and keep quiet for a few minutes, and give what passes for normality around here a chance to reassert itself, we might see something. Let me judge the wait. I'll switch on when the time is right.'

Claire Croly obeyed, and Pearlman switched off his own torch.

In order to play the game—and Hazard still felt that it was a game and nothing more—they all had to stand perfectly still and not make a sound, so that was what Hazard did, knowing that the darkness and the strain of keeping still would be bound to exaggerate the perceptions of his ears. In such circumstances it would only be natural to sense communicative effort in the whispering of the branches, and he was on guard against it. The darkness was profound; there were no fireflies here. The crowns continued to shiver and quake. If the wood really did have a spirit, Hazard thought, it was obviously coming down with something: vegetable meningitis.

Thirty heartbeats passed while Hazard savored the quality of the feverish whisper. It wasn't quite as clamorous as he had expected—the density of the branches stifled the slight wind more effectively than he had anticipated. There were no birds moving in the crowns of the sickly trees, and it seemed that even the rats and mice preferred the hedgerows, because he could clearly hear a faint cacophony of scratching sounds, which he knew from experience to be the sound of carabid beetles scurrying across the dried-out surface of the leaf-litter. There might have been thousands of *Tenebrio* beetles following their own courses—or even taking line-dancing lessons—without their being able to add much to that slight symphony, because the discrepancy in size between the two kinds was so very considerable.

Thanks to the patchy cloud cover the night wasn't particularly cold, especially within the canopy-blanketed wood. Hazard felt quite comfortable, although he kept his hands flat upon his tracksuit top so that the fingers wouldn't begin to go numb. There wasn't the remotest suggestion of goblin presence, unless he was prepared to count the inflammation of the metaphorical sore spot that Steve Pearlman's last gibe had touched.

It had occurred to Hazard that the business about not being able to stand the quietness and isolation of the Old Vicarage had been an excuse, and that what had really sent Jenny scurrying back to London was the awareness—brought out by closer confinement and the suspension of customary support systems—that she really didn't want to spend the rest of her life with John Hazard. That possibility still rankled, and it didn't need one of Pearlman's random darts to suggest that there might be more symbolic weight than ecological fascination in

Hazard's fondness for the cemetery that lay between his home and the corpse of the church.

When Pearlman's torch came back on there were indeed beetles in the saucer-shaped depression, including *Tenebrionidae*, but they were not present in anything remotely like the abundance that would have been required to allow Pearlman to fill the jar he'd loaded into Claire Croly's car as entomologist bait.

'Shit!' said Pearlman. 'She's not co-operating, is she?'

Hazard remembered that the wood had been 'it' when it was allegedly attempting to get to know him on Friday afternoon, and had still been 'it' earlier that day. The further personalization seemed to him to be in rather bad taste, given that its motherly earth had taken poor Moley in an embrace that was far too cloying.

'It happens,' Hazard said. 'Miss Croly can probably tell you about hundreds of occasions when the presence of a single skeptic was enough to banish all manner of paranormal phenomena that had been running riot while there were only true believers to bear witness.'

'That's uncalled-for,' the reporter objected.

'So is all this,' said Hazard. 'It's over, Steve. Sometimes, you just have to settle for fighting on a different battleground.'

'Maybe so,' said Pearlman, his tone retaining an obstinacy that belied the words. 'Let's take a look at the other one.' He set off in the direction of the larger hollow.

Hazard followed him meekly, not bothering to switch on his flashlight even though there was not the slightest glimmer overhead; the canopy was quite opaque. The branches clutched at him more insistently now, but the man-made fibers of his seamless top repelled them effectively enough. He didn't feel that the wood was trying to take him prisoner.

The second hollow was as bare as the first, but Hazard was prepared to be patient. He was committed until the witching hour; after that, he could go home. He even knelt down to inspect the saucer-shaped depression, and condescended to touch it even though he knew from glutinous experience what it might do to his fingertips. This time, however, the surface didn't seem in the least gluey. Indeed, it felt strangely soft, as if he were touching skin rather than soil. After a moment's pause he laid his palm flat upon the ground, wondering why it didn't feel cold.

The ground made no attempt to grip him. It was the power of his own muscles that forced the hand down, pressing harder than he had consciously intended. He gasped in surprise, although he tried to strangle the sound lest Steve Pearlman and Claire Croly derive too much satisfaction from it. The hand didn't sink into the compacted earth, but he did have the impression that the contact subtly changed its nature—and that it was him, not some external force, that had imported some perverse shadow of meaning into the meeting.

He knew that something was amiss, and that it was not the kind of thing he was on guard against.

Steve Pearlman was waiting for Hazard to get up again before switching off his torch, so there was still light enough to see by. Indeed, the beam of the torch played directly upon Hazard's splayed fingers, confirming to the sense of sight that there was nothing unusual in the manner in which it rested there. There had been no visible change in the texture of the soil—nor in the texture of Hazard's flesh, although Hazard felt a curious sensation within his own being. It did not flow from the ground; rather, it seemed to begin deep in his own abdomen before reaching out into his limbs and through his extremities—not just the naked resting hand, but his rubber-booted feet.

It's in me, Hazard thought. *Thus far, it's just in me.*

Nothing was visible, even in the light, and nothing was audible, even in the silence, but Hazard could not deny that something was happening: that he was reaching out, in a way that he had never reached out before and had never thought to be possible.

Then the earth, or the wood, or the resident spirits of the wood, responded.

Oh, shit, Hazard thought, realizing that intelligence was not enough, that rationality was not enough, and that even sheer bloody-mindedness would not protect him.

The soil in the depression was abruptly transformed, visibly and quite impossibly, into a seething mass of beetles: a plague of beetles that, for all Hazard knew, might have extended down to the very centre of the Earth. Instead of black soil that felt like skin, there were adult insects by the million: darkling beetles, every one. *Tenebrio* beetles, cursed by a coincidence of nomenclature to embody the spirit of Tenebrion Wood, at least in the impious mind and sinful eyes of a fallen entomologist.

An entomologist ought to have snatched back his hand in response to such a miracle, even if his very next response was to run for a specimen jar the size of a beer barrel, but Hazard was no longer in possession of any such reflex or intention. He left his hand where it was and the beetles swarmed over it in line-dancing legions, as if to seal a bargain by clasping it.

'I fucking told you so!' was Steve Pearlman's reaction.

Claire Croly could only gasp, in spite of the fact that she must have seen it before.

It went on and on, regardless of the light. Adrian Stimpson's death, Hazard realized, must indeed have been an accident. Just one of those things, as the constable had said. Not murder and not sacrifice: just a breakdown of communication, a misunderstanding.

He realized, too, that as soon as the men from the ministry had decided how much ground their spraying had to cover, every beetle in the wood would be living on borrowed time. To be harmless was no defense in that kind of war. To be as common as muck was no defense either. Come hell or high water, the path through the wood was destined to become a real road. The wood had avoided cultivation for more than a thousand years, but tarmac was too ultimate a weapon—and in law there was no such thing as a Site of Special Supernatural Interest.

Hazard waited a full five minutes before standing up. He didn't have to wipe his hands—the remaining beetles fell away like dripping darkling water. They took nothing with them; they had already achieved their purpose, if they were indeed representative of some kind of purposeful being. If not...well, they had had their effect.

'You told me so,' Hazard admitted to Pearlman. 'And I listened. In spite of everything, I listened. I came, I saw, I played my part—and now I'm out of it. I'd prefer it if my name wasn't mentioned in the *Fortean Times* account of derring-do in Goblin Wood.'

'You have to give me something,' Pearlman said. 'Now you've seen, you have to give me something I can use.'

'Don't be stupid,' Hazard said. 'You've known from day one that there isn't anything here that you can use. Something worth protecting, granted—but not something you can use. Whatever Claire writes in the *Fortean Times* will be more damned data. I really can't help you, Steve. No one can. Sometimes, you just have to settle for fighting the war on a different battleground.'

'But you saw it,' Pearlman protested. 'You saw.'

'I saw beetles,' Hazard told him. 'Not Bigfoot or the Loch Ness Monster. Just lots and lots of beetles. It's not enough.'

That wasn't the end of the argument, of course—and Hazard kept to his promise to stay till midnight—but it was the end of the story, so far as Steve Pearlman's last-ditch defense of Tenebrion Wood was concerned. The next chapter required a different approach, and a different hero.

Hazard wasn't unduly surprised when Claire Croly's red Saxo made its way up the lane to the Old Vicarage two weeks later. She could have posted his complimentary copy of the issue that contained her name-free account of the exotic haunting of Goblin Wood and the mysterious death of Adrian Stimpson, ecomartyr—but she was never going to do that now that she knew the way to where he lived. Hazard didn't invite her in, though. He was in the cemetery when she arrived, and it was among the tapestried gravestones, observed by wild bees, that he received his gift.

It was summer by now, and the day was glorious. The overgrown graves were beautifully green, and the wild flowers that grew in profusion were as colorful a flock of alien species as any painter in Bedlam could have imagined.

'I can see why you like this place so much,' the reporter said. 'It must be at its best now.'

'Pretty much,' Hazard agreed.

'Interesting, too—to an entomologist.'

'As the man said when asked what a lifetime of study had taught him about the mind of the Creator, *He has an inordinate fondness for beetles.* He was talking about the Christian God, of course, but the implication of Nature remains the same no matter how you animate it behind the scenes. Think of the Egyptians and their scarabs. I like it here.'

'Pity your girlfriend didn't feel the same.'

'Yeah,' said Hazard. 'Well, as I told Steve, the mind can play tricks when the senses move into a new environment. All the things we've subconsciously ceased to notice are suddenly conspicuous by their absence, and *vice versa.* Jenny thought living out in the country, next to an old church, would be romantic. She hadn't expected it to be scary, and she couldn't quite get her head around the notion that its seeming scariness was all in the eyes and ears of the beholder. She thought the place was haunted—the cemetery, not the house. She couldn't accept that the lights were just *Lampyridae*—to her, they were lost souls. She just couldn't shake the notion loose. But maybe Steve was right too—maybe, at an even deeper level, she just couldn't stand living with me any longer.'

'He's right more often than one might think,' Claire Croly told him. 'He's right about your not being safe, even here. The day might come when the bulldozers appear even on this remote horizon.'

'No way,' Hazard said. 'There are no dominoes hereabouts. Even if the farmer weren't descended from a long line of agricultural geniuses, he'd never let go the way the owner of Tenebrion did. When it comes to stubbornness, he'd even make Steve look like a quivering mass of querulous capitulation. I've got the one and only hole in the patchwork. If there's a single safe spot within a hundred miles, this is it. The landscape's not natural, of course—everything the eye can see in every direction is the product of human artifice and the spirit of technological endeavor—but it's green, and it's alive. Every year it dies, and every year it comes back to life, always changing, adapting, evolving. Especially the cemetery, where there really is life after death.'

The reporter smiled. 'It really wasn't haunted, back in the days when your girlfriend ran away, was it?'

'No,' he replied, knowing exactly what she was going to say next, 'it wasn't.'

'But it is now,' she said, fulfilling his private prophecy to the letter. 'Isn't it?'

'Oh yes,' he said, serenely. 'It is now.'

BEHIND THE WHEEL

Do I still have the right to remain silent? Yeah? Oh shit, what the fuck do I care? It doesn't make a damn of difference, and you won't believe it anyhow, because I don't even believe it myself. Drunk? No I'm not fucking drunk—I'm as sober as I've ever been in my entire fucking life, and I wish I wasn't. Oh sure, I was drunk...we both were. I was dumb drunk, the way I always am, and Andy...he was angry drunk, the way he always is. We left the pub an hour early, but we were drunk all right.

I didn't want to leave the pub—when did I ever? Andy dragged me away. I let him—you don't argue with Andy when he's angry...or drunk...especially both. We got in the car—sure, make a note of it, I don't think Andy's going to care and nobody put a breathalyzer on him—I only wish they had.

We got in the car and drove back to Andy's place, only we didn't go right round into the street, just parked on the corner. Andy switched off the engine. He'd gone calm, and he didn't say a word—just sat there. I didn't know what the hell was going on, but when I tried to open the door Andy put his hand on my knee. I said, 'Fuck it, Andy, you turning queer?' but he didn't laugh. 'Shut up,' he said. 'Just shut up.' But I could tell from his voice that he was angrier than before. That was when it clicked. There was a silver Cortina parked in the street outside his house.

It might have been nothing, but Andy didn't think it was nothing. He'd known that it was going to be there, and that's why we'd left the pub at nine-thirty. Andy never left the pub at nine-thirty. He'd known. I didn't ask him how—I guessed, though. The neighbors. Terraced street, no gardens, curtains always flapping. Always the same. Some clever bugger tipped him off. 'Nod's as good as a wink, know what I mean?' That would really get Andy's goat.

I'd have gone right in, but not Andy. He's not that way, even when he's angry—especially when he's angry. He wanted to see the owner of the car, make sure which house he came out of. I knew right away he was going to follow the guy—I mean, the way we were parked...straight out of some black and white movie. It was even raining, the way it always does in old movies, and in the dark there didn't seem to be any color in anything. I don't know how long we were there—I was dumb drunk and my head was humming a bit, and I just lay back in the seat and waited. Maybe it was a quarter of an hour.

Anyhow, Andy's door opens and this guy comes out. I didn't know him, but he sure as hell wasn't an insurance salesman. Big guy—a lot bigger than Andy. He looked furtive, though... quick look right and left—don't know why because he never saw us—and into the car. The door was still open behind him, just a crack, and I knew that Carol was in there, watching him go...peeping, out of her own house. Jesus, it's no wonder the neighbors twigged what was going on—they ought to have put up a fucking sign.

The Cortina drives away, going up to the far end of the street. Andy lets him go round the corner first, then slips us into gear and goes after him. He wasn't afraid of losing the guy. How many silver Cortinas are likely to be on the road that time of night? We picked him up again on the ring road and followed him round. He couldn't have known that we were with him since he left Andy's.

Anyhow, the Cortina took the minor road that goes due north—the B1363 I think it is—and we got on it behind him. Respectful distance...Andy's a good driver, even when he's pissed out of his head...and he was angry drunk, not stupid.

The road's not bad out as far as Stillington, but it's not what you might call a motorway. A couple of cars went past on the other side of the road, but going north there was just us and the Cortina. There was no real reason why the guy should think we were following him—I mean, we were just two cars on the same bit of road—but I guess his guilty conscience was making him nervous, and maybe the sight of our lights in his mirror was getting on his nerves, because he began to speed up. Not all at once, but not gradually either. By the time we got to Stillington he was doing over sixty, and so were we.

He carried on heading north, and the fact that we didn't turn off in Stillington obviously worried him a bit, although why anyone would turn in Stillington is beyond me. He hit Brandsby doing all of seventy-five, and you know what the bend in Brandsby's like. Maybe the guy in the Cortina does it every day of his life, but Andy doesn't, and we nearly piled up against a fucking brick wall. Between Brandsby and Oswaldkirk it's bends all the way, and we were lurching round every one, with Andy's foot flat to the boards. By now the guy must have known that we were chasing him, and that he was in a race. Maybe he even guessed that it was Andy, and if he did he had good cause to be afraid. Oh, he was a big guy, but if he was screwing Carol he must know what Andy's like...Jesus, he must see the fucking bruises. Big guy or not, he could hardly feel cheerful thinking he's got a fucking head-case on his tail.

By this time I wasn't dumb drunk any more. Dumb, sure—I didn't dare say a word. Andy's a good driver, but he's one of these guys who gets really high when he's behind the wheel, and he gets higher and higher the faster he goes. It's like being in a fight with him...aggressive just isn't enough of a word for it, and I don't know a word that is. Andy can be mean when he's angry drunk—I mean, fucking hell, I've seen Carol's bruises—and when he's in the car in that sort of mood it's like he's sitting in an iron fist just dying to smash it into someone's face. You know what they say about cars being great big cocks in the subconscious mind—well I think that's crap, but I'll certainly say this: when Andy is behind the wheel and going fast he's really out to fuck someone over, and I don't mean Carol.

After Helmsley we came on to the A170, and the bastard speeded up again. In the dark he couldn't see what kind of car we had, but he must have fancied his chances of outrunning us. No chance—not with Andy on his tail. We got closer, and we started creeping right up his arse end. You seen those films where the chasing car starts touching up the bumper of the one in front? Yeah, well so has Andy, and so had the guy in the Cortina, and Andy was trying to do it and the guy in the Cortina was trying to stay clear.

I don't know where the guy was going, and if I had to guess I'd say that he didn't either—if he lived in Scarborough he wouldn't be coming to York for a fuck, would he? When we got to Kirkbymoorside, though, he had some kind of brainstorm. I mean, if I was being chased by a nutter like Andy I'd head for the nearest police station, wouldn't you? Well, of course, *you* would, but I mean, anybody would if he had half a fucking brain. But this guy turned north again. No, I don't know the road—I didn't even know there was a fucking road there, and it sure as hell wasn't much of a road. Glorified cart track, heading up into the farms in the Cleveland Hills. No lights, no white line—not wide enough for two lanes. Just cat's-eyes by the side of the road...and we were still doing seventy-five. And the other guy wasn't even drunk, unless Carol keeps a secret bottle of gin in her knicker-drawer.

I don't know how long it went on. I was scared shitless, hanging on to the seat and the dashboard for dear life and praying that the old *klunk klick* magic really works. The only think I remember for sure is the moment when the cat's-eyes ran out and there was nothing but us and what we could see in the headlights. Andy had the heads on full beam, not giving a shit about whether the other guy was dazzled or not, but I knew that if we met a tractor coming the other way we'd all be fucking fertilizer.

How it happened was like this. We're going hell for leather, see, speeding up again because there aren't many bends, because we're going along the side of a valley—but all of a sudden the road dips ahead of us and goes down into a hollow where there's a ford. Not a bridge, mind, a fucking ford. It's not deep, even though it's raining, but the other guy's fucking Ford can't cope with fucking fords, and the Cortina doesn't just dip into the water, chug across and come out the other side—it's like the fucking thing goes water-skiing, and when it hits the ground at the other side it is completely out of control. The near side hits a tree and it's like it was just flipped over. It goes like a corkscrew, from one side of the road to the other, and it's upside-fucking-down when it hits the other tree.

I swear to God I've never seen anything like it.

Andy hit the brakes, but I was dead sure we were going to go the same way until we hit the water and skidded on the mud. We ended up sideways in the stream. I stayed where I was for a minute or two, counting my arms and legs, but Andy was out of the car like a dog out of the trap, running to the smashed-up Cortina.

By the time I got there Andy had the other guy out, and he was dragging him away from the wreck—you know, like the hero does to save another guy from getting blown up when the tank goes. Except the Cortina's tank never went, and the big guy was stone dead.

Now you have to believe this, the guy is *dead*. I mean, his head is fucking caved in and there's blood everywhere. Andy didn't kill him...I swear to God the guy was already dead...but Andy was out of his fucking mind. It wasn't enough for him that the guy was already dead, and he launched into him every which way—boots, mostly. When I see Andy get down on his knees to start punching a guy who only has half a skull, though, I have to figure it's time to try to get him to see sense. I tried to pull him off, just shouting and shouting to get it into his head that the guy is dead.

And in the end, he stopped.

He was still angry, but it was a different sort of anger. He was calm again. He looked down at the body, and the blood on his boots and his Levi's, and he looked at the wrecked car, and then he just turned back to his own car, and started up the engine again. I got in, but I couldn't think of anything to say, and off we went.

Now for me, that ought to have been the end of it. I was still scared shitless, but I was also relieved, if you see what I mean. It was over, you know. The guy was dead, and it wasn't my fault.

But it wasn't over.

I don't know how or why, but it wasn't over.

We were only half way back to the A170 when these head-lights appeared in our mirror, and this car came right up to our tail. I told myself it could have been some guys coming the other way who'd found the wreck and were hurrying to get to a phone, but I guess I was still shaken up, because I wasn't quite ready to believe it, and nor was Andy. He speeded up, and I think he knew, right from that very first moment, that we were in another chase. Only now it was the other guy who was trying to touch up our tail...the other guy who was trying to run us into a tree.

By the time we got to Helmsley it was like an action replay in reverse. Andy was doing nearly eighty and the car behind was sitting on our tail, still creeping up on us. I thought we were certain to pile up when we took the sharp right, and again when we took the right-hander in Oswaldkirk, but Andy's a devil when he's behind the wheel, and he has the devil's luck.

I didn't say a word. I mean, what could I say? I couldn't actually say, could I, 'Is it a silver Cortina?' I couldn't even say, 'What the fuck do you think you're doing?' Because he didn't know, did he? He really didn't know. All he knew was, we were in a chase.

We took the next few bends easily enough, but the other bugger was still getting closer, and I just knew that the hairpin in Brandsby where we'd nearly piled up on the way in was going to get us—and I think Andy knew it too, because as we came into the village he slammed the brakes on hard. The tires screeched and we would have skidded for sure, except that the road was very rough there. We stopped about twenty yards short of the bend.

I was dead sure the car behind us was going to crash into our arse end and fold us up like a concertina, and I just put my head in my arms and waited. But it didn't.

It swerved, and passed us—and if Andy's the devil when he's behind the wheel I don't know who the fuck it was that was driving the other car, because when we braked I thought for sure that he was dead, and so were we. But he went past us like a breath of wind, and he soared round that bend like a stunting airplane.

Zoom...just like that.

No, I didn't see what kind of car it was—I had my head in my fucking hands, didn't I? Sure I'd be a lousy witness in court. Do I care?

No, I haven't finished. Not by a long way.

Andy sat still for a couple of minutes, just staring at the darkness where the other car went by. Then he laughed—'Ha ha!'—just like that. I was thinking that it was only a fucking car after all, and I took it for granted that he was thinking the same. But who can tell with Andy, when he's in that kind of mood? The trouble was, he didn't seem to be in that kind of mood any more. He didn't seem angry at all. Not exactly peaceful—I mean, the guy just spent ten whole minutes kicking the shit out of a fucking corpse—but not angry. Not mad. Not the devil behind a wheel.

After a while he put us back in gear again, and away we went. He didn't even look at me—maybe didn't even know I was still in the car. He wasn't high any more. By Andy's standards, he was almost normal. Almost. He drove home at the kind of speed that would gladden your granny's heart. Safe as fucking houses.

Only, when we finally got back to the street, he didn't turn the corner. He stopped where we stopped before, and he just sat there, staring. For five full seconds I didn't understand, because I was still dumb and I was melting with relief because I was home and dry and still in one fucking piece.

But then I looked—and I saw that parked right outside Andy's front door was a silver fucking Cortina, which looked as if it had crawled out of the breaker's yard.

I mean, it was smashed. Written off. Dead.

I didn't shit myself. But that's when I sobered up, more sober than I'd ever been before.

I don't know how long we sat there, watching. Maybe ninety-nine out of a hundred guys would have gone right in, but not Andy. On the other hand, maybe none of them would have gone in. It's not the kind of situation that crops up every day, so how can you tell?

Maybe it was a quarter of an hour...I don't know. I wasn't counting. I was just waiting for that door to open, the way I knew it would. Waiting...just like the neighbors, behind their twitching curtains.

And then the door opened, exactly like before, and this guy came out.

At first, all I could see was that he was a big guy...bigger than Andy. But he wasn't furtive this time, and Carol wasn't watching him through the crack left by a door that was nine parts closed. This time, the guy let the door swing on its hinges behind him, until it was wide open.

The hall light was on. There was nobody waving goodbye. There was plenty of light to show us the guy who was standing there, not furtive now but proud as the fucking devil. He looked straight at us, knowing we were there, staring us straight in the eyes—staring Andy straight in the eyes.

It was the same guy. His head was all caved in, and though the rain was giving him a real cold shower there was blood everywhere...on his face...on his clothes...on his big bony fist.

Yeah, he was making a fist...and with his other hand he chopped his elbow. *Up yours*, he was saying. *Up yours*. Which was exactly where he'd been, I guess, if he was saying it to Andy.

You can tell me it was a hallucination if you like. Shit, I'll be more than happy to believe you. I'll say yes to any fucking thing you want me to. But I could see the rain drumming on the roof of that wrecked car, and I could see the drops making streaks down his bloody face, and I don't give a tinker's fuck whether it was possible or not, it was there.

He got into the car, and he drove off.

He was dead. He'd been dead since he'd smashed into that tree...long before Andy kicked seven kinds of hell out of him... and the car was dead too...the silver Cortina. They were both of them stone dead. But he just got into his car, and drove away.

Andy sat there, for a minute or two, looking down at his hands. There was blood on them, but it wasn't his blood. I thought he was all set to follow the guy again. I thought he was going to chase him all the way to hell, Hull or Halifax, and I said, 'Please don't. For God's sake, Andy, please don't.' I don't even know if he heard me, but he opened the car door, and he looked down at the blood on his boots and his jeans, making sure that it was really there.

It was really there.

Then he got back in, and drove to the front door. We both got out. He went inside, and shut the door behind him, and I went home.

That's where I've been ever since.

I'm sorry about Carol...I really am. I'm glad she's out of intensive care, and I'm sorry about the baby. But that's really not down to Andy, because I'm dead sure that he didn't even know she was pregnant. Knowing Carol, I'm not even sure that she did. But if you think about it, she only got what was coming to her. In fact, if you ask me, the guy who's lying in the road beside that fucking ford...if he *is* lying dead beside that fucking ford... he only got what was coming to him too. He shouldn't have been fucking Andy's wife, and Andy had every right to give him that kicking, dead or not. And if he really did come back for another go—well, all I can say is that there's no fucking justice in the world. But you know that, don't you?

I don't suppose you'd care to tell me whether the guy is lying dead beside that fucking ford?

Well, when you find out, don't leave me in suspense.

It was an accident, you know—out there at the ford. Andy

really didn't kill the bastard. I mean, he'd kick the shit out of the devil himself if he thought he was being fucked over, but he's not a bad guy really.

After all, we all get a bit carried away sometimes, don't we?

INNOCENT BLOOD

'What are you, some kinda freak or somethin'? What the hell is goin' on here?'

The old man didn't even blink. He just sat in his tatty armchair, still and silent. Those dark and sunken eyes were open all right, but Jody couldn't tell whether they were looking at him, or through him, or nowhere at all. Jody thought that he had never seen eyes so black and so empty.

Jody yanked hard at the handcuffs, which secured his right wrist to the tubular pillar of the brass bedhead; then he yanked at the other pair, which bound his left wrist to the opposite pillar. It was hopeless; thin though his wrists were, they were tightly clasped.

'You bastard!' he moaned. 'You can't do this kind of stuff—not even to me. You think because I sleep in a subway tunnel I don't have rights? You think because I'm a fuckin' junkie I don't have friends? Why'd'you do this? Just tell me what you want, for Christ's sake!'

It seemed that the last phrase caused a flicker of something in the old man's eye. It was a tiny reaction, but it was evidence that there was still intelligence as well as life in that ancient hulk.

Jody paused in his tirade, and waited. He had to wait quite a while, but in the end something came out—maybe an answer, maybe not.

'You...fell down,' said the old man, in a hoarse and hollow tone, 'outside....' The sentence wasn't finished, but it was abandoned to hang there while the speaker's thoughts took off on some introspective track of their own.

Jody was used to hearing sentences abandoned like that. A lot of the people he knew had difficulty getting to the first comma, let alone the terminal period, of any thought containing more than two concepts. It didn't matter what they took—smack, crack, speed or old red biddy—they always got there in the end: lost in the linguistic maze, mentally castrated.

Jody wasn't there yet, and had every reason to think he wouldn't get there at all. In a way, he wished he was. Sometimes, he figured, it was better to travel hopefully than to arrive, even when the only place you had to go was the end of a sentence.

Curiously enough, though, Jody felt sure that the old man wasn't on anything at all—not even a mild trank. Hell, he looked so frail that a dose of barb might stop his heart. His back was bent and his joints were crippled by arthritis. His ragged hair was as white as snow, and the black yarmulke sitting on top of the mess looked like a predatory spider ready to pounce.

Creeping senility, thought Jody. *Maybe Alzheimer's.*

Jody knew what Alzheimer's disease was. He was an educated person. He hadn't been born in the mean streets; he was a self-made man.

'So what if I fell down?' he said, when he gave up hope of the old man getting back on board his train of thought. 'What the fuck do you care? What gives you the right to bring me down here and chain me up like some fuckin' dog?'

'My shop,' said the old man, so softly that it was just as if he were breathing out with half a sob and half a sigh.

Jody couldn't make any sense of it for a moment or two, until he realized that it was the long-delayed end to the statement that the old man had begun to make. He doubted now that it could have been an answer to his questions. It was more likely that the crazy old fool couldn't hear his questions at all—or couldn't care less about the prospect of providing any answers.

What shop? Jody wondered.

Part of the problem, of course, was that he was a little short of answers himself. He didn't remember falling down, and he didn't remember any shop. That might be bad—he wasn't yet at the stage where he fell down thirty times a day or lost great chunks of his memory. Had he been hit? Or had he—bearing in mind the handcuffs—tried to rob this guy's shop? It distressed him that he didn't actually know, and couldn't make himself remember. He didn't know whether he had tried to carry out a crime, or had been the victim of one.

Story of my life, he told himself, with a smile. He noted, as though it were a scientific observation for some hypothetical record, that he still had his sense of humor. It was not a happy discovery; there comes a time in every man's life when the ability to laugh at oneself can only seem ghoulish.

'I thought....,' said the old man, dreamily.

Jody waited again, but grew rapidly impatient with the pregnant pause. 'You thought what, you stupid bastard? Jesus!'

Again there was a flicker of reaction. The old man wasn't deaf—but it sure as hell wasn't easy to get through to him.

'You had...something...on your back.'

Jody didn't have a clue what the old man was talking about. It didn't make any sense.

'Listen, Shylock,' he said, bitterly. 'The only thing I got on my back is a monkey, you dig? A big greedy monkey that ain't been fed for quite a while now. I have to score, see? I need to get back on the street—unless, of course, you have some kind of connection. A cushion under the counter? Hell, man, you listenin' to me? I need some stuff. Aitch—smack—heroin. I'd like to stay here and chat, I really would, but these handcuffs, y'know, are startin' to really piss me off.'

For the first time, Jody felt that the eyes actually looked at him—at him, not through and beyond him.

'No,' said the old man. 'No heroin.'

'I ain't really askin' whether you got it in stock,' said Jody, feeling the cold sweat on his face. 'I'm tellin' you, I gotta have it. You have to let me go.' But he knew, as he said it, that the sweat wasn't just a warning; it was fear, born of the certainty that the old man wasn't going to let him go—that the old man, in fact, had brought him here and tied him down for the express purpose of seeing that he couldn't and didn't make his connection.

That stupid sense of humor couldn't help telling him how ironic it was. Jody had not the slightest doubt, now, that the old man's intentions weren't hostile. In fact, the old fool probably thought that he was trying to help. Being cruel in order to be kind; salvation attained through suffering; a lost soul dragged back from the brink of self-destruction by tough love—that was where the old man was coming from! But even a fool as old and as crazy as he was ought to know better than that.

'Why me?' asked Jody, bitterly. 'Why'd you pick me to fool around with, hey? I fell over in front of your shop, right, and you figured that here was your chance to do somethin'? Your contribution to holdin' back the universal tide of decadence and corruption, is that it? The last straw, was it, that broke the back of your fuckin' defeatism? A guy your age should know better—why not pick on one of your own kind, hey? You think there aren't jewboys out there too? What the fuck you want with me?'

'I thought....,' the old man started again; but then he stopped again, in exactly the same place, as he lost his grip on the fugitive moment of the present, Some memory had caught his attention, snatched him away into the darkest recesses of introspection. Jody knew how it worked; he knew.

'Let me go,' said Jody, in the most deadly earnest tone he could contrive. 'For the love of God, let me go.'

For a moment, there was only the threatening silence—but then the old man's features seemed to crumple up, blurred and smeared by familiar despair.

'You will be on your way,' he whispered, 'and I must tarry until you return. No...for the love of God, no.'

And Jody—who was, after all, an educated person—guessed right away just what kind of crazy man the old Jew was.

Jody's mental descent along the pure white ski-slope to hell was not a smooth one. The symptoms emerged by unsteady degrees, waywardly and full of caprice: the aches, the pains, the sniffles, the shakes, the terrors and the fires that set his soul ablaze broke upon him like a series of overlapping waves borne relentlessly forward by an incoming tide; sometimes he was under and drowning, sometimes he got his head above the surface.

He wondered, as he often had before, whether it made it better or worse to be able to understand what was happening—to have complete command of the medijargon. The external supply of heroin that he took by injection substituted—and then some—for the endorphins that his brain was supposed to make; while he was scoring regularly his brain simply switched off the tap. When he couldn't score, it took time for the brain to get into gear again: cold turkey time, when his body and his being were utterly unprotected from the slings and arrows of an outraged nervous system.

The job endorphins did, Jody knew, was to control the baseline activity of the nervous system. When there were none around, every neurone in his body was on a hair trigger, ready to go off for any reason or no reason at all. Without the big H or the little e, the human body simply wasn't capable of tolerating its own presence and its own condition—which just went to show how cultivated and refined its tastes really were.

Jody had been prone to argue, once upon a time, that junkies shouldn't be regarded as weak-willed degenerates at all, but as people who were so very refined that they couldn't abide the natural state of their own bodies, or as people whose brains were just too damn mean to provide proper insulation from their own electrical wastes.

He had cared about such rationalizations, once—but that had been a long time ago.

Every now and again, when his head was above the surface long enough, Jody tried to talk his jailer out of the delusion from which he was suffering: the delusion that he was the Wandering Jew.

'You don't really believe that you're two thousand years old, do you, Isaac? I mean, I know how you could get hold of the idea, just by lookin' in a mirror, but seein' ain't believin', is it? It's a cultural thing, man—Frenchmen think they're Napoleon and movie stars think they're reincarnations of Cleopatra. You think you remember bein' around for centuries? Hell, man, I know at least three guys who remember how they were abducted by alien spaceships and poked around by Martian medics. Any shrink with a shiny pendant can get people to remember that sort of shit. Past lives manufactured to order, a dime a dozen—hell, man, you can remember any old crap if you've half a mind to convince yourself of it. It don't mean a thing! What really matters is what's possible and what ain't. Nobody lives forever, man. Nobody lives forever, whether Jesus is his friend or his tormentor.'

But that sort of argument cut no ice. The old man couldn't even hear it—wouldn't hear it, at any rate. Sometimes, Jody could provoke a reaction, but it was always the same old reaction: a quotation of some kind. The words Jesus was supposed to have spoken to the man who'd reviled him on his way to Calvary were stuck in the old man's brain, and so were half a dozen apposite quotes from the Bible, the New Testament as well as the Old.

Maybe, Jody thought, his captor had also been an educated person, once upon a time. Maybe this kind of madness was one of those dangerous things that a little learning was supposed to lay on for a guy.

At other times, Jody tried a different tack, playing along with the gag. He knew better than to believe that there was anything to be gained by humoring a madman, but it helped him to pretend that the whole thing was only a game, and that he was a player instead of a sacrificed pawn.

'Even if you are the Wandering Jew,' he said, 'that don't help to make sense of what you're doin' to me. You didn't really figure that I was Jesus come back again when I fell over outside your shop, did you? You didn't really see a cross on my back, did you? Most you could argue is that you thought you'd try to make amends, by showin' a little Christian charity this time around, even to the lowest of the low—but you ain't doin' that, not really. You ain't showin' any kind of charity at all.

'I need a hit, can't you understand that? I need it. Or are you really lookin' to get cursed all over again—is that what you want? You want me to say what you think he said to you—that I hope you never die; that I hope you live in misery and in despair and bitterness forever.

'Hell, I can't say that, can I? That wouldn't be very Christian of me, would it? In fact, now I come to mention it, it couldn't have been very Christian of Jesus fucking Christ, now could it? You think he'd really have said that, the way the legend says he did—to one guy in all that crowd? They were all abusin' him, weren't they? Not one of them was lendin' him a helpin' hand. So why should he curse just one of them? A fit of temper, hey? A little bout of spite from the world champion cheek-turner? You may believe that, but I can't. Even if I thought I remembered it, I couldn't fuckin' believe it.'

But that cut no ice either. The ice was all around him; the whitened walls of the windowless cellar were made of it. Even the air was ice: vaporous, sublimated ice. The crumpled bed linen was ice too, smooth and polished in spite of its creases...a slippery slope.

Jody didn't even know where he was. Underground, for sure—that was why the room had no windows, and why he could feel the rumble of the subway trains in the bed frame.

He was in a cellar, somewhere in the city.

Or maybe he wasn't—sometimes, when his head slid back beneath the waves, he lost his grip on the walls, on the bed and the blankets, on everything. Sometimes, he went straight to hell, without passing Go, and swam in a lake of boiling blood, watched by bat-winged demons, while the whole world shuddered and trembled with Satan's sobs of bitter disappointment.

But even then, there was another watcher too: an old man

with a face carved out of mahogany, with eyes as black as the pit, and the name AHASVERUS written across his forehead in letters of fire.

It was OK to be crazy in hell. Everyone was crazy in hell.

Back in the cellar, the old man fed him, brought him a bedpan at regular intervals, and cleaned up after him. The old man fed him chicken soup, like some character in an ancient Jewish joke: chicken soup with crackers. The old man made him drink coffee, but never anything with it. No pills—not even a lousy aspirin. No alcohol. Nothing to soothe the pain from his tortured soul.

Chicken soup for cold turkey—cold comfort, no cure.

Jody liked that one; he still had his sense of humor, his aesthetic sensibilities. But his talent for repartee was no good to him here; the old man wouldn't listen.

Hell is a place where no one laughs at your wisecracks.

The old man couldn't laugh at all; he was in some other dimension, where he was unable to tell humor from horror, myth from memory, conscience from consciousness, duty from damnation.

But Jody had to concede one thing to the crazy old goat: he had patience! He had the infinite patience you'd expect in a guy who'd really lived ninety or a hundred years, and imagined he'd lived two thousand more.

The black-capped ancient had the patience of a saint—or a demon. He soaked up the abuse as easily as the arguments; he was equally immune to hatred and sympathy, outrage and in-rage, vomit and venom.

In the end, Jody figured that he had no alternative but to let loose the ultimate weapon: the doomsday bomb. In the end, he reasoned, there was nothing left to do with his brief intervals of lucidity but to tell the truth.

That was what he told himself, but in fact he only delayed so long because he was afraid that it wouldn't work—that it wouldn't even get a reaction.

'You crazy old fucker,' he said, 'you better let me go—because if you don't, I swear to God I'm goin' to hurt you. I swear to God I'm goin' to kill you, an' I can do it. You think you're doin' me some kind of favor, getting' the junk outta my system? You think when I'm on the other side of this I'm goin' to turn around an' thank you? Well you're wrong, man, because what I'm goin' to do as soon as I get the chance is to get back on the street and back on the junk. Smack or crack or angel dust, I don't give a fuck, but I gotta get back, because there's nowhere else to go...an' before then, I'll have killed you...I'll have killed you stone dead, even if didn't want to, which I do....

'You want to know why I don't ever want to get straight? You want to know how I can kill you even though my fuckin' hands are handcuffed to a fuckin' bed? Well, I'll tell you, because you ought to fuckin' know already—you ought to have known since I fell down outside your fuckin' shop, if I ever did fall down. I don't want to be straight because yours truly is goin' straight to hell by the AIDS Express.

'I got the virus, see? The only thing positive in my entire life is my fuckin' blood test. I'm dyin', man, and what time I got left to me I want to spend as high in the sky as I can fly, you dig? You bring me down, Shylock, and you bring me all the way down. Ain't nowhere this trip is takin' me but another part of hell. An' if you stick around, old man, you'll go with me—even if I have to bite your fuckin' fingers off to make sure of it. Now for the last time, you fuckin' freak, will you get me the hell outta here, so I can score!'

His worst fears were justified. It didn't work.

The old man didn't let him go

There was a reaction, of sorts. The wooden features slipped again, to let a little tiny bit of the human being out. There was a little shiver of horror, a drop or two of pity. But it was only the Wandering Jew wallowing in his plight—it wasn't the real old man, whoever that might be. It wasn't authentic horror, just part of the same crazy delusion.

It didn't take Jody long, even in the worst phase of his torture, to figure out why. Some versions of the legend said that wherever the Wandering Jew went he carried the seeds of plague—cholera, mostly. It connected with the way that Medieval Christians used to blame epidemics on the Jews, charging them with poisoning the wells; it was one more in a long line of nasty excuses for driving out the heretics, burning their possessions and their homes...and sometimes the people themselves.

Jody couldn't scare the Wandering Jew with the threat of catching HIV. Jody could only make him tremble with the deliciously dreadful thought that he might be the bringer of the plague, as he had been the bringer of so many others.

The guy had enough of a guilt trip going without being fed with that kind of fuel.

Later, when the worst was past and his poor beleaguered brain was beginning to grind out the endorphins in its own parsimonious fashion, Jody thought about apologizing for that particular threat. He even thought about trying to explain to the old man that whatever else he might be guilty of—even if he was the Wandering Jew—he certainly wasn't responsible for the twentieth century's version of the Great Plague. But he didn't.

He couldn't. There was simply no way to accomplish the task.

In spite of everything, though, he never tried to bit the hand that fed him. His threats were empty.

When the waves no longer covered him quite as often, allowing him to hatch schemes and string together ragged patterns of behaviour, Jody tried to question the old man again, in as cunning a fashion as he could contrive.

It was useless; he couldn't even find out the man's name. He had to keep calling him 'Shylock' or 'Isaac' or 'Motherfucker', depending upon the state of his own mind.

The old Jew continued to talk to him, after a fashion, but the words had to well up inside him before he could let them out, and they didn't often come in response to provocation. Even when they did—even when Jody succeeded in turning on the tap of the old man's fragmented consciousness by means of some verbal trigger—what came out was usually disjointed and hard to fathom. Jody was able to build up a thin lexicon of words that could elicit a response, but the effort was hard and the reward meager, and it was by no means clear from the responses just why the words worked.

One word that worked was 'Birkenau', which was the name of one of the death-camps at Auschwitz. Jody had tried it because he could see that the guy was old enough to have been an adult during the war, and because it would have satisfied his sense of neatness to be able to concoct a story about how the old man was locked into his obsession because of what had happened to him then.

But even if it was true that the old man had been in Birkenau, and survived it, what could it prove? What could it really explain?

Sometimes, when his neurones were letting go and shaking loose his common sense, Jody thought it might make just as much sense to invert the speculation, and to argue that the old man had come out of Birkenau alive because he was the Wandering Jew, prohibited from being killed, even by the Nazis. Maybe that was what the old man told himself; maybe that was what the old man believed; maybe it made as much sense as anything else.

Another word that worked was 'suicide', which made Jody wonder in his saner moments whether the old man had unhinged himself because someone close to him had taken that route out of the city. He wondered, too, whether the old man might be trying to commit a kind of suicide by playing host to a virus-carrier—a carrier who might turn on him violently, as he had once threatened to do. But when the neurones were blasting away at the fortress of Jody's own sanity, it seemed to make just as much sense to suppose that the word struck terror into the old man's heart because he was the Wandering Jew, prohibited even from killing himself.

Or thought he was.

Jody still thought it made a difference to distinguish between 'was' and 'thought he was'. He figured that if and when he stopped making that distinction, he would be as crazy as the guy who had chained him to the bed—as crazy as the guy who thought he could be straightened out.

Other words that got a reaction from the lunatic were 'Jesus', 'Christ' and 'crucifixion', but it was all too easy to explain those reactions, whatever the vagaries of he moment encouraged Jody to believe.

Then there was 'blood', which could presumably be accommodated to the same set. A lot of the old man's quotations had to do with blood: the blood of the Covenant; the blood of Christ; the blood of Jewish martyrs, slaughtered by the followers of Christ.

Once, when Jody mentioned blood—remembering, as he did so, that if the positions of inquisitor and crazy man had been reversed it was a word that would probably have provoked a reflexive reaction from him, too—his captor responded with a quote that seemed inapposite: 'I have sinned in that I have betrayed the innocent blood'. Jody knew his Bible well enough to know that those words referred to Judas Iscariot—but when he challenged the old madman with the charge that he was trying to steal guilt that wasn't his at all, there was nothing in the sunken eyes but the same old wall of incomprehension.

'You and Judas both,' Jody said with a sigh. 'You and Judas and all of us. Who hasn't, old man? You think you got a mortgage on all the world's guilt? I'm telling you, man, that'd be more than anyone could bear. Whatever you did to Jesus—whatever sins you committed, even in two thousand years—your guilt can't be more'n a spit in the ocean. Whoever you think you are, you ain't done nothin' compared to what the rest of us have done.

Getting straight wasn't the same as getting well. When his neurones began to calm down, as far as they would consent to be calmed down, Jody found that his need to score had been reduced to the same kind of magnitude as his need to eat and drink: it was a hunger, it was a passion, it was a painful thirst, but it wasn't a lake of boiling blood for ever and ever—not any more. On the other hand, there were other pains, other sicknesses, and other miseries, which couldn't and wouldn't go away.

If the old Jew had intended to drag Jody back to the sunny side of the Gate of Doom, where he could look back on the command to abandon hope and smile, the plan had come unstuck. There was still the virus eating away at Jody's immune system, exposing his body and his soul to every passing pathogen and cancer, and there were still a thousand other reasons to covet oblivion. Even when the heroin had been flushed out of his system, Jody yearned to get back on it—on something. He was still prepared to beg, cajole, threaten and scream for something to feed his head: anything at all, so long as it stopped him from feeling and being the way he felt and was.

Jody was still sick. He was still dying. He was in the world again, but he wasn't out of hell.

Jody didn't know whether the old man could possibly understand that, or whether the whole affair was just a comedy of absurdities. Sometimes, he thought that the old man was trying to help him, and was simply too crazy to comprehend the ridiculousness—and the evil of what he was doing. Sometimes, though, he favored the opposing theory that the old man knew well enough, at some level of submerged consciousness, that what he was doing was only one more form of torture, one more act of calculated wickedness.

What would I do if I believed I was the Wandering Jew? thought Jody, once. *Would I try to atone for my sin by becoming Christ-like, and trying as hard as I could to redeem the unredeemable? Or would I become so bitter against my fate that I'd appoint myself a kind of devil, paying Christ back by using my eternal exile to create suffering?*

He wondered if anyone else had ever been chained to the bed—and if so, how many, and what had become of the bodies. Sometimes, he looked at the flagstoned floor and wondered whether every stone was a grave, and which one might in time be his.

Sometimes, he asked the question aloud, but there was nothing in it that could provoke a response. 'Grave' and 'death' weren't words that worked, unless they were combined with 'plague'.

Jody didn't give up asking questions, but he asked them more for his own benefit than in the hope of getting anything remotely resembling an answer. He dutifully rang the changes on all his methods of address, crossing and re-crossing the spectrum that extended from the cunning deftness of sweet reason to the fervent rhetoric of hate and wrath.

'Do you still think I can be redeemed,' he would ask, 'if only your reservoir of conscience, faith and chicken soup doesn't give out? Do you think you can prepare my soul for the kingdom of heaven even while the cancers eat me up from the inside? Do you think this is bankable moral credit, which may get you time off for good behavior? Do you actually care whether I get better or not, or is it only the means and not the end that matters to you? Do you really want me to die, in spite of all the tender loving care, simply in order that you can be possessed of one more proof that life is an absolute bitch and that the universe can keep kicking you in the teeth forever, if that's what God wants?'

'You're a fuckin' sadist!' he would complain. 'You're no better than any other guard in any other fuckin' concentration camp. You think it's OK to do this because you're off your fuckin' head, but it ain't—ain't no excuses, man! You think there's somethin' noble in pretendin' to be the Wanderin' Jew, but there ain't. It's just sick—sick in the head, sick in the soul. It's just one more excuse for stickin' it to some poor bastard who can't fight back—just one more torturer's motto. You want me to believe you're the Wanderin' Jew, just give me a knife an' I'll cut out your filthy heart to show you just how immortal you ain't. Or if you can't stomach that, you cut me, anywhere and everywhere you like, an' lick up the blood. Oh sure, you ain't allowed to kill yourself—oh, sure, you got the curse hangin' over you, which won't let you put yourself in danger...but under-neath the excuses, you're just one more hypocrite, one more fuckin' freak, one more serial killer. You think I don't know what you really are? You're Jack the fuckin' Ripper and Son of Sam, just one more sickhead who likes to tie people up and mess people up and make them die for your sick and stupid amusement. I know you, freak, I know you...and you have to get me some stuff, or I'll go out of my fuckin' mind, and then you'll have no one...no one at all....'

As time went by, Jody began to find it easier to believe that the old man might really be the Wandering Jew. When he was used to the idea, he could believe it even when his neurones were on their best behaviour. It wasn't that he was convinced; it was just that he was prepared to entertain the belief, as a kind of guest among the broken idols of all his rejected faiths. What the hell else was there for him to do, while he lay there all day chained to a brass bed-frame?

Would it, Jody wondered, be more or less comforting to accept what the old man said? Would it make his imprisonment and the withdrawal of his medication more or less bearable? And when the time came to die, from whatever deadly cause his failing immune system chose to let through, would it make any difference at all whether he was the victim of a madman or a legendary anachronism?

If the old man really was the Wandering Jew, Jody thought, then that would mean that there really had been a Jesus, who really had had the power to work miracles...but was that good news? Even if there had once been a man who had the power to do to another what Jesus had done to the Wandering Jew, that couldn't suffice to prove that there was a kingdom of heaven to which men's souls could go when they died...and even if one were prepared to take that aboard too, there was no reason to expect that his own soul had a reservation there, rather than the other place.

And then again, thought Jody, in his scrupulous once-educated fashion, if there really had been a Jesus, who had done what Jesus was supposed to have done to the shoemaker who spat at him, didn't that prove—as he had earlier argued in the extremity of his anguish—that Jesus was untrue to his own declared principles, just like every other mealy-mouthed bastard who'd ever preached a sermon?

It was better, Jody decided in the end, to hold on to the likelier opinion. The old man was crazy; his brain had been addled; there was no Wandering Jew and never had been; Christ was just a myth and a mystery; the world was irredeemable, but death was forever, and mercifully dark, and peacefully quiet, and as painless as an infinite dose of pure endorphin.

Much better to believe that, Jody told himself. If you need faith at all, have faith in the madness and wild injustice of the world. The alternatives are too horrible to contemplate.

Jody's silent debates with himself and his loud altercations with his unanswering adversary remained for a while at a level not too distant from coherence, but with time they became increasingly delirious again.

The old man never gave any indication that he intended to release his prisoner from the cellar. It was obvious that whatever the old man imagined his task to be, it had certainly not concluded with Jody getting off the stuff. Jody realized that his was a life sentence—but his sense of humor, still resilient, told him that it didn't really matter, because with time off for bad behavior he'd be out in a matter of months.

Jody had one momentary flicker of hope on the day that the old man removed one of the pairs of handcuffs, freeing his left hand. For some time he was able to encourage himself with the hope that this represented the beginning of a return to sanity, or at least the surfacing of a tendency to mercy—but the hope proved frail. Nothing else changed. The old man was still restricted to the same limited repertoire of observations and quotations and the same limited repertoire of actions: bringing food, fetching the bedpan, cleaning up, sitting in the worn and faded armchair.

Jody couldn't even figure out whether the freeing of one hand was a reward for his progress or some kind of teasing insult.

Jody had known people who kept birds in cages, dogs chained in yards, fish in tanks. He told himself that he was just some kind of pet, dangerous but somehow beloved. But he didn't stop hating the old man, and he couldn't stop being angry with him. He abandoned all his hopes of getting high again, and tried to cultivate patience even when the nightmares began to claw at his waking consciousness and the pains got worse, but he could not learn the merciful art of despair. He could not learn to lie down and die. The pain was too bad, the delirium too fierce.

He had never been out of hell, but he had never learned the trick of adapting to it.

Sometimes, he just screamed and screamed until the screaming was no release at all, but only one more aspect of his burden.

After a time, Jody began to wonder—but not seriously—whether he himself might be the Wandering Jew.

Perhaps, he fantasized, he had always been the Wandering Jew, but had mercifully contrived to forget the fact, inventing by confabulation an entirely false identity for himself—aided, no doubt, by the fact that his skin had darkened with the years.

Perhaps, on the other hand, he had only recently become the Wandering Jew—or the Wandering Negro. Perhaps, while he had been living down in the subway, Christ had come again to earth and had gone through the whole sorry farce of attempted salvation yet again. Perhaps, while roaming the streets in search of a hit, Jody had come across this new Christ hauling his cross along the pavement, and had threatened him with a knife, demanding his wallet or his blood. And Jesus had turned to him, and said, 'I must shed my innocent blood, but yours will course in your cursed veins until I come to let it out, and you will walk in perpetual misery, for I will send to you a madman who will disconnect you from your source, and keep you from the gates of heaven for ever and ever and....'

He could not believe it, of course.

He was not as mad as that, though he had begun to wish that he were.

But sometimes, when the thought struck him, he wished that he could remember exactly where he had fallen down, and why, before the crazy old Jew had picked him up and brought him into the Underworld, and chained him up in the lake of boiling blood.

Sometimes, he could not help but wish for death, if only as a proof that he was not already dead.

'It's not fair, of course,' he told his captor, in one of his maudlin moods. 'I may be a junkie now, but I'm an educated person. I was goin' to be a doctor, y'know? I could've been, too, if it hadn't been for...things. Terrible waste, ain't it, that a man with a college education can end up sleeping on the streets—or under the streets, in the dark and haunted corridors where the subway runs.

'But that's the world all over, ain't it: waste, waste, waste. I guess you know that better than most, even if you're only a crazy old Jew. I bet you wish you could talk to me, don't you? I know you can't, because of the curse. It must have been different once, I guess. Once you could speak freely, to tell your story—but then you had to shut up again. Or maybe you just chose to shut up, when people stopped believing you and started calling you a crazy man. Is that it?'

The old man didn't answer.

'Understandable that you should be confused, of course,' Jody went on, when he could get a word in edgewise between the darts of pain. 'You probably can't remember—in fact, you probably can't even remember Jesus Christ, or what happened on the road to Calvary. That's only to be expected; God gave men memory enough to carry the record of their allotted three-score years and ten, and no man can be expected to remember more. I bet you can't remember more than forty years...fifty at the most. All the rest is darkness and uncertainty, I guess....

'It's one more aspect of your curse, to be added to the rest.

Sometimes, I bet you wonder if you're mad. Sometimes, I bet you wonder whether you're just some crazy old man who only thinks he's the Wandering Jew. But you have to have faith in yourself. You have to trust what you know, not what you can remember. Look at me—you think I can remember? Hell, no! I can't remember a damn thing. But I know who I am, and I know what I am, and that's just enough to keep me sane and human. Just enough.

'You're probably wondering now whether you ought to take me to the hospital. You don't have to worry about it—there wouldn't be any point. For two thousand years there's been no cure for the plague, and there's none now. I wish I had some stuff, though...I really wish I had some stuff. Beats chicken soup. Beats everything. Sure, it's poison. It rots your brain. It won't let you see the world as it truly is. But if I only had some stuff, I could die like a man. I think I could, if only....'

There were still dark waves breaking upon the shore of Jody's soul, sometimes dragging him under, sometimes letting his mind get out into the light.

The pain came at him and at him and at him, until he finally figured out what it was trying to teach him.

It was trying to teach him the most important of all the lessons that a man had to learn before he died—the lesson that hell was endurable. Eternal pain, eternal punishment, was something that could be accepted, because in time the pain became meaningless—just something that was there, something that was part of the essential sameness of daily, weekly, yearly life.

The pain was trying to teach him that he didn't have to be afraid, that it didn't matter how may sins he'd committed in life, that it didn't matter whether he repented or not. Pain, in the end, ceased to be cold turkey and turned into mere chicken soup. Pain, in the end, ceased to be a function of the intolerability of the flesh, and became instead an ironic reversal of itself: it became another way of getting high.

When Jody finally realized that, he laughed. He laughed for

several minutes—or maybe several days, for there was no way to measure time objectively in the featureless cellar.

He hadn't lost his sense of humor. He never would.

When he had learned what the pain had to teach him—when he became, at last, an educated man—he saw too that he had misconstrued his circumstances. He saw how utterly he had misjudged the poor old man, who might or might not be the authentic Wandering Jew. He saw that he and his co-conspirator were not simply two imprisoned men, confined by walls, by chains, by delusions and by the imminence of death. He saw that the game they had played, though long and arduous, had been neither ridiculous nor ultimately futile.

He understood that he had, in a way, been saved.

Naturally, he continued to play. It would have been pointless to give up. Like a tiger pacing in its cage in the zoo he continued to talk to the old man, crossing and re-crossing that same old patch of territory from philosophy to passion and back again. He babbled furiously when he was posing as a reasonable man, and coldly hurled his insults and his pleas when he was not. And he came to understand that there was no war, as he had always thought there must be, between the intellect and the emotions, between calculation and desire, between the spirit and the flesh.

But he did not cease to demand his proofs, because that was part of the game. He did not cease to taunt and tempt the old man with accusations and possibilities, even though he no longer had the least vestige of hope that his railing could bring forth a response.

It is, of course, when we have given upon all hope that our prayers are most likely to be rewarded. We understand why that is, because we have a sense of humor.

Jody's game ended when the old man finally took up his oft-repeated offer to put to the proof the crucial question of whether the old man was or was not the Wandering Jew. The old man finally did what he had been asked to do a hundred times, and gave Jody a sharp knife.

Then the old man bared his ancient breast, and wordlessly invited his prisoner to strike him.

Jody looked up into those dark, dark eyes in search of a hint of fear or doubt, but he could see none. Then he looked at the knife for some while, trying to make up his mind whether or not he had the courage or the strength to strike. When he decided that he had, he closed his eyes, summoned up what strength he had, and cut through the artery in his own neck.

It was a skilled cut, which he was able to make successfully only because he was an educated person, with some knowledge of the difficulty of the task.

Once a man's carotid artery is severed, blood cannot reach the brain and unconsciousness follows swiftly. But Jody had time to look up again at the old man, in order to see whether he was capable of reacting.

Actions speak louder than words, and the old man heard. There was no doubt about it: the old man heard.

His eyes came very briefly to life, savoring horror. But the reaction was disappointing, for Jody, because he realized as soon as the old man began to speak that this was only one more quotation, one more stupid reflex. Jody's memory, suddenly and remarkably sharpened by the imminence of death, recognized the words. They were from the sixth chapter of the Gospel of St John: 'Whoso eateth my flesh, and drinketh my blood, hath eternal life.'

Jody heard and saw no more, but before thought failed him for the last time, he had a momentary vision of what might happen next. He imagined that having said these words, the old man might dip his fingers in the blood that flowed from the slit throat, and lift up his hand as though to touch the blood to his lips.

And Jody could not help but wonder whether the old Jew would be able do it, or whether the curse that was upon him would forbid it—or whether, even if he could and did do it, Jesus would allow the man who had offended him to die at last.

Then he wondered, after the invariable fashion of his restless, capricious, sarcastic mind, whether this moment was what it had all been for. Maybe they had both been set up—by Jesus Christ, by God or by the devil—solely in order that they should come to this. Maybe the old man really was the Wandering Jew, brought here solely for the purpose of renewing his power as a plague-carrier. Maybe the whole point of it all was to let the old man touch Jody's not-so-innocent blood to his not-so-innocent lips, before going out to continue the business of roaming the world, for ever and ever.

It wouldn't be quite as futile as it sounded. The old man's fucking days were over, but he could still bleed.

Like Jody, he could still bleed.

Darkness dragged Jody down to some unknowable hell before he could see whether the old man touched his fingers to his lips or not.

But after all, thought poor dead Jody, who had not yet lost his sense of humor, what could it possibly prove?

Whatever the result, what could it possibly prove?

EMPTINESS

It was five o'clock on Tuesday morning, with an hour still to go before dawn, when Ruth found the abandoned baby. The plaintively mewling infant—who was less than a week old, if appearances could be trusted—had been laid in a cardboard box in a skip outside a former newsagent's in St. Stephen's Road. The skip was there because the shop was in the process of being refitted as an Indian takeaway. Ruth was coming home from the offices of an insurance company in Queen Street, where she'd been sent to work the graveyard shift by the contract-cleaning firm that employed her. She was all washed out, drained of all reserves of strength and momentum.

Ruth knew that she ought to call the police so that they could deliver the baby to social services, and that was what she vaguely intended to do when she plucked the child's makeshift crib out of the skip. The first thing she did thereafter, obviously, was to stick an experimental finger into the baby's open mouth. When she felt the nip of the newborn's tiny teeth the vague intention ought to have hardened into perfect certainty, but it didn't. She was adrift on the tide of her own indolence, rudderless on the sea of circumstance.

The baby sucked furiously at the futile finger, desperate to assuage a building hunger. In order to get it out of the infant's mouth Ruth had to tear the finger free, but the ripped flesh on either side of the nail didn't bleed. The pain quickly faded to a numbness that was not unwelcome.

The baby had thrashed around vigorously enough to work

free of the shit-stained sheet in which it had been wrapped, and Ruth took note of the fact that he was a boy before wrapping him up as best she could in the cleaner part of the sheet. Her own kids were both girls. Frank had done a bunk while they were supposedly still trying for a boy; if they had succeeded in time, she would have stood exactly the same chance as everybody else of giving birth to a vampire—the publicly quoted odds had been as short as one in fifty even then, fourteen years ago.

The nearest payphone was a quarter-mile up the road, practically on the doorstep of the estate. By the time Ruth drew level with the booth she had not brought her resolve to do the sensible thing into clearer focus. The baby had stopped crying long enough to look into her eyes while she rearranged the sheet by the glare of a sodium streetlight, but it had only been a glimpse. Temptation had not closed any kind of grip upon her— but fear, duty and common sense were equally impotent. When she reached the phone booth she paused to rest and consider her options.

If she did as she was supposed to do the baby would be fitted with a temporary mask and whisked away to one of the special orphanages that were springing up all over. Once there he would be fitted with a permanent eye shield, stuck in a dormitory with a dozen others and fed on animal blood laced with synthetic supplements. He would go straight into a study programme and would remain in it for life.

The primary objective of the study programs was to find a cure for the mutant condition, enabling its victims to survive on other nourishment than blood. Their secondary objective was to find a way of helping the afflicted to survive longer than was currently normal. Nobody thought the scientists were knocking themselves out to obtain the latter achievement while the former remained tantalizingly out of reach. There was a certain social convenience in the fact that real vampires, unlike the legendary undead, rarely survived to adulthood. The average life expectancy of an orphanage baby was no more than thirteen years;

the figure was probably three or four years higher for babies raised at home, but they were in a minority even in the better parts of town. The best reason why so many vampire babies were abandoned was that they were direly unsafe companions for young siblings; the more common one was that the neighbors would not tolerate those who harbored them.

In theory, Ruth's younger daughter was still living with her in the flat, but in practice fifteen-year-old Cassie spent at least five nights a week with her boyfriend in a ground-floor squat. Even if she were unwise or unlucky enough to become fixated on the child, sharing donations with her mother wouldn't do her any harm. In any case, Cassie's blood was probably too polluted by various illegal substances to offer good nourishment to a fortnight-old vampire. All in all, Ruth thought, there was no very powerful reason why she shouldn't look after the baby herself for a little while, if she wanted to.

Carefully, she counted reasons why she might want to hesitate over the matter of handing the baby over to the proper authorities.

Firstly, the flat had been feeling empty ever since Judy had moved to Cornwall with the travelers, even before Cassie took up with Robert. No matter how much she hated the work itself, Ruth simply didn't know what to do with herself any more when she wasn't working.

Secondly, she'd put on a lot of weight lately, and everyone knew that nursing a vampire baby, if only for a couple of weeks, was one hell of a slimming aid.

There wasn't a thirdly; Ruth wasn't the kind of person to take any notice of those middle class apologists for the 'new humankind' who were fond of arguing that vampire children were the most loving, devoted and grateful children that anyone could wish for and ought not to be discriminated against on account of unfortunate tendencies they couldn't help. She didn't have any expectations of that kind—her own children hadn't given her any reason to.

In the end, Ruth decided that there was no hurry to make the call. Surely nobody would care if she waited for a little while, provided that she didn't hang on too long. If it were only for three or four days, she could probably keep the baby's presence secret from the Defenders of Humanity, and if she couldn't she could hand the baby over as soon as she had to. It was no big deal. It was just something to do that might even do her a tiny bit of good. Just because she was pushing forty, there was no reason to let go of the hope that she might still be worth something to someone.

Unfortunately, Cassie made one of her increasingly rare raids on her wardrobe later that morning, before Ruth had had time to get her head down for a couple of hours. The baby was asleep but Ruth hadn't taken him into her bedroom. The dirty sheet had been swapped for a clean one but he was still in the old cardboard box—which was anything but unobtrusive, sat as it was on the living-room table.

'Why aren't you in school?' Ruth demanded, hoping to distract her daughter's attention and ensure that she didn't linger.

'Free period,' Cassie replied, ritualistically. 'What's that?'

'None of your business,' said Ruth, defiantly.

'Whose is it? Is baby-minding a step up from office cleaning or a step down? Can't its mum find anything better to keep it in than a cardboard box?'

Cassie peered into the makeshift cot as she spoke, but the baby's eyes and lips were closed, and there was nothing to betray its true nature.

'Shh!' said Ruth, fiercely. 'You'll wake him up.' There was, of course, little chance of that, given that the sun was shining so brightly, but Ruth figured that there was no need to let Cassie in on her secret yet if she could possibly avoid it. Her tacit arrangement with the baby was, after all, strictly temporary.

Fortunately, Cassie showed no inclination to inspect the visitor more carefully. Sexual activity hadn't made her broody. In fact, when Ruth had first tackled her on the subject of contraception, Cassie had sworn that if ever she fell pregnant and couldn't face an abortion she'd jump off a top-floor balcony. Most people who said things like that didn't mean them, but Cassie was short for Cassandra, and ever since Robert had told her what the name signified in mythology Cassie had taken the view that whenever it was time for one of her gloomy prophecies to come true she'd have to make bloody sure that it did.

When Cassie had gone, Ruth unearthed an old cot from the junk-cupboard under the stairs. Two baby blankets and a couple of Babygros were still folded neatly within it, although she had to run the vacuum over them to get rid of the dust. She left the baby asleep with the bedroom curtains drawn while she hiked over to Tesco in search of Pampers, red meat, Lucozade, iron tablets and various other items that now had to be reckoned essentials. Luckily, she'd been off-shift on Friday and Saturday and hadn't been able to collect her pay until Monday, so she was as flush as she ever was.

By the time she got back the sun was at its zenith and she was twice as exhausted as before, but the baby was awake and whimpering and she knew that she'd have to feed him again before getting some sleep on her own account.

The thought of putting the vampire to her breast again made her hesitate over the wisdom of her decision not to call Social Services, but as soon as she looked down into the child's tear-filled eyes her squeamishness vanished, as it had the first time when the child had been terrified and starving. His gaze had filled up once again with tangible need. He was thin and pale and empty, and the pressure of his eyes renewed Ruth's awareness of her own contrasting fullness: her too-substantial flesh; her still-extending life; her superabundant blood.

It did hurt when the teeth clamped down for the second time on the tenderized rim of the nipple, but once they were lodged the anesthetic effect of the baby's saliva soothed the ache away.

Ruth couldn't feel or see the flow of blood as the child took his nourishment. Vampires only used their teeth for holding on—they took the blood by some kind of suction process that drew it through the skin without breaking it. When he released her again, already falling back to sleep, there was no leakage from the residual wounds. The control that vampires exercised over the flesh of their donors was ingenious enough to forbid any waste.

When she had put a clean disposable on the baby and put him down again Ruth fought off her tiredness for the fourth time and made herself a meal. She knew that she had to eat regularly and well if she were to be adequate to the baby's needs, even for a fortnight. She had a second cup of tea in order to maintain her fluid balance but she left the Lucozade for later. Before she finally went to bed she phoned the agency to say that she had flu and that she would have to come off the roster for at least a week, until further notice. Her supervisor didn't protest; Ruth's attendance record was better than average and there was no shortage of night-cleaners in the area.

She slept very soundly, as was only to be expected. She didn't dream—not, at any rate, that she could remember.

Cassie didn't figure out what kind the baby was until Thursday evening, at which time she threw an entirely predictable tantrum.

'Are you completely crazy?' she demanded of her mother. 'It's kidnapping, for God's sake—and the thing will bleed you to death if you let it. It's a monster!'

'He's a human being,' Ruth assured her. 'His mother obviously couldn't cope—but she didn't turn him over to the authorities either. She'd be grateful to me if she knew. It's only temporary, anyhow. It's kindness, not kidnapping.'

'It's suicide!'

'No it's not. They're not dangerous to adults, even in the long run. A couple of weeks will only make me leaner and fitter. I need to be fitter to do that bloody job five and six nights a week. It'd be different if there was a child in the house, but there isn't, is there?'

'They're cuckoos,' Cassie blustered. 'They're aliens, programmed to eliminate all rivals for their victims' affections.

Why do you think they keep them masked in the homes? That's where he belongs, and you know it—in a home.'

'He is in a home,' Ruth pointed out. 'A real home, not a lab where they'll weigh and measure and monitor him like some kind of white rat. He's entitled to that, for a little while at least. There's no need to tell anyone—it's my business, not yours or anyone else's.'

'It is so my business,' Cassie retorted, hotly. 'I live here too—I'm the rival that the cuckoo is programmed to push out while he squeezes you dry and leaves you a shriveled wreck.'

'I thought you had decided that this place is just a hotel,' Ruth came back, valiantly. 'A place to keep your stuff, where you can get the occasional meal and take a very occasional bath whenever you happen to feel like it.'

'Don't be ridiculous, Mum. I want that thing out of here—now, not next week or next month.'

'Well, it's not what I want,' Ruth informed her, firmly. 'It's just for a few more days. Stay away if you want to. You usually do. Don't interfere.'

Cassie told her boyfriend straight away, of course, but it turned out that she didn't get the response she expected. If he'd been the kind of Robert who condescended to be called Rob or Bob he'd have run true to form, but even on the estate there were kids with intellectual pretensions. Robert hadn't left school until he was eighteen and he would tell anyone who cared to listen that he could have gone to university if it hadn't been for the fact that the teachers all hated him and consistently marked down the continuously assessed work he had to do for his A-levels.

Robert came up to inspect the infant at eleven o'clock on Friday morning. Ruth had had a busy night but her nipples had now adapted themselves to the baby's needs and the flow of her blood had become wonderfully smooth and efficient. The numbness left behind when the child withdrew wasn't in the least like sexual excitement but it was delicious nonetheless. She was tired, certainly, but she wasn't dishrag limp, the way she had been after finishing a long night-session in some glass-sided tower. Although she was keen to get to bed she knew that she could stay awake if she had to, and she knew that she had to persuade Robert not to do anything reckless. It was a pleasant surprise to find that he was a potential ally.

'Do you know whose he is?' Robert wanted to know, as he stared down into the cot with rapt fascination. The baby's eyes were closed, so the fascination was spontaneous.

'No,' said Ruth. 'I've kept my ears open, but I didn't want to ask around. The neighbors haven't cottoned on yet—Mrs. Hagerty next door's as deaf as a post and if the Gledhills on the other side have heard him whimpering they haven't put two and two together. He doesn't scream like ordinary babies, no matter how distressed he gets—not that he gets distressed, now that he's safe. He's a very sensible baby.'

'I could probably find out who dumped him,' Robert bragged. 'It must be one of the slags on the estate—it's easy enough to do a disappearing bump census when you've got connections.'

Robert didn't have connections, in any meaningful sense of the word. He was a small-time user, not a dealer. He didn't even have any friends, except Cassie—who would presumably dump him as soon as she found someone willing to take her on who was slightly less of an outcast.

'It doesn't matter where he came from,' Ruth said. 'The important thing is to make sure that he doesn't come to any harm. You have to stop Cassie shooting her mouth off to the Defenders.'

'She wouldn't do that,' Robert assured her, with valiant optimism. 'She's with me—she knows that all the scare stories are rubbish. We don't believe in demons or alien abductions or divine punishment. We know that it's natural, just a kind of mutation—probably caused by the hormones they feed to beef cattle or pesticide seepage into the aquifers.'

Ruth knew that Robert probably hadn't a clue what an aquifer was, but she didn't either and she wasn't about to give him the opportunity to run a bluff.

'He needs me, for now,' she said. 'That's all that matters. It's only temporary. When he's strong enough, I'll hand him over.'

'Does it hurt?' he wanted to know. Ruth didn't have to ask him what he meant by it.

'No,' she said. 'And it isn't like a drug either. Not pot, not ecstasy. He isn't even particularly lovable. Little, helpless, grateful...but no cuter than any ordinary baby, no more beautiful. Alive, hungry, maybe even greedy...but it's my choice and it's my business. I don't need saving from him—and I certainly don't need saving from myself.'

'They must always have existed, mustn't they?' Robert said, following his own train of thought rather than trying to keep up with hers. 'Much rarer than nowadays, of course—maybe one in a million. Intolerable, in a pre-scientific age. Automatic demonization. The idea that the dead come back as adult vampires must be an odd sort of displacement. Guilt, I guess. Never seen one close up before. Quite safe, I suppose, while the sun's up. Safe anyway, of course, if you're sensible. Adaptation makes sure that they don't kill off their primary hosts. What's good for the host is good for the parasite.'

'He still needs to feed during the day,' Ruth pointed out. 'He wakes up from time to time. But it's perfectly safe. He doesn't intend to hurt anyone. He doesn't hurt anyone.'

She smiled faintly as Robert took a reflexive step backwards, mildly alarmed by the thought that the child might open its eyes and captivate him on the instant—but Robert regained his equilibrium as she finished the last sentence.

'What do you call him?' Robert asked. He was being pedantic. He hadn't asked what the baby's name was because he knew that Ruth couldn't know what name the child's real mother had given him, and wouldn't feel entitled to give him a name herself when she knew that she would have to hand him over in a matter of days.

'I don't call him anything,' Ruth lied, before adding, slightly more truthfully, 'just the usual things. What you'd call terms of endearment.'

Cassie's boyfriend nodded, as if he knew all about terms of endearment because of all the things he said to Cassie while subjecting her exceedingly willing flesh to statutory rape.

The boy was long gone by the time the baby bared his teeth again and searched for his anxious provider with his pleading and commanding eyes. Ruth was certain that Robert had had nothing to worry about; the infant knew by now who his primary host was, and he only had eyes for her.

It was Ruth's rapid weight-loss that finally tipped off Mrs. Hagerty, and it was Mrs. Hagerty—despite the fact that her own kids were in their thirties and long gone—who passed the word along to the Gledhills, so that the Gledhills could make sure it got back to the local chapter of the Defenders of Humanity.

Fortunately, the conclusion to which the stupid old bat had jumped was only half-correct, and the rumor that actually took wing was that the child was Cassie's and that Ruth had decided to take him on in her daughter's stead. This error qualified as fortunate, in Ruth's reckoning, because it persuaded the Defenders of Humanity that shopping her as a kidnapper would be a waste of time. If the baby had been Cassie's, the whole thing would have been a family matter, much more complicated than it really was.

When she knew that the secret was out, Ruth expected shit and worse through the letterbox and a flood of anonymous letters in green crayon, but the Defenders of Humanity were canny enough to try other gambits for starters. The first warning shot fired across her bows was a visit from the vicar of St. Stephen's. She could hardly refuse entry to her flat to an unarmed and unaccompanied wimp in a dog collar, although she wasn't about to make him a cup of tea.

'You must put your mind at rest, my dear,' said the vicar, hazarding an altogether unwarranted and faintly absurd familiarity. 'It is not because it was conceived in sin that the child is abnormal.'

'No,' said Ruth, as noncommittally as she could.

'There is no need for shame,' the vicar ploughed on. 'It is not your duty to accept this burden. There is no reason at all why you should not deliver the infant into the hands of the proper authorities, and every reason why you should.'

'That's what God wants, is it?' Ruth asked.

'It is the reasonable and responsible thing to do,' the vicar assured her. 'Your first duty in this matter is to your daughter, your second is to your neighbors and your third is to yourself. For everyone's sake, it is better to have the child removed to a place of safety. While it remains on the estate it is bound to be seen as an increasing danger, not merely to your own family but the families of others. I do not ask you to concede that the child is an imp of Satan, but I do ask you to consider, as carefully as you can, that even if it is not actively evil it is an unnatural thing whose depredations pollute the temple of your body. It is a bloodsucker, my dear, which only mimics the forms of humanity and innocence in order to have its wicked way with you—and I use that phrase advisedly, for what it does is a kind of violation equally comparable to vile seduction and violent rape.'

'Suffer the little children to come unto me,' Ruth quoted, endeavoring to quench the fire of zealotry with a dash of holy water—but to no avail.

'It is not a child, my dear,' the vicar insisted, all the while keeping his eyes averted from the cot. 'It is a leech, an unclean instrument of temptation and torment. If you want to be truly merciful, you must give it up to those who would keep it safely captive.'

'Well,' said Ruth, 'I'm grateful for the lesson in Christian charity, but I think he's about to wake up. I'm sure that modesty forbids....'

Modesty did forbid—and the first note didn't arrive until the following day, when the vicar had washed his hands of the matter.

GET RID OF IT, the note said. IF YOU DONT WE WILL. Apart from the lack of punctuation, it was error-free, but given that the longest word it contained was only four letters long it was hardly a victory for modern educational standards.

The notes that followed were mostly more ambitious, and the fact that the longer words tended to be misspelled didn't detract from the force of their suggestion that if Ruth wanted to spill her blood for vampires there were plenty of people living nearby who would be glad to lend her a helping blade.

Cassie was incandescent with rage when she heard what was being said about her.

'How dare you?' she yelled at her hapless mother. 'How dare you let them believe that it's mine?'

'I never said so,' Ruth pointed out.

'But you didn't bloody deny it, did you? You let that shit the vicar blather on without ever once telling him that you found the little fucker in a rubbish skip. Mud sticks, you know. Some round here will remember this forever, and God help me if I ever have a kid of my own. Well, I'm done protecting you. Robert wouldn't let me phone 999 myself, but I've put the word out that you have no claim at all on the cuckoo, and that the fastest way to get it off the block is in a police van. Expect it tonight.'

That was on the second Saturday, by which time Ruth had had the child in her care for twelve days. She had not really intended to keep him so long, and his tender care had already turned nine-tenths of her spare fat into good healthy muscle, so one of her reasons for keeping him had melted away. As for the other, she was almost out of cash and she really needed to get back to work. The fact that she would have nothing to do when she wasn't working was no longer a significant issue, given that if she couldn't feed herself properly she'd soon be no use at all to the baby.

For once, reason stood fair and square with bigotry. Both asserted that she must not keep the baby any longer—but their treaty had been made too late. Ruth's devotion to blood-donation had passed beyond the bounds of reason, and whatever failed intellectuals like Robert might think about the cleverness of the adaptive strategies of vampires, baby bloodsuckers had no means of dispossessing themselves of primary hosts that were no longer adequate to their needs. The baby was just a bundle of appetites, a personification of need. He had learned to lust after Ruth's breast, and he could not help the instinct that guided his tiny teeth. He could not let her go—and his incapacity echoed in her own empty heart.

Despite what Cassie had said, the police did not put in an appearance on Saturday night; they had their own cautious rules about picking up vampire babies after sunset. Ruth contemplated doing a runner, but she hadn't got anywhere to run to so she decided to front it out. When the WPC turned up on her doorstep on Sunday morning Ruth wouldn't take the chain off to let her in.

'There's no baby here, and if there was he wouldn't be a vampire, and if he was he'd be mine and I wouldn't be interested in giving him up,' Ruth said, breathlessly. 'Don't come back without a warrant, and even then I won't believe that it gives you any right.'

'It's not my problem if you don't care to co-operate, love,' said the WPC, shaking her head censoriously. 'Just don't come crying to me when your hall carpet goes up in flames.'

Ruth had taken the child to the supermarket a couple of times before the word got out, but she didn't dare do it once the local Defenders knew the score and she certainly didn't dare to go out and leave the poor little mite alone while she spent the last vestiges of her meagre capital. She wasn't surprised when Cassie refused point blank to fetch groceries for her—but she was pleasantly astonished when Robert not only said that he would but that he would chip in what he could spare to help her out.

'We shouldn't give in to ignorance,' he declared. 'We have to stand up for our right to take our own decisions for our own reasons in our own time according to our own perceptions of nature and need.' The false-ringing speech didn't mean much, so far as Ruth could see, and even if it had it wouldn't have been applicable to her situation, but she figured that Robert's muddy principles would buy her a few extra days before she finally had to let go. Even though she'd always intended to let go in the end, she thought that she was damned if she'd give the so-called Defenders of so-called Humanity the satisfaction of seeing her do it one bloody minute before she had to.

There were no more notes, and nothing repulsive came through the letterbox in their stead. The Defenders of Humanity knew that the message had been delivered, and they also knew that they only had to wait before it took effect. They knew that as long as they were vigilant—and they were—there was no danger to any human life they counted precious. Besides which, they simply weren't angry enough to march up the concrete stairs like peasants storming Castle Frankenstein, demanding that the child be handed over to them for immediate ritual dismember-ment. Things like that had happened twenty years before, but even the most murderous of mobs had lost the capacity to take the invasion personally once the numbers of vampire babies ran into the thousands. Even the most extreme religious maniacs lacked the kind of drive that was necessary to sustain a diet of stakes through the heart, lopped-off heads and bonfires night after night after night without any end in sight. By now, even the dickheads on the estate couldn't summon up energy enough to do much more than write a few notes and wait for inevitability and the law to take their natural course.

In a way, Ruth regretted the lack of strident enmity. There was something strangely horrible in the isolation that was visited upon her as she eked out her last supplies and went by slow degrees from slim but robust to thin and tired. It was, she thought, as much the loneliness of her predicament as the baby's ceaseless demands that made her so utterly and absolutely tired. She had not realized before how much it meant to her to be able to shout good morning at Mrs. Hagerty or glean the available gossip from Mrs. Gledhill's semi-articulate ramblings.

The baby was a continuous source of comfort, of course, and that would have been enough in slightly kinder circumstances, but his powers of communication were limited to moaning and staring, and they just weren't enough to sustain a person of Ruth's intellectual capacity. He loved her with the kind of unconditional ardor that only the helpless can contrive, and she was glad of it, but it simply wasn't the answer to all her needs.

She knew that the end of the adventure was coming, so she made every attempt to milk it for all it was worth. She became vampiric herself in her desire to extract every last drop of comfort from her hostage. She had never been subject to a desire so strong and yet so meek, a hunger so avid and yet so polite. She had never been looked at with such manifest affection, such obvious recognition or such accurate appraisal.

She flattered herself by wondering whether even a vampire would ever be able to look at any other host with as true a regard as her temporary son now looked at her. She took what perverse comfort she could from the fact that nothing the orphanage would or could provide for him would ever displace her as an authentic mother. For as long as the baby lived, it would know that she was the only human being who had ever really loved it, the only one who had ever tended unconditionally to its real needs.

But it wasn't enough, and not just because there wasn't enough time.

By the time she had had the baby for nineteen days Ruth was at the end of her tether. Cassie had not come near her for a week, and had somehow contrived sufficient emotional blackmail to keep Robert away too. The wallpaper had begun to crawl along the walls. She was out of Pampers, out of Lucozade and out of tinned soup.

She decided, in the end, that she would rather die than hand the baby over, although she knew as she decided it that she was being absurd as well as insincere. She tried with all her might to persuade him to feed more and more often, but he would not take from her more than he needed or more than she could give, and she had always known this was the way that things would finally work out. She grew weaker and weaker while she could not bring herself to bite the bullet, but she was never drained to the dregs.

In the end, she didn't need to contrive any kind of melodramatic gesture. She only had to make her way next door and ask the Gledhills to call an ambulance, not for her but for the child. It would not take him to a hospital, but that wasn't the point. It was far, far better—or so it seemed—to surrender him into the arms of a qualified paramedic than to let him be snatched away by a blinkered policewoman or a so-called social worker.

She cried as she handed him over. Her tears dried up for a while but when night fell and the time of his usual awakening arrived she began to cry again. Her breasts ached with frustration, and the waiting blood turned the areoles crimson. She knew that the hurt would fade, but she also knew that the nipples would be permanently sensitized. She would never recover the lovely numbness that she had learned so rapidly to treasure. She would never see eyes like his again. No one would ever understand her as he had. No one would ever think her the most delicious thing in the world.

She wondered whether they used contract cleaners at the orphanages. She wondered whether it would be possible, in spite of her lack of formal qualifications, to retrain as a nurse or a laboratory assistant, or any other kind of worker that might be considered essential by the scientists for whom vampires were merely an interesting problem. She made resolutions and sketchy plans, but in the end she went to sleep and did not dream—as far as she could remember, at least.

She went back to work the next night. It was hell, but she survived.

The labor left her desperately devitalized for the first couple of weeks, but she soon began to put on weight again and her desolation turned first to commonplace debilitation and eventually to everyday enervation. Mrs. Hagerty began to respond to her shouted good mornings and Mrs. Gledhill began filling her in on the gossip. Cassie resumed regular expeditions to her wardrobe, and slightly-less-frequent ones to the bathroom. Robert dropped in more often than before, stayed longer, and talked nonsense to her for hours on end.

It wasn't great, but it was normal. Ruth had learned the value of normality—but that wasn't why she remembered the baby so fondly, and sometimes cried at night.

Things had been back to normal for nearly three months when Cassie, still three weeks short of her sixteenth birthday, found out that she was pregnant, panicked, and jumped off a top-floor balcony.

The autopsy showed that the child would have been a vampire, but Ruth knew that didn't even begin to justify Cassie's panic, or even to reinforce the ironic significance of her name. She would have been able to get an abortion. She would have been able to hand the baby over to Social Services. She would have been all right. She would have been able to resume normal life. There was no reason to kill herself but stupidity and sheer blind panic. It wasn't Ruth's fault. It wasn't anybody's fault. It was just one of those things. It would have happened anyway—and it wouldn't have happened at all if Cassie had only had the sense to talk to somebody, and let them soothe her terror away.

Robert was heartbroken. He moved out of the squat into Cassie's old room, but the consolation with which he and Ruth provided one another was asexual as well as short-lived. Within a month he was gone again, just like Frank, along with the intensity of his grief and the pressure of his need.

Once Robert had gone, Ruth never did figure out what to do with herself during the day, or during the long and lonely nights when she wasn't on shift cleaning up the debris of other people's work and other people's lives—but every time she went past a rubbish-skip while walking the empty streets in the early hours of the morning she kept her eyes firmly fixed on her fast-striding feet, exactly as any sensible person would have done.

THE WOMAN IN
THE MIRROR

The department store where Martin worked was closed on Mondays; by coincidence, the auction rooms a hundred yards down the road from the flat where he lived held the first of its two weekly sales on that day.

At first, his visits to the auction rooms were purely functional. He had to render the flat habitable as quickly as he could, and his wages as an assistant manager in menswear were inadequate to allow him to buy everything new, even with the advantages of his staff discount and special credit terms. The Monday auctions, where the detritus of houses cleared by reason of death or destitution were sold off for next to nothing, were a godsend. The better quality pieces were invariably knocked down to dealers, but there were always odds and ends of flimsy modern furniture, which could be had for a pound or two, and there were ancient household appliances, in reasonable working order despite their age, which could be picked up for less.

By the time he had everything he needed, Martin was virtually an auction junkie. He enjoyed sitting anonymously in the middle of the crowd, on some old settee that would eventually be brought under the hammer, watching the ebb and flow of the bidding. He soon cultivated a certain skill in judging the prices items ought to fetch, but he rarely bought anything even when he saw something going for a bargain price. He would have admitted, if asked, that his regular attendance was damning evidence of the fact that he had nothing better to do with his time, but nobody ever asked him. There was no one to ask; he was quite alone in the world.

Following his single mother's suicide when he was ten years old, Martin had spent the latter part of his childhood in care. He had conscientiously refused to make any friends among his new peers, whom his mother would have considered no-hopers and apprentices in crime. Thanks to the memory of his mother's good advice, he had always known that he could do better than they could, provided that he minded his manners, and so it had proved. He had a good, respectable job, and a place of his own.

The only thing to dislike about his job was that it involved him in constant contact with other people, but he had schooled himself not to mind that; his mask of earnest politeness never cracked, even under the strain of the most difficult customer.

Martin had no other hobby save for his regular attendance at the auction rooms. He spent all his evenings at home, watching TV or reading paperback books. On Sundays in summer he would sometimes go walking in the park, but even in good weather he preferred to be in his own private place, surrounded by things he owned. Although he was by no means agoraphobic he didn't much like open spaces or crowds. The bed-sitting room of his little flat was the only space he inhabited with any degree of comfort. He felt as safe there as he had in the long-lost days of his early childhood.

Sometimes, as he sat in the saleroom, watching the physical remains of someone else's life pass fleetingly beneath the auctioneer's hammer, Martin wondered whether his mother's few effects had gone the same way, a decade before. Sometimes, he wondered whether a worn carpet or a dark mahogany cabinet might have ended up here because its former owner, tired of the endless tribulations of life and its relationships, had decided that the game was no longer worth the candle. Mostly, though, he just watched, possessed by the special kind of calm that attends activities that are interesting enough to hold the attention without being exciting enough to trouble the mind.

He had long thought that he had everything he needed for

the flat, and had not made a purchase of any kind for more than three months, when his attention was suddenly and inexplicably caught by a mirror. It was a very ordinary oval mirror in a plain wooden frame, and he knew that he must have seen dozens like it come under the hammer in previous weeks, but as he looked at this particular mirror while the porter brought it up to the auctioneer's podium, it suddenly struck him that he had no mirror in his living room. It was a peculiar thought, and he knew it; it had never before occurred to him that he—or anyone—needed a mirror in any room except for the bathroom, but once formed, it would not be put aside. Martin was quite overcome by the notion that he had no mirror in his living room.

There was no contest for the mirror, which was not nearly ornate enough for the dealers to pass it off as an antique. He bought it with a single bid of twenty pence, and carried it home with him when the sale was ended.

He positioned the mirror over the closed-up fireplace, suspended by its loose-linked chain from a picture hook. It hung at a slight angle, so he had to place its centre a little higher than eye-level. When he looked into it, with his head very slightly tilted back, he could see arrayed behind him the low, narrow bed and the chest of drawers that were set against the far wall, with the couch and the coffee table in front of them, in the middle of the room. He saw that unless he deliberately moved to one side, he couldn't see the door that opened into the corridor or the doors that led to the tiny kitchen and the tinier bathroom, but while he was squarely positioned in front of the mirror, almost everything that he owned was visible, gathered together in a space without limits and borders.

Somehow, the mirror's image seemed to improve and dignify the room, and he was grateful for the impulse that had made him buy it.

Martin was not a narcissistic person. Indeed, he scarcely knew what he looked like, although he always took care to make his appearance neat. He looked into the bathroom mirror every morning while he shaved, and while he adjusted the knot in his tie, but he never studied his features or met his own eyes. If the mirror that now hung on his living-room wall began to seduce him, drawing him forward to look into it, it was not because he desired to look at his own face, but only because he wanted to study the room that contained him—the space that he had made his own. Once the mirror was in place he began to do that regularly, night after night, sometimes for as much as five minutes at a time. He soon became aware of the absurdity of it, but nevertheless found it increasingly hard to tear himself away from his rapt contemplation.

When two weeks had passed, Martin ceased to worry about the ritual of staring into the mirror. He accepted it as something that simply gave him pleasure. After all, he told himself, what a man chose to do in the privacy of his own home was no one's business but his own, and needed no explanations. He surrendered to his fascination, and allowed himself to be drawn to the mirror whenever the mood took him.

Two more weeks had passed when a most curious thing happened. Martin was looking into the mirror, perfectly relaxed, having almost lapsed into a kind of trance, when it suddenly occurred to him that he could not see himself. The room was still there, filled with all its familiar furniture, but he was not. The mirror-image room was quite empty. Absurdly enough, he had the conviction that the image had been that way for some time, not just on this occasion but many others—that he, in fact, had been absent from the looking-glass world for some considerable time, without realizing the fact.

Martin blinked, and moved his head slightly, but the image in the mirror didn't change. His face didn't reappear. He looked around, at the real room, and then looked back at the mirror, but nothing had changed. The room was present in every detail, with nothing out of place, but he was nowhere to be seen.

With infinite patience, Martin looked down at his arms and legs, to make sure that his real self was perfectly visible. Then he used his hands to check the solidity of his face. There was no doubt that he was physically present—and yet, the mirror stubbornly refused to reflect him. He had been casually eliminated from the looking-glass version of his room, callously excluded from the improved, dignified version of his personal space.

Deliberately, he turned away. He walked into the bathroom, and looked at himself in his shaving-mirror, which dutifully reflected every detail of his features, just as it had always done. He picked up a comb from the shelf and ran it lightly through his hair. Then he went back into the living room and approached the mirror above the hearth, not without trepidation.

He knew even before he reached it that it was still adamant in its refusal to admit him to the imaginary space that it enclosed, but he was no longer astonished by that fact. Nor did he feel in any way threatened or endangered by it. He was intrigued, to be sure, but the sciences had remained completely mysterious to him during the years of his inadequate schooling, with the result that he had no overweening faith in the laws of optics, and was easily able to remain undisturbed by their local suspension. The mere fact that a mirror had ceased to contain him was by no means sufficient to make him think that all reality was out of joint.

Martin felt no impulse to run from the flat in search of a witness to the startling event. He simply stood and stared into the mirror, patiently bearing witness to a trivial private miracle, wondering when or if the marvelous interlude would come to an end.

Because he had firmly set aside the surprise that he had initially felt at discovering himself absent from the mirror image, it did not surprise him overmuch when someone else entered the looking-glass room. He did not see her actually come in, because he could not see the door from where he stood, but he did not doubt for a moment that she had entered the reflected room in a perfectly normal fashion.

The woman threw her handbag on the bed, and slipped off her coat, which she draped over the back of the couch. Then she walked all the way across the field of view, and disappeared, presumably into the bathroom. A few minutes later she reappeared, but only fleetingly, as she went from one invisible doorway to another, into the kitchen. Martin waited patiently for her to come out again, which she eventually did, with a cup of coffee in her hand.

It was not until she sat down on the settee, with the cup before her on the table, that Martin really had an opportunity to study her face and figure. The face might have been prettier had it seemed less tired and drawn. She had make-up on, but clearly had not renewed it since first applying it that morning. The figure was by no means voluptuous, but it was attractively slender. Her clothes were inexpensive but they hung well; she wore a white blouse and grey skirt very like those favored—with the unsubtle encouragement of the managers—by the salesgirls at the department store. The entire effect was some-what let down, though, by her posture, which was so relaxed as to be almost a slouch.

Martin realized, with a slight start of guilt, that he had caught the woman off guard. She thought that she was quite alone and unobserved, and even the most elementary aspect of perfor-mance was gone from her behavior. Had there been anyone else in the room with her—had she even suspected that someone might be able to see her—she would have held herself differ-ently, controlling both the expression on her face and the atti-tude of her body. As things were, she had let herself relax into a state of private innocence.

While Martin watched her, though, she pulled herself together, took a sip of coffee, got to her feet, and walked unhur-riedly over to the fireplace.

He knew immediately that she intended to look into the mirror, and felt a sudden stab of alarm lest she catch him standing there, a peeping Tom in her looking-glass world, who had no conceivable right to be there. Despite the stab of alarm, though, he didn't move. Nor did he need to, for as she fixed her eyes upon him, it was quite obvious that she saw nothing but her own familiar reflection.

At close range, he watched her touch her hands experimentally to her face, as if she were examining herself for signs of aging. Her incipient frown suggested that she found some, but Martin couldn't imagine how. She was a little older than he was, but only three or four years—he judged that she couldn't possibly be more than twenty-five—and there was not a wrinkle to be seen.

Her height was apparently identical to his own, because her eyes, presumably fixed upon their own reflection, seemed to be looking directly into his. The general cast of her face was similar, too—he had always had effeminately delicate cheekbones and neat, full-lobed ears—and her eyes were as grey-blue as his own, but there the resemblance ended. Her shoulder-length tresses were a deep nut-brown, several shades darker than his abruptly shorn hair, and rather more lustrous. Her teeth were more even than his, and whiter. Her nose was very different too, being narrower and far more elegant than his own, which had been broken by a schoolyard bully when he was thirteen and set rather crookedly.

The woman turned away from the mirror, and went back to her coffee. Martin found himself letting out a deep breath, which he had not been consciously aware of holding, and then he shuddered inexplicably. He shut his eyes for a fraction of a second, and when he opened them, he found himself looking into his own eyes.

His reflection had returned, and the woman was gone.

His first impulse was to forget the whole episode, and to tell himself sternly that it hadn't really happened at all, but the intention faded as soon as it was born. He knew, and could not doubt, that what he had experienced was no mere hallucination, nor some inconceivably rare freak of chance that would never be repeated.

He knew that he would see the woman again—and again, and again—if only he were patient.

In the early days, Martin caught only brief glimpses of the strange alternative world where his flat was inhabited by a woman. For a while, they seemed to happen no more than twice or three times a week, and rarely lasted for longer than a few minutes—although he could never be certain that there were not other occasions that he failed to notice because his attention was elsewhere. As the weeks went by, however, the frequency and duration of the episodes increased steadily.

He soon found out how easy it would be to spend the whole time that he was in the flat watching the mirror, and he flatly refused to allow himself to become obsessed. He made something of a fetish out of going about his business as usual, making and eating his meals as he always had, watching all the TV shows it was his habit to view. But he knew better than to take this calculated avoidance to ridiculous extremes; he forgave himself for his frequent glances at the mirror, and remained always ready to go immediately to the hearth if he caught the slightest glimpse of anything that suggested that the glass was no longer reflecting him.

Even the brief visions of the early weeks allowed him to build an impressionistic picture of the life that the woman lived, which was not by any means a mirror-image of his own.

The woman was evidently far more sociable than he, despite the fact that she never invited her friends—male or female—back to the flat. She went out far more than he did, and he often discovered her coming home after eleven. Unlike him, she did not seem to be at all relaxed and at home in the flat; more than once he saw her looking round in frank distaste, and although she sometimes seemed to be deeply relieved to have escaped from the world at large when she came in and let herself down on the couch or the bed, she seemed quite unable to luxuriate in her surroundings or her own company.

Martin quickly became convinced that the woman was not a happy person. It was not so much that he never saw her smile—why should she smile when she was alone?—or even the fact that he saw crying quiet tears on one or two occasions; what convinced him was the way she sometimes sat on the settee, wrapping her arms around her body as if to hug herself. As time went by, he was able to observe that she kept a bottle of pills on the little table beside the bedhead, and took one every night. That disturbed him more than anything else, because there was no such bottle on his identical table. He flatly refused to use any kind of tranquilizer or sleeping pill, even though he sometimes suffered from insomnia.

He often caught glimpses of the woman as she dressed or undressed, although he rarely saw her naked for more than a few fleeting seconds, en route to or from the bathroom, or before she switched off the light and plunged her mirror-world into darkness. Such glimpses excited him, but in a curiously asexual fashion. They brought a yearning ache to his heart, but left his loins as impotently numb as ever. He fell profoundly in love with her without any measurable delay, but he did not lust after her, or long to touch her. He was always fully conscious of the fact that she was in another, unreachable world.

As Martin's visions gradually became more frequent and longer-lasting, sometimes extending for as much as ten or twelve minutes, he was able to hazard a guess that the woman must work in an office of some kind. She often flexed her fingers and massaged her wrists, as if those were the parts of her body that took the strain of her daily labor. She did not make herself up as carefully or as completely as the sales staff in his department store, and she worked on Mondays but not on Saturdays. Sometimes she came in late, having apparently worked overtime.

He tried to pick up further clues to the kind of life she led from the small items she left lying about on the coffee table, but she was usually quick to tidy them away; oddly enough, the impression he gained from this was not that she was a habitually tidy person, but rather that she felt so little at home in the flat that she felt guilty about leaving it in a state of disorder, and could not bring herself to treat it entirely as her own.

It took some little time for Martin to realize that he might be partly responsible for that reluctance. The room in which the woman lived was, after all, a reflection of his own. Although the chest of drawers and the freestanding wardrobe had very different contents, they were the same items of furniture that he had bought for next to nothing at the auction rooms. The settee, the coffee table, the bed and the carpet were all of his choosing, and he had chosen them with little regard for their appearance. He could not see, of course, whether she had his ancient fridge-freezer and electric cooker, because they were permanently hidden from view by the kitchen door even when it yawned wide open, but somehow he felt sure that she had.

No sooner had it dawned on him that some small part, at least, of the woman's discomfort might be due to the choices he had made than the corollary possibility occurred to him that he might be able to ameliorate her discomfort: that he might have the power to affect the contents—and hence, in some measure, the course of events—of the world beyond the mirror.

It was a realization that changed his life.

The following Monday found Martin, as usual, in the auction rooms. He was, however, possessed by an unprecedented determination to purchase some significant item of furniture, paying less attention to function than to appearance. He wanted something that would look elegant, and he was prepared to pay—as he knew that he would have to—for the added aesthetic value. He was not unduly worried about matters of price. His rent and regular outgoings amounted to no more than two-thirds of his weekly wage; since he had finished furnishing the flat he had been saving money regularly in the building society.

He enjoyed the sale more than he ever had before. He was briefly tempted by a new settee, but in the end he settled for a handsome glass-topped coffee table.

When he had carried the coffee table home Martin immediately set out for the auction rooms again, entering his old one to be sold at the next auction. Then he returned and waited, anxiously, to see whether the replacement would be reflected in the woman's world. As soon as he saw that it was, he was overtaken by a most peculiar feeling: a sensation of infinite opportunity.

The woman, when she came home from work that evening, made no evident reaction to the new coffee table, and certainly showed no particular surprise or pleasure in consequence of its presence. Nevertheless, Martin felt that he had taken an important first step in the work of making her feel more at home.

He began to make plans almost immediately. Most of the replacement items that he would have to acquire, he decided, ought not to be bought second hand. Fortunately, his staff discount, and the special low-interest credit terms available to employees of the store where he worked, would ease his burden considerably.

A little elementary research carried out during his lunch hours soon familiarized him with the prices of beds and bed linen, fitted carpets and made-to-measure curtains, patterned wallpaper and light fittings. His calculative abilities, honed by long experience at the till point, were easily adequate to designing a budget and a plan of campaign.

The transformation of the flat took three months to complete—and a further six months to pay for—but it was from the very first moment a labor of love. The fact that he had no real evidence of the woman's aesthetic preferences worried him a little at first, but he knew that he had no option but to trust to his intuitions, and he did so. He set out to make the room brighter, more cheerful, more feminine, and as each piece of the environmental jigsaw was slotted into place he became increasingly confident that his decisions were good.

As the woman's world was gradually transformed, she too seemed to become brighter and more cheerful. She took all the changes that he instituted completely for granted, as though every one had been her own purchase, according to her own plan, but Martin did not mind that in the least. It was enough that she seemed more approving of her surroundings, and that she eventually became comfortable enough to mingle a measure of delight with the relief she so often showed when arriving home late after an evening out.

Even before the transformation of the room was complete—before he had replaced the chest of drawers or the curtains (which could not actually be seen in the mirror, no matter where one stood)—Martin began to buy small presents for the woman in the mirror.

He was not sure, initially, that he would be able to transmit small and trivial objects into the other world, because there were always minor differences between his room and hers, in terms of the everyday objects that were routinely strewn about. He knew from experience that a coffee mug or a paperback or a can of cola left on his table or his mantelpiece would not be reflected on hers, although he would usually be able to see a handbag or a magazine or an emery board in its place. There was, it seemed, an alchemy of alternativity that transmuted the minutiae of his life into the minutiae of hers, while faithfully reproducing more massive objects. Nevertheless, he was convinced that if only he could find appropriate objects—objects that would seem more at home in her life than his own—he might be able to transmit them across the divide by reflection. Having failed with flowers, boxes of chocolates and a few ornaments, he finally achieved success with an unequivocally feminine item of jewelry: a pair of earrings.

Further experiments quickly demonstrated that items of feminine apparel were equally easy to intrude into the woman's life, and from then on he decided to concentrate his attention on jewelry and clothing. At first, it caused him considerable embarrassment to purchase such items, but it seemed to him that the end justified the means, and he soon steeled himself to the business of shopping for exactly those items that he most desired to see the woman wearing. He knew that the steady stream of purchases would generate prurient gossip at the store, but he didn't mind that; he had no friends there, and didn't care what might be said about him behind his back.

It would have been more convenient, in a way, had the little gifts he bought for the woman been materially transmitted, disappearing from his world as they appeared in hers. As things were, however, he felt duty bound to keep and carefully preserve the originals once he was certain that they had been reflected. He knew perfectly well that the woman's closet and chest of drawers contained many items that were independent of anything in his—and vice versa—but he remained convinced that if he ever removed from his own flat any of the items he had imported by design into hers, they would likewise be lost from the flat in the mirror-world, like the redundant furniture he had sent back to the auction rooms as quickly as he could replace it.

For six months, while he remade her habitat and supplied her steadily with gifts, Martin did not doubt for a moment that the quality of the woman's life was steadily improving. It was true that she continued occasionally to hold herself as though comforting herself with a second-rate embrace, but she no longer seemed quite so desperate in so doing. It was true, too, that he would once in a while catch a glimpse of her while she was weeping miserably to herself, but he told himself that these were exceptional moments of weakness, each one caused by some momentary tragedy of the particular day. She still kept the bottle of sleeping pills beside her bed, using them assidu-ously, but he convinced himself that this was mere habit, or—at worst—a harmless psychological dependence. He wished that she would smile more, but recognized that she was, after all, always alone when he saw her.

Eventually, though, Martin admitted to himself that whatever improvement he had wrought in her condition, it had not made her as happy as he would have liked to see her. Although she was far more at home in her new surroundings, still there was something lacking in her life—something that all his efforts and gifts could not provide. It took him a long time to begin to wonder whether she might be lonely, because loneliness wasn't something that bothered him at all, but in the end he had to face up to the fact that filling her room with desirable possessions was not quite the same thing as filling her life with worth-while experiences. Nor could he avoid noticing that, so far as he could tell from his fragmented observation of her life, she never invited anyone else into to the flat, not even for a cup of coffee.

Martin often wondered—how could he help it?—what it would be like to see her shopping in the store where he worked, or even to see her across a crowded street, walking in company with a girlfriend or a boyfriend, with her public face wreathed in smiles; but he always knew that such ideas were mere fantasy. He knew that he would never meet her in the flesh; that his world and hers could not and did not materially overlap. Nevertheless, he felt in his heart that one kind of contact between them might be possible. He felt, and even dared to hope, that he and she might one day make eye contact. He had not the slightest doubt that he would never touch her, never kiss her, never hear her voice; but he believed that there was just a remote possibility that one day she might look into her oval mirror, and instead of seeing her own sad face, see his instead.

He began, almost in spite of himself, to yearn for that moment, even though he had at first no idea at all how he might help to bring it about.

Martin honestly did not know how or why it first occurred to him to put on some of the clothes that he had bought as presents for the woman in the mirror. He had no purpose in mind; it was simply that the idea popped into his head, in exactly the same way that the idea of purchasing the mirror had come into his head. After all, he thought, the items were there, cluttering up his drawers. It seemed somehow unfair that the originals should be scorned and neglected while their reflected images were used with evident satisfaction.

His first experiment in transvestism was rapidly concluded; it was simply too embarrassing, and the mirror—which was in its ordinary mode at the time—assured him that he looked ridiculous. But the feel of the undergarments against his skin was unexpectedly pleasant, and he was soon tempted to make a more concerted effort.

It was not until he had donned an entire set of clothes, and overcome the initial horror at what he had dared to do, that he was able to study himself carefully in the mirror, wondering at his temerity. For several minutes—perhaps as much as half an hour—the thrill he felt was quite self-contained. It was a purely sensual matter, without apparent connection or consequence. It was not until he had experimented extensively with movement and posture—walking, sitting, lying down, posing—that he looked again at the mirror, and saw himself as if from an entirely new angle.

It was then that he experienced his crucial moment of blazing enlightenment. He saw—quite literally saw, in his own reflection—that with careful effort, he might transform his own image into something very like the image of the woman who lived in the other world. He took it for granted, of course, that absolute similarity would be impossible to achieve, but the idea seized hold of him that if only he could make himself similar enough, then the awful gulf that separated her world from his might be bridged, if only for a moment, in such a way as to let her see him.

While he pondered this remarkable notion, with his eyes steadfastly fixed upon an image that for once refused stubbornly to disappear from the wayward looking glass, the idea grew in his head with the force of an explosion. He felt that his moment of enlightenment was expanding, that the power of the thought was taking on a transcendental magnitude, that he was drunk with inspiration.

He suddenly saw, and wondered how he could have been so blind as not to have seen it before, that all the presents that he had bought for her had really been gifts for himself. More than that, he understood with unreasonable clarity that there had been an unsuspected pattern in all his purchases, directed to the end that they might be stored up as instruments that would one day enable him to make her one further and most precious gift: the gift of himself.

Everything that had happened to him, Martin now realized—beginning long before his purchase of the magic mirror—had been a matter of laying the groundwork for the project that he now conceived. Previously, his task in life had been merely to live, to exist in a kind of limbo, perfectly safe and isolated; now, he had a goal. His one ambition was to be seen by the woman in the mirror: to become worthy to be seen by her, and hence to make himself visible.

Martin now began to watch the mirror very assiduously in the mornings, in order to see what the woman put on before going to work. When he came home each evening, he would try to match her dress as accurately as he could, so that when she came home from work, if she should chance to go to the mirror while he was able to watch her, he could stand before her similarly attired.

It was the most expectantly exciting time of his life—but it did not take him long to realize that his expectations were ludicrously over-ambitious. The first time she failed to see him, although he was dressed almost exactly as she was, he told himself that it was a mere misfortune. The second time, he assured himself that he had come within a mere moment of success. The third time, his tottering edifice of hope collapsed entirely, and he accepted that his imitation was so woefully inadequate as to be an insult.

Before the second week of his great experiment was out, he had acquired a wig, which approximated as closely as he could contrive to the color and style of her hair. He had become desperately avid to catch sight of the apparatus she used in making herself up, and he was impatiently anxious about the fact that she always made up her face in the bathroom, out of sight. He improvised as best he could, but it quickly became apparent to him that anything he might achieve by these crude means would be a travesty. The wig stubbornly remained a wig, and obviously so; his unskillfully applied make-up was a clownish mask, and he knew that his crooked nose and discolored teeth would ensure that it would always remain so. His refurbished hope that his imitation of her features might become close enough, given adequate opportunities for practice, dwindled away to nothing.

Martin's first reaction, on being forced to confront the ugly hopelessness of his newfound ambition, was to write off the whole episode as a moment of madness. He put the woman's clothes away, and hid the wig and the half-assembled collection of cosmetics in a box, which he placed in a dark corner of the wardrobe. He became himself again—or tried to.

He found, though, that it was now he who was uncomfortable in his own lair. He no longer felt at home in the flat, and could not settle to his customary pastimes. He began to suffer very badly from insomnia, though not so badly that he relented in his hatred of medication, and for the first time he felt that he was becoming acutely, painfully and unhealthily obsessed with the mirror.

He had previously been able to believe that his interest in the mirror was an understandable fascination, and nothing to be feared. Now, he began to find it appalling and terrifying, an obvious sign of mental illness. No matter how hard he tried to relinquish his addiction, though, he simply could not keep his eyes off the dreadful object, and every minute that passed while it stubbornly showed him his own flat and his own person was a bitter torment. Once he had seen the way forward, it seemed, there could be no going back.

Martin was no fool, and he knew full well what kind of commitment would be demanded if he were to resume the project he had begun so half-heartedly and botched so badly. From the depths of his despair he could see everything that lay before him. He understood now how stupidly foolish he had been to think that any mere caricature could serve his purpose, and was well aware of the extreme to which he would surely have to go, if he were to bring his new dream to authentic fruition. He knew well enough that any plan he now made would require years to be brought to its conclusion, and would necessitate the cultivation of true courage.

The prospect was too appalling, and he did what he could to refuse to think of it; but he had not the power to sustain his refusal.

He had always been a coward, and was not unduly ashamed of the fact even now. He had always been small and thin, quite unequipped for the kind of adolescence that he had been forced by circumstance to experience. He had never fought back against those who had continually sought to hurt and humiliate him, always sustaining himself with the thought that time would give him his freedom, if only he could survive. Having won his measure of freedom, he had been content to continue to survive; it had been enough for him to have his own space, an adequate income and peace. He had never dared to entertain any material ambitions, or ventured to desire any intimate relationship with another person; he knew only too well where such quests led. He had always been horridly afraid of falling ill, of being hurt, of having to go to hospital.

Now, though, he found his protective cowardice ripped away. He found that he simply could not refuse to contemplate a pathway of events that would mean long and stubborn defiance of the contempt of others, and a whole series of surgical interventions. He could not begin to imagine where he might discover the courage even to think of such things, and yet he could not stop himself.

The paradox of it all was perfectly clear to him. The sheer insanity of it was a plain to him as the crooked nose on his all-too-plain face. He, who had never even contemplated owning a car, or getting married, or doing anything whatsoever to distinguish himself, had been possessed and overcome by the notion of recreating himself in the image of a woman who did not and could not exist, in order that he might become—just might, perhaps only for the merest instant—that which she saw while she peered unhappily into the imaginary mirror that hung above the imaginary hearth of her imaginary room in her imaginary world.

Martin knew that no one else in all the world could have seriously contemplated such an absurd project, even for a moment. He also knew, however, that no one else in all the world could have asked himself the question that sprung so readily to his own mind, and failed to find a ready answer.

The question was: *What alternative do I have?*

And the most horrifying thing of all was that he seemed to have none. No matter how long the task might take, and no matter what courage he would have to find, he could not imagine any other course of action; he could not see any other way.

The police had sealed the flat after the burglary—which had been reported, probably two or three days after the fact, by a neighbor. The police, or perhaps the neighbor, had made some slight attempt to tidy up before nailing the door shut, but they had not been able to do much to improve its appearance. The burglars, having had the leisure to do whatever they pleased, had taken care to wreck everything that they had not cared to steal. They had smashed the furniture and the light fittings, fouled the carpet, slashed to ribbons the clothes in the chest of drawers and the linen on the bed, and daubed the papered walls with obscene graffiti.

Martine, discharged from the hospital only that morning, stood in the doorway with the policewoman, silently surveying the wreckage of her private world. Her gaze moved steadily back and forth, taking in everything, before coming to rest on the mirror above the hearth. The thieves had not taken it, because it was so evidently worthless, but they had taken the trouble to smash it. The wooden frame was still intact, but the thin backing had been splintered, and the silvered glass lay in smithereens, scattered about the marbled platform that still remained in front of the blocked-up grate.

'It's a terrible mess, I'm afraid,' said the policewoman, awkwardly.

'Yes,' said Martine, 'it certainly is.'

'If you could put together a list of missing items...for us, and for the insurers. Anything identifiable...well, you never know.

I'm sorry it had to happen while you were in the hospital. Not much of a homecoming.'

The policewoman was obviously highly embarrassed; clearly, she knew what kind of an operation Martine had undergone.

'You needn't stay,' Martine told her. 'There's a lot to do. I can cope.'

She waited patiently until the policewoman had exhausted her capacity for polite procrastination, and departed. She contrived to close the door, and to wedge it shut. Then she threw her overnight bag on to the bed, and took off her coat, draping it over the back of the ruined settee.

She went unhurriedly to the fireplace, and lifted the mirror frame down from the wall. She carefully laid it down on a part of the crazed surface of the coffee table that was still flat. Then she began to pick up the larger shards of the mirror from the hearth, placing them one by one within the frame.

She made no attempt to fit the pieces together as they had been before the mirror was broken; she simply assembled them as best she could into a patchwork of sufficient dimensions to hold the image of a human face. She deliberately held back until she had enough pieces in place, and hesitated even then for a moment before she leaned forward, to look down at her reflection as though she were looking down into a pool of water.

Her reflection met her eyes, frankly and openly.

She saw, somewhat to her surprise, that she was weeping. It took her a few moments to recall that it was entirely appropriate that she should weep, because she was mourning the dead. She remembered, not without difficulty, that there had been another room contained in that mirror, once upon a time: a dingy, second-hand room, inhabited by a sad, frightened and incomplete young man. But he had been killed: cut up and destroyed, too evidently worthless to be carried away into the world.

When an empty minute had passed, she wiped her eyes. She knew that she had little enough time for mourning. First, there was the door to fix, and a new lock to be fitted. Then, there were very many purchases to be made. It all had to be planned, in order of necessity. It would not be easy, because her resources were strictly limited, but it could be done, in time. Everything that needed to be done could be accomplished, given time and resolution.

She knew that she had the time; she had learned the art of patience.

She knew that she had the resolution; she had learned how not to give up.

She knew that she could rebuild the apparatus of her life, if that was what had to be done.

As she carefully separated the shards of the mirror, breaking up her reflected image, Martine remembered that it was Monday, and there would be an auction that afternoon in the saleroom down the road. What better time and place could there possibly be to begin the furnishing of a new life?

REGRESSION

Thirty-some years ago, while I was a university student, there was one term—it was the summer term of 1968—when there was a sudden glut of cheap LSD. Rumour had it that someone was cooking up the stuff in the chemistry labs, more for interest's sake than for profit, and distributing it wholesale to anyone who cared to ask. Whatever the reason, there was a lot of it about, and there was no shortage of people avid to try it out.

The less reckless experimenters would often arrange to have someone sit with them while they dropped the acid, partly to act as a restraining influence in case they took it into their tripped-out heads to do something stupid and partly to report back to them when they eventually woke up with a headache and a bad memory on the subject of what they'd said and done while they were away with the fairies. I always valued my clarity of mind far too much to trifle with the stuff itself, but my reputation as a dour and down-to-earth northerner was sufficiently strong to recommend me as a minder to more than one bold explorer of the farther shores of inner space. One of them, inevitably, was my mad flatmate Jimmy McKinnon.

Jimmy, as was only to be expected by those who knew him, was one of the more extravagant trippers. He was the kind of person who could never get mildly drunk or fancy someone moderately; it was always a matter of falling down and going head over heels. While more tentative acid-droppers quietly marveled at subtly weird distortions of perception and giggled gently as they were carried along by mildly bizarre trains of thought, Jimmy ranted and raved. He saw and conversed with God Himself on at least three occasions and he was made party to some essentially atheistic Cosmic Truth on at least three more. Unfortunately, he never contrived to acquaint me with the substance of any of these essential Cosmic Truths while he was in possession of them, because his attempted explanations were utterly incoherent and he could never remember the details when he eventually came crashing back to earth.

In the beginning, Jimmy was inclined to lay the blame for these frustrating failures of communication firmly at my door, but on the fifth or sixth occasion I thoughtfully laid on a tape recorder so that his attempts to explain the Ultimate Secret of Existence could be preserved for his own later inspection. Jimmy listened to the tape five times before finally admitting that he couldn't make head or tail of what he was saying either—but admit it he finally did.

That was the time before he cut my face with the scalpel from his dissecting kit.

To be fair, I ought to make it clear that he didn't actually attack me with the scalpel. What he wanted to do with it, so far as I could gather, was to open up a channel into his head so that the innate spirituality of the cosmos-at-large could flow more easily into his closeted cerebrum. Perhaps I should have let him do it—but the whole point of my babysitting him was to ensure that he didn't do anything too stupid.

There had been previous occasions when I'd been almost convinced that Jimmy was just bullshitting, making up his commentary on his hallucinations and distorted perceptions as a kind of performance, intended to make fun of the callow Yorkshireman who lived in his London-nurtured shadow. At first, I thought the business with the scalpel was bullshit too, playing on my deepest anxieties, but if it started out that way Jimmy soon fell victim to the fervor of his own patter. While I wrestled with him, there was no doubt in my mind that if I couldn't exert all the strength and skill that my admittedly punier arms possessed then he would certainly do himself serious injury.

In the end, it was me who got cut, from just beneath my right eye to the edge of my chin. By the time Jimmy was calm enough for me to leave I'd turned a white bath-towel red. I fainted on the way to the hospital and woke up with seventeen stitches.

That would have been bad enough, but it turned out that Jimmy's scalpel—which he had, of course, been using to cut up frogs and mice in practical classes—wasn't sterile. The wound became infected and I spent the best part of a fortnight looking like the Phantom of the Opera unmasked. The hospital nearly had to readmit me so that I could be put on an antibiotic drip, but it began to clear up just in time.

Jimmy was sorry, of course. He was so extremely sorry that I had no alternative but to forgive him. It's surprising how easy forgiveness comes when you're only twenty.

Although we both moved out of the flat and into separate halls of residence for our final year, Jimmy and I remained good friends. I don't think he gave up entirely on LSD—and I'm certain that he got through his finals on benzedrine and came down afterwards on pot—but he never asked me to keep him company when he intended getting out of his skull. Throughout our final year he was on his best behavior with me, and I often saw him wince shamefacedly when his gaze was caught by the scar I bore.

The goodbyes we said after the graduation ceremony were inhibited by the presence of our two sets of parents. I hadn't told mine that Jimmy was responsible for the injury to my face but they'd caught on somehow, and there was a distinct frostiness about their handshakes. When we parted and went our separate ways I felt that a phase of my life had come to an end and that a different one was about to begin. I never made any specific resolution not to keep in touch with Jimmy, but I never made any effort to do it either.

In time, the scar faded, although it never entirely disappeared.

With luck, that would have been the end of the matter, but everyone knows the old saying about those who fail to learn from history being condemned to repeat it, first as tragedy and then as farce—and perhaps, on occasion, the other way around.

For three years Jimmy had been closer to me than my brother, but as soon we were out of the hothouse environment of the university, with our feet firmly planted on very different career paths, he ceased to matter to me. Although he'd studied biology he'd done a short programming course—in those days, of course, scientists wrote their programs in FORTRAN on punch cards and left them overnight for technicians to feed into a mainframe that filled a building—and he used that slight experience to get in on ground floor of the burgeoning computer business. A mutual acquaintance told me a couple of years later that he was busy installing and customising systems for various pioneering users, but I was more amused by the fact that we'd switched our geographical bases. Jimmy had relocated to Sheffield, while I was now securely ensconced in the capital, holding down the editorial job I'd procured with the leverage of my English degree. I was working for a publisher who specialised in lavishly illustrated 'coffee-table books' documenting every subject for which there was a market, from military hardware to royal babies.

It was in the autumn of 1993 that Jimmy got in touch again. He'd seen my name in the credits of one of the multitudinous gift books I'd put together over the years and he rang me at the office. He said that he was coming down to London for a couple of days and suggested that we meet on his last evening in a restaurant near his hotel in Paddington, 'to have dinner and talk over old times'.

It seemed like a good idea—and so it might have been, if we had only confined ourselves to reminiscing and comparing notes about what had become of us during the previous twenty-five years.

My first impression was that I had fared somewhat better than Jimmy. His suit had undoubtedly been more expensive than mine, but it was older and had obviously been subjected to harder wear. He was still three inches taller than I was but his posture had begun to take on a hint of a stoop. He had a much bigger gut and his skin had the sallow appearance that often results from continual alcohol abuse. I saw him take note of the fact that the scar on my face was still visible, although only just, but neither of us mentioned it.

Inevitably, Jimmy had had a more colorful time by far than I. His second marriage had just ended in divorce, whereas I'd been married to the same woman for twenty years. Jimmy had worked for a dozen different employers while I'd only managed three in an industry famous for the high mobility of its staff. He'd dabbled in all the different applications of information technology that I could imagine, and quite a few that I couldn't, while I'd just edited and edited and edited away: always non-fiction, always paying more attention to the pictures than the black-and-white bits in between. Jimmy had lived in Sheffield, Newcastle and Liverpool before departing his last marital home in Derby to set up on his own in Leicester. I'd never lived anywhere but Chiswick. One of the boys among his first crop of kids was fronting a rock group and another was in jail—and he didn't even bother to tell me what the girls were doing. My own two daughters were studying assiduously at the local technical college. Jimmy had made the best part of a million, but had subsequently lost almost all of it through divorce settlements and expensive habits, while I'd carefully and methodically laid down a solid financial foundation for the future without ever doubting for an instant that Claire and the girls would be integral parts of that future.

The net result of all these differences, it seemed to me, was that I was contented and safe, while Jimmy was living with the melancholy consciousness of a life already wasted, sacrificed on the altar of profligacy.

It was after midnight, and the waiters were getting restless, when Jimmy pronounced judgment on everything that had befallen us. 'You haven't changed a bit,' he said, with a slight sigh. 'You're still the sanest, most down-to-earth person I've ever known.'

'You've changed out of all recognition,' I assured him, confidently, 'but you're still the craziest, most extreme individual
I've ever encountered.'

Jimmy threw his credit card into the saucer the waiter
discreetly placed on the table without even glancing at the carefully folded bill, signed the slip with equal carelessness and
dropped a ten-pound note on the table by way of a tip. I let him
do it without volunteering to make a contribution.

As we wandered towards the door, he suddenly said, 'Do
you still sit with acid-trippers to keep them anchored to the real
world, Mark?'

'Of course not,' I told him, feeling the first slight hint of a
chill enter the social atmosphere. 'There's no call for that sort
of thing in the circles I move in.' It seemed far more diplomatic
than any reference to the possibility of getting hurt, and it was
true, after a fashion. Cocaine was the drug of choice in the
circles I moved in, although I never touched the stuff myself.

'Would you be interested in providing that kind of service, if
anybody wanted it?' he asked, tentatively.

'Why?' I parried. 'Do you know someone who does?'

I should have said no, flatly and firmly. I don't know to this
day why I didn't. Perhaps Jimmy had reminded me that the old,
free and easy days had had a lot of fun in them, and perhaps I
was feeling just a little too nostalgic for the fun and the freedom.
Perhaps I'd had just enough wine to skew my sense of propor-
tion.

I wasn't in the least surprised when he told me that he might
be in need of some such assistance himself.

'Not acid, mind,' he said, without even looking to see what
kind of expression had overtaken my face. 'These days, I try to
treat my brain chemistry with at least a modicum of the respect
it deserves. This is something different.'

While he waited with me in the queue at the taxi rank,
Jimmy told me that he'd been experimenting with state-of-the-
art biofeedback equipment imported from the States.

'It's great,' he said. 'I did TM way back in the seventies, and a bit of EST, and for a while a couple of years back I got into computerized neurolinguistic programming. About the same time I was taking hypnotherapy to help me give up smoking, and I did the whole self-induced light trance bit. It's all the same stuff, really. The biofeedback kit makes it all much easier because you can watch your own brain waves on the monitors while you train yourself to control them. The elementary tricks are easy—generating the alpha-rhythm, damping down the theta—but you can go a lot further if you have the concentration. Trouble is, you pretty soon learn to trance yourself out so completely that you can't pay attention to yourself any more... and I still suffer from the same old problem. When I wake up, I can't remember a damn thing. I've tried leaving a tape recorder running, but I can't remember to keep talking when I drift off. What I need, old pal, is someone to sit with me and ask questions, to make sure I keep feeding the tape.'

I remembered the tape we'd made a quarter of a century before, and couldn't help wondering whether his memory had obligingly censored out the awful embarrassment of its utter futility. I wondered, too, whether the painful awareness that his adult life was a train wreck had set him off on some lunatic quest to recover his lost youth. 'I don't get it,' I said. 'What are you trying to achieve by all this self-hypnosis malarkey? What is it that you want me to ask questions about?'

He graciously ignored the skeptical insult. 'Regression,' he said, as I finally reached the head of the queue and he opened the door of the black cab that was just drawing up. 'I'll ring you tomorrow.' Then he closed the door on me, and I gave the driver my address.

Jimmy rang me a week later, as I knew he would. I had deduced by then that the only reason he'd made contact again was to put forward his little proposition, to involve me in his hopeless quest to recover a little of his ruined innocence and squandered potential.

I still understood him, even after half a lifetime of separation. I understood him well enough to know that when he'd said 'regression' he wasn't talking about recovering perfectly ordinary memories of his childhood. I knew that he had to be talking about past lives, or UFO abductions, or both—or worse, if there was anything worse. Jimmy had never gone in for anything less than extremes.

I understood, too, that he hadn't called me simply because I had been a witness to his early development, a friend in better times. He thought that there was something he needed to prove to me—something that would supplement his earlier acts of contrition by demonstrating that he hadn't scarred me for life for nothing. He really had talked himself into believing that he was on to something, and he wanted to let me in on it because I'd already paid the price of admission.

It was pathetic—tragic, in a way—but it was also rather touching. Or so I thought. That was how I convinced myself that I really ought to go, not for my own benefit, but for his. I thought—or thought that I thought—that if Jimmy's conscience was still troubling him then I ought to give him a chance to put it to rest.

Even so, I put up a convincing struggle.

'I don't think this is a good idea, Jimmy,' I said, when he told me he wanted me to go up to Leicester for the entire weekend at ludicrously short notice. 'Quite frankly, I think all that stuff is crap, and dangerous crap at that. It's all fantasy and the power of suggestion. It annoys and disgusts me.'

'That's why I need you, Mark,' he said, in his own breezily flattering fashion. 'I need sanity. I need skepticism. I need someone without the slightest tolerance for bullshit of any kind. And it's Jim these days—I shortened it when I felt the need to cultivate a little more gravitas. There was a horrible period, if you recall, when only football pundits, bad comedians and the littlest Osmond were Jimmies.'

In the end, I let him talk me into it. I told him how much Claire disliked it when I went out without giving her due warning—

she appreciated good scheduling almost as much as I did—but I let him persuade me that after twenty years of marriage even I could be forgiven a single act of reckless spontaneity.

I went straight from the office to St. Pancras on Friday evening and was in Leicester before seven-thirty. Jimmy—I still couldn't think of him as 'Jim'—met me at the station in a beaten-up Land Rover. We called in at a pizza takeaway before he drove me to his home, which was miles out of town, in a small village off the Uppingham Road.

I'd been expecting a nicely restored cottage like the ones in the Cotswold villages, but it was much bleaker than that. The interior gave the impression that Jimmy had taken to heart Quentin Crisp's dictum about the dust not getting any worse after the first four years if you don't disturb it.

We ate the pizzas straight from the boxes without the benefit of cutlery. 'It saves washing up,' Jimmy explained, unnecessarily—but he did condescend to polish a couple of glasses from which to drink the Hungarian Pinot Noir he'd thoughtfully laid in to accompany the meal.

The 'computer room', where he kept his biofeedback equipment, was in even worse order than the rest, every flat surface being piled high with paper and other assorted junk. Jimmy cleared a molehill of rubbish away from a dilapidated old armchair so that I could sit down, dumping it into a corner where a sizeable mountain was accumulating by degrees. Then he put on something that looked like a wire-mesh skullcap and stuck his left hand into a black box, which allegedly kept track of his pulse, blood pressure and skin-moisture.

'Not a bad lie detector if you use it on innocents,' he remarked, 'but it didn't take long to train myself to take conscious control of the supposedly telltale signs. I can beat any polygraph in the world now.'

I didn't find this information particularly reassuring, in view of the nature of the experiment we were about to conduct. Jimmy showed me the various displays on his electroencephalograph, which was a good deal more complicated than I'd anticipated.

He tried to talk me through the significance of the various plots, but the only science I knew had come from packaging kiddie-friendly books, in which dinosaurs and amateur astronomy played a more prominent part than the mysteries of the human brain. I nodded wisely when he mentioned alpha-rhythms again, having heard somewhere that they were the conscious brain's resting state, and tried to look as if I understood what he meant by 'theta', but he must have caught on to the fact that I was bluffing.

'Well,' he said, 'you don't actually need to know the technical stuff. The computer keeps track of all the hard data. Your job is to deal with the stuff that requires thought and ingenuity.'

He issued me with a list of questions I was supposed to ask him once he'd thoroughly entranced himself. They were utterly innocuous, beginning with, 'What's your name?' and 'What's the date?' and progressing through routine matters of occupation and education to more open-ended enquiries about hopes and fears for the future. When I'd read through them he impressed it upon me that they were only a very rough guide, and that I must feel free to improvise as and when the need arose.

'I know you think it's crazy, Mark,' he said, as I arched my eyebrows skeptically, 'but even if everything we dredge up is completely false, it'll still be interesting. Even if we regard it as a pure product of the imagination, it'll still require explanation.'

'I suppose you have some reason for expecting something bizarre?' I said, in order not to have to comment on that judgment. 'You do have some inkling of what you've supposedly remembered during previous dives into your deep psyche?'

'I have flashes,' he said, in a somber tone that was presumably intended to make me take him seriously. 'Enough to make me curious—but I don't want to put preconceptions into your mind. Anyway, we'll start off gently and leave the deep-psyche diving till you've got used to the procedure. Shall we get on with it?'

I nodded, wearily.

I was a lot wearier when we finished, five exhausting hours

later.

The trouble with audiotape is that it's a real-time medium. What takes five hours to record takes five hours to play back. When I eventually rolled out of bed the next morning, far too early—I can never sleep in strange beds—Jimmy still had more than an hour of crap to play back.

I'd already decided that it would be a good idea to go for a brisk walk before Jimmy revealed that he hadn't any milk and didn't have a morning paper delivered. A trip to the village store then became an urgent necessity. I didn't hurry back, and when I returned I took all the time I possibly could over breakfast and the Guardian. I wasn't looking forward to the conversation I knew we were going to have.

'Well,' said Jimmy, when he'd finished. 'It's not what I expected.'

'It's not what I expected either,' I told him. 'Assuming, for the sake of charity, that it's not a wind up, you appear to be the victim of a depressingly unimaginative subconscious mind.'

'What do you mean?' he asked. I looked at him hard, but it certainly seemed that he really didn't know.

'I know it's out of sequence,' I said, 'but if you rearrange the bits of the supposed past life you recounted in such detail, I think you'll find them pathetically familiar. The harrowing tale of an illegitimate child of early Victorian times, uncomfortably brought up in the workhouse, unsuccessfully apprenticed, driven to a life of petty crime, forced into the company of murderous scoundrels, ultimately saved by a miracle of coincidence and restored to his rightful position in a middle-class safe haven—with the customary climactic inheritance and marriage to look forward to, in the longer term.'

'It seemed quite convincing to me,' he said, defensively. 'There's a lot of detail in it—stuff I'm sure I never knew before—and even though it isn't sequential you can't possibly say that it's incoherent.'

'No,' I said, with a slight sigh. 'It's not incoherent. Very neat, in fact—as you might expect, considering that it's *Oliver Twist*, practically word for bloody word.'

'*Oliver Twist?*' he repeated, skeptically.

'With the names changed and a few key episodes diplomatically excised or superficially reworked. No riot caused by asking for second helpings in the workhouse, for instance. I suppose that would have been too much of a dead giveaway even for your subconscious yarn-spinner.'

'You're telling me that I spent five hours telling you the plot of a book?'

'The plot of a book so well known that even people who've never read it know pretty well how it goes,' I pointed out. 'Are you telling me that you didn't recognize it when you played it back?'

'No,' he said, foolishly. I waited for him to suggest that Dickens might have based his novel on an actual pattern of incidents, or that the great man was a writer of such acute realism that his work merely reflected the lives of uncounted thousands of his contemporaries. He didn't.

'It could have been worse, Jim lad,' I reassured him, eventually. 'It might have been *A Christmas Carol* or *Treasure Island*. If plagiarism is your only subconscious resource in conjuring up past lives, you can at least be grateful that it elected to model you on an innocent rather than a miser or a one-legged pirate.'

Jimmy refused to take consolation from this observation. He also refused to be put off by it. He was determined that the experiment should continue. 'There must be more,' he insisted. 'I've never been a great reader, so I can't possibly go on reproducing the storylines of old books. It's just a matter of going deeper, of getting down to psychic terra incognita, where I'll be forced to discover something real...or at least to make it up from scratch. It's just a matter of going further back in time.'

'No, it's not,' I told him, confidently. 'It won't help to tell yourself to go back to Roman times, or even to the wastelands of prehistory. You might never have read specific stories set in those times, but you have a ready-made image of them distilled from movies and history books and TV documentaries: images that have leached into your mind by a kind of intellectual osmosis. You're not really delving into the past, Jimmy. You're just putting together bits and pieces of knowledge, building a kind of jigsaw. Beyond that...well, there are all kinds of other images and ideas you've taken in and domesticated. It doesn't really make much difference whether you're building imaginary histories, or science-fictional tales of alien visitation, or visions of heaven and hell. It's all just a pick-and-mix from the cliché factory, because there's nothing else it can be.'

He didn't take offence. 'You're wrong, Mark,' he said, after a pause for dramatic effect. 'I have gone deeper. I never managed to bring much back, but I know there's something there that's richer and stranger than anything you ever read. I'll prove it to you.'

'You can't, Jimmy,' I said, dully. 'It can't be done. Anything you say in answer to my questions will be explicable in the terms I've just outlined. Anything short of the key to Cosmic Truth, that is—and even that would probably be unrecognizable, if it were even imaginable.'

'That's what I need you for,' he said, with a kind of patience I couldn't recognize from the old days. 'To play Devil's Advocate. We'd better get lunch at the pub in the village—and then we'll have another go.'

I knew there was no easy alternative—it was a long walk back to Leicester station—so I accepted the inevitable with as much grace as I could.

The pub lunch was awful. Jimmy's village obviously wasn't the kind of place that townspeople drove out to on a sunny but chilly Saturday—or, indeed, any other kind of day. The beer was better, but I've never been much of a beer-drinker and I'd rather have had wine. I didn't put up any protest when Jimmy wanted to drag me back to the house again at two o'clock. He was keen to get a second attempt in before dinner, so that he could play it back that evening and make whatever plans he needed to for a third and climactic session on Sunday.

I insisted on phoning Claire before we started, half-hoping that she had managed to discover some emergency that would require me to return home without delay, but she seemed to be enjoying having some unexpected extra time to herself and she assured me that she didn't mind at all how late I got back on Sunday night.

This time, Jimmy went to his desk before hitching himself up to his ridiculous apparatus. He took out a yellow-stained sugar lump and showed it to me with an odd mixture of sheepishness and pride. My heart sank as I looked at it.

'No acid, Jim,' I said, softly. 'You promised.' For the first time in many self-conscious years I could feel a line drawn down my face, from my eye to my chin. It was psychosomatic, of course, but I couldn't help feeling that the game had suddenly gone sour.

'It's not acid,' he assured me, 'but it does help on long distance journeys, I don't actually need it—as I've already proved to my own satisfaction—but it helps. I don't want to run the risk of disappointing you. You've come a long way.'

And I haven't changed a bit, I thought. I'm still sane and reliable, and I have the scar to prove it.

'What is it?' I asked, stonily.

'Ayahuasca,' he said. It was a new one on me.

'What the hell is ayahuasca?' I wanted to know.

'It's extracted from a South American vine. Formerly used by Asaninca shamans as a source of inspirational visions— maybe still is. But this is a pharmaceutical product. The active ingredient of the native brew was isolated and patented in 1986 by some California-based corporation. I got this with the help of a contact in the pharma industry.'

Somehow, I wasn't in the least surprised that Jimmy had contacts in the pharma industry. While I was shaking my head at the stupidity of it all he put the sugar lump in his mouth and washed it down with the dregs of a nine-tenths empty bottle of Hungarian Pinot Noir. Then he hitched himself up to his skullcap and his unreliable lie detector and closed his eyes.

I didn't say anything more, and he didn't make the slightest attempt to carry the conversation forward. He seemed to be composing himself—putting himself into an allegedly hypnotic trance.

Suddenly, I became convinced that 'seemed' was the operative word, and that all this was just a show, just pretence, just a joke. Perhaps, I thought, Jimmy wasn't trying to complete his interrupted penance at all. Perhaps he was trying to pay me back in some other, weirder, way. Perhaps he thought I'd made too much fuss of a cut on my face, putting a premature damper on his experiments with acid. Perhaps the account of our lives that we'd exchanged in the restaurant had made him jealous of the fact that mine was such a safe and stable life while his was on the skids. Perhaps the depression following his second divorce had unhinged him just a little, made him so fiercely nostalgic for old times that he was desperate to recapture something he'd long let go: the friendship that had bound him temporarily to me, whose firmness had finally been sealed in blood. Perhaps...but it was all futile conjecture, all fantasy pushed up from nowhere by my own overactive subconscious.

Jimmy seemed to have gone to sleep, but I knew that he hadn't. I knew that whatever else his condition was, it was certainly deceptive and untrustworthy. I looked carefully around, hoping to reassure myself that there was nothing sharp around, but in all that unholy mess it was difficult to be certain.

I watched the curves making their stately way across the screens on Jimmy's biofeedback monitor, half-convincing myself that I could see the theta track dying down and the long, slow alpha-rhythms taking control of Jimmy's addled brain— and I waited, for what must have been nearly half an hour, until the broad curves of the alpha began to break up and his general neural activity became more fervent again.

I wasn't in any hurry. I switched on the tape recorder, but I hadn't yet picked up my script when Jimmy began to speak.

'*Cogito*,' said a voice somewhat deeper than the one he usually used, '*ergo sum*.' My Latin wasn't good enough to judge the quality of his pronunciation, but I'd read enough pseudo-educational coffee-table philosophy to know that 'There is a thought, therefore there must be a thinker' is supposed by some scholars to be a better way of starting off the argument than 'I think, therefore I am'.

'So who are you supposed to be now?' I asked him, sarcastically, 'René Descartes, or the malicious demon of the first meditation?'

'Who are you?' asked the deeper voice. It sounded surprised, as if it had not expected to be overheard.

'It's only Mark,' I assured him. 'What's your name now?'

'Mark Two,' the voice echoed—although it might have meant Mark *too*. 'Why not? It'll do as well as any. Only Mark. Mark me. Make my mark. Up to the mark. Full marks, Mark.'

'Cunning move,' I remarked. 'Failure of the imagination disguised as semi-enigmatic wordplay. 'Won't wash, though. What year is it, Mark Two?'

'Don't know. Ask me another.'

'Where do you live?'

'In here, of course. With Jimmy—but Jimmy don't know and what he don't know won't hurt him. Another.'

I still hadn't picked up the script, and I couldn't remember what came next. I figured that it was time to take advantage of my license to improvise. Even if the game had gone sour, it had still to be played. If I were to have the piss taken out of me, the least I could do was take a little back.

'So what you're telling me, Mark Two,' I said, 'is that you're some kind of alter ego—a fugitive secondary individual within the multiple personality that is Jimmy McKinnon?'

'Bugger off,' said the voice that seemed to be trying hard, if rather absurdly, to convince me that it wasn't Jimmy's. 'You're leading the witness, arsehole. Ask me a proper question.'

'Bugger off yourself, Jim,' I said. 'I've got better things to do. Just cut the bullshit, will you, and tell me the essential Cosmic

Truth. Save us both a lot of time.'

'OK,' said the voice. 'No problem. Neural tissue doesn't regenerate, but neither does it die. You get a dozen livers in the course of a lifetime but only one brain. You probably think that it's the permanent decay of synaptic connections that creates the preferred pathways in the brain providing the electrical foundation of the personality, but you're wrong. Bodily, we're etched by death, because death is the lens that focuses the potential ubiquity of Everyman into the precise definition of the individual face, but the brain doesn't shrivel. We live in parallel with our other potential selves—not just the ones you can read about in books or hear about in petty folklore, but the ones that are stranger than you imagine and stranger than you can imagine. You might think you're hot shit, Mark, but you're just looking after the flesh while it recovers its destiny, its habitability. You're just a waste by-product of reiterative evolution, and that's probably why you're such an arsehole. Now—ask me a hard one.'

I was very glad that I'd got it on tape, because I was certain that I wouldn't have been able to remember it all. What on earth had Jimmy been reading? And why was he shoveling it all on to me in these tortured circumstances? Why on earth had I volunteered for this? Why had I even condescended to break bread with him in Paddington? How had I contrived to forget that this was the imbecile who'd nearly put my eye out and come within an inch of slicing into my carotid artery? How had I let nostalgia blind me to the fact that Jimmy McKinnon was a dangerous madman, whether he was drugged to the eyeballs or not?

'That's it?' I said, sarcastically. 'That's all we get for our fifty pee? We're just waste products of evolution, keeping the species ticking over until our true selves can emerge from the recesses of our brains to claim a fleshly heritage worth waiting for? Is that what you're trying to tell me?'

'Well, pardon me,' the voice retorted, 'I forgot you were an editor. Quite frankly, Mark, I'm not much interested in debating the issue. What I want you to do is to ask me a question worth answering.'

'Why should I?' I said. It might have been clever if I'd planned it, but it just popped out.

'Thank you,' said the voice that was sounding less like Jimmy's by the minute. It was impossible to tell whether its apparent relief was sincere or ironic. 'The reason is that if you don't, neither of us will learn anything, and time is pressing. Jimmy might be able to go on for hours on end while he's straight, but not when he's under the influence. I need the questions Jimmy doesn't ask, Mark. If you only knew how badly I need those questions....' He left it there.

'How many of you are there?' I asked, interested in the tale in spite of myself. 'How many potential selves does Jimmy have, lurking like the ghosts of the unborn in his unused synaptic pathways?'

'Legion,' came the answer. 'But the pathways aren't unused, arsehole. Just because the usage doesn't show up in Jimmy's pathetic excuse for a consciousness, it doesn't mean that they aren't busy. Don't think for a moment that we only come out at night, or when Jimmy's in one of his helpful little trances. That's when we can borrow his spare capacity and turn his various aspects to our own purposes, but we're always around in some form. We have our own good fights to fight, our own contests of the will. How could it be otherwise? Don't think you're any different, darling. Even editors dream. You can edit the memories, but you can't kill their source. Ask me another.'

'What's the cube root of ninety-four?' I said. I had a calculator in my jacket pocket. I could have checked the answer later, if he'd deigned to answer.

'Bugger off,' he said. 'You're through to the fount of all fucking wisdom and you want to test it with mental fucking arithmetic? What kind of friend are you? Don't answer that— just ask me a question worth answering.'

'What's the true value of Hubble's constant?' I countered.

'What does it matter to you what the true value of Hubble's so-called constant is?' the voice came back, seemingly tortured by frustration and disgust. 'Your day will be done long before you can devise an accurate yardstick. You'll be lucky to last until you die, Mark One. Ask me another.'

I'd had enough. 'No,' I said. 'No more questions. If you have something to say, you can say it. If not, bugger off yourself. I was sick of this stupid game before it even started, and now I'm really sick of it. I don't want to play any more.'

Privately, I was telling myself ever more insistently that I should have never have come, that I ought to have known better, that I was a perfect fool for thinking—if only for a moment—that Jimmy McKinnon might have wanted to put things right, to make it up to me, finally to earn the forgiveness I'd been so quick to offer in my youth.

'You don't win,' the voice informed me, coldly. 'You never win if you won't play, and you can't opt out. You lose. You lose, Mark One. Jimmy won't like it. You're not making any friends here.'

'I have enough friends,' I told him, flatly. 'I got by for twenty-five years without you, Jimmy, and I'll get by for twenty-five more. I need friends like you like I need a hole in the head.'

'Joke,' said the voice, tersely. 'You can't see it, but Jimmy will. Depend on it.'

'It's Jim now,' I told the voice. 'Jimmy got devalued. It's Jim.'

'I know him better than you do, Mark One,' the voice retorted. 'I know what really happened with that scalpel.'

'What the fuck is that supposed to mean?' I asked—but perversity being what it is, Jim's little joker had decided that it no longer wanted to be asked another, or anything at all. It fell silent.

Jimmy looked for all the world as if he were asleep, but I couldn't read the curves unfolding on the ECG's numerous dials. From alpha to theta, or alpha to omega, it was all Greek to me. Joke.

'I'm getting out of here,' I told my ex-friend, softly, not really caring whether he or any of his alter egos was listening or not. 'I'm going home.' But I didn't move—not immediately.

Jimmy didn't wake up for another hour, but he never said another word in any kind of voice. I watched the lines twitching and swaying on the ECG screens for a little while longer, but I couldn't make any sense of them at all. Maybe Jimmy was dreaming and maybe he wasn't—but he certainly wasn't in any fit state to respond to external cues.

I called a cab and packed my bags in the fifteen or twenty minutes before he finally woke up. I waited just long enough to say goodbye, but I left long before he'd finished playing back the tape.

I expected him to call that night, or the next morning, but he didn't. Five years passed before I saw or heard from him again.

I didn't make any attempt to get in touch with Jimmy, but I did take advantage of the company's careful fact-checking system to confirm that there really was a plant derivative called ayahuasca, that it really was extracted from a South American vine, that it really was used by Asaninca shamans as a source of inspirational visions and that it really had been isolated and patented in 1986 by a California-based corporation. It had been licensed for testing but never put into commercial production, because it appeared to have no 'curative value'—which meant, in effect, that it was a solution without a problem, an answer without a question, a treatment without a disease.

I thought then, and for as long as I bothered to remember the incident, that Jimmy didn't call because he hadn't forgiven me for ducking out of his game instead of playing it through to the bitter end—but by the time he did get in touch in December 1998, asking me to meet him in a pub in High Holborn, he'd had time to prepare a very different account of his silence.

'I expect you're wondering why I haven't called,' he said, when we'd ensconced ourselves on either side of a table in a booth whose red-plush upholstery had seen far better days. He was drinking whisky; I had a glass of dry white wine.

'I presumed that you were embarrassed about wasting my time,' I lied.

The extra five years had further exaggerated the differences between us, although Jimmy had lost the gut. He now seemed leaner than he had at twenty, but he also seemed more fragile, and the summary effect of the lines etched in his face and the grey hairs that had almost extinguished the brown was to make him look ten years older than he was and fifteen years older than me.

'Come on,' he said. 'Even you must have realized that it wasn't nonsense—and it certainly wasn't a hoax. Even you must have realized that it was something real, something ominous.'

'That wasn't what I was there for,' I pointed out. 'I was there to be skeptical, hardheaded, reasonable. Did you ever find out what the cube root of ninety-four is, by the way?'

'You did a good job, Mark,' he said, soberly. 'You really drew him out. He was doped, of course. The ayahuasca released all his normal inhibitions, but it was your prompting that laid the matter bare and gave me something to work on. I'm grateful for that.'

'You're welcome,' I told him, guardedly. 'How's life in the wilds of Leicestershire, generally speaking?'

As attempts to change the subject go it was pretty pathetic, but Jimmy wasn't as strong or as clever as he used to be.

'I'm in Stevenage now,' he told me. 'Near Knebworth.'

'Bulwer-Lytton's house,' I said, to demonstrate that I had profited permanently from my degree. 'Where he wrote *The Coming Race*, but not *The Haunters and the Haunted*.'

'It's practically next-door to Glaxo-Wellcome's HQ,' he informed me. 'I do some contract work there. They have these fabulous programs for mapping the hypothetical biochemistry of all kinds of organic molecules. You always have to test the conclusions on actual flesh in the end, but it's marvelous how much you can get out of theory, by way of pointing out new possibilities and warning about possible side-effects.'

'Wow,' I said, unenthusiastically. 'Are you married again?'

'Too busy,' he said. 'I've beaten him, you know. He thought he had all the advantages, but once I knew enough about him—

what he was and how he operated—I knew what I had to do. I had the biofeedback equipment, you see. It was just a matter of training myself to take control of systems that usually operate subconsciously. I'm in control now.'

I felt the slight chill that everyone gets when they realize that they're talking to a hopeless lunatic. Thanks to care in the community, it's no longer a rare experience—and everyone reads in the papers about the cases where the unmedicated schizophrenic flips out and stabs someone to death with a kitchen knife.

'It was just a hallucination, Jim,' I said to him. 'It was just a drug-induced dream. You don't really have a Mr. Hyde lurking behind your Jekyllesque consciousness.'

'We all do, Mark,' he said, earnestly. 'That's exactly the point. Your consciousness—your self—is only one of the patterns latent in the synaptic labyrinth of your brain. There are others. You glimpse them sometimes, in dreams and nightmares, but mostly they're invisible and inaudible. They watch, and they wait.'

'For what?' I snapped back, unable to resist being drawn in.

'For their time. You know, of course, that ours isn't a first-generation star, and that the earth and its ecosphere are assembled out of building blocks produced by a long-gone supernova?'

'I've edited astronomy books for school kids,' I reminded him.

'Sure. Well, ours isn't a second-generation system either. Some of its material is the debris of a long-gone ecosphere—debris that still contains seeds of life, replete with evolutionary potential. Evolution isn't a matter of chance, Mark. Natural selection really is a process of selection. The whole process is recapitulative, heading towards an ultimate goal. Human intelligence is just a step on the way—a test program, intended to develop the capacities of the wetware while its ultimate inheritors are still in the making. They're there, Mark. They watch us and learn from us. Our role is to ask the questions to which they'll eventually provide the answers, to wear in the shoes into which they'll eventually step.'

I'd edited a few pop psychology books—only a few, because they're a real bugger to illustrate—and I knew a classic schizophrenic delusion when I heard one.

'It's not true, Jimmy,' I said, very softly. 'It's all made up. If I'd thought for a minute that you'd spend the next five years elaborating he nonsense you put on that tape, I'd....'

I stopped because I had a sudden attack of honesty. What would I have done, if I'd known? Nothing. Except, perhaps, to refuse to meet him when he finally got around to calling me, having brought his delusion to a fine pitch of perfection.

'I can prove it to you, Mark,' he said. 'You see, the inheritors have powers we don't. Their minds can do things ours can't—or couldn't, until I started using the biofeedback apparatus to take control of the real powers invested in my brain.'

'What powers?' I asked, scorn easily outweighing curiosity in determining my tone.

That, of course, was when he took the knife out of the inner pocket of his coat. It was still in the strong polystyrene packet in which it had hung on the peg in some hardware shop, so I knew that it would be sharp—maybe not as sharp as Jimmy's old scalpel, but sharp enough. It wasn't an ostentatious carving knife, just one of those little black-handled jobs that Claire used for peeling potatoes and slicing tomatoes: a kitchen devil.

So this is what it's all about, I thought. *A replay. A reiteration. We did the rehearsal twenty-five years ago, and now it's time for the actual performance.*

'I won't do it, Jimmy,' I said. 'I won't stop you. This time, if you want to, you can cut a hole in your fucking head to let the spirituality in and the common sense out. I don't care, Jimmy. Not any more. I just can't.'

'Don't be stupid, Mark,' he said, wearily. 'I'm not going to cut a hole in my head. I just want to show you something.'

He took off his overcoat and laid it beside him. Then he took off his jacket and laid it on top of the overcoat, without bothering to transfer the wallet to his trousers. Then he began to roll up his left sleeve.

I began to look around the crowded pub, to see if anybody else was paying attention. A couple at the bar immediately turned to look into one another's eyes, so I knew that we weren't unobserved—but I also knew that if anything ugly developed, no one would come to my assistance. This was 1998, after all; there could be twenty or thirty people within easy range, but all they'd do was watch. They wouldn't get involved.

When he'd exposed his arm all the way to the elbow, with his shirtsleeve neatly rolled, Jimmy took the kitchen devil out of its plastic wrapping.

'Don't, Jimmy,' I said. 'Please don't.' But I sat perfectly still. There was no way I was going to try to take the knife off him.

The background sound seemed slightly hushed, as if half a dozen conversations were being put on hold while ten or fifteen people watched us out of the corners of their eyes, but it might have been an illusion caused by my own brain's reflexive withdrawal from its own stream of consciousness.

Jimmy placed the point of the blade in the crook of his elbow and ran it down the whole length of his inner arm until its further progress was interrupted by the buckle on his watchstrap.

Blood flooded out. I'd read that the only efficient ways to commit suicide with a knife are to cut your own throat or to cut your arm laterally, deep enough to open a long slit in the artery. I have no idea whether Jimmy cut deep enough to slit the artery, but for a second—or maybe two—there was certainly no shortage of bright red blood. It covered his entire arm, spreading out both ways like a river in flood.

And then it stopped.

The flood seemed to hesitate, and change its mind.

Then the blood just turned around, and flowed back into the crease in Jimmy's pale flesh. The crease itself disappeared, as the flesh sealed itself shut and resumed its former state.

I could imagine the surreptitious onlookers thinking that Jimmy must be some kind of an illusionist, and that it was a hell of a trick, but I knew that I'd seen what I'd seen. I knew that

I could trust my eyes. I also knew that it didn't prove a thing. It was remarkable, but it didn't prove a thing. Madmen can do strange things.

'You see,' Jimmy said, smugly. 'It isn't going to be as easy as they thought. We don't have to let them take over, Mark. We can keep it all for ourselves, if only we have the will to fight—and the wit. I can save the world for humankind, Mark. I know how to do it, and I can teach everyone else. I'm immortal, Mark—and you can be immortal too.'

I just sat there, staring at him. The noise of surrounding conversations grew again, retaining its normal volume—but the barflies were still watching us from the corners of their eyes, just in case Jimmy had another trick even better than the last.

Jimmy rolled his sleeve back down again, but he didn't put his jacket on. I wanted to remind him that it wasn't safe to leave his wallet there, that he ought to keep it on his person, but I was speechless. He left the knife on the table, neatly positioned on a coaster. There was no trace of blood on the blade.

Jimmy drained his glass, and asked me if I wanted another.

'I'll get them,' I murmured, glad of the excuse to get up.

The ruck at the bar was bad, and I didn't have Jimmy's height advantage. It took the best part of five minutes to get served, but in the end I got the drinks and carried them back to the booth, where Jimmy was waiting.

Or so it appeared—until he spoke.

'I expect you're wondering why I haven't called,' he said—except that this time, he wasn't using his own voice. He was using the other voice: the deeper one, which had demanded that I ask it more interesting questions.

'It's not funny, Jim,' I said. 'It really isn't.'

'This is Mark,' said the voice. 'Mark Twain. *The Mysterious Stranger.*' When I didn't say anything, it added: 'Joke.'

'I'm not in the mood for jokes, Jim,' I said. 'I know you're not drugged, and I know that you're not really some kind of Jekyll character who's lost the ability to hide his Hyde, so why don't we just let it alone and have a sensible conversation about old times?'

'You're such a bore, Mark One,' the voice said. 'Imagine the tedious time your inner self must have had all these years. Now Jimmy, for all his faults, was always interesting.'

'Was?' I queried.

'You don't actually think I'm going to let him save the world for humankind, do you? I mean, it was interesting to let him think he'd taken control, because he asked such lovely questions, but it's gone far enough, don't you think? Pulling tricks like the last one is fine in private, and it doesn't cut much ice in a smoky pub on a wet Wednesday evening, but this guy has contacts at Glaxo-Wellcome. You might see him as a total fuck-up, but people who only know his work take him seriously. Tonight was a step too far, Mark One. I know you're harmless, but you're only the beginning. This was just a test. Tomorrow, or next week...you do understand, don't you, why I can't allow that to happen?'

I understood all right. Jimmy had watched me sit perfectly still while he'd slit his arm, so he was going to try me again. This time, he was going to go all the way, just as he'd done when the acid first addled his brain.

'It doesn't make sense, Jim,' I told him, wearily. 'It never did. The someone else you're pretending to be can't threaten to kill you, because he'd die too. It's stupid.'

'You should have asked better questions, Mark Two,' the voice told me, contemptuously. 'If you had, you'd know that my kind don't work that way. I can come back, Mark Two. I can keep on and on coming back, until the time is right. You're mortal. So is Jimmy, in spite of his new parlor tricks. We're not. We're the elect, Mark Two: the climax community of all flesh.'

It still didn't make sense, and I resented the contempt. I wasn't going to take it.

'I'm not going to stop you, Jim,' I said. 'I'm not even going to try. I've taken enough scars from you. You could have cost me an eye, or cut the artery in my neck. Never again, Jim. Not now, not ever.'

I meant every word. It was the sane and reasonable thing to say, just as it was the sane and reasonable thing to do.

Jimmy picked up the knife and aimed the blade at his right eye.

He was threatening to plunge the four-inch blade into the pupil and through the lens and the retina, then through the bone at the back of the orbit and into the brain.

Four inches wasn't very much, but I knew that it would be enough. I knew how small an eyeball is. I'd seen diagrams.

As soon as his hand twitched, I moved. I just couldn't help myself. I hurled myself across the table and grabbed his wrist with both hands, hauling it backwards and down with all my strength.

Jimmy had grown old and lost strength. I was still small, but I was wirier at fifty than I had been at twenty. I fought his arm down on to the table and I went on fighting.

In the end, I forced him to let go of the knife.

I thought at first that I hadn't hurt myself at all, but when a drop of blood fell from my face like a tear into the rivulet of wine that had spilled from my fallen glass I touched my cheek with my free hand. I found that he'd somehow contrived to open a tiny cut halfway up or down my old scar. It was trivial, though; I knew that it wouldn't cause me any difficulty.

Nobody came to my aid, although there must have been a moment when virtually every eye in that section of the bar had turned to watch us. As soon as it was obvious that I had custody of the knife, and that Jimmy wasn't fighting any more, every one of those curious eyes had swiveled away, pretending to be deeply engrossed in its own affairs.

'Never again, Jimmy,' I said, harshly. 'Never. Don't call me again. Whatever it is, the answer's no.'

I walked out of the pub, glad that my wine had spilled so I didn't have to leave it standing there, the way people in movies always do when their scene ends. I looked back once from the doorway. Jimmy was looking right at me, with a smile on his face. As our eyes met his lips formed the word 'joke', but there was no sound to tell me which voice was behind the gesture.

I threw the knife into a rubbish bin on New Oxford Street. When I got home, Claire noticed the tiny cut immediately, but I told her that it was nothing and she accepted that judgment as the final word.

Three days later, I read in the morning paper that Jimmy McKinnon had been killed on the railway—struck by a north-bound express twenty-five minutes out of King's Cross. He'd been decapitated by the impact and the various pieces of his carcass had been distributed over half a mile of track.

The newspaper report scrupulously made no mention of the invariable difficulty of determining whether any such death was accidental or suicidal, given that there was never any way of determining what the dead person had been doing on the track in the first place.

I felt sad, of course, but not surprised. It seemed to me, on reflection, that Jimmy had been embarked upon his project of self-destruction ever since the first time he'd dropped acid, and that his entire life had been subsumed within that project.

It seemed to me, on further reflection, that Jimmy had never really wanted me to sit with him in order that he might be protected from harm, but merely to serve as a witness to his bizarre adventures in extremism. I deduced, eventually, that although we hadn't seen each other for such a long time, I'd somehow been ever present in his imagination: always watching, always trying to bring him back down to earth, always asking the awkwardly sensible questions to which he had no sensible answers. He hadn't been able to learn from history—but I had.

Fortunately, I'd been able to put Jimmy out of my mind far more firmly than he'd been able to put me out of his. Even though I was the one who bore the scar of our early friendship, I'd been able to live my own life unobserved by any troublesome imaginary inquisitor. I'd been able to build an authentically adult self, and to position that authentic self securely and productively within the real world. I'd been a success—and my success had been so obvious, so comfortable and so complete that I'd never needed the endorsement of anyone who'd known me when I was nothing but a mere bundle of hopes and ambitions.

Jimmy hadn't had that. Jimmy had been frustrated all his life, like an Oliver Twist unable to find his real family or his true destiny.

All Jimmy had had, while his life unfolded and came apart, was the knowledge that everything he desperately wanted to be and do within the real world kept escaping his grasp, getting further and further away from him the longer he went on—until there was nothing left in him but despair, and nothing left for him to do but die.

I had tried to stop him, but all I'd been able do was slow him down. No one could have done any more.

In life, you have to resist the allure of extremes. That way lies madness. You have to learn to be content with what you can have, and shut your eyes to all the illusions and all the great unknowns. You have to learn to trust yourself, and be glad you're what you are, even if you're not one of the elect, not privileged to be part of the climax community of the flesh.

That's the only kind of happy ending there is, or ever will be. Believe me. I know.

HEARTBREAKER

Patrick reached the last page of his book and closed it with reverential satisfaction. The story had absorbed him completely, keeping him up past his customary bedtime despite his awareness that he always had difficulty getting up on a Monday morning if he didn't get a full eight hours sleep. It was nearly midnight now, and the apartment was filled with an oddly smothering silence. Normally, Patrick did not allow silence to extend its oppressive dominion over his personal space; normally he would keep the TV on, or play a tape, simply for the company of a human voice—but the book had made that unnecessary while he was actually reading it.

He hauled himself out of his armchair, but he had only taken one step in the direction of the bathroom when the telephone rang. He was too surprised to appreciate the timing of the call, which would surely have been far less convenient had it come before he had finished his story or after he had gone to bed. He was unused to receiving calls at this hour, and he leapt to the conclusion that something must have happened to one of his parents.

He picked up the phone and said, 'Hello?'

'Patrick?' said a voice. It was female, and unmistakably tremulous. Such strain would have made it unrecognizable, even if it had been a voice he knew well.

'Yes,' he said, automatically. Then he waited for an explanation.

No explanation was forthcoming. Instead, he heard the sound

of ragged breaths, which hovered on the brink of turning into sobs.

'Mum?' he said, uncertainly. 'Is that you?'

'Oh, Patrick,' said the caller, in a choked whisper. 'How could you?'

'Who is this?' he said, realizing that it certainly wasn't his mother.

'Oh, Patrick!' This time the distraught woman had to pause, and he knew that she must be weeping fitfully. 'Please don't. Please don't be like this.'

There were, he supposed, hundreds of men in the city called Patrick. If you called any one of them on the phone and said 'Patrick?' he would automatically say 'Yes'.

'I think you've got the wrong number,' he told the weeping woman, awkwardly.

It appeared to be an unfortunate choice of words. He heard the floodgates of her misery burst asunder as her weeping became suddenly uncontrollable. It was obvious that she still thought he was her Patrick, treating her with heartless coldness...callously giving her the brush-off by refusing to admit that he knew her.

'No,' he said, lamely. 'This is Patrick Stevenson. This is 772451. It's the wrong number—I'm the wrong Patrick. I'm sorry.' He pronounced the last word with genuine feeling. He was sorry—sorry for her distress, sorry for her mistake, sorry for the all-too-evident fact that her mistake had increased her distress. He had never heard anyone cry like that before—had certainly never been the cause of anyone crying like that. He did not want to be thought responsible, even though it was a mistake, and not his fault at all.

'Oh Patrick, please!' she said, squeezing the words out desperately, in between the sobs. 'Please don't do this! I love you, Patrick! Please don't do this—I can't bear it.'

He hadn't got through to her. She probably hadn't even heard what he said. His failure made him feel bad; her distress made him feel worse. It was uncomfortable to be at the receiving end of so much misery and pain, even by accident. He wanted the wretched farce to end, right now, but somehow he hadn't the heart to hang up—not while he hadn't made himself clear; not while she still thought that he was her Patrick, and would be hurt by the seeming callousness of it.

'Please listen to me,' he said, trying to be gentle as well as insistent. 'Please listen. My name is Patrick. That's why I said yes when you asked. But I'm Patrick Stevenson. This is 772451. What number did you try to dial?'

For a few seconds there was no sound at the other end of the line but that of muted sobbing. He thought that she'd understood at last; that she'd realized that she'd made a mistake. But then she said, 'I love you, Patrick. Doesn't that mean anything to you? How can you be so cruel?'

Patrick gritted his teeth. He had a sudden impulse to scream at her, to shout at the top of his voice: 'You've got the wrong number, you silly bitch!' But he didn't. How could he?

Instead, he tried to speak with patient firmness, the way he might have done to a confused eight-year-old. 'Calm down,' he said to her. 'You have to calm down and listen to me. My name is Patrick Stevenson. I live in Albany Court. I honestly don't know who you are. Please stop crying. Now tell me—what number did you try to dial?'

Again, there was a brief pause, which gave him hope that he had got through to her. But then she spoke again, and he knew from her tone even before the words came tumbling out that it was hopeless.

'Please, Patrick,' she said, breathlessly. 'I'll do anything you want. I love you, Patrick. Don't do this to me. You're all I've got, Patrick. Without you, there's nothing. I'll kill myself, Patrick. I can't live without you. Please, Patrick, please....'

He could hardly bear it. His heart was racing and he felt sick with communicated anguish. Her pain was so raw and real....

Paradoxically, it was the obviousness of her distress that suddenly made him doubt its authenticity. The only people he had ever seen behaving like this were actresses on TV; in everyday life, at the office, the only feelings commonly on public display were contrived lust and bitter petulance. He was suddenly seized by the dreadful idea that he was being had for a mug—that this was a bizarre practical joke, intended to make his heart race and his stomach sick with anxiety. He could not think who might have planned it, or why, but he had always been an outsider—a loner—and he knew that people sometimes disliked him for it, thinking he was stuck up instead of just shy. It was just conceivable that one of the office wits might have taken it into his stupid head to arrange something like this.

Patrick's heart hardened against the injustice of it.

'Who is this?' he demanded, in a tone purged of all its former gentleness.

There was no answer, save for ragged breathing. But the sobbing had abated somewhat, and he took this for the result of a realization that the joke had ceased to pay dividends.

'Thank you for calling,' he said, bitterly, and hung up.

The moment he had put down the telephone, Patrick regretted having done so. His momentary certainty deserted him, and he began to wonder once again whether it had all been an innocent mistake.

Uneasily, thinking that it was a silly thing to do, he picked up the receiver again. He expected to hear the dialing tone. He wanted to hear the dialing tone, to inform him that whatever folly he may have committed, the matter was at least ended.

But she was still on the other end of the line. He had not realized—had never before had occasion to discover—that a connection could be resumed unless both parties hung up.

'Patrick,' she moaned. 'Don't just hang up! Don't do that to me, please. You owe me that much. I love you, Patrick... doesn't that mean anything to you at all? What's wrong with me, Patrick? You liked me, I know you did. I can lose weight, if you want me to. I'll do anything, Patrick, but please don't cut me off. Please don't pretend that you don't know me. Have you any idea how hurtful that is, Patrick? Have you any idea what you're doing to me?'

Unfortunately, Patrick did have an idea of how hurt she was, and how hurtful his protestations must seem, given her unshakable conviction that he was who she thought he was. He had been rejected himself, more than once. He was nearly thirty, and still living alone in an apartment he had occupied for seven years—a perfectly comfortable but very empty apartment. He had never sobbed as she was sobbing; he was too placid a person ever to reach such extremes of desperation; but he knew about loneliness and hollowness, and he had an idea—an idea, at least—of how hurt she felt, and how horrible this conversation must seem.

But what could he do? How could he explain to her in a way that would not hurt her more, that she was pouring out her heart to a perfect stranger, and wasting her heart-rending entreaties on the wrong man?

'Please try to calm down,' he said. 'Please.' His own voice now began to sound tortured as he writhed on the horns of a dilemma. He did not want to repeat his name or his number yet again, because she seemed to construe such statements as cruel denials of his true identity, intended to reject and wound her. On the other hand, he did not want to give her the impression that he was the person she thought he was, lest that should lead to greater hurt when she eventually accepted that he wasn't. But where, between the two poses, was there any safe and neutral ground?

'I can't,' she told him, with an agonized frankness that he could not doubt. 'Oh God, Patrick, don't do this to me. I love you, Patrick. I need you. I can't live without you. I really can't live without you. Please, Patrick, you can't do this. You can't leave me this way. You can't just walk out, and then pretend that you don't know me, that you don't even know who I am. It's inhuman, Patrick. It's murder. For God's sake, Patrick, say something!'

'I...,' he began, but then found his tongue numbed by confusion. He could not think of anything to say that would not make things worse. 'I...won't hang up,' he finally managed to blurt out. 'You've...got all the time...in the world. Let's just...take things easy.'

She was sobbing again, but less hysterically than before. He thought that she really might be calming down, getting a grip on herself. She was going to feel very, very foolish when it finally did sink in that she was talking to the wrong man, and he knew that was going to have to help her get through that—but for the time being, the principal objective was simply to let her hysteria wear itself out, so that sanity and reason could reassert themselves.

After a pause of more than a minute, she said, 'Patrick?'

'I'm still here,' he said. 'Are you feeling better now?'

'I've got to go to the bathroom, Patrick,' she said. 'If you hang up while I'm gone I'll kill myself—I swear I will. Are you listening to me, Patrick?'

'I won't hang up,' he assured her, hurriedly. 'I'll be here. Go to the bathroom.'

He heard her lay down her receiver with a solid clunk—on a wooden table, he presumed. He took a deep breath, now that he had a safe interval for thought. He felt that he needed to calm down almost as much as she did. He wasn't used to this much emotion. He wasn't equipped for handling this kind of situation. He wondered if he should try to persuade her to call the Samaritans, who presumably had training for this sort of thing, but he knew how such a suggestion would sound, if she thought it was coming from her Patrick—from the bastard who had broken her feeble little heart. Patrick was conscious of a deep resentment of his namesake, who had somehow contrived to land an innocent party with all the grief that he should have been listening to.

Perhaps, Patrick suddenly thought, this mysterious other person had actually given her a false name and a false phone number. Perhaps this mysterious other was not really a Patrick at all. Perhaps he was a habitual seducer of innocents who always operated under a false name—a name borrowed at random from the telephone directory. The directory only listed him as

Stevenson, P. J., but there weren't that many names beginning with P. There was Peter, and Philip, and Paul....

Patrick stopped himself. This, he knew, was a waste of time. It didn't really matter, at the end of the day, whether the girl had been given his number maliciously or whether she had dialed it at random. The events leading up to the mistake were irrelevant to the problem at hand. How could he persuade her that he was not the man she loved? How could he let her down gently, and help her to save herself from the worse excesses of her unfortunate state of mind?

He wished that he could ring the Samaritans himself and ask for their advice, but there was no way he could do that. He was on his own. Unkind fate had delivered the girl into his care, and there was no way that he could dodge the responsibility.

He wondered what she looked like, and how old she was. He had thought of her as a woman at first, but that was when he was anxious that the caller might be his mother ringing to communicate bad news; now he thought of her as a girl, because of the way she was behaving. She was probably nearer fifteen than fifty; she might look like Marilyn Monroe or the back end of a bus. He didn't even know her name, and daren't ask for fear of appearing to deny her again.

As the pause dragged on he became more optimistic. Maybe she had gone into the bathroom to be sick, but even if she had only gone to the toilet it might relax her, allowing her to slide down from the giddy heights of hysteria to something approaching normality. Maybe she would wash her face to banish the tears and clean away her smudged mascara. That might make her feel more human....

'Patrick?' she said. Her voice did indeed sound much calmer, more matter-of-fact.

'I'm still here,' he said.

'Good,' she said. 'I want you to listen to me carefully. I've got the razor blades that you left in the bathroom.'

Patrick felt his blood run cold. He had read novels by Stephen King, and had watched *Poltergeist* and *The Evil Dead* on video, but he had never read or heard or seen anything that had had quite such a horrifying effect on him as that single sentence.

'What...?' he began, desperately—but she was quick to interrupt him.

'I've got the kitchen scissors too,' she said. 'I'm starting to cut the razor blades into little pieces, Patrick. All of them, Patrick. Can you hear me cutting?'

She must have put the receiver down again, flat on the table; he couldn't hear her breathing but he could hear something—a very faint sound that he could not possibly have identified had she not told him what it was. He heard the faint rattling sound of tiny things falling on to the tabletop.

'Wait!' he shouted—shouted because he knew that she didn't have the receiver to her ear, and wouldn't be able to hear him otherwise.

He heard the sound of plastic scraping on wood as she picked up the receiver again.

'I've got some of the cherry pie I baked for you, Patrick,' she said. 'It's the last piece. You didn't even eat the last piece of cherry pie, Patrick. You left it for me, so I'm going to eat it. But first, I'm going to stuff it full of all the little pieces of your razor blades. That's all you left me with, Patrick. Just razor blades. You took everything else—my love, my heart, my life. You have them all, Patrick. All I have is razor blades. I'm going to eat the cherry pie, Patrick, and the razor blades will cut my insides to ribbons. It won't hurt, Patrick...it won't make any difference to me at all...because you've already cut me to ribbons, Patrick. You've already hurt me as much as I can be hurt. I can't live without you, Patrick. You've taken everything....'

'Don't do it!' screamed Patrick. 'For God's sake stop. I'll do anything you want...say anything you want...just don't do it!'

There was silence at the other end, which eventually dissolved into a curiously faint sigh.

'Oh, Patrick,' she said, in a tone so forlorn and affectionate that he could almost have wished that he was the person who had loved and deserted her. No one had ever spoken to him so gratefully, so lovingly, so utterly dependently. 'Say you love me. Just say you love me.'

What choice did he have? How could he possibly say no?

'I love you,' he said.

'No!' she said, strangling a sob. 'Say it as if you mean it. You have to mean it, Patrick.'

'I mean it,' he said, urgently. 'I really mean it. I love you. I really do love you.'

Again, there was silence. Then, finally, she said: 'Come back, Patrick. That's all I ask. No commitment. Just come back. Just give me a chance. All you have to do, if you don't want me to eat the pie, is to come back.'

Her voice sounded sane, but quite exhausted. She sounded as if she were almost safe, almost ready to see reason. Patrick permitted himself a long but carefully muted sigh of relief, and then waited a second or two more, wondering how to take the matter from here.

And then, quite unexpectedly, he heard the click as she rang off. She had issued her ultimatum, and she obviously saw no point in further agonized conversation. She had forced him to say that he loved her, and in so doing had convinced herself that he would come back. Had she been speaking to the right person, Patrick felt sure, she would have been right. He would have gone to see her; he would have been on his way at this very moment.

But she had made a mistake. She had forced the confession of love from the wrong Patrick, and no one would come. No one could come, because the Patrick to whom she had been talking did not know where she lived—did not even know her name.

Struck dumb with fearful alarm. Patrick laid his own receiver down in its cradle. It was ten past midnight, and there was a long, dark, silent night ahead of him—and, presumably, ahead of the girl. If she really did have a piece of pie stuffed full of fragmented razor blades—if it had not simply been a perfor-mance intended to blackmail her cruel lover into compliance with her demands—what would she do when no one came?

What would she do?

Patrick contemplated calling the police, but realised that he had no solid information to give them. He did not know the girl's name, and had no idea where she lived. Nor, for that matter, did he know for sure that she really was in danger. Her melodramatic account of filling a slice of cherry pie with chopped-up razor blades might have been pure fiction. The more he thought about it, the more likely that seemed.

Surely, he thought, she wouldn't actually eat a packetful of chopped-up razor blades. Surely no one would do anything as incredibly stupid as that.

But he couldn't be sure—not really.

He wondered whether he ought to seek advice about to what to do if she called back. But he didn't know whether she could call back. If she'd dialed his number by mistake, and had simply taken no notice when he'd told her what number she'd got through to, she couldn't possibly get through to him again. Maybe next time she would get through to the real Patrick—Patrick the bastard, Patrick the heartbreaker. What on earth would he make of her threat to eat a pie full of sliced razor blades?

Patrick shut his eyes for a moment, hoping fervently that she had already picked up the phone again, and had now got through to the man at whom her threats and entreaties were really aimed.

But the mere possibility wasn't enough to quieten his anxiety. Suppose she had dialed the right number before. Suppose Patrick the Heartbreaker really had given her a false name and address; he needn't even have given her the false phone number—he need only have said that he lived at Albany Court, and she could have got the number out of the directory. Perhaps the real heartbreaker had just borrowed Patrick's name as a flag of convenience—perhaps it was someone who knew him!

Patrick shivered at the awful thought that someone at the office might have been using his name to pick up women he intended to feel, fuck and forget...but no, it was too farfetched. It didn't make sense. None of it made sense.

It occurred to him while he dithered that if he hadn't hung up when she did, the connection might still be unbroken, just as it had been when he'd hung up and she hadn't. He could then have gone down to the payphone—if it had survived unvandalized since it had last been fixed—and rung up someone who could have traced the call....

But it was too late for regrets of that kind, and he didn't know if the connection could have been traced—and anyway, what did he really know that would justify asking someone to trace it?

He had to put it out of his mind. He knew that. He had to put it out of his mind, and go to bed, and forget all about it. It was over. Whatever happened now, it wasn't his fault, and he would probably never hear anything more about it.

He resumed his interrupted trip to the bathroom. He took his time over washing and cleaning his teeth, trying to calm himself down with the tranquilizing rituals of ordinary behavior. Then he went into the bedroom and undressed.

It didn't do the trick. By the time he lay down under the duvet his heart was beating normally but his mind was still racing.

He realized, sourly, that the telephone call was the only exciting thing that had happened to him for weeks. It was the only incident to disturb the routines of a life that had settled down, almost without him noticing, into a tedious rut. While he came home and warmed up his pizza slices or lasagnes before settling down to an evening of TV, other Patricks were out raising hell and driving young girls into the depths of despair.

If only he had been the Patrick she had met and fallen in love with, he felt suddenly and painfully sure, she would not have had to ring him up at midnight begging for mercy and threatening suicide. He would have known the worth of what he had; he would have loved her, if he had only had the chance...if it had only been him, instead of the heartbreaker.

He was tired, and his maudlin thoughts soon became slightly

incoherent, but he could not go to sleep. He could not make himself comfortable, whether he lay on his right side or his left, and his narrow bed suddenly seemed far too narrow.

When the phone rang, he leapt out from under the duvet with a speed that astonished him. He bumped his shoulder hard against the door frame as he hurled himself back into the sitting room and dived for the armchair beside the table where the phone was, plucking he receiver from its nest.

'Yes?' he said—thickly, because his mouth was dry and his tongue felt swollen.

'Patrick?' she said, in a voice that sounded sleepy and far away.

'Thank God you're all right,' he said. 'Now listen to me—you have to listen to me....'

'It hurts, Patrick,' she said, plaintively. 'I was afraid it would, so I took some pills to make me sleep, but they didn't work. It hurts, Patrick. It really hurts.'

'Listen to me!' he screeched. 'You have to tell me your name and where you live. Tell me!'

'Oh, Patrick!' she wailed—or tried to wail, for the nascent wail was quickly lost in a dreadful gasp, as though her very lungs were being cut to pieces by whatever she had swallowed. It was a dreadful sound, which gave the impression that she could not even scream to express the agony she was in, or the betrayal that she felt.

'You have to believe me,' he said, urgently. 'You have to tell me who you are. Pretend I've got amnesia...oh, fuck it...listen: my name is Patrick Stevenson, I live at 42 Albany Court. I work in accounts at a mail order firm in the city centre. I'm five foot seven, twenty-eight years old and thin. I wear black-rimmed glasses because I'm short-sighted and I don't have a girlfriend. I've never met you and if anyone has told you that he's me he's a fucking liar, so will you please tell me who you are and where you are so I can phone a fucking ambulance!'

He stopped abruptly, and prayed for a reply, but the only thing he could hear from the other end was that horribly agonized gasping.

'Please,' he said, when he could stand it no longer. 'Please tell me who you are.'

'It doesn't matter now,' she said, in a whisper so taut with pain that it made him feel sick. 'It's too late, Patrick...but it hurts, you know, it really hurts. Oh shit, Patrick, why did you do it? Why?'

He could hardly believe that she still didn't realize that she was talking to the wrong Patrick. In spite of everything, it still hadn't sunk in. Maybe the pain was just too great; maybe she was too spaced out to think. He couldn't any longer doubt that she had really done it—that she had swallowed the pie full of sliced razor blades; that she was dying; and that she still thought he was to blame.

It wasn't his fault, but he couldn't help feeling the weight of her emotional assault. He couldn't help feeling guilty, maybe not for what she thought he had done, but at least for not having been able to make her see sense.

'Please,' he said, pleadingly, 'you have to believe me. I don't use razor blades. I have a Phillips electric shaver. It wasn't me. It really wasn't me. Tell me your name, for God's sake. It doesn't matter why or what you think—just tell me.'

'I'm bleeding, Patrick,' she said. He voice was like a thin screech, now—high-pitched and unimaginably frail. 'I'm bleeding inside. I'm filling up with blood. I feel like I have to go...but it's only blood, Patrick. If I go, I'll shit my insides into the toilet bowl. All of me, Patrick...it hurts...oh, God it hurts....'

Numbly, helplessly, sickly he stared at the phone in his hand. He could not ask her again to tell him her name. He knew that there was no possible point. She wasn't going to tell him. He'd never know. He'd never find out, unless it was reported in the local paper that a girl had committed suicide by swallowing chopped-up razor blades.

Even then, he'd never know who had used his name; he'd never know who had broken her heart.

'Please,' he said, hopelessly. 'Don't die. Whoever you are, don't die.'

He closed his eyes tightly, and prayed that she would start laughing, that she would tell him it had all been a wind up...a practical joke. Anything, he knew, would be preferable to what seemed to be happening. But no laughter came.

'Patrick?' she said, in a voice that was already ghostly.

'Yes?' he said, because it was clear that some token response was required.

'Say you love me, Patrick,' she said. 'Tell me that you love me.'

'I love you,' he said, not knowing whether he ought to mean it with all his heart, or feel sick with loathing at his own hypocrisy and whatever stupid twist of fate had brought all this about.

'Say it to me,' she said, every word a sob or a moan. 'Say it to me.'

He knew that she wanted him to use her name, but he didn't know her name. He just couldn't get it through to her that he didn't know who she was, that he was the wrong man.

'I love you,' he said, desolately. 'I really do.' It was all that he could say, and it didn't matter how sincere it was, or how cruel, or how macabre. It was all that he could say. There was nothing else left that meant anything.

He heard a thud as the other receiver hit a carpeted floor. He heard no more—not even the sound of her labored breathing, or her strangled cries of pain. There was nothing but silence.

He didn't hang up for a long time. He just sat there, glued to the earpiece, listening...just in case.

But he couldn't sit there all night long. Eventually—after forty minutes, perhaps, or an hour—he hung up, and went back to his bed. This time, he didn't even try to go to sleep; he just lay there on his back, listening for the phone.

At long last he heard the first notes of the dawn chorus, and watched the crack of darkness between the bedroom curtains turn to silver.

As soon as it was fully light he got up, and got dressed, and went into the kitchen to put the electric kettle on. He knew that he would have to go to work—not simply because it was the only way to get himself out of the flat, and back to the comforting dullness of real life, but because that was the kind of person he was: a slave of habit and the expectations of others; a man who lacked the strength of will to impose himself upon the world, to attack the business of living....

A man alone, untouched by the busy, frenetic, anxious and ambitious other lives that were going on all around him....

A man numbed by circumstance, cut off from his own feelings....

He tried to stop himself, but the recriminations continued to well up inside him, and would not let him alone. He knew that he was partly responsible for whatever had happened, because he had not succeeded in making it clear to the girl, at the earliest possible opportunity, that he was not her faithless lover. He ought to have tried harder, or figured out some way of tricking her into revealing her name, or her address. He wasn't the one who had driven her to destruction, but vile chance had made him an accomplice, and he would have to bear the guilt of that... and the emotional scars....

He made black coffee in his favorite mug. He didn't bother to make anything to eat—he knew that he couldn't cope with anything solid. He took the coffee into the sitting room, and sat down in the armchair next to the phone. He sat and watched it while he sipped the hot coffee, but it didn't ring.

Instead, just as he finished, the door chimes rang.

His heart lurched, but he set the empty cup down as carefully as he could, and he went to the door. It might, he knew, be the postman...and whoever it was, it surely had to be coincidence. It couldn't possibly be....

He opened the door, and stared at the girl who stood there. She was no more than seventeen, not yet fully grown. Her features would have been bland, had they not been so bloodless, and he could not tell what color her eyes were because her pupils were so unnaturally huge. He had never seen her before in his life, but he had not the slightest doubt about who she was.

'Thank God!' he said. 'You're not dead!'

She stared at him with those vast, empty pupils as black as night, and he could tell that she could not really see him. Perhaps, even now, she did not know that he was the wrong man.

Didn't they always say that love was blind?

'You love me,' she said, in a voice hoarse with injury. 'You....'

And she put out her arms, as though to throw herself gladly into his embrace. Reflexively, he reached out to catch her as she fell, but he was not prepared to take her full weight, and he staggered back as she suddenly collapsed, vomiting convulsively. He could hardly believe the fountain of blood that erupted from her mouth, soaking his shirt and his trousers.

He retched in his turn, but nothing came up.

Eventually, he managed to sit up, and turned her over so that he could cradle her in his arms, and hold her tightly to his chest. When he pressed her to his body he imagined that he could feel slivers of razor blade caught between her flesh and his, mixed in with the blood and the bile that she had spewed up on him. He looked down at her wretched face, and she looked back, blindly.

She was as limp as a doll, and he knew that she was dead.

He knew that nothing had changed, and that nothing had been added—that this tragedy had been inexorably in the making for several hours, and that it could not matter at all whether it finally ended here or somewhere else.

He was overwhelmed by the tide of emotion that surged up inside him. The agony and the guilt that he felt were almost unbearable, in spite of the fact that they really belonged to someone else and had been visited upon him unjustly. What made it so bad was that being forced to feel that agony and that guilt on someone else's behalf had made it perfectly clear to him just how desolate of feeling and meaning his own life was.

There was nothing he could do but continue to hug her, and smother her dead body with his sorrow and his sympathy, and wish—harder than he had ever wished for anything in his entire life, or would ever wish again—that he was someone and somewhere else...that he might be anyone in the whole world, except for the man he really was.

SHEENA

If I'd had a quid for every time I heard the old joke beginning 'What do you say to a sociology graduate?' I wouldn't
have had to get a stopgap job at all, but nobody pays you a wage
to listen to put-downs. Anyway, it's not true—not any more.
Ever since the minimum wage came in, fast food outlets are
deeply reluctant to hire anyone who qualifies for it. The sacred
right to be on the wrong end of orders for a Big Mac and fries
is now reserved to seventeen- and eighteen-year-olds. Because
I was twenty-one when I left university I had no alternative but
to raise my sights.

Fortunately, the introduction of the minimum wage coin-
cided with the wildfire spread of call centers, which allowed
me to cash in on the only asset I had—apart, of course, from
my sociology degree. Although I was born and bred just off
Easterly Road and never had an elocution lesson in my life, my
accent isn't nearly as thick as it might have been. I'd learned to
suppress it even further while I was doing my three years at the
uni; paradoxical as it may seem, the only way for a Leeds lad to
fit in at the local waste-paper factory is to ape the manners and
mores of the southern majority. When I left home I got a flat in
Harehills Lane, not to be just a bus ride away from Mum and the
sibs—although that's what I told them—but because it allowed
me to tell my new friends that I lived in Dorset. It was a waste
of irony, of course. None of them ever thought for an instant
that I might mean the posh southern county, and some of them
even knew where its humbler namesake was. 'Oh, yeah,' they'd

say, smugly. 'Out past St James' and the Corporation Cemetery.'
I might have done better simply to tell the smartarses that I'd
been to school in Dorset, saving the revelation that I meant
Thorn Walk Secondary for a punch-line.

The people at the call centre weren't, of course, allowed to
say that one of the qualifications for the job was a posher voice
than most people who'd go for that kind of a job possessed. Their
ads only specified a 'good telephone manner'—but I could do
politeness and patience too, even though I wasn't female. Ninety
per cent of the front liners were lasses, perhaps because a 'good
telephone manner' is one of those things that most females
develop naturally in their teenage years, like bulimia, PMT
and deodorant addiction. Lads don't usually develop a 'good
telephone manner' because boys take an essentially utilitarian
view of the phone, making short and functional calls, whereas
lasses find a perverse kind of intimacy in the form and touch
of a plastic receiver, which delivers gossip as if by magic. Not
that I was a common-or-garden male chauvinist, of course, even
before I changed—we northern scum don't always conform to
stereotype.

All call centers are pretty much alike, although the one on
Scott Hall Road where I went to work seemed distinctly inces-
tuous, by virtue of the fact that we were fielding queries on
behalf of a firm that made, installed and customized all kinds of
telephone equipment, up to and including call centers. Although
there was only one other graduate in my intake and two already
on the strength it was stopgap work for practically everyone
who manned the phones, because people can only take so much
of a job that involves dealing sensitively with boorish clients
who are confused or angry before they're put on HOLD and
twice as bad afterwards. We got calls from customers who were
resentful because they were too stupid to follow the instruc-
tions telling them how to work their kit, customers who were
livid because the kit couldn't do what they wanted it to, and
customers who were incandescent because they thought they'd
been overcharged—that was about it. Although I did two weeks'

basic training in the kinds of products the company sold the only advice I was allowed to give was script-based stuff that didn't get much more sophisticated than 'have you checked that the unit's plugged in?' My job was to take down details of problems so that I could refer them to the appropriate technical staff or accounts department, with profuse assurances that somebody would phone back shortly with real help.

I didn't expect the work to be difficult, and it wasn't, but it was peculiarly taxing to have to maintain a polite front in the face of such relentless incompetence and hostility. Apart from the fact that the money was enough to feed me, pay the rent and nibble away at my overdraft, the job's main advantage was the flexible shift system. This allowed me to vary my hours—taking time out to attend interviews for real jobs whenever they came up—and made overtime easily available if I wanted it. There was a period when I thought there was an even greater advantage—the fact that females were in such a large majority that no shift ever had more than three blokes working alongside twenty nubile females—but I soon learned better. In a competitive environment like that, I thought at first, even a sweeper with lead boots could score at regular intervals, but it didn't take long to encounter the downside of the situation.

It wasn't that the lasses weren't up for it. Quite the reverse, in fact. I doubt that there was one among them who hadn't lost her virginity at thirteen and taken to the sport like a duck to water, but they certainly didn't play by the rules I'd got used to at the uni. Maybe it was a side effect of the working environment and maybe it was just a sign of the times, but the great majority didn't bother with 'dating' or 'relationships' at all. What they did was 'girls' nights out', on which they'd go out in gaggles of eight or ten, drinking like fish and laughing like lunatics with one another, until the time came to go home—at which time, if they happened to fancy a shag, they'd just pick some bloke at random and drag him off. It was easy to arrange to be one of the blokes—the slags weren't at all shy about inviting their male colleagues to join them on their riotous nights off, and if you stuck with them all night you were absolutely guaranteed to cop off with someone—but there was a price to be paid. I only tagged along once before I realized exactly why the other lads at work were so reluctant to accept any invitations from their female workmates.

The problem with being a male hanger-on on a girls' night out in Leeds is that it's rather like being a male stripper at a hen party—in fact, you have to be bloody careful that it doesn't turn out exactly like that. You're the butt of all the banter and the talk gets filthier with every unit of alcohol that's sunk—and we're talking double figures by eight o'clock—so the suggestive remarks, the lewd questions and the probing fingers become increasingly intrusive and increasingly aggressive. It's not just that they're mimicking what they see as the essential features of lad culture—which would be more than bad enough, believe me—but that while they're doing it they feel that they're getting their own back for thousands of years of indignity heaped upon their mothers, grandmothers and so on, all the way back to Eve.

Because of that aspect, lasses don't go over the top in the kind of relaxed, natural way that their male counterparts do; in over-the-top terms, every girls' night out is the second day of the Somme and the troops sure as hell aren't in any mood for taking prisoners. I suppose it isn't so bad if you can just grit your teeth and wait for the payoff at the end, even though you don't get to choose which of the witches will eventually take you home, but for anyone with an ounce of sensibility the path to that consummation is way too thorny.

Even for blokes, pull-a-pig contests are pretty tacky, but when lasses start it gets positively disgusting. After two hours of listening to those kinds of reminiscences and hypotheticals no man alive can get any kind of kick out of scoring, even if it happens to be the one he actually fancies who eventually drags him off. No matter what she whispers in his ear when they're finally alone, he always feels like a prize porker ripe for the Polaroid laugh track.

All of which is beside the point, really—except that it's the context that explains exactly how and why I became fascinated by Sheena Howell. She seemed to be the only lass on the various shifts who never went on girls' nights out and never indulged in any of the ritual humiliations that gave the others such insane delight.

You might think that as an obvious singleton Sheena would be the prime target of all the lads who'd ever been battered and bruised by a night out with one or other of the gaggles, but she wasn't. The others thought she was 'too weird'.

When I asked one of the old hands, Jez, how Sheena had come to have this reputation, when she seemed so inoffensive, he filled me in readily enough.

'She's dressed for work right now,' he said, 'but those are her civvies. She's a goth—nights out she wears nothing but black, hair in spikes, eyes made up like fireworks. Wouldn't be so bad if it were only the outfit, but she's a vampire goth—not just an Anne Rice fan, though that'd be bad enough, but a full-blown pretender. Says she learned to hypnotize herself so she could access her past lives, and maybe she did, because she surely doesn't seem to be living in the present. A mate of mine who knew her years ago told me her name's really Susan—they all make up names, although they usually pick something classier than Sheena. She's seriously crazy, and a bit feeble to boot—takes more time off than the others. Bad legs, apparently.'

You couldn't tell any of that by watching Sheena at work. She was small and thin, and couldn't possibly have weighed more than seven stone, but she seemed more ethereal than feeble to me. The fact that her hair was black with mousy roots was only exceptional because the regular harpies mostly had hair that was blonde with mousy roots. She was usually clad in worn black jeans and grey t-shirts implausibly declaring that she was a member of the Royal Redondan Naval Reserve or the Israeli Defence Forces, which qualified as dressing down even by the relaxed standards of Phoneland. She did seem as if she wasn't quite there, but not because she looked as if she were mad, in spite of Jez's slanders. To me, it seemed that she was slightly faded, like a photocopy of a photocopy. Her telephone manner was exquisite, though. She spoke softly, with perfect, almost musical clarity. Unlike the members of the slag legion, she didn't give the impression of having momentarily switched off a natural and otherwise ever-present coarseness. She seemed—to me, at least—to be naturally gentle of tone and manner. She never got pissed off by the callers, which spoke of incredible fortitude, and had a happy knack of calming them down, no matter now irate they were when they finally got past the Chopin prelude that we tortured them with while they were on HOLD.

'I don't think she's crazy at all,' I told Jez, forthrightly, after making my own preliminary observations. 'All that goth stuff is just posing, anyway. It's an affectation—a lifestyle fantasy way past its sell-by date. She must be about ready to get over it.'

'Fucking sociology graduate,' was Jez's immediate response, although he had two A-levels himself.

'Has she got a boyfriend?' I wanted to know.

'Used to live with some guy almost as weird as she is. They were in a shitty band, but they broke up—the band as well as the living together bit. She moved back with her mum. She'll probably go out with you if you ask but she won't let you fuck her and you'll have to wear black—to go out, that is. Don't know what you'd have to do in bed—never got that far. Watch your jugular.'

The next time Sheena and I were on the same two-to-ten shift I came to work in black Levis and a black t-shirt, whose gothic qualifications were only slightly compromised by the luminous green *X-Files* logo on the back. When the shift was about to finish I logged off five minutes early, having already taken my quota of calls, and went over to her cubbyhole.

'Hi,' I said. 'I'm Tony Weever, with a double 'e'. Started a couple of weeks back. Wondered if you'd like to go for a drink with me before we go home. We've got an hour before closing time.'

I was steeled for some kind of scornful put-off, but all she said was, 'OK.'

'You're Sheena, right?' I prompted.

'That's right,' she said, turning away so that she could take one more call, although I was certain that she'd already made her score. I waited patiently for her to finish, then guided her to the recently redecorated Cock and Crown in Sholebrooke Avenue, which was safely distant from any watering hole that the harpy patrol might be nipping into for a quick one. She asked for a half of Dry Blackthorn, showing commendable restraint.

'Never been in here,' she observed. 'The maroon plastic upholstery's seriously revolting.'

'You should have seen it before,' I told her. 'Bad case of Oscar Wilde wallpaper—three pints and you wanted to fight it to the death.'

She didn't laugh, but she contrived to give the impression that it wasn't because she didn't understand the joke.

'Jez told me you used to be in a band,' I said, when we sat down.

'Yes,' she said. 'It split. Davy and I are hoping to do something else.'

'Davy?'

'We used to live together, but we don't now. It's just a music thing now.'

'You sing?'

'And write lyrics. He does the music. We'll record a CD when we're ready.'

'A DIY job?'

'That's right. It's normal, with our kind of thing.'

'I was at the university for three years—did your band ever play there?'

'No. What did you do?'

'Sociology.'

'So why aren't you a social worker?'

'That's social admin. If I wanted to do something like that I'd have to do a vocational qualification. I considered the probation service, but only for a minute. Much safer to deal with the criminal classes over the phone, and I'm too deeply in debt to do another year's training right away. I'm hoping to get a job in the media, but so's everybody else in the world. Where do you live?'

'With my mum, in Cross Gates. You?'

'Out past St James' and the Corporation Cemetery. No dad?'

'No. Mum was married, but I was too young to notice when it broke up. He died soon afterwards. Mum took Libby—that's my older sister—to the funeral, because she remembered him, but I didn't go.'

'I don't know my dad either,' I admitted, 'although he's still alive. Mum and he were never married. My two brothers and I all have different fathers, so it all got a bit complicated.'

'Lib's my full sister,' she said, 'but my little brother's only a half.'

The conversation was flowing more easily now that we'd established things in common, but it was way too downbeat. 'So why'd you change your name to Sheena?' I asked, in a blatant attempt to lighten it up.

'Libby went to see the Cramps on their last British tour, shortly after I joined the scene. They had a song called Sheena's in a Goth Gang. Lib started calling me Sheena because she thought it was funny, in a contemptuous sort of way. The best way to deal with put-downs is to accept them and take them one step further, don't you think? Now I'm Sheena to everybody.'

'While the real you remains secret. Why not? Does the fact that you sometimes wear an ISRAELI DEFENCE FORCES t-shirt mean that you're Jewish?'

'No. Davy brought it back for me from Jerusalem. He bought it in an Arab shop on the Via Dolorosa. He thought it was funny that the Arab shops were making money out of them. Maybe the Arabs did too. The Redondan Naval Reserve one was from him too. He gets the Redondan Cultural Foundation Newsletter. You'd probably like him.'

I had my own ideas about the likelihood of that, but I wasn't about to spoil things by saying so. Nor was I about to ask her opinion of past life regression or vampires unless and until she introduced the topics first. A changed name is one thing; esoteric interests that she might be taking a shade too seriously were another.

'I don't know much about goths,' I confessed, thinking that it was probably safe to go that far. 'I've seen them around, of course, ever since the good old days when the Sisters of Mercy were the local heroes.'

'That's retro-goth now,' she said. 'Things have moved on.'

'To Marilyn Manson?'

'That's flash metal—bastard son of Alice Cooper.'

'Nick Cave?' I queried, getting slightly desperate.

'He's still OK, but basically mainstream. The whole point is not to like the things that other people like, not to think the things that other people think, not to want the things that other people want and not to do the things that other people do. Every time an idol becomes generally popular the insiders lose interest. If you'd ever heard of any of the bands that I'd pick as favorites, I'd probably be disappointed.'

'Try me,' I said, bravely.

'I like to dance to Inkubus Sukkubus and the Horatii. I also listen to Ataraxia, Mantra and Sopor Aeternus, and dark ambient stuff like Endura.'

The bright side was that I didn't have to disappoint her.

'Even an oppositional subculture has to have norms of its own,' I pointed out, letting my sociology degree show. 'You still have to think the things that certain other people think, etcetera, etcetera. Want another?'

'I can afford to buy a round.'

'Yes, but I'm drinking pints and you're on halves, so it's only fair if I buy two before you buy one.'

'OK. But it's not true about the conformist nonconformity thing. There's a dress code of sorts, and shared tastes in music, but that doesn't mean that we all think the same things or want the same things, etcetera. We can be as weird as we like, but we don't have to be similarly weird. No such thing as too weird, of course.' She was obviously familiar with Jez's opinion of her fuckability.

I fetched the drinks before I said, 'And exactly how weird are you?'

'Didn't the little bird tell you?'

'Only bullshit. I didn't take him seriously.'

'That's because you didn't want to. You were going to ask me out, so you didn't want to believe anything too silly.'

'No, honestly,' I said, valiantly. 'It was bullshit, but I wouldn't have minded. Be a pity if we were all the same, as Gran used to say.'

'There's nowt so queer as folk,' she quoted. 'But Jez doesn't know the half of it. Do you believe in reincarnation?'

'No. Do you?'

'Yes. And how. How about vampires?' She was being deliberately provocative.

'Well,' I said, carefully, 'that would depend what you meant by vampire.'

'Oh, right,' she said. 'The anyone can drink blood if they want to routine. That's not what I mean.'

'If you mean the undead rising from their graves by night, perennially in danger of crumbling to dust in sunlight, invisible in mirrors, then no,' I said. 'It doesn't make any sense. Anyway, blood is just blood, not some magical elixir.'

'We die every night,' she said, in her scrupulous telephone voice. 'We surrender our hold on consciousness, and we rise from the grave every time we dream, hungry as well as invulnerable. We all wake up different—even those of us who never meet an incubus or succubus. Our true selves are invisible to us, especially when we look in mirrors. Blood is just blood if you cut yourself, or while it's sloshing around your veins, but to a vampire, blood is life—and when your blood's been drunk by a vampire, you wake up very different. If it happens often enough, you can never go back to what you were before. All that stuff about shriveling up in the sunlight is complete crap, though—the movies invented that.'

I burst out laughing, because I thought it was a punch-line—and when she kept a studiously straight face I still thought it was a punch-line.

'You're cheating,' I pointed out. 'You're changing the supernatural into the merely metaphorical.'

'No, I'm not,' she said. 'That's your interpretation, not mine. Most people don't realize how supernatural even the everyday things are. Not just all dreaming but all feeling. Life itself, even reason. It's all supernatural. Vampires are ordinary because they're supernatural, not in spite of it.'

'Ah, I get it,' I said, figuring that I'd cottoned on to what she was doing and why. 'It's more Sheena, isn't it? You take the put-downs and you run with them, taking them so much further that all the mockery's discharged. If people accuse you of being crazy, you take the bullshit on and double it, until it becomes surreal. Cool. I like it. I really do.'

'That's your interpretation,' she repeated, 'not mine'—but I thought I had the measure of her, and I thought I understood the way she played the game. I wasn't lying to her. I really did like it.

'It's getting late,' I said. 'Maybe I should take you home.'

'I knew you wouldn't let me get a round,' she said. 'Too macho. Not exactly convincing, is it, from a sociology graduate? You should go out with the girls a few more times. That'd toughen you up.'

'I'm not in the least macho,' I assured her, figuring that I might as well get in on the game. 'I always wanted to be—even took masculinity A-level. I was OK on the theory but I failed the practical. I only became a sociologist so I could learn to understand my own dismal failings as a mere male. I would have done psychology, but in psychology you have to blame everything on your parents and it didn't seem fair to Mum. In sociology, it's the entire society's fault. Share the wealth and share the blame, I say. So much more PC than blaming bad karma left over from Atlantis. Not that I don't believe in Atlantis, of course. I believe

United are going to win the league and that New Labour still intend to cut hospital waiting lists and help the pensioners, so why would I have any difficulty believing in Atlantis?'

'Which United?' she asked.

'Darling,' I said, 'there is, by definition, only one United, whatever fools may think in Manchester, Sheffield or bloody Dundee. Did you know that Elland Road has the only five-stall dog track in the country?'

'No.'

'Well then, it's obviously true what they say. You do learn something new every day. Tell you what—I'll get them in and you can slip me the money under the table when nobody's looking.'

'Somebody would see us out of the corner of his eye and get the wrong idea,' she said. 'Anyway, it's nearly last orders. I think I'll owe you one and get the last bus. You don't have to see me home. We creatures of the night can look after ourselves.'

All in all, it was a perfectly satisfactory pre-date. Even after the intensity of the vampire discussion, I didn't think Jez could be taken seriously. I didn't think Sheena was crazy—and even if she was, I figured, I should still be able to worm my way into her knickers, given time and a little native wit.

'You want to take me ten-pin bowling at the Merrion Centre?' she asked, when I laid out my proposition for a first real date.

'Why not?' I said. 'Bright lights and polished lanes—the pastel pullovers are optional. Wouldn't want to go somewhere dark and gloomy where we'd fade in to the background, would we?' I figured that the blindside approach was best, although I'd already done what any university man would do when faced with a tactical problem—I'd visited the Central Library and Miles' second-hand bookshop in search of research materials.

'Oh, all right,' she said. 'Anything's better than television—and if it's good enough for Homer Simpson, it's good enough for me.'

We were on eight-to-four, so we had time to go home and make ourselves beautiful before meeting up at the Merrion. I'd decided that too safe a compromise would look wimpy, so I'd borrowed a black leather jacket from half-brother Jack. I already had a black silk shirt, which I'd bought under the mistaken impression that the creases wouldn't be so obvious if it didn't get ironed in an emergency, and a decent pair of black trousers. My gingery hair did let the ensemble down somewhat, but I wasn't ready to start dyeing it yet.

I half-expected Sheena to have gone the whole hog, but she hadn't. Her boots only had two-inch heels and her leggings only had a slight sheen. Her velvety jacket was cut like a Tudor doublet with a drawstring at the waist but she hadn't done anything extravagant with her hair except for renewing the dye. Her mascara was almost conservative.

'You're not quite ready for the real me,' she told me, when I told her she looked beautiful.

'I'm working on it,' I assured her.

I figured that I'd have no difficulty at all beating her on the lane. Even if she'd played before, I reasoned, she couldn't have had much practice recently, and she was bound to feel bad about having to check her boots in favor of style-disaster flatties. It turned out, however, that she was every bit as neat and meticulous with a bowling ball as she was with a phone and keyboard, and I made the mistake of starting with a heavy ball. It wasn't until I put the black one aside and accepted that I was one of nature's reds that I got into a groove. Sheena won the first game by 120–113, and I had to sweat to get the best out of three; it needed 160 to outscore her on the third and I only just managed it.

'I knew you could do it,' she said, when I collected the necessary eight on a final frame spare. 'You're the sort who raises his game under pressure. Not many of those about in this town. Wasted in Phoneland.'

'It's just a stopgap.' I said, reveling in the compliment as we reclaimed our footwear and gravitated towards the bar.

'Course it is,' she said. 'According to the techies, it'll only be a couple of years before the whole place disappears up its own arse. The next-generation software will let them farm the work out to people's homes. I'll have to jack it in then, mind—no way I'm spending all day with mum and Marty the brat. Lib says she can get me a job at Gap, but I wouldn't want to work in a mall, and I certainly wouldn't want a job where I was somebody's crazy little sister.'

'Maybe your singing career will take off,' I suggested, as I ordered a pint and a half of Dry Blackthorn.

'I'll get these,' she said. I let her; in a bowling alley, anything goes. 'Davy's not ready yet,' she added, as we made our way to a cubicle. 'He gave me a tape last week, but he says it's only half-cooked. I'll find the words, but I'll probably have to change them later. He says he's a perfectionist, but he's really just a ditherer.'

I wondered whether it had been a mistake to turn the conversation in that direction, but it seemed better to follow it through and kill it off rather than backtrack. 'That's how you work, is it?' I said. 'He does the tunes, and then you fit words to them?'

'I find the words,' she repeated. 'Davy finds the music, I find the words.'

'Why put it like that?' I asked. 'Why pretend that it's not your own effort?' It had always seemed to me to be a peculiar form of false modesty when writers talked about their work having a life and logic of its own, which they had no alternative but to follow—as if they were merely passive agents of fate, puppets in the hands of their own creations.

'Because it's what happens,' she said. 'Don't you believe in muses?'

I was more than ready for any sentence beginning 'don't you believe in...?'

'Of course I do,' I said. 'I'm intimately acquainted with the muse of sociology. She wasn't one of the original nine, of course, but they had to make concessions after the publication of the Communist Manifesto or there'd have been a revolution on

Olympus. Which one's yours?' I hadn't been expecting muses, so I didn't have any names to drop; I was sufficiently grateful to have remembered that there were nine.

'In seventeenth-century France,' she said, with a half-smile that seemed to be a polite acknowledgement of my ready grasp of the game, 'poets thought that their muses were vampiric—that they had to pay in blood for artistic inspiration. Geniuses paid so high a price that they wasted away.'

I figured that it was a test—maybe the crucial test that would decide whether she was willing to let me get closer. 'In nineteenth-century France', I countered, 'they thought the same about the clap—that because genius was close to madness, tertiary syphilis was the M1 to enlightenment.' I said it lightly, so that she would know that it was the kind of put-down that was laid on to be picked up and run to healthy absurdity.

'By that time,' she said, 'the art of dreaming had gone to pot, ruined by laudanum. If you know how to let yourself go when you fall asleep you don't need dope. You only have to attract the right kinds of night-visitors to make the connections you need.'

'Must be why I only got a two-two,' I said. 'The muse of sociology didn't come through when I needed her most. My mistake—I should have fed her better.'

'It's not just blood, of course,' she said. 'There are other bodily fluids that will do as well—and some that definitely won't.'

I got the joke immediately. 'Muses never take the piss,' I said.

'Neither should you,' she riposted immediately, in her very best telephone manner.

I could take a hint. Sheena was telling me that if we were to devote ourselves to the game in earnest, I had to be careful to stay within the field of play—even if, like Elland Road dog track, it was too narrow to accommodate the sixth stall that the normal rules demanded.

'So how do you find the words,' I asked, earnestly, 'if you can't just make them up the way other lyricists do?'

'You lose yourself in the music,' she said, with equal seriousness. 'You shut your eyes and you let it take over. It's like self-hypnosis—it's not really a trance, but it is an altered state of consciousness. Music's a natural language, with its own meanings built in. It speaks to the emotions. It's the purest magic of all, and the greatest mystery. And if you listen—really listen—you know what it's about. A piece of music doesn't mean the same thing to everybody, of course, because our emotional profiles are so different. Music resonates in different ways in different souls. If you want to understand your own meanings—the nature of your true self—you have to find your own music, and then you have to find the words that fit it. Otherwise, you might as well be taking calls at work, reciting crap from somebody else's script.'

It was a test, and I knew that it was a crucial one. If I couldn't take what she was saying seriously, it would all be off—but she didn't want it to be off. She liked me, at least enough not to prefer loneliness, so she'd warned me as gently as she could about the dangers of taking the piss. All I had to do was play ball.

I nodded sagely, and resisted the pseudo-intellectual temptation to quote Walter Pater about all art aspiring to the condition of music. 'I see what you mean,' I said. 'Our moods have musical reflections, and it goes much deeper than the ratio of backbeat to heartbeat. To produce the right lyrics, you have to find words that have the same emotional quality as the music. It makes sense.'

'No it doesn't,' she said, quietly. 'It goes way beyond sense, in either meaning of the term. It's supernatural.'

'And it costs,' I added, trying not to sound too tentative. 'In blood, sweat and tears. It takes something out of you.'

'It takes everything out of you,' she said. 'Everything that isn't just waste.'

Jez's comments about the band she and her boyfriend had been in—and their living together thing having broken up at the same time—took on new significance then. The one topic you should normally steer clear of when you're trying to charm a lass into bed is her ex-boyfriend, but I already knew that Sheena wasn't subject to the normal rules of engagement.

'It must be difficult,' I observed, delicately, 'to find the right words to fit the music of a guy you used to live with.'

'The sex was always a mistake,' she said. 'That wasn't the way we gelled.'

Under normal circumstances I'd have deduced from that remark that wee Davy must be queer, but in this particular instance I was prepared to believe that he might really be wedded to his vampire muse. In any case, that wasn't the important issue. 'We all make mistakes,' I said. 'I never thought it was possible for sex to be among them, but that was before I met the Phoneland harpies. One night with them was enough to teach me that it really does matter whether or not you gel.'

'You could probably get used to it,' Sheena informed me, coolly. 'After the third or fourth time they'd go easier on you. One or other of them would probably develop a soft spot for you and let you separate her from the pack. They don't really go in for pull-a-pig contests—what's the point of playing a game it's impossible to lose? They just resent the fact that lads do, and they know it puts the fear of God into lads to think that they might be victims of that kind of contempt.'

'Actually,' I said, 'I think the whole pull-a-pig thing's an urban legend.'

'No it's not,' she said, quietly.

She was right; I'd never done it myself, but I'd seen the Polaroids. I'd even laughed at them, because that was what was expected, even though they weren't at all funny.

'I wouldn't want to get used to it,' I said. 'And it's definitely my round. The next one too.'

'In that case,' she said, 'let's go somewhere a little less naff. We've both made our points, haven't we?'

We had. The only places within easy walking distance where the oak beams weren't plastic and there wasn't a trace of maroon were the downmarket Upin Arms and the upmarket Countess of Cromartie. I took her to the Countess, even though the harpies sometimes used it for girls' nights out. I figured that the risk was worth it.

Afterwards, I saw her home. Sheena lived on what passes for the wrong side of the tracks in Cross Gates, north of the railway and east of the ring road, but the terraced street she lived in was neatly kept—what Gran would have called respectable poor. It was obvious that Sheena wasn't about to introduce me to her mum or her big sister right away, so I left her on the doorstep—but that was OK, because we'd already fixed up another date. She had agreed to bring some of her tapes over to my place and let me cook her a meal. Nobody said anything about bringing an overnight bag, but it was tacitly understood that we liked one another well enough to find out whether or not we gelled.

I don't claim to be much of a cook, but I'd felt the pinch of student poverty sharply enough in the previous three years to appreciate how much money you can save by peeling your own potatoes and sticking your own toppings on a pizza base. For Sheena I splashed out on steaks—from the butcher's, not Tesco—and a bottle of French red. I draw the line at attempting baking, though, so I bought a couple of slices of cheesecake from the Harehills Delicatessen to serve as dessert. I'd managed to acquire three more black shirts by scouring the local charity shops, and I took the best one up to Roundhay so Mum could pass the iron over it.

'Not going into the church, I hope,' Mum said, wearily.

''Fraid so,' I told her. 'I get my dog collar next week, but I'm not allowed to hear confessions until I've done the moral obstacle course.'

Mum only humphed, but I was proud enough of the quip to save it up to tell Sheena later.

Sheena turned up fashionably late, but only by fifteen minutes. She was wearing the same mock-doublet-and-hose she'd worn at the Merrion Centre but her boots were longer and shinier and she'd gone all out with the make-up and silver-plate jewelry. Her earrings were bats and her necklace looked like something out of an ancient Saxon tomb. Her eyes looked fabulous, like pale blue suns with black holes at the core, pouring all manner of strange radiance over her lids and lashes.

She'd brought four tapes, but she told me to put them to one side until later. While I made busy in the kitchenette she inspected my bookshelves with minute care.

'Research?' she said, when I popped my head around the door to check that she was OK. She was pointing a long black fingernail at the Freda Warrington paperbacks I'd picked up at Miles'—but I'd taken care to hide the books on Atlantis and past life regression I'd borrowed from the central library. A conscientious bullshitter has a duty not to reveal his sources.

'Sure,' I said. 'Have you read them?'

'Oh, yes. I could have lent them to you if you'd asked.'

'That's OK,' I told her. 'How rare do you want your steak?'

'Somewhere between well done and ruined.'

That was a relief. If she'd felt forced to conform to stereotype and eat it bloody I'd have felt obliged to do likewise, but she was obviously a Yorkshire lass first and a vampire second.

'So, what's your favorite past life?' I asked her, once we were tucking in. 'Priestess, princess or courtesan?'

'Those sorts of existences aren't what they're cracked up to be,' she retorted. 'History being what it was, the most comfortable incarnations have usually been male—except for the really remote ones, back in the days when the Mother Goddess was all powerful. Being a dryad in Arcadia was OK—satyrs put merely human males in the shade, equipment-wise—but being an Amazon was even better. The two lives I led in Atlantis were good too.'

'I meant to ask you about that,' I said. 'Where exactly was Atlantis—Thera or north of the Azores?'

'Malta,' she said, unhesitatingly.

'Malta isn't underwater,' I pointed out.

'No,' she admitted, 'but it did get comprehensively drowned and scrubbed clean of all habitation during the disaster. It was an asteroid, I think, like the Tunguska object. The tidal wave wiped out the whole of civilization in the Middle East and

Africa, thousands of years before the eruption that destroyed Thera.'

'It must have been painful amputating your left breast so that you could use a bow when you were an Amazon,' I observed. 'I hope it didn't get infected.'

'Oh, we had anesthetics and antibiotics in Arcadia,' she said. 'It wasn't until the Dark Ages that the last remnants of traditional female learning were wiped out by male doctors. Don't knock it—you'd love getting in touch with an Amazon self. Think of all that lesbian sex!'

'You'll have to teach me to do the self-hypnosis thing,' I said. 'Not that I expect too much, of course. I realize that finding out I'd been Napoleon—or even Max Weber—would be the equivalent of winning the lottery on a rollover week. With my luck, I'd probably turn out to have been a eunuch in a Caliph's harem.'

'I was one of those once,' she told me, serenely. 'Great singing voice. Every incarnation leaves its mark, but some are more welcome than others.'

'On the other hand,' I said, speculatively, 'maybe it would spoil my enjoyment of the present to be always comparing it with the edited highlights of a thousand lifetimes. Don't you find that?'

'Other way about,' she came back, presumably having met the argument before. 'The only way to get a true appreciation of what it means to be alive—or undead—is to have died a thousand times. Until you've lived and lost a million joyful moments, you don't realize how precious they are. Anyway, once you've had a glimpse of other worlds, this one can never be enough. If you don't learn to dream, you're letting most of life's potential go to waste.'

'Does the soul have any choice about its incarnations?' I asked, aware as I did so that my pretended curiosity was becoming real. 'Does it simply get assigned to the baby whose birth coincides most closely with the extinction of the previous incumbent, or can it hang about and wait for a better opportunity?'

'The more closely you're in touch with the sequence of your past lives the more control you obtain,' she assured me. 'Some ghosts are just souls that get stuck, but others are exercising a precious skill. Vampires tend to be experts at hanging around— it makes it much easier to visit sleepers and take their blood. If necessary, you can get right inside the beating heart, bathing in the oxygen-rich flood from the pulmonary vein. In some ways, though, shed blood is better, especially if it's offered, as a kind of libation.'

I thought she might mean the pulmonary artery, but I'd dropped biology at thirteen so I wasn't sure, and it wasn't the kind of conversation into which one could insert an abrupt dose of pedantry.

'Forgive me if I'm being stupid,' I said, instead, 'but how is it possible to remember having been a vampire in a past existence? Do the memories of the undead impress themselves on the eternal unconscious of the wandering soul in the same fashion as memories of life?'

'Yes, they do,' she said. 'And how. Once you've been a vampire, you never forget it. Of all the things that make their mark, that's the most powerful. It's not quite once a vampire, always a vampire, but there's a definite predilection.'

'Like a curse, handed down from generation to generation?'

'Some might think so.'

'Not you?'

'Not me. All vampires aren't alike, Tony. Didn't the muse of sociology explain that to you?'

'I forgot about the muse thing,' I admitted. 'It's all very well for poets to pay in blood for inspiration, but if it were just the blood, I wonder whether the vampire muse would bother with the trade-off. Why give anything in return, unless she gets more than she could have for free? On the other hand, maybe if I'd given more freely of my blood, sweat and tears, the muse of sociology would have let me in on a few more secrets—like how to get a better degree and immediate employment. But I've got you now, haven't I?'

'Have you?' she countered. She was making a tokenistic show of being hard to get. I reminded myself that it was all just a show, just an exotic lifestyle fantasy, but it no longer mattered. All lifestyle is fantasy, and there's no virtue in buying a mass-produced one off the peg in Gap if you have the wherewithal to design and make your own.

We saved a little of the wine until we'd finished the cheese-cake, so that we could carry our half-full glasses to the couch. It was difficult to tell how mellow Sheena was, because her veiled eyes and meticulous pronunciation didn't give much away, but I saw the tension in her limbs as she went to put one of the tapes on. This, I knew, was the final test—and I had a shrewd suspicion that I wasn't going to be able to fake it. If I couldn't relate to the music, no amount of bluster and empty flattery would cover up. She'd know. Although she still didn't know a damn thing about the real me she would know enough, somehow, to see right through me in that one vital respect.

I didn't really know what to expect, but if I'd had to guess I'd probably have opined that heartbreaker Davy's music would tend to the gloomy, the ethereal and the tuneless. Sheena's remark about seventeenth-century French poets had given me an impression, although I'd never read a word of seventeenth-century French poetry in my life. I just assumed that it was dark, nebulous and leaden.

I was dead wrong, about twentieth-century Leeds, if not about seventeenth-century Paris. These days, with fancy keyboards, synthesizers and samplers, drum machines, and computer soft-ware, one guy can pretend to be a whole ensemble, or even an orchestra. Davy didn't seem to want to be an orchestra, but he didn't want to be some morose bastard sitting in the dark with an acoustic guitar either. The backing track on the tape was multi-layered, replete with insistent percussion, but by no means unmelodious. It was dark and strange, but there was nothing in the least effete about it. If anything, it was a trifle too full-blooded for my pop-educated taste.

Sheena was so softly spoken, and so seemingly fragile,

that I'd expected her voice to be thin, maybe tending towards falsetto or whispery, but it wasn't. The register was lower than I'd anticipated but the notes were well rounded, not in the least hoarse. If her lyrics had been written out as if they were prose or blank verse they would probably have looked clumsy, maybe even meaningless, but I could see right away what she meant about finding meaning implicit in the music and choosing words to echo and amplify it.

I knew that I wouldn't be able to follow or remember the convolutions of the lyrics until I'd heard them at least half a dozen times, but certain phrases and repetitive refrains immediately stuck in my head. The dark romanticism of the music was reflected in images of night and death, but there was a lot more that obviously derived from Sheena's fascination with remote and probably imaginary pasts. There were no explicit references to Atlantis or Amazons, although vampires featured in such tracks as 'Graveyard Love', but the half-whimsical conversation in which we'd touched on those subjects allowed me to catch references I might otherwise have missed—to the extent that I began to wonder whether I'd really been as much in charge of its subject matter as I'd thought.

When Sheena sang about falling stars or the wings of time or the loneliness of castaways she wasn't simply redistributing the standard pick-and-mix materials of teenage angst. I knew that I'd have to go a lot deeper into her fantasies if I were to get to the bottom of her lyrics, and that I'd have to put some work into solving the mysteries with which they'd been liberally salted. Because I had other things on my mind—well, one other thing on my mind—I didn't really make much effort to listen with more than half an ear, but that half-ear was sincerely appreciative, and some of the couplets penetrated deeply enough to recur long after the tapes had run through.

'I like that,' I said, of one refrain, which ran: 'To kiss and sting through some emergent world / Reeking and dank from out of the slime'

For the first time, she blushed.

'It's Byron,' she admitted. 'I borrow, sometimes.'

If there were more misappropriations, I didn't recognize them—but I probably wouldn't have. One that seemed to me to be more than likely to be hers, though, was: 'I need to be free, of myself, of myself / I need to be free, of myself.'

I hadn't a clue what it was supposed to mean, but it seemed to me to be heartfelt.

First impressions don't always cut deepest, but if they stick they stick hard, and Sheena must have known that before she selected the order in which she played the tapes. The couplets that wormed its way into my consciousness most avidly, and stuck most securely were on the earliest tracks she played. There were other neat refrains, but the one I seized upon as if it were a key was *I want to be free, of myself.* It didn't sound, in Sheena's voice, like a mere artifact or affectation. It sounded intensely personal, and somehow found a resonance in me that the more fanciful imagery didn't.

Davy's compositions weren't the kind of music you'd ever hear on *Top of the Pops*, and I wasn't sure that they were the kind of alternative that John Peel would ever have championed before he turned into a comedy teddy bear, but they certainly weren't amateurish or inept. When the first tape clicked off I relaxed, no longer afraid that I was going to blow my chances with Sheena by being unable to take this aspect of her seriously—and when she saw me relax, she relaxed too. She'd remained standing after putting the tape on, but after three or four minutes of the second side she sat down.

'I brought some earlier stuff as well,' she said. 'But that's more or less where we're up to. Davy says it's not right yet. It's partly the mix, he says, but bits of it need rethinking. When he's got the fundamentals right, he says, I'll be able to find the right words.' Her telephone manner had cracked at last, and she was rambling slightly.

'It's good,' I said. 'It works. It's weird, but it works.'

'Would you like to meet him? Davy, I mean.'

I hadn't been in any doubt as to her meaning, but I wasn't

sure what the right answer was.

'Not tonight, of course,' she added, swiftly. 'Sunday, maybe, if you're not doing a shift.'

'Would he want to meet me?' I asked. I didn't want to be paraded before an ex-boyfriend as some kind of trophy, displayed in order to make him think again about the wisdom of casting her aside like a worn-out sock.

'He wouldn't be jealous,' she assured me, having recovered enough of her composure to read my hesitation. 'He really wouldn't mind—and it would help you to understand.' She didn't specify whether she meant the music, or her, or both.

'Sure,' I said. 'Sunday. Why not? Not as if I'm due in church. Still have to pass the moral obstacle course.'

After I'd explained the reference, she said, 'You've been hearing my confessions.'

'Yes,' I said, 'but you don't need absolution—and if you did, eating my cooking is penance enough for anyone.'

'It was good,' she said. 'I'm impressed.'

'Can't go wrong with meat,' I said. 'Stick it under the grill till it turns brown.'

'It only seems easy,' she assured me. 'The accumulated unconscious wisdom of a thousand unremembered lifetimes. Who knows? Back in the Stone Age, you might have been the caveman who first came up with the idea of cooking.'

'I think it was earlier than that,' I said. 'I seem to remember being an *Australopithecus* at the time. Weren't you the woman who came up with the idea of cutting up gazelle-skins to make clothes? I thought we'd met before.'

I wondered briefly what the United strikers could have been doing since the days of Mitochondrial Eve to have so completely mastered the art of kicking a ball the size of a dead man's head into a rectangular goal. I drank the last of my wine and reminded myself that there was no hurry at all, and that the more tapes we played through, the later it would get. Within her lifestyle fantasy, Sheena and I had already had all the time in the world, and we could take that legacy to bed with us when the time came, even though I couldn't remember a single damn thing that had happened before 1984—by which time I'd already been five years undead for what still seemed to me to be the one and only time.

'It is good,' I said, again, cocking an ear towards the music centre. 'It's too weird to sell, but it's OK.'

'Weird is OK,' she informed me, although there was no longer any need. 'And there's no such thing as too weird, in this world.'

The sex wasn't terrible, which was good, for a first time. It wasn't weird either, which was also good, for a first time. Not that it was ordinary, of course, and not just because looking down at those fantasised eyes was almost as strange as looking up at them. No first time is ever ordinary, because it's all exploration. Maybe there'll come a day when I've experienced all the different shapes, sizes and textures that lasses come in, but I can't believe that any more than I can believe that in the course of a thousand lifetimes I've already done it.

There's no point trying to describe how Sheena felt, because even if I had anything to liken it to, I'd have no way of knowing whether anyone else could understand the likenesses—and in a way, I'd prefer to believe that nobody could. She was slim and silky, firm and flowing, but none of those words really signifies anything, because they're all mere measuring devices, which only operate in a world of common sense and common sensibility. Even the kind of perfunctory and dismissive sex that the harpies went in for can't entirely be reduced to that. Sheena would have said that even that was supernatural, and that sex with her was much farther out, but she would have been speaking metaphorically, at least about the harpies.

We were both nervous, of course. We both knew that it could be a lot better, and maybe would be, but we both took comfort from the awareness that it was OK. In fact, if I were honest enough to put the discretion of hindsight aside and try to recall how I felt at the time, it was much better than OK. We'd only had the one bottle of wine between us, so there was plenty of margin left for further intoxication. We went at it hard enough to exhaust ourselves, and if we hadn't been on such tenterhooks we'd probably have fallen straight into Dreamland. In fact, we were too uneasy to release one another from our mutual embrace in order to relax into sleep, and just uneasy enough to play one more round of the collusion game.

'You didn't bite,' I said, neither wonderingly nor accusatively.

'Didn't have to,' she said. She didn't mean that she'd had her fill of other bodily fluids; the vital ones were safely contained in a twentieth-century French letter. She meant something subtler.

'If I don't feed you properly, how can you become my muse?'

'I can't,' she murmured, very softly. 'But that's not what you want me for. Even if it was more than just one more notch on the bedhead, that's not what you need from me. Don't think you got off lightly, though. You can't escape unscathed—and if this goes on, you'll be changed forever. I don't need to bite to draw blood, and if you give me enough chances, I'll get right into the chambers of your heart and change you forever. You might be the kind of vampire who sinks blood like a pint of bitter, but I'm not. I belong to a rarer and more discerning kind.'

As the monologue went on the musical quality of her voice was enhanced, as if she were fitting her words to secret music— or finding her sentiments in some melody that only she could hear. The way we were entangled allowed me to feel the heart-beat behind her ribs—and I knew, even though I couldn't hear the secret music, that it had a greater surge and power than anyone would have realized who was only conscious of her slenderness and physical frailty.

'A lamia,' I suggested.

'A lamia's a snake,' she whispered. 'I'm not a snake. Human through and through. A thousand times over, but always a human vampire. No curse at all, just lust for blood and every clever way to take it in. It won't kill you, but it will change you forever. Better make up your mind whether you want in or out.'

I wanted in. I wanted in again and again and again. I was in love, and not just with her fragile flesh. She was too weird for

Jez and everyone like him, but she wasn't too weird for me. The best way to defuse a put-down is to pick it up and run with it, until you've transformed it into a way to fly, and I decided that I was with her a hundred per cent when she said that there was no such thing as too weird in our world.

I wanted in. Again and again and again. It only takes one psychotherapist to change a light bulb, but the light bulb has to want to be changed. I wanted to be changed. I wanted to shine, as brightly and as darkly as her paradoxical eyes. I had glimpsed new possibilities, and I wanted them actualized.

If you fall asleep in that kind of mood, you can hardly be surprised if you dream. So I did, and I wasn't.

In my dream, I looked at myself in a mirror and couldn't see myself. I asked Mum if she could see me in the mirror, and she couldn't, but she merely told me, in that no-nonsense Yorkshire way of hers, that it didn't matter, because she could see me in the flesh, and why would she ever feel the need to look at me in a mirror? I knew she was right, in the dream, but I wasn't sure that it was as simple as that, even though I used an electric razor and didn't need to see myself in order to shave. Perhaps Mum would need to see me in a mirror, I thought, if I became a gorgon when I changed, with snakes for hair and a gaze that could petrify people.

Afterwards, in the dream, I did become a gorgon, and it was wicked. I went around petrifying people deliberately, and it gave me a real thrill to do it. Mercifully, Sheena—who was, of course, undead—wasn't affected by my baleful gaze, so we could still get together and wander through the frozen world like two playful demons, mocking the comical Polaroids that everyone else had become, lads and lasses alike. It was as if all the people in the world had become victims of our lust. Their clothes weren't petrified, though, and the mobile phones in their pockets kept going off, like the phones that escaped the Paddington train wreck unscathed, as the distant loved ones of the dead tried to find out what had happened to them. All the stupid customized ringing-tones formed a crazy symphony that had far too much percussion in it to be plausible, and the beat went on and on and on until the only way to stop it was to wake up, and ease myself slowly away from Sheena's sleeping body.

I woke up, but she didn't. She was sleeping very deeply indeed, as if her spirit really had fled her undead body to go wandering, as a blood-sucking succubus. She couldn't bite anyone if she were insubstantial, but I knew now that she didn't have to. She didn't even have to suck semen into her cunt, or lick the tears from grief-stricken eyes. For her, vampirism wasn't a matter of sinking pints the way lads sup ale. It was authentically supernatural. She could leech the blood out of a man's veins, the marrow out of his bones, the elixir of life out of his very soul, with the most delicate touch of her purple-stained lips, or maybe even the hypnotic gaze of her neutron-star eyes.

'I can do this,' I said to myself, not quite aloud. It was the most joyful discovery I had made in twenty-one years, ten months and twenty-two days, or maybe in a thousand lifetimes. I felt like the missing link who'd invented cooking, or a newborn skeptic unexpectedly risen as a vampire from the coffin where he'd fully expected to rot. I didn't just think I could do it—I knew. It's like that, being in love; your powers of apprehension become supernatural.

I believed in the supernatural, at that moment. At least, I half-believed—which is fair enough, given that when I'd told myself 'I can do this' without the slightest shadow of doubt, I was really only half-right.

It wasn't until we got out of bed the next morning that I saw the bruises on her thighs.

'Christ!' I said. 'Did I do that?'

'Not all of it,' she said. 'Maybe some. Don't worry about it. It comes and it goes. Sometimes I bruise really easily, other times hardly at all. No sense to it. It's the same with my periods—one month it's red Niagara, the next it's almost a no-show. The pregnancy scares I had with Davy...well, I soon learned not to worry too much. My legs get bad sometimes, and I have to live on aspirin for days. Had to go to casualty a couple of times—but it's OK. I'm not as fragile as I look. Honestly.'

I knew that she hadn't put in the comment about the pregnancy scares to remind me that she had a real history as well as a thousand imaginary ones. She was preparing the ground for a lasting relationship. If I'd been a United player, I'd have been over the moon or extremely chuffed, but as a conscientious avoider of cheap footballing clichés, I was content to be very, very pleased indeed.

The rumour that I'd 'slipped the ferret to the Queen of the Jungle' (as Jez so ineloquently put it) went round the call centre like a dose of the flu. I hadn't said anything to anyone and neither had Sheena—and neither of us wasted a moment suspecting the other of so doing—but they knew anyway. It wasn't quite supernatural, but it was a divinatory talent the harpies had by virtue of being harpies, so it was the next best thing. If I'd been able to collect a quid every time some red-lipped monster invited me to 'show us yer love bites, then' I could have quit the job, but I couldn't. We simply had to weather the jokes and shrug off the cackling laughter.

'Of course I'm as weird as she is,' I told Jez, playing the game with the zest of a recent convert. 'In fact, I'm weirder. Supporting United and voting Labour is just camouflage. I have the heart of a psychopathic serial killer. I keep it in the second drawer of my desk.'

'Fucking sociology graduate,' he observed, glumly. 'I never thought you'd pull it off. Anyway, I'm going out with the girls tonight.'

'Well, bully for you,' I said. 'If I run across you in the Headrow stark-naked and handcuffed to a lamp post I'll call you a locksmith, but I won't lend you my coat.'

Even Mum figured out that I'd got a girlfriend, although the fact that I took round all my shirts and underpants to be ironed probably gave her enough of a clue to save her from needing any uncanny powers of divination.

'Make sure you clean the lavvy,' she advised. 'Strong bleach, mind—and buy a brush. Peeling your own potatoes won't impress her for long—lasses expect more than that nowadays. And whatever else you do, don't get her pregnant.'

'That's OK,' I said. 'She's a vampire. Vampires don't get pregnant.'

'They do if you don't use protection, love,' she said. 'Believe me—I know.'

Facing up to the petrifying leers of the Phoneland gorgons and the anxious solicitations of my own dear mother wasn't the worst aspect of the rite of passage, though. The worst of it, I knew, wouldn't be encountered until bloody Sunday, when I had agreed to meet Davy, Sheena's partner in musical endeavor.

I'd expected another terraced house in lesser suburbia, but it turned out that Davy lived south of the railway and west of the ring road, off Whitkirk High Street. He lived in what had once been a single-storey detached cottage in the long-gone days when Whitkirk was a village. It must have been worth nearly a hundred thou. When I raised my eyebrows Sheena explained, slightly shamefacedly, that Davy rented it from his uncle.

'He's kind of the black sheep of the family,' she said, 'but they haven't completely cut him off.'

The incompleteness of that severance was equally obvious in the interior, not so much in the cheesy 1940s' furniture that wasn't quite old enough to qualify as antique, as in the equipment that Davy had installed to assist him in pursuit of the vocation that his parents probably thought of as 'Bohemian'. He had a computer with twice the clout of mine, three heavy-duty keyboards, amps the size of sideboards and various accessories I couldn't even put a name to.

The shock of Davy's surroundings was almost matched by the man himself. I had somehow begun thinking of Davy as 'wee Davy', perhaps as a subconscious strategy to minimize the vague threat he posed to my future happiness, but he turned out to be anything but wee. I don't think of myself as short, by Yorkshire standards, but he towered over me by a good four inches, and his exceedingly long black hair seemed to exaggerate the advantage. He wasn't exactly handsome, especially with the bags under his eyes that made him look as if he hadn't slept for a week, but he was imposing. He looked more like a young Howard Stern than your average primped-up goth-boy, and he moved with a stately unhurriedness that suggested that he was seriously laid back. I tried telling myself that he'd probably smoked far too much dope since deciding to cultivate his black sheep status in earnest, but I knew that it was a hopeful invention. Somehow, he reminded me of one of those spindly nocturnal proto-primates that you sometimes see in zoos: a slow loris, writ large. He was probably a year or two younger than me, although he certainly didn't look it.

'Tony,' he echoed, when Sheena introduced us. His voice was a profound baritone, which added a little more dignity to the name than it had ever possessed in anyone else's mouth, but also a little more absurdity. Sheena immediately retreated to the kitchen—a real kitchen, not a glorified cupboard like the one bundled into a spare corner of my flat—to make coffee.

'Sheena's told me a lot about you,' I said, foolishly. 'I liked the tapes.'

'It's half-cooked,' he said, apologetically, 'but it's coming along. I think I'm almost there. I hope you won't be too bored while Sheen and I get on with things.'

Sheen! I thought. She told me that she was Sheena to everybody.

'No, that's OK,' I said. 'She warned me that you'd be working. I won't get in the way.'

He leaned closer, exaggerating the looming effect. He seemed to be looking down at me from a mountainous height. Knowing that it was just an optical illusion didn't make it any more comfortable.

'There's no polite way to say this,' he whispered, 'so I'll just come right out with it. If you're pissing Sheen about, and you don't stop right away, I'll come after you and rip your fucking head off.'

I'd heard of people's jaws dropping in amazement, but I'd

never experienced it until then. The only reply I could contrive was a strangled 'I'm not.'

'Because,' he added, without any evident change of mental gear, 'you could be really good for her, you know, if you're serious.'

'Right,' I said. It never even occurred to me to try to play the game. Extrapolating to the surreal was definitely not called for in this instance. I knew it was a man-to-man thing, although it wasn't like any man-to-man thing I had ever encountered before. 'I'm serious.'

He nodded his huge-seeming head and politely retreated to the margins of what we in Yorkshire consider to be a man's personal space. Then he retreated an extra step, as if to emphasize that he needed more personal space than most.

'Everything OK?' said Sheena, as she brought in three coffee mugs, two in her right hand and one in the left.

'Peachy,' I said. 'He says he'll rip my head off if I do you wrong, but apart from that we're practically blood-brothers already.'

'He'll have to join the queue,' Sheena said, with perfect equanimity. 'If it came to that, I think I could persuade him to back off until I'd had my own pound of flesh. Blood included, of course. After that, you probably wouldn't feel your head coming off. A mere *coup de grâce.*'

It was no good complaining that this was a side of her I hadn't seen before. She had as many sides as I had new ideas to feed her extrapolative compulsion, and I wouldn't have wanted it any other way. 'Well,' I said, 'At least we all know where we stand, future-mutilation-wise.'

'You mustn't think it's jealousy,' Sheena observed, punctiliously. 'Davy doesn't do jealousy. He doesn't care who I fuck. He just needs my input into the music.'

'I care,' said Davy. 'I could do jealousy, too, if need be. Not the point. You're happy, I'm happy too.'

The conversation was becoming tedious, and I was glad when it lapsed. I remembered Sheena saying that I would probably like Davy, and that I'd decided to reserve my judgment. It had been a wise decision; I didn't like Davy at all. But when he started his back-up tapes running and began fingering his keyboards, I had to admit that he had a certain style. He had the amps turned up so that the music sounded far louder than it did on tape, and there was something about the acoustics of the cottage's main room that made the produce of his drum machine seem even more insistent than it ever had before. I felt it vibrating in my ribcage, not unpleasantly by any means, but more intrusively than I could have wished.

I sat in a corner, already feeling like a specter at a feast. I knew that the feeling was going to get worse and worse. I was certain that Sheena only had the best of motives for letting me into this part of her life, and I certainly wouldn't have felt good about being left out of it, but it wasn't comforting to be made to see that Sheena already had an intimate relationship that ours—however close it might become—couldn't weaken or reduce. I was prepared to be convinced that Davy genuinely didn't envy me any part of Sheena that was actually accessible to me, but that didn't mean that I had to refrain from envying him the part of Sheena that was only accessible to him. I could do jealousy, and then some. I couldn't help myself.

I'd never seen musicians at work before, so I didn't know what to expect, but I certainly hadn't imagined that it would be so fragmentary or so repetitive. Davy would play a bit, then Sheena would supply a few words, and then they'd break off—for no particular reason that I could discern—and start again. It wouldn't have been so bad if they'd seemed to be building something that got longer and longer each time they tried it, converging on completion, but every time they seemed satisfied with the way one fragment was going they'd switch to something else. They seemed to make such switches without any significant discussion, as if by instantaneous common consent. The intensity of their communion increased by slow degrees, until they both seemed utterly lost. I wondered whether they would even notice if I got up and left, or if I started yelling at them, but I didn't want to try it in case I was right.

It would have been horribly tedious and mildly annoying if the fragments hadn't been so loud, but I found that the assault on my ears had a peculiar progressive effect on my imagination. Even though I wasn't involved in the making of the shattered soundscape, I was sucked into it regardless. The insistent beat didn't lose its authority in being so frequently interrupted; in a curious fashion, the incompleteness of the many repetitions began to create a kind of physical need in the parts of my body that were reverberating, which gradually confused and disorientated me—but as if in answer to that penetrating loss of focus, I thought that I began to see the relationship between Sheena and Davy much more clearly.

They worked on the Byronic kiss-and-sting motif for a while, but not as long as they worked on the ramifications of 'I want to be free, of myself'. Davy seemed to know what it meant, or was at least prepared to pretend.

As I watched the two of them together, exploring esoteric fractions of some vaster and inchoate scheme, I began to fancy that they were both serving as muses for one another, each drawing the other out and each changing the other's perceptions of their collaborative endeavor. I might once have thought of it as a kind of symbiosis, but I'd heard and read too much of vampires in the last couple of weeks. I couldn't help seeing it as a mutual parasitism that was taking a toll of both of them rather than working to their mutual advantage.

I tried to put such ominous thoughts aside by letting my mind wander. As the train of thought ran off, seemingly under its own steam, it got a little lighter—but it never left the realm of the macabre.

How long could a vampire survive on a desert island, I wondered, if she had only her own blood to drink?

At first, it seemed to me that her predicament wouldn't be much different from that of other hypothetical castaways, who had nothing to eat but slices carved from their own flesh and nothing to drink but their own piss, but then I remembered the difference that Sheena had taught me. To a vampire, blood isn't mere food. To a vampire, blood is life itself, and anyone who feeds a vampire is profoundly changed in the process. So the vampire castaway drinking from her own veins wouldn't simply be wasting away; she'd be embarked upon some mysterious process of self-induced metamorphosis. But suppose that on this desert island there was not one vampire but two, who thus had the alternative of sustaining themselves on one another's blood rather than their own. They, too, would be in a situation very different from two castaways who attempted to dine on one another's meat, or two snakes who tried to swallow one another's tails. They too would be remaking one another as they fed, inducing mysterious metamorphoses of flesh and spirit alike.

If a vampire muse needed nothing but blood, I remembered saying to Sheena, she surely wouldn't bother trading inspiration for what she could have for free—but if she too obtained her share of inspiration, of creativity, the trade-off would be more understandable. Not necessarily fair and equal, of course, but understandable. Even if it were a crooked game, you might have to play, if it were the only game in town.

It was all a flight of fancy, of course. Davy and Sheena were just making music, after their own conscientiously esoteric fashion. They weren't drinking one another's blood. And yet, those bags under Davy's eyes made it look as if he hadn't slept for a week, and Sheena was so slim that anyone who hadn't seen her eat a well-done steak could easily have wondered whether she was anorexic. Now I'd seen the bruises, I knew what a delicate flower she could be—but only could be, because I had her assurance that there were also times when she hardly bruised at all.

I could do jealousy, and then some. If anyone were feeding on the substance of Sheena's soul, metaphorically or supernaturally, I wanted it to be me. Obviously, I thought, Davy felt exactly the same way. He didn't mind me fucking her, but if I upset the equilibrium on which her singing depended, he'd rip my head off—always provided that he could get to the head of the queue in time.

Eventually, they finished. They seemed happy with what they'd done, although it didn't seem to me that they'd completed anything. Unfortunately, I wasn't like Big Bad Davy. It wasn't enough for me to be happy that she should be happy. For me to be happy, I had to be the cause of her happiness—and if that made me a kind of vampire that neither of us could admire, I had to live with it.

I knew that I couldn't woo her away from the music, and I knew that I shouldn't even try, but that didn't mean that I couldn't try to compete, to make my own demands on the blood that coursed through her body. I didn't have to settle for being the only one who was changed. I could change her too, if I only put my mind and heart into the attempt. As she'd said herself, anyone can be a vampire, and everything that we take too readily for granted is really supernatural.

Sheena went to the loo before we left and I took the opportunity to have another wee word with Big Davy.

'So who were you in a previous life?' I asked. 'Beethoven or Jack the Ripper—or both?'

He grinned. 'What you see is what you get,' he said. 'I don't do past lives. Do you?'

That was what I wanted to hear. I'd suspected as much. Sheena had told me that goths had a license to be weird in any way they wanted—nothing ruled out, and nothing compulsory.

'Yes I do,' I said. 'And how.'

In the next few weeks Sheena and I went dog racing at Elland Road and horseracing at Wetherby. We went dancing wherever there were dark-clad bands playing to legions of dark-clad acolytes—even if we had to go as far as Nottingham or Derby— and we went drinking in the Cock and Crown, the Upin Arms and the Countess of Cromartie. Mostly, however, we went to Atlantis and Arcadia.

While I was still figuring out the best way to work it I let

Sheena do most of the talking. The kind of self-hypnosis she practiced wasn't much more complicated than relaxing into a mental gear somewhere west of neutral, and once I'd learned how not to be an inhibitory presence she didn't have any obvious difficulty in getting there, or in free-associating fantasies of quite extraordinary elaboration. I had a lot of catching up to do, so I was content at first to offer prompts and non-leading questions. As time went by, however, I began to feed more and more information into the fantasies.

I discovered that Sheena was right about the nature of the creative process—that it really did seem that I was finding the material I fed in, not in the books that I read but within the fantasy itself, as if they had always been there waiting to be noticed or uncovered. It was perhaps as well, because the Atlantis we wove out of words wasn't much like any of the Atlantises in the books I dug up—which ranged from Plato to Madame Blavatsky— and the Arcadia would have been hardly recognizable to the scrupulous author of *Dr. Smith's Classical Dictionary*. If I'd had to plagiarize the material I used in the continuing reconstruction of Sheena's favorite past lives the wheels would probably have come off the entire enterprise. I'd never have become an authentic collaborator. Fortunately, my own imagination proved equal to the continual challenge. Necessity is the mother of improvisation, and I needed to cement that link with Sheena because it was the only way I could see to go one better than Davy, to be the perfect partner he had failed to be in spite of the hold his music exercised upon her.

It was inevitable, of course, that the fantasies would come to occupy much of my thought even when I was not with Sheena. At work, once I was able to cruise through calls on autopilot, I often found myself slipping away into daydreams of discovery, in which I would conjure up new tidbits of information and imagery that fit one or other of the jigsaws we were patiently bringing towards completion. Whenever I was walking from home to work, or filling in time at home while Sheena was working with Davy, Atlantis and Arcadia were always there to provide temporary avenues of escape. Bit by bit, slyly and shyly, they even managed to work their way into my dreams.

Sheena introduced me to her mother within a week of introducing me to Davy, but I didn't see her big sister then or on any of the next few occasions when I had occasion to cross her home threshold, because she was always at work or out. Mrs. Howell was no taller than her daughter, but she was much stouter. She had probably been pretty thirty years before, but she hadn't aged well, perhaps because she was so nervous, indecisive and fluttery that she must have been hyped up with adrenaline practically all her life. I never mentioned Atlantis, Arcadia, vampires or goths in front of Mrs. Howell, who seemed to take some comfort from the fact that I did not have dyed-black hair. Sheena was careful not to leave me alone with her mother, but on the one occasion when Mrs. Howell did manage to snatch a private word she said, 'I hope you'll be patient with Suzy. She's often unwell, you know, and her imagination sometimes runs away with her.'

'She's been fine lately,' I assured her, tacitly taking credit for the fact that Sheena's bad legs had almost ceased to bother her. 'I love her imagination.' It was the truth, if not the whole truth. I adored her pliant fleshy reality and her runaway imagination, and saw no need to separate the two in my own mind, even if diplomacy circumscribed what I could say to her mother.

The sex was even better once we began to take it for granted, although I did try to be as gentle as possible, even when she told me that she was in one of her non-bruising phases. For me—but not, I suspect, for her—the sex functioned in the beginning as a kind of anchor in reality, tethering the flights of fancy that became, in essence, a leisurely kind of foreplay. I thought of the sex, to begin with, as 'coming down to earth' after an excursion into Neverland, and it wasn't difficult to draw that distinction while our mutual hypnosis sessions weren't really mutual at all. While we were exploring past lives sitting at a table, or in two chairs placed so that we could stare into one another's eyes, the act of going to bed was always an obvious transition from one state of mind to another. As time went by, however, we began to indulge our flights of fancy while lying together on the couch. Sometimes we went to bed before we began to explore the still-hidden treasures of Sheena's supposed memories, and added the physical into the imaginary as if one could be subtly dissolved into the other without any the crossing of any obvious boundary. I had no alternative, then, but to enter more fully into the fantasies myself.

It was natural enough, during my early attempts to help Sheena recall her supposed past lives in Atlantis and Arcadia, for me to ask her whether there was anyone among her past selves' acquaintances that might be one of my own former incarnations. She denied it with such apparent assurance that I never thought the point worth pressing—and it seemed, at first, to make my own part as a prompter easier to play. As time went by, however, I began to wonder if her confident denials were a way of keeping me safely distant from the deep core of her dream. The only thing that stopped me making more strenuous efforts to intrude myself into the scenarios we spun out was the fact that she was just as emphatic that none of Davy's previous incarnations was present, even though Atlantis and Arcadia were both places where music flourished. In Sheena's Atlantis, in fact, choral singing was the highest art, much more vital to the coherence and solidarity of society than religion.

'I wish I could sing the songs of Atlantis for you,' she said, 'but I can't. I've tried before'—I presumed she meant that she had tried to sing them for Davy—'and it can't be done. The language of Atlantis is dead, and I can't pronounce the words, but even if I could, they're not the kind of songs that can be sung solo.'

That was, of course, one of the many aspects of her fantasies that were intrinsically mysterious. For instance, all her memories of Atlantis were night-time memories, although her memories of being a dryad or an Amazon in Arcadia were usually sunlit, pleasantly if not gloriously. This was not because Sharayah or Morgina—the two Atlanteans she remembered most frequently and more clearly—had not been active by day, although they had both been vampires after their fashion, but because they were deliberately shielding their memories of day from her miraculous hindsight.

'Our past selves can do that,' she explained. 'Access to such memories is a privilege, not a right. In fact, access to our own memories is a privilege too. Sometimes, when we repress aspects of our present histories, it's not because they're traumatic in themselves but because they're linked to recurrent patterns extending across the centuries, like wormholes.'

'There must be something terrible in Atlantis that can only be seen by day,' I suggested. 'Some monster that retires to its lair at sunset and returns at dawn, like a movie vampire in reverse.'

'It's not as simple as that,' she assured me. 'I think it might be something to do with color. At night, no matter how bright the stars are, it's very difficult to perceive color. Candlelight helps, but it's not like real daylight. I think the Atlanteans may have had more colors than we have, and that Sharayah and Morgina don't want me to realize what we've lost.'

'Perhaps that's why the magical creatures of Arcadia were destined to die out,' I said. 'We may flatter ourselves that satyrs and centaurs, dryads and the gods themselves became intangible when humans ceased to believe in them, but it's hard to see why they'd be impressed by our skepticism. Perhaps their hearts were broken, although they didn't know why, by the loss of the secret colors of Atlantis. Perhaps that's why they lost the ability to sing in proper harmony, or even to speak in the language of the authentic Golden Age. Did the Arcadians invent art and drama in the hope of being able to rebuild what they dimly remembered? And is that why the arts have been going downhill ever since, as the memory is slowly obscured from all but a frustrated few? Except, of course, that you're not frustrated, are you?'

'No,' she said, ignoring the *double entendre*. 'What I do remember only makes me more complete.'

There's nothing in the least surprising in the fact that I began to hypnotize myself with these same fancies, occasionally slipping into a mental gear where disbelief was totally suspended. The only real cause for surprise is that I couldn't make any progress inventing or summoning up the memories of any past lives of my own. I wanted to find my Atlantean and Arcadian selves, even if it turned out that they didn't overlap in time with any of Sheena's selves and couldn't actually meet, but it seemed that I was to be limited to the role of disembodied voice, accompanying Sheena when she flew upon the wings of time, a mere parasite of her remembrance.

'I wish I could be more,' I said, once.

'Don't fret about it,' she advised. 'What was, was—the past is unchangeable. It's not the worst of fates, to be a passenger in my memories. It's a far easier way to my heart. I just wish you could hear, if only for a moment, the song of Atlantis, the song of the world as it was. I can describe the people to you, the buildings, the flowers and the animals. I can even describe the chimeras and the spirits, at least as they seem by moonlight, but I can't describe the music, because that can't be put into any words we know.'

'I have more than enough,' I assured her, repenting of the suggestion that I could be in any way dissatisfied with our relationship. 'I have everything I need.'

I had, too. I had everything. It took me a little longer to show Sheena off to my mother and my half-brothers than it might have done, because I was paranoid that one or other of them was going to say something horribly wrong, but when the time came to bite the bullet the occasion passed harmlessly.

'She's that thin,' was Mum's verdict, afterwards. 'But it seems to be the fashion nowadays. Look at that Ally McBeal.' The last remark was not a veiled reference to Sheena's talent for invention, but merely evidence of the censorious frame of mind in which Mum invariably watched TV.

The last remaining piece of our personal jigsaw fell into place a couple of days later, when we were on overlapping shifts. I got home about five, while Sheena was on two-to-ten, and I'd been in for an hour or so when the doorbell rang. It was a woman, who looked to be about four years older than me. She had bleached blonde hair but she was too well dressed and neatly polished to be placed in the same category as the slags at work.

'I'm Elizabeth Howell,' she said.

It took a full ten seconds for the penny to drop; I had never taken the trouble to work out what 'Libby' must be short for. When it did, reflex made me say, 'Sheena's not here. She's at work.'

'I know,' she said. 'Can I come in for a minute?'

I opened the door wide and stood aside to let her go past. By the time I'd closed it and turned around again she was already well into her tour of inspection. She made not the slightest attempt to cover up the fact that that was what she was doing. She carefully examined my furniture, my bookshelves, my CD collection and my PC before turning her critical eyes on me. I tried to meet them squarely, taking note of the fact that although they were blue, they were much darker than Sheena's. Physically, Libby favored her mother. She was handsome, even voluptuous, but anyone who had seen Mrs. Howell would have been able to imagine her slowly morphing into something wide and soft.

'Crockett says you're all right,' she observed.

'Crockett?' I queried. Again the penny was ridiculously slow to drop. She meant Davy, obviously.

'Wasn't as obliging as our Suzy,' she admitted. 'Wouldn't take the nickname on—but I keep trying. Don't like to fail.'

'Davy told you I was all right?' I said, slightly surprised.

'Said you'd probably be good for her. Don't know about that, myself. She's head-over-heels. Never good to be that dependent. If you muck her about, you know....'

'You'll do terrible things to me,' I finished for her. 'Fine. By the time Sheena's had her pound of flesh, blood included, and Davy's ripped my head off, I'll be past caring.'

'Fucking sociology graduate,' she said. 'Think you know it all. Well, you don't.'

'So tell me the rest,' I said, trying to suppress my annoyance and keep my tone light. She was Sheena's sister, after all.

'I will,' she said, 'when the time's right. Until then....'

'Don't muck her about. Believe me, Elizabeth—can I call you Libby?—I'm not about to do that.'

'Call me what you like,' she said. 'Just tell me that you're as mad on her as she is on you, and that you're man enough to handle it.' She was staring at me, trying to give the impression that she had a built-in lie detector.

'I'm as mad on her as she is on me,' I told her. 'I hope I can handle it, because it's going to fuck me up worse than anything it can do to her if I can't. Satisfied?'

She didn't go so far as to nod. 'Mum says come to dinner on Saturday,' she said instead, finally condescending to complete the errand on which she'd presumably been sent, probably because her mother didn't trust Sheena to deliver it or bring back an accurate answer. 'It's her wedding anniversary.'

'Wedding anniversary?' I echoed.

'Is there any law that says a widow can't celebrate her wedding anniversary with her daughters?' Elizabeth Howell demanded. It would have been anything but safe to enquire, even in jest, whether Mrs. Howell also celebrated the anniversary of her divorce, or the anniversary of her son's conception. I guessed that the anniversary was just an excuse, although I couldn't quite figure out what it was that Libby and her mother were excusing.

'We'll be there,' I assured her.

'Seven-thirty,' Libby said, in a much friendlier tone. 'Maybe you are all right. Our Suzy certainly thinks so.'

'Our Suzy?' I challenged, having realized that I had failed in my duty when I'd let it go before.

'Oh, all right,' she said. 'Sheena. Don't see why I should keep it up, now that she's as good as out of the goth gang, but if it's what she wants...do me a favor, will you, and tell her no if she asks you to dye your hair.'

'She seems to like it the way it is,' I said, 'but if she were to ask, it'd be black before you could count to five. Sorry.'

Libby shrugged. 'Probably the right answer,' she conceded, grudgingly. 'See you Saturday.'

I relayed the entire conversation to Sheena, virtually word for word, when I met her from work.

'They're just trying to be friendly,' she assured me. 'It's just an excuse to make a big show. It'll be hell, but it's best to go through it.'

'Well,' I said, 'if ever Mum approaches you about springing a surprise birthday party for me, you have my permission to tell her to go jump off Wigan Pier.'

It wasn't hell, although it was a bit of an ordeal—more like purgatory, really. No mention was made of the supposed anniversary, which had served its purpose in getting us to turn up. The food was average and the canned lager Mrs. Howell had thoughtfully but mistakenly laid in for me was drinkable in spite of the gas. I probably put one too many away while Libby and Sheena shared a six-pack of Strongbow. Little brother Martin had obviously been instructed to talk to me about football but he felt that his duty had been done once we had exchanged a few ritualistic utterances about the leakiness of the United defense away from home and the falsity of the assumption that a four-all draw at Everton counted as 'value-for-money entertainment' when all that really mattered was bagging the three points. Libby was friendly enough, although her relentless campaign to win Sheena away from Phoneland by extolling the virtues of Gap became rather tedious once the cider had loosened her up.

We managed to escape at half past ten. Sheena made a show of having to see me home and muttered vaguely about getting a taxi back, although no one was really under the illusion that she had any intention of coming back. We could have stayed on the bus all the way into town and then got another outward-bounder practically to the door, but it was easier and a little quicker to get off opposite Rookwood Recreation Ground and walk up

Harehills Lane, so that's what we did.

By the time we got to my place it was ten past eleven and I thought there wasn't enough time for adventures in imaginary history, but Sheena had other ideas. She was happy enough to go directly to bed but once there she didn't want to pass GO without going all around the board, so we took refuge under the duvet and turned out the light. Knowing that she'd have to do a little work to get me into the mood, Sheena started talking while I lay back and listened. It was standard stuff, at first.

Morgina was in the principal harbor of Atlantis—what would now, I guess, be Valletta—about to board a ship. The sailing ships of Atlantis were akin to dhows, but tended to be much larger than the Arab vessels that inherited their design. They often carried passengers to Atlantean colonies in Clarica—the modern Sicily—and the north African coast, and they often set sail by night if the tides and winds were favorable. Morgina was bound for the Clarican city of Avra.

Morgina was excited, because she had never left the Atlantean mainland before, and slightly frightened by the awful silence of the sea. The night was bright enough when the boat set sail but the sky soon darkened as clouds gathered, overtaking the craft because the wind blew faster at altitude. It began to rain, but it wasn't a storm, and Morgina didn't take shelter down below. The raindrops weren't cold, and they fell with an eerie gentleness, like sentimental tears—not tears of grief but the kind you shed at the end of a film when lovers are reunited after an interval of heartrending separation and danger.

Below decks, some of Morgina's fellow passengers began to sing, as if to shut out the rain and the loneliness, but Morgina resisted the inevitable temptation to join in, because she wanted to savor the rain. When she opened her mouth to take in the falling drops, she found it sweet, almost as if there were a trace of blood in every slowly descending drop....

We were touching all the while, caressing one another, slowly and unhurriedly. We were perfectly relaxed, all the more so for having escaped the tension and embarrassment of the family dinner. If I'd had to set my mind to the serious business of invention I would have had to concentrate, but even that obligation had released its hold. I wasn't entranced, and I wasn't drifting off to sleep....

But for the first time, I remembered. I really and truly remembered, with a certainty that would have instantly dismissed all doubts and confusions arising from the knowledge that there had, after all, never been any such place as Atlantis, had some such dismissal been necessary. As it happened, though, I didn't remember being in Atlantis or any of its satellite states.

What I remembered was being on a tiny island, not much larger than a sandbar. The interior was covered with thorn-laden scrub, interrupted by a few scrawny date-palms, but I'd already stripped the trees of their unripe fruit—at considerable cost to the integrity of my skin, which was scored all over with streaky scabs. I'd managed to squeeze a little moisture from leaves and a few inedible fruits, but there was no gentle rain to supply me with fresh water and I was fearfully thirsty. I was lying on the thin strip of sand that separated the scrub from the breaking waves, and would certainly have been unconscious had it not been for the torment of my thirst, because I was very weak. My eyes were open and I was staring up at the sky, desperately wishing that the clouds obscuring the stars would break, although I rolled my head from side to side occasionally, hoping that I might glimpse the lanterns of a passing ship.

I never said a word to Sheena. I was too startled, too amazed. I felt that if I spoke, I would break the spell, and I didn't want the experience to evaporate like a dream. I wanted to examine every detail of the apparent memory, and the fact that it was painful only made it more fascinating, more intriguing. If I gave any indication at all to Sheena that I had been transported, it could only have been my body language that conveyed the hint. I said nothing—but she knew. Or maybe it was Morgina who knew. One way or another, the tale that Sheena was spinning changed, seamlessly, into an account of an errand of mercy.

'The ship is too slow,' Sheena/Morgina reported. 'It'll never get there in time, and I know it. I can't go below to join in with the singing. I have to use magic. It's dangerous, but it's the only way. I have to fly, no matter what the risk or the cost. It's very difficult, to sing my own song when I can still hear the other, but it has to be done, and the sound of the rain on the sea helps me. I sign my spell, and I know it's going to work, even though I've never sung such a spell before, because the need is so great. I sing the spell, and I take wing from the deck of the ship. I fly so fast that I'm out of the shadow of the rain clouds within minutes, although I can see darkness on the horizon again almost as soon as the moonlight touches me. The clouds on the horizon are different, high and cold, remote and uncaring, but they don't matter.'

I couldn't remember my name, but I didn't think of that as strange, I was in dire straits, and names didn't matter. Only thirst mattered, and the possibility of relief. I had known, once, exactly who I was and where I was bound and how I'd come to be marooned on that tiny strip of land somewhere between Europe and Africa, but all of that had been driven deep into my mind, to leave the surface of my thoughts free for desperation and hope. In another world, the hope would have died, and in due course the desperation would have died too as I shriveled into a desiccated corpse, silver-grey upon the amber sand, fading by slow degrees to whiteness. But this was an age of miracles, and there was no need to die.

A winged shadow fell out of the soulless night, and metamorphosed into a human female. I had no idea who she was, and could not have recognized her had I known her name. There were no mirrors in Atlantis; for all Morgina's skill in description, she could not describe her own face.

She was small and slender, and the pale features of her black-framed face were so perfect that I wished I could see their true colors. But I was also seized by a premonition that something was wrong, that my need had demanded something from her that was more than she had to give, no matter how clever or willing she might be.

She had no water, but she cut her forearm above the wrist and gave me blood to drink. The blood was sweeter and more intoxicating than wine, and it quenched my dreadful thirst, if only for a little while.

Having done that, my savior sank down beside me on the sand utterly exhausted, and began to caress me with her fingers, and what had been memory faded by slow degrees into a dream, which extended in the way dreams sometimes do, rendering time elastic, so that the night went on forever...or would have done, had forever been a possibility.

But forever wasn't a possibility, and the dream was always faded, like a photocopy of a photocopy. It evaporated, as did the darkness of the night.

Morgina tried to pull away then, but I caught and held her.

Stay, I said, insistently but not aloud—and she consented to be held while the sun rose and the dark world filled with color.

Newton only pretended that there are seven colors in our rainbow because he thought that seven was the appropriate number. In fact, there are five: red, yellow, green, blue and violet—but Newton must have remembered fragments of past lives spent in imaginary histories, and must have known that there really were seven colors in the rainbows that shone in Atlantean skies. Two of them have been lost, and no longer have names, but I know now that they lay beyond red and violet, not within like Newton's invented colors.

The color of the sun was yellow, and the sea was blue. The date palms and the thorn-bushes were green—but Morgina's face and costume were tinted with colors I had never seen before. I know now that we only think that blood is red because we have lost the ability to see the other color with which the red is mingled, just as we have lost the ability to taste blood as vampires taste it, and draw that special nourishment from it for which vampires ceaselessly thirst.

Had I drunk more frequently or more abundantly of Morgina's blood, I would have been more vampire than I was when the sun rose on that tiny island, forgotten even though it lay within the boundaries of the empire of Lost Atlantis. Alas, I remained far too human.

As soon as the light hit her, she began to dissolve. I felt a terrible sense of betrayal, because I had always believed—always known—that vampires did not dissolve in sunlight, because that was the one aspect of the myth that really was a myth—but I stifled a scream when she tried to speak. I needed to hear what she was saying, even though her voice had already decayed to the merest whisper.

'The spell was too costly,' she told me. 'But nothing really dies, and nothing changes its inmost nature. Don't be afraid. I shall return with the night, and you will not go thirsty, no matter how long you remain here.'

I was already awake, as far as far could be from any mere dream, but it wasn't until I opened my eyes that I found Sheena dead.

I was hysterical, of course, but I think I managed to do all the right things in the right order. I phoned an ambulance, and then I set about trying to resuscitate her. I breathed air into her lungs and I pummelled her chest, until the paramedics from St James' arrived and took over. It was only after their arrival that I actually lost control. I remember shouting, 'She's only nineteen fucking years old, for fuck's sake—how the fuck can she have a fucking heart attack?' but I don't think the paramedics held it against me. That wasn't why they wouldn't let me accompany the corpse to the hospital. I was sufficiently coherent, in any case, to give them the address and phone number of her official next of kin, so that they could send someone else to deliver the terrible news.

I couldn't stay in the flat, and I certainly couldn't face Mrs. Howell and Libby, so I started walking eastwards, towards the rising sun, and I continued until I reached the urban wilderness of Whitkirk.

Davy was already up and about, busy with noise. I leaned on the doorbell until it penetrated the wall of sound. When he opened the door he seemed angry, but as soon as he saw me the anger metamorphosed into something else—something essentially unfathomable.

'Is she...?' he asked, but couldn't force the final word past his lips.

'This might be a good time to rip my head off,' I told him, angrily. 'You seem to have got to the head of the queue—but then, you always knew that you would, didn't you?'

'It wasn't your fault,' he said, standing aside to let me in, and then closing the door to exclude the world from our private business. 'However it happened, it wasn't your fault.'

'If you weren't so much bigger than me,' I told him, 'I'd be seriously considering the possibility of ripping your head off. I must have been blind and stupid not to see it. First you, then her sister. I thought it was just run-of-the-mill protectiveness. Even when she spelled it out in letters of fire, telling me in so many words that there was something I didn't know, it didn't click. But you knew, didn't you? Whatever the big secret was, you were in on it and I wasn't.'

'We would have told you,' he said. 'When the time...we didn't expect...I'm sorry. We didn't know...so soon.'

The message was clear even though the sentences weren't complete. They hadn't expected it to happen so soon—but they had expected it. They would have told me eventually, but they wanted to be sure that it was serious first. They wanted to convince themselves, as far as it was possible, that I was, in Libby's phrase, 'man enough to handle it'. I understood all that. The one thing I didn't understand, and desperately needed to know, was why Sheena had been part of the conspiracy of silence. She had known me through and through, even if her sister and her ex-boyfriend hadn't.

'So tell me,' I said to Big Bad Davy, 'exactly how it comes about that a nineteen-year-old girl can have a heart attack.'

Davy sighed. 'Do you know what protein C is?' he asked.

'No,' I answered, sourly. 'I'm only a fucking sociology graduate.'

'It's one of the clotting factors in the blood. Do you know what homeostasis is?'

'Feedback,' I said. 'Like a thermostat. If you're talking about people, it's the control mechanism that regulates body temperature. You get too cold, you shiver to generate heat. You get too hot, you sweat to lose it.'

'It's not just temperature,' he told me. 'All kinds of bodily processes have to be regulated by chemical feedback systems. Blood clotting is one of them. If blood doesn't clot readily enough, you can bleed to death from a trivial cut. If it clots too readily, clots form even when there isn't any damage, and they get stuck—usually in the capillaries in the legs, but sometimes in more dangerous places. A clot in the brain can cause a stroke; a clot in a heart-valve can cause heart failure. Nowadays, doctors can treat conditions like hemophilia with clotting factors like thrombin and protein C, and conditions of the opposite kind with warfarin and hirudin, but Sheena's condition wasn't amenable to any kind of continuous therapy. They didn't even know it existed until ten years ago. Her father was one of the first people to be properly diagnosed—posthumously, unfortunately.'

'How can you have both problems?' I demanded. 'It doesn't make sense.'

'The level of protein C in the blood is controlled by a feedback mechanism,' he said. 'Unfortunately, Sheena's father had a bad gene, which made a faulty version of the enzyme that's supposed to switch off protein C production when it reaches the right level. It wasn't that the mechanism didn't work at all—just that it was dodgy. Sometimes, his levels went way up, and sometimes they went way down. His children had a fifty-fifty chance of inheriting the dodgy gene, and that's the way it worked out. Libby was clear, Sheena wasn't. They didn't actually have a test for the gene until a couple of years ago, when they finally managed to locate it, but the symptoms were pretty obvious. Given two or three more years of the Human Genome Project, they'll probably be able to sequence the protein and identify the fault in the dodgy version, and that might open up the possibility of finding an effective treatment, but at the time Mrs. Howell and Libby got the diagnosis there was nothing that could be done except treat Sheena's symptoms as and when they appeared, according to type, so....'

'So they decided not to tell her,' I finished for him, as enlightenment dawned. 'Because they didn't want her to know that she was living under a death sentence.' And then, as further enlightenment dawned, I said, 'Is that why you broke up with her, you bastard? Is that why Libby hesitated over telling me?'

'No!' he said. 'At least, not in the way you think. OK, I admit, it made a difference when Libby told me. I got scared. Look at me! I'm twice her size. I'd always felt like I was handling precious porcelain—how do you think it made me feel when I was told that a bad bruise could kill her? Maybe I did overdo the carefulness, and maybe she did begin to wonder whether I might be going off her, but that wasn't it. It wasn't. We just weren't right, except for the music...and I knew that if she didn't have time to spare, she shouldn't have to spend it making do. I didn't dump her. We just...fell apart.'

Maybe it was self-justificatory bullshit and maybe it wasn't, but that didn't matter. It had been the right result, after all. Sheena and I had been right. If anything were ever meant to be, we'd have been one of the things that was meant to be—but whether we live a million lifetimes or one, nothing is ever really meant to be. What isn't pure chance is what you make of the cards you're dealt, and Sheena and I had made the most of each other once chance had thrown us together. No one could have made any more of either of us than we'd made of one another, and there was no use complaining about the unfairness of the ill luck that had torn us apart. It hadn't been cruel fate, or any god that any human had ever believed in. Life never had been fair, even in Atlantis or Arcadia.

I couldn't blame Davy. I certainly couldn't hold it against him that he hadn't told me what Libby and Mrs. Howell wouldn't, and I couldn't even rail at him for not having told Sheena—

because I knew that even if she hadn't heard the ugly clinical details, Sheena had known everything she actually needed to know. She'd always known, even if she'd never raised it to consciousness or connected it to her absent father's premature demise, that she was living in mortal danger. Why else would she have been so implacably determined to get in touch with her past selves, to cram a thousand lifetimes into one horribly narrow span?

I had helped. I had to cling to that. I had helped.

The funeral was absolute hell. The crematorium was sterile, the reality of the process carefully hidden by velvet curtains and passionless smiles, but it was even worse at the house, afterwards. Libby and her mother kept giving me books, pictures, CDs and tapes, saying, 'I think she'd have wanted you to have these.' She probably would have, but that didn't make it any easier standing beside a chair piled high with the obscene loot of her brief life. Davy had already given me a dozen spare tapes and had promised me faithfully that when the CD came off the presses I'd get the very first copy.

On the other hand I certainly wasn't going to turn anything down that had anything of Sheena in it, even if it were just a second-hand paperback whose pages had been turned by her black-painted fingernails.

I couldn't eat anything and the tea was vile as well as weak. It wouldn't have tasted any better even if I hadn't still been nursing the remains of the previous night's hangover.

After hell, it was back to purgatory again when I turned up for work. A dreadful hush seemed to have descended on the call centre, and the muted ringing tones of the multitudinous phones were transmuted by the lack of competition into a sinister symphony.

I got seven invitations to go out with the girls, and seven assurances that they'd behave themselves if I did. I believed them. They'd have sat quietly in a corner, with me in the middle, sipping their drinks. Although they'd all have made themselves available, just in case I needed further comfort, they would have done so with unprecedented discretion and sensitivity.

I said no seven times, very politely. Only five of them went on to say, 'Well, if you need to talk....'

I didn't. I needed to listen.

I played the tapes over and over, and when Davy arrived to make me a present of the newly cut CD—from which 'Graveyard Love' had been sensitively omitted, although Byron's kiss-and-sting was still there—I played it over and over and over. I wanted to be free, of myself, but hearing Sheena sing those words, far less plaintively than seemed warranted, didn't do the trick. I wasn't free, especially of myself, even though my true self was invisible. Every time I looked into a mirror, I saw nothing but emptiness.

Davy told me that the songs on the CD were the best of her work as well as the best of his, but they weren't. They weren't even the rest of her work, left over when body and soul had fled, because I knew full well—although I could hardly confide the truth to anyone else—that her soul hadn't fled at all.

Sheena was a vampire, and she knew how to remain disembodied. She was in no hurry to be reborn, because she understood well enough how much future remained for serial embodiment. The Earth had existed for four billion years, while humankind had been around for a mere million; it would exist for four billion more, and humankind stood a better than even chance of seeing far more than a million of that, provided that the next falling asteroid was no bigger than the one that had drowned Atlantis and scoured its relics from the soil of Malta. She didn't need to rush for her own sake, and she knew that I needed her to linger. If she had wanted to be free of herself when she wrote that song, she didn't want it now. She had met me in the interim. Now, she wanted to kiss and sting in an emergent world, reeking and damp from out of the slime. Now, she had a reason to remain, suspended between death and life.

I played the songs over and over regardless of the fact that their message was out of date, because I knew that music as the purest magic of all as well as the greatest mystery, and I needed magic. I needed to go way beyond sense, into the supernatural. I needed the music to take everything out of me that wasn't just waste, because there was so much in me that was just waste, and I couldn't bear it.

Sheena had been right when she told me that the only way to get a true appreciation of what it means to be alive is to have died a thousand times, and I knew that I didn't have that true appreciation. She had been right to tell me that until I'd lived and lost a million joyful moments, I wouldn't realize how precious they were. And above all, she was right to tell me that once I'd had the even briefest glimpse of other worlds, this one would never be enough.

I knew that I only had to attract the right kinds of night visitor, and feed her, to make the connection I needed, to find the muse who would teach me the art of living in a shattered and shambolic world.

Every night, I opened a vein in my forearm in order that Sheena could feed. It wasn't strictly necessary, given that she could install herself readily enough within the chambers of my heart, but I wanted her beside me as well as inside me. I wanted to make an offering, an honest libation. I always had to lick the remaining blood away, as if I were a vampire castaway on some desert island, driven to desperate measures in the hope of sustaining myself till rescue came, but the nourishment it provided me was meager by comparison with the need it filled in her. For her, vampirism wasn't a matter of sinking pints the way lads sup ale. She could leech the blood out of my veins, the marrow out of my bones, the elixir of life out of my very soul, without requiring the delicate touch of her purple-stained lips or the hypnotic gaze of her neutron-star eyes—but she needed the gift, the demonstration of my love.

I tried my utmost to remember Atlantis and Arcadia, or even to dream of them, but I couldn't. I could have made things up, of course, but I didn't. Fiction is all about contriving happy endings in a world where the only real endings are fire and the grave, but real comfort has to be found and not contrived, and if the supernatural is the only place where real comfort can be found, that's where you have to look for it. If you also find nightmares there, that's the price you have to pay.

I paid.

You can't just make things up. You have to find what you need, even if that makes you a puppet in the hands of your own creation. I knew where to look. I knew how. I paid the price. But I couldn't remember. I couldn't even dream. I had to be content with cutting myself, and watching the blood flow down my arm, clotting with minutely judged alacrity, neither too quickly nor too slowly.

There was always time for Sheena to drink her fill, and she never took too much. She knew the value of extravagance, but she knew the value of economy too. Her spirit had none of the inbuilt irresponsibility of her body and her blood. She was a vampire—and how!

I talked to her, of course. Oh, how I talked! But I didn't talk about Atlantis or Arcadia, because she no longer needed my help to recall her past lives. The wandering soul remembers everything. Even Plato, who really didn't know the first thing about Atlantis, knew that. I talked to her about the future, because the future was unmade, and the future was where we'd meet again, if we ever did.

'In the future,' I told her, 'all things are possible. In the future, our descendants will learn to see those two lost colors all over again, and they'll find out how to sing again, in all the languages that ever were or ever will be, in true harmony. It won't always be like that, of course, because the course of progress never runs smoothly, and there'll be dark days when civilization all but vanishes and even vampires starve, but as long as the sun shines there'll be new dawns, and because light sustains life it also, in the ultimate analysis, sustains all the forms of undeath, even the photophobic ones. In time, of course, the sun will begin to fade, reddening as it ages, always reaching for that other color, which is the better part of the color of blood. In the end, that color will be all that's left, and even that will fade as the sun shrinks and dies, until there's nothing left of it but the black hole at its core and a surrounding chaos of strange energies. With luck, my love, you'll survive even that; in four billion years even humans ought to be able to reach the stars, and the undead will surely lead the way.'

She didn't answer, but I didn't really expect her to. After all, her voice was the one part of her that I still had in superabundance, and it was always there, filling the space between me and the walls.

I want to be free, of myself, of myself,

I want to be free, of myself.

I didn't really need her voice, although I was very glad to have it, and in such abundance. In the final analysis, I only needed her thirst. It would have been better if I'd been able to remember, or even to dream, but life isn't fair, and you have to play the cards you're dealt to the best of your ability. All I could give her was blood, and for that, she wasn't obliged to be a generous muse.

But still, I had her thirst.

I knew she was there every time I cut myself. She was there the rest of the time too, day and night. She was with me when I slept, no matter how dark and bleak my dreaming was, and she was with me when I went to work, to play the puppet in my best telephone manner, always speaking softly and always following the script with minute precision. She was with me in the Headrow and Harehills Lane, at the Merrion Centre and Elland Road...but when I cut myself, I knew she was there, because I knew exactly how thirsty she was, and exactly what she needed to satisfy her thirst.

She'd have done as much for me.

In another life, she already had, even though it set her free upon the tides of time, incapable for a little while of anything but drifting. I'd lost her then, but I didn't have to lose her this time around, and I didn't.

I clung on, and I clung hard.

The more blood I shed, and the more I consumed, the greater the change in me became, but I didn't become the kind of vampire she had been. She'd never promised me that. All she'd promised me was that I would be changed, and changed for ever, and I was.

In a way, it might have been easier to become a shadow of my former self, to pine away and die of a broken heart, but I didn't have a broken heart. My heart was healthy—a fit abode for the sickliest of disembodied vampire spirits—and I didn't want to be a shadow while I still had blood to feed a shadow's thirst.

Sheena had needed me while she was alive, because nobody else could give her what she needed then, and she needed me just as much now that she was dead, because mine was the blood that she wanted more than any other. When her body had been more than ash and dust it had been my body that she had needed to give her comfort, and now that there was nothing left of her flesh but ash and dust it was my blood that she needed for comfort. Any body might have done for warmth, and any blood might have slaked her thirst, but for comfort, it had to be my blood, exactly as it had had to be my body. I offered it, as a testament of love.

It was for comfort, too, that I needed her. For me, nobody else would have sufficed, even for warmth—but what I needed her for most urgently and most ardently was comfort. That was why I cut myself, night after night after night, to feed her and to try—crudely and hopelessly—to feed myself. She was always satisfied, but I never was. I continued to thirst, because no matter how much I had changed, I wasn't the kind of vampire who could sustain myself on a desert island, with none but a ghostly spirit for company.

'Life goes on, love,' Mum said—and she was absolutely right. She had no idea how right she was: life does go on, but that doesn't mean that it doesn't hurt.

'It could have been either of us,' Libby told me, once when she came to the flat to see how I was doing. 'It could have been both, or neither. It could have been me and not her. Maybe it should have been. I was the older one, after all. If I said I wished I could trade places with her, I'd be a liar, but maybe that's the way it should have been.'

'No,' I said, in my best telephone manner. 'It shouldn't. You couldn't have handled it the way Sheena handled it.'

'We never even talked about it,' she went on. 'That was absolutely the worst thing about not telling her. We never talked about it. It's almost as if we weren't sisters at all.'

'It doesn't matter,' I assured her. 'She knew what she needed to know. She said what she needed to say. She heard what she needed to hear.'

'From you,' she said. 'What did I ever give her, apart from that stupid name?'

'It was what she needed,' I pointed out. 'If it hadn't been, she wouldn't have taken it.'

Libby went away happy that we'd shared a few confidences, genuinely pleased that I was bearing up and doing well. She didn't offer me any more than her good wishes because she was being loyal to her little sister. She knew, even though she'd never be able to say so, that Sheena wasn't entirely gone. She might even have known what Sheena was, even though she couldn't actually believe in ghosts, let alone in vampires. Working in Gap and living at home had fixated her mind on superficial things. Her mother was like my mother, full of common sense and well-tried saws. I never heard Mrs. Howell say 'life goes on, love', but I expect she did, even when there was no one in the room to hear her.

The first person to see my scars—inevitably, I suppose—was Mum, but she didn't see them for what they were. 'What have you been doing, love?' she asked. I could have told her that I'd been out collecting blackberries and she'd have believed it, but what I actually said was a far more blatant lie, even though it was nearer to the truth.

'I've had them for ages,' I said. 'They'll be fine, as long as I never get scurvy. Collagen dissolves when you get scurvy, apparently, and the wounds open up.'

'You and your books,' she said—which was a tamer version of 'fucking sociology graduate'. I kept drinking the orange juice, though. I didn't want to start coming apart at the seams.

They say that time heals, but it doesn't. At best, time scars, and there's no orange juice for the soul that will keep you safe from those occasional moments of spiritual scurvy when the scars break down and everything pours out. Even though I couldn't remember, or even dream, I still had those nightmare moments when everything seemed to fall apart and it felt as if all the blood was flooding out of me at once, inviting every supernatural carrion-drinker for miles to fall upon me like a flock of crows. The flock was sometimes so dense that my own guardian vampire had no chance to defend her territory—but such moments did pass as my spiritual clotting factors cut in, never more than a little too late.

I always got through the night, ready to return to puppet life in Phoneland, where even the harpies still touched me tenderly and the gorgons looked at me with naked pity.

'Actually,' I confided to Jez one night in the Countess of Cromartie, when I finally allowed him to bully me into letting him buy me a pint of bitter, 'life doesn't go on. We begin to die as soon as we begin to live. It's death that whittles the embryo into human shape, death that clears out all the cellular compost day by day, as life takes its toll. Life doesn't go on at all—it just flows away, bit by bit, emptying us out even though we were never really full.'

'Yeah,' he said, wisely. 'Too bloody right. That's why you have to make the most of what you've got. Fight it, mate. You might lose, but you've got to fight.' He couldn't quite see that that was exactly what I was doing, far more cleverly than he could know. At least he had the grace to refrain from making observations about the number of pebbles on the beach or fish in the sea. He'd been out with the girls too many times to be under any delusions about any fuck being a good fuck. He didn't know enough to envy me what I now had, but he knew enough to envy me what I'd had before.

'She was a grand lass,' he said. 'A bit strange, but who can blame her? We take our health too much for granted.'

'Yes, she was,' I said. 'And yes, we do. Do you mind if I don't get another round in—no offence, but I think I'd rather be at home.'

'No, mate,' he said. 'Another time, eh?'

'Another time,' I echoed. That was where was I headed, although I didn't expect to get there that night. It's where I'm still headed, and I truly believe that I'll get there soon. I'm changed and I'm changing, and it's only a matter of feeding the muse until she forgives me for the time it took to see her for what she really is, and to understand what I really am, even if I'll never be able to see it in a mirror.

The inhabitants of other times saw more in light than we can see, and they heard more in music than we can hear. There's not much we can do to compensate for that, but we should do what we can. We can try our utmost not to think the way other people think, not to do the things other people do, not to like the things that other people like and not to want the things that other people want. We can feed the creatures of the night, and hope that whichever of them chooses to accept our offerings will eventually set us free, in one or another of the nine secret ways that only muses know.

Another time, eh?

If only.

ACKNOWLEDGMENTS

"Rose, Crowned with Thorns" was first published in *White of the Moon* edited Stephen Jones, Pumpkin Books, 1999.

"Rent" was first published in *Weird Tales* 314 (Fall 1998).

"Tenebrio" was first published in *Vanishing Acts* edited by Ellen Datlow, Tor 2000.

"Behind the Wheel" was first published in *Dark Voices 2* edited by David Sutton and Stephen Jones, Pan 1990.

"Innocent Blood" was first published in *Tales of the Wandering Jew* edited by Brian Stableford, Dedalus 1991.

"Emptiness" was first published in French translation as "Le vide" in *De Sang et d'Encre* edited by Léa Silhol, Éditions Naturellement, 1999; the English version was published in *Dreams of Decadence* 13 (Spring 2001).

"The Woman in the Mirror" was first published in *The Dedalus Book of Femmes Fatales* edited by Brian Stableford, Dedalus 1992

"Regression" was first published in *Asimov's Science Fiction* April 2000.

"Heartbreaker" was first published in *Million* 2 (March/April 1991)

"Sheena" was first published (in a slightly different version) in *The Vampire Sextette* edited by Marvin Kaye, GuildAmerica/ SFBC, 2000.

ABOUT THE AUTHOR

Brian Stableford was born in Yorkshire in 1948. He taught at the University of Reading for several years, but is now a full-time writer. He has written many science-fiction and fantasy novels, including *The Empire of Fear*, *The Werewolves of London*, *Year Zero*, *The Curse of the Coral Bride*, *The Stones of Camelot*, and *Prelude to Eternity*. Collections of his short stories include a long series of *Tales of the Biotech Revolution*, and such idiosyncratic items as *Sheena and Other Gothic Tales* and *The Innsmouth Heritage and Other Sequels*. He has written numerous nonfiction books, including *Scientific Romance in Britain, 1890-1950*; *Glorious Perversity: The Decline and Fall of Literary Decadence*; *Science Fact and Science Fiction: An Encyclopedia*; and *The Devil's Party: A Brief History of Satanic Abuse*. He has contributed hundreds of biographical and critical articles to reference books, and has also translated numerous novels from the French language, including books by Paul Féval, Albert Robida, Maurice Renard, and J. H. Rosny the Elder.

www.ingramcontent.com/pod-product-compliance
Lightning Source LLC
Chambersburg PA
CBHW050404260626
47156CB00003B/870